A Place by the Sea

By

Simon Clayton

Published by New Generation Publishing in 2015

First Edition

www.newgeneration-publishing.com

New Generation Publishing

Dedication

This book is dedicated to Esmilly and the Twins.

Contents

Prologue

A large, dark man with a peaked and braided hat, climbed up the steps to the pulpit and raised his right hand, in which he held an automatic pistol. He pointed it at the nearby nun standing in front of the altar then, in a firm loud voice, called out, "Kill all the cockroaches!" as he pulled the trigger. The back of the nun's head burst as she slumped to the floor and, in the centre aisle, silvery pangas flashed up and down in the beams of fading sunlight coming through the remains of the stained glass windows.

The terrified screaming of the women and children, herded together in the middle of the church, quickly turned to dying moans as the sharp blades cut deeply into flesh. In less than five minutes, the noises had all but gone and the pews were spattered with thick patches of deep red blood. The bodies, about thirty or so, were heaped in groups across the floor, still oozing crimson, pulsing over their black skin and those of their dead neighbours. One or two feeble groans were abruptly terminated with single shots to the head, from one of the dozen soldiers, then all was quiet.

One woman remained standing, stiff, upright and just behind the altar. She had been held firmly by two soldiers, one hanging on to each of her upper arms, facing the scene. Her eyes were open and her facial expression blank as she glanced up to the pulpit. She stared at the officer there and spoke in little more than a whisper, "Why did I trust you?"

"You would question me?" he replied with a hard edge to his voice.

"What would be the point?" she said, turning her head back to the bodies.

"I think you need to know your place...Woman." Looking across at the half platoon of troops, he ordered them to go outside, and to get petrol ready before it got dark.

He then dismissed her two guards and took hold of her with a big hand to her throat. Without another word he dragged her to a rough wooden desk at the very back of the church and bent her over it. Her struggles and cries were useless as he held her down firmly and ripped her cotton dress from her shoulders, all the way over her hips, to the floor. He fumbled briefly with his uniform and she felt the force of him behind her. He entered her painfully with a roar and dug his fingers into her flesh as he pounded her repeatedly, before grunting in satisfaction and holding her tightly as he finished.

They left the church and, waiting only long enough to supervise the burning, the officer threw the woman into the back of his 4x4. He smiled at her and suggested that perhaps she could have a hot bath at his house, then his house-girl would cook dinner for them. Her face remained impassive as she looked and gave the barest of nods, while clutching her tattered dress around her. Any further communication was interrupted by a loud 'whoomph' as the petrol-soaked bodies and pews in the church ignited.

The officer looked at the flames already licking though the absent church windows and called out of the car, "Sergeant, once that's done, get the men back to barracks and I'll see you at 07:00 tomorrow." With that, he nudged his driver and said simply, "Home".

-+-

Part One

Chapter One

Lydia Hockley-Roberts turned on her laptop, then leaned back in her plush revolving chair and lifted a huge cardboard coffee mug to her lips. She sipped at the foam and watched the big screen come to life. After a few more sips and the dab of a napkin on her full lips, she put the mug to one side and clicked to open her Outlook program. She displayed no surprise when, scrolling down the list of submissions in her inbox, she saw the email she was looking for and selected it.

From: Robindc58@gmail.com

To: Lydia@rivetingread.co.uk

Sent: Sun 12/10/14 11:56

Subject: AONAG - First Chapter

Message: AONAG - C1

Hello Lids,

As per your relentless nagging over the last three weekends, here is the first draft of Chapter 1! No doubt you'll give it some treatment and get back to me. In the meantime I'll just bash on with the next bit, Ok?

Cheers,

RDC.

Lydia smiled, then opened the Word attachment and settled back, finishing her coffee before looking closely at the screen. She smiled again as she saw the title they had agreed and scrolled down to the first page of text:

I was born in the back of a Land Rover and delivered by the muddy hands of a gamekeeper in the middle of a grouse shoot, on a wet autumn day in 1958. By the time they got my mother and me to Darlington hospital, apparently I had stopped crying and was asleep in a big tartan blanket. Although two weeks premature, I weighed in at seven pounds, so pretty respectable. I was also greedy and couldn't get enough of the milk my mother provided, so went onto a bottle after a few days.

My father was hundreds of miles away at the time, taking on Icelandic gunboats in the first Cod War. He'd just been given his virgin command, a brand new frigate called HMS Zephyr and, in between bullying the Icelanders, he sent a quick radio message in reply to my mother's news. I still have the transcript of it, framed behind my desk, to this day. It reads;

"Well done old girl, glad you banged the sprog out with no fuss. Must have made a mess of the Landy. Should be a good start for the little bugger, toughen him up from day one. Just off now to take a few pot shots at Johnny Viking, chin up!"

The next few pages continued in a similarly brisk fashion and Lydia leaned closer, reading eagerly and making a few notes on her iPad while doing so. After a short while she reached for the phone to her right and pressed a button.

"Morning Francis," she said breezily into the mouthpiece, "Good Weekend?"

"Why is it that you are the only member of the entire London publishing industry who won't call me Frank? And, no, I had a crap weekend, thanks for asking. Jen had to have her mother round for some reason."

"Well, I think this will cheer you up. You remember your old friend from the club, the one with the chequered history?"

"Of course, my pet project. What of him?"

"I've had his first chapter and, so far, it's looking quite lively."

"I told you he had potential, and at no cost so far."

"Do you want to have a look... Frank?"

"Good God no, that's what I pay you for. But keep me informed and polish it as you go."

"Ok, no problem."

"Oh, and Lydia?"

"Yes."

"You do know that it's not compulsory for literary agents to sleep with their writers... Don't you?"

After the slightest hesitation, Lydia replied, "I'm sure I don't know what you mean... Francis," then put the phone gently down.

She decided that she would read the chapter again later before replying. Far from the only question in her mind was, email or phone?

-+-

Chapter Two

The man pulled his bulky waterproof around him tighter as he came around the corner from the shelter of a rocky crag that came almost down to the shore, and was hit by the sharp westerly wind and the cold rain it carried. He continued on the snaking path towards a looming, smooth grey building. A blue and white saltire cracked out from a dirty flagpole jutting diagonally from where the second floor came under the protection of a sharply pitched tile roof. The building looked cold and uninviting, the large windows shuttered with no lights breaking the early evening gloom. The man barely gave it a glance as he walked straight past the front door then angled to his right and walked around the side.

His face lifted and he could see smoke being blown horizontally from a squat chimney stack on top of a low rugged stone structure, tucked at the rear of the building he'd just passed. He noticed orange light flickering out from two small, deep set windows on either side of a black painted entrance. Above it he could make out a small sign with hand painted letters declaring 'Dion'. Higher up, on the front of the slate roof, was perched a big timber board, on a simple frame, with the word 'YES' in metre high letters.

The door was stiff to the man's push, as if it wanted to keep the elements at bay, but he was soon inside and removing his coat as he looked around. His eyes were drawn first to the warm, fluttering glow of the peat fire at the centre of the back wall. He approached it with palms outstretched and glanced to his right. The only other person there was an unshaven, burly man sitting behind a basic bar which filled that side of the building.

"Good evening Finn," said the newcomer, "All well with

you?"

The barman got up and his head almost touched the low ceiling, "Aye, fine. What will you have?" he replied in a deep, gruff, accent.

"Half and half please."

"Right you are."

"Weather's on the turn?"

"It always is, on Harris," said Finn with what sounded like animosity, "And you've not had your first winter here yet, have you... Englishman?"

Finn put the half pint of heavy and the single whisky on the bar, then returned to his stool behind it. The Englishman turned from the fire and hopped up onto a bar stool in front of his drinks.

"Come on Finn, you're not still brooding about your countrymen voting No to independence, surely? And, by the way, isn't it time you took that board off the roof now? The vote was about three weeks ago."

"Well, maybe I will, maybe I won't."

Additional political debate was curtailed by the sound of the door opening and both men turned to see a bald headed man, in a thick, dark blue, heavy knit jumper, with jeans tucked into Wellington boots, entering the bar. His old, weather-beaten, face smiled as he got near the fire and he asked Finn for a large Talisker.

"Evening Neil," said the barman as he reached for the bottle of single malt, "I saw your boat coming in, and if you're drinking Skye's finest, I'm guessing you've had a good catch?"

"It could have been worse, aye, the lobster god was with me today I'm thinking."

The fisherman took in the stranger on the bar stool and saw a man of medium height, with very short black and grey hair. His face was tanned and shaved, with wrinkles around his grey eyes that deepened from the cheery expression around his mouth. He looked, if not fighting fit, then in good condition for his age, which Neil guessed was around 50. He stepped to the bar and held out his right hand, as he reached out with his left to pick up his drink, "Neil Mackenzie, pleased to meet you."

"Likewise Neil, my name's Rob, glad you had a good day out there today."

"You must be the Englishman who's moved into Uisge Bothan?"

"Water Cottage, yeah that's me, got here about a month ago, keep myself to myself most of the time, only my third time in here tonight... Wanted to celebrate."

"So what are we drinking to, Rob?"

"Well, I've come here to write a book, and I sent off the first chapter last night to my agent in London."

"What did he say?"

"He's a she, and I don't know yet... It was just good to get it done."

"A toast then, to 'getting it done' and," proposed Neil, "Finn, have one on me so you can join in."

The evening continued in good spirits, even though Rob refused to tell Neil, Finn, and the couple of other locals who joined them later, what his book was about. He said they would have to wait, and buy it one day.

Rob walked, somewhat dizzily, from the pub to his cottage, late that night. After fumbling to put his key in the lock, he remembered he hadn't locked it, and opened the fresh pine door. The stone cottage was ancient - a converted Blackhouse - but, in the words of the estate agent he'd got it through, 'beautifully and tastefully renovated, to retain the essential character of the location'. This didn't stop it being cold at that time on a windy night, but he was too drunk to do any more than tug off his clothes, climb into his big oak framed bed and snore the night away.

-+-

Chapter Three

"Early lunch Carla," Lydia called to the girl sitting behind the curved reception desk, who glanced at the retro clock face on the opposite wall and nodded in acknowledgement.

"Shall I say when you'll be back, Ms Hockley-Roberts?"

"Shouldn't be more than a couple of hours?" And with that, she pushed through the smoked glass double doors, and strolled down the one flight of stairs to the street. Glad of her scarf against the wind whistling through Kings Mews, she walked quickly to the junction with Grays Inn Road and walked towards the sun that was piercing the scudding cloud cover intermittently.

Within a few minutes she had reached The Printers Devil and went inside, then upstairs where she squeezed into a small table for one that just fitted into what was a turret-like corner of the old building. She got herself organised with iPad and phone and waved to the barman. He turned to a colleague, "Do you know that nice bit of mature in the corner?"

"Calls herself LHR, starting to bulk out a bit, but I still would. Comes in, couple of times a week. Likes to get in early so she can camp out in the hobbit-hole, and drink Pouilly Fuisse while watching the world go by. Tips well if you don't mess up."

The new barman busied himself and then appeared through the hatch with a frosted glass half full of the wine he now knew she liked. As he approached the table he could appreciate her thick auburn hair, cut roughly to the shoulder with curls that looked natural. She turned her round face to him and her blue eyes reflected the sunlight at him, "Thanks, well done, but I think you'd better bring the whole bottle today. Could be intense. Don't forget the ice bucket."

The barman stole a quick look down her blouse as he backed away to get the necessary. As he got a chiller sleeve out of the freezer and the bottle out of the cooler, he told his colleague that he agreed with him, "She might be a full size 12, and probably in her forties but still a great body." The older barman grunted his assent then said, "By the way, when she says ice bucket, she means exactly that, prefers it to the sleeve. You want to make a good impression, I assume?"

She had started her third glass when she finished re-reading his first chapter again, and looking through her notes. It was already more than 24 hours since she'd first seen the work and so, with one more swig of wine she reached for her phone. She found his name then, after the barest hesitation, pressed it.

"Ms Hockley-Roberts," said a welcoming but mildly croaky voice.

"Rob?"

"Yeah, it's me, still a bit fragile from last night."

"Celebrating getting some work done at last?"

"Kind of... you Ok?"

Lydia hesitated, then with a deep breath and in a softer voice said, "I miss you Cat."

Rob's end of the phone went quiet, before he coughed and replied, "You said no strings attached Lids, that you could handle it."

"I can, and I will, but I can't help my feelings sometimes, especially after three glasses of Pouilly." She laughed, and it seemed to work. The tension went out of Rob's voice and he sounded brighter, "So, you're in the Devil then?"

"Am I that predictable?"

"Maybe... What do you think? About chapter one, I mean."

"Right, yes, it's good, really good. A bit like a runaway train in terms of pace. You've crammed about seven years into the first chapter."

"But, like anyone, I can't really remember most of being a kid, and there's no-one left to ask."

"I know, it's not a problem, really Cat, just keep it going. We'll worry about editing later."

"I thought we were sticking to the 'nom-de-plume'...less of the Cat?"

"Sorry, yes, you're right... Rob."

"You'll be pleased to hear that, in spite of serious queasiness this morning, I've already made a start on chapter two, in my head. Once it's underway, it's really satisfying keeping the momentum going."

"A bit like relationships?"

"Lydia, let me repeat what I told you before. Those two weeks we spent in and out of the Savoy in the summer, were fantastic. I've never enjoyed myself, or London, as much. We had a great time but, whatever your feelings are for me, it would be wrong to tell you that I felt anything more. I couldn't have had a better date, or better...well, you know."

"Sex? Is that all it was to you?"

"Of course not... But it really was good, wasn't it?"

Lydia went quiet for a few moments, then went on, "Look, I don't take it back, I've never had a better lover than you, but to me it was a lot more. I know it's one way and the main thing is, we need to work well together on the book. Frank will entirely blame me if we fuck it up. He idolises you, for some reason, and I'm sure he knows about us."

"He's not said anything to me."

"Well, you boys don't talk about specifics do you? You just assume that it's part of life's game to shag anyone you fancy."

"Change of subject please Lids? So, we're agreed? Let's be mates? And you must tell me everything I do wrong, in the book I mean... I trust you Darling, really."

"Ok, as my best girlfriend tells me, 'At least you know where you are with a bastard'."

"A brutal stab Lydia, but a fair one," chuckled Rob.

"Right then, I'll email you with some detailed points to help with the next few chapters and we'll talk at the end of each one?"

"Or earlier, if I get stuck?"

"Indeed."

"Thanks, Lydia. I wouldn't have started this without you."

"I know. Now bugger off, so that I can finish my bottle in peace."

"Ok, see you soon."

"You never know, I might surprise you. Bye."

Lydia didn't wait for acknowledgement, just clicked the 'end call' box on her touch screen. She shrugged, drained the last of her wine then waved the same waiter back over. As he leaned in to collect the glass, bottle, and bucket, Lydia said quietly to him, "I'll have the bill please...and stop looking at my tits."

-+-

Chapter Four

After Lydia's phone call had roused him, Rob decided that a shower was just the thing to bring him round completely. He luxuriated for some time as the power shower (installed as part of the 'tasteful renovation') gently pummelled his head, shoulders, and chest. Suitably rejuvenated, he threw on a tee shirt and track suit bottoms then brewed some coffee in his galley kitchen. He made and buttered some toast and took it with a mug of black coffee into the study. This had originally been a second bedroom and, although there was still a bed settee against the inside wall next to the door, this was now most clearly a room celebrating things other than sleep.

Rob walked over to a large, solid looking, antique pine desk, and put down his very late breakfast. He pulled back the leather 'swivel and tilt' chair and sat in it, before pulling it up to the desk front. The view he faced, through the large double-glazed picture window, was impressive. To the far left and going down the sloping hillside was a gravel track, just wide enough for one vehicle, that joined a larger rough road which was mainly hidden by the central part of the slope. To the far right was a small burn, bubbling down the slope through a narrow channel that it had clearly carved for itself out of the bare, rocky hillside. The road reappeared here and the burn went under it through a culvert. In the centre the slope had some sparse tufted grass and heather, interspersed with bare rock. Beyond the end of the slope, where the road ran unseen in the lee of its base, the view went straight out to sea. To the left, was a small island, about a mile offshore, breaking the vista. Apart from that, and dominating the whole scene, was the North Atlantic and the grey sky above it, merging on a hazy horizon.

The wind had dropped since the previous night and such

waves as could be seen were small and with little foam on top reflecting the cloudy sky. Most of the waves broke onto bare rocks, some being huge from being dumped there in the last ice age, some worn small and round forming a partly pebbled beach. Rob knew that along the bay, nearer the pub, was a sandy beach but this couldn't be seen from Water Cottage.

He munched some toast and drank his coffee as he took in the view. Lydia had been right, this was perfect. He glanced around the room and it gave him a contented feeling. There were lots of books in two tall and deep pine bookcases, many of them with military titles. Also, plenty of biographies featuring famous adventurers, explorers, soldiers, sailors and airmen. On top of both bookcases, were about forty different bottles of single malt whisky, with varying content levels. Resting on an antique blotter in the middle of the desk, was a new looking laptop connected to a printer on a small side table. Sharing the table was a wireless router for internet connection and a battered looking pair of naval binoculars. Apart from this there was a locked filing cabinet, and a wide shelf fixed to the wall, with a chess set on it, the pieces of which looked like Napoleonic soldiers. Most of the wall space was taken up with dozens of framed photographs. The common feature about them was that they all featured people, mostly in uniform but some in suits or casual clothing. Rob appeared in some but from most of them, he was an absentee.

He turned on the laptop and rummaged in one of the desk drawers, withdrawing an A4 size, distressed leather covered, notebook. He undid the leather bootlace style fastener and flicked through some pages, stopping to scribble here and there with a biro. Turning back to the screen and keyboard, Rob slid his finger over the touchpad and opened the Word icon, then the 'AONAG.docx' file he needed.

He glanced through chapter one, in the light of LHR's comments, and grinned to himself, then started typing. With occasional looks out to sea, and glances into his notebook, Rob's fingers moved speedily over the keyboard. There were plenty of touches on the backspace key but after around an hour and a half, he leaned back in the chair, stretched his fingers in turn until they clicked, and gave a satisfied sigh. He scrolled the screen up until he saw *'Chapter Two'*, then read his words:

So, after a disruptive early life, moving to and from various homes in naval bases around Britain, and usually brief, disappointing stints in local infant schools, I reached the ripe old age of eight. By this time I knew that my mother came from something called a 'good family' that had apparently fallen on hard times. I often heard my father going on about the 'Bloody skinflint Admiralty' and this all seemed to lead to my parents often being short of money. From the noisy arguments at whatever home we were in at the time, this seemed to be something that always provoked rages in my father. I remember over the breakfast table once, when my father was home on leave, I asked if I was ever going to have a brother or sister. My father turned to me and with the coldest eyes I could remember, shouted at me, "Don't you think that you're enough of a burden already, without adding another bloody mouth to feed?" I kept quiet on the subject after that.

Actually, getting to eight was a bit of an achievement for me. My father almost drowned me before I got to that age. I don't think he meant to do it, his need for economy probably didn't drive him to measures that extreme. On a rare bit of Navy leave, he declared that we were going to go to the west coast of Scotland for a holiday. A fellow officer had a small sailing cruiser and he had said my father could use it for a fortnight. We lived in Devonport then, so the drive north, in our Morris Minor (the 'birthing'

Land Rover had long since given up the ghost), took over two days.

We arrived in a tiny bay near Oban, tired and irritable from sleeping in the car, and it was raining. We found where the boat was moored and got a local to row us out to it, with our luggage. My mother put the kettle on the tiny stove for tea, and my father got our wet cases stowed away. It was late morning before we were organised and then it was time for the holiday to begin in earnest. My father went around the deck sorting out ropes (or 'sheets' as he insisted on calling them) and soon announced that we were ready to 'cast off'. My mother and I sat in the cockpit, her hand on the tiller, while my father disengaged us from the mooring buoy and looked up at the mainsail starting to fill. The rain had faded to a sort of drizzle by then and we slowly edged our way to the end of the bay, heading north-west for the Inner Hebrides.

After about half an hour on the open sea, pitching gently over the small waves as we continued our course, I started to feel very ill. The motion made my insides churn and I groaned helplessly. This was my first time on open water and it was completely different to the odd motor boat trip around a naval dockyard. I clung closer to my mother and continued groaning. My father, having grabbed the tiller from my mother and corrected our course with a look at the centrally mounted compass, looked at me with disdain and barked, "What's wrong with you boy? It can't be seasickness, this is like a bloody millpond!"

"Don't John," said my mother as she held me tighter.

"What do you mean, 'Don't John', he's being pathetic. How will he ever become a naval officer if he can't cope with the slightest swell?"

"Perhaps he might not want to?"

"Don't be ridiculous, of course he will. If Nelson could beat the entire Frog Navy while being seasick, there's no way a boy of mine can't take it in his stride. All he needs is something to take his mind off it. Right Margaret, you go below for a while, get another brew on, I'll get laddie here, busy."

With that, my father pushed my mother out of the cockpit towards the cabin and took her seat at the helm. He then told me to go forward and bring the mainsail in a few notches on the starboard winch, as the south-westerly wind was getting a bit stronger and we could speed up. I didn't really understand it all and just sat there, still moaning.

"Get your useless lump to that handle there," he shouted at me, pointing to a round metal thing on the right of the deck, "And turn it, quickly."

I still sat, rooted to the cockpit bench, trying to keep swallowing back the pressure that had built up in my stomach and throat. After a few seconds more, it was too much and I turned my head to the left, throwing up straight into the freshening breeze. Much of it was thrown back by the wind, over me and my father, sitting behind me to the right of the tiller. His face was splattered by my vomit and he lunged out an arm, grabbing me by the slack of my anorak and hurling me forward. "Turn the fucking handle boy," he screamed as he wiped his eyes with his hand. I stumbled forward and, just before I bent down to the winch, the slack sail suddenly filled with wind and the boom flew across from the top of the cabin catching me on the left shoulder, pushing me easily over the rail. The water in those parts is never warm and, being Easter, no long days of sunshine had yet been of effect. The piercing cold went through my clothes instantly and the thought I remember most clearly was, 'It's not my fault'.

The screams of my mother, my father lifting me out with a boat hook caught in my anorak, and having hot chocolate after the rescue, were all a bit of a blur. More vivid was the comment afterwards that, 'If he'd got the sail in when I told him to, the whole debacle would never have happened.' My mother's protestations, mainly pointing out that I was only seven years old, cut no ice. 'I could sail before I could walk, no bloody excuse', and suchlike.

Anyway, that was the first day of two weeks of hell for me. My father was determined to toughen me up and, as events many years later would tend to show, he may have been partly successful. One thing that I never got to cope with however, was seasickness. It was ten times worse when, later on our cruise, we crossed the Minch to the Outer Hebrides. My mother always recounted that my face actually went green for that whole day, as we struggled to make headway in seriously strong winds.

The most positive aspect of that holiday for me, was that I developed a love of the islands. The whole west coast of Scotland is, to me, a wonderful place. The scenery, the people and the whole environment, are sensational. Quite simply, I started then to grow up as a man who loves the sea, but would rather not be on it, if alternatives are possible.

Anyway, part of growing up is going to school and that takes me back to my eighth birthday. Father's ship was on the Hong Kong station and my mother made a small cake onto which she had placed eight candles. We'd just moved to Rosyth and didn't yet know the other naval families on the base. We sat at our small dinner table eating the cake and drinking lemonade, after I had blown the candles out and made a wish. I wished that my mother's smile could come back. She seemed sad most of the time but, curiously, this got worse when she knew my father was due on leave.

"I've got some news for you," she said to me after she finished her lemonade, "Now you're eight, you can go to a proper school."

"But, Mum, I've been to lots of schools."

"This is different, my son. I've had your name down for Bainbridge, since not long after you were born. I put aside the last of my inheritance to pay the fees, and your father never knew."

"Where's Bainbridge?"

"It's in North Yorkshire, not that far from where you were born, near Uncle Hugo's house."

My mother was obviously pressing the right buttons as she knew I enjoyed the adventures we had when we visited the Pennines, and the way Uncle Hugo would spoil me when we stayed at his sprawling Manor House. However, one thing concerned me, "How will I get there every day when you are here?"

"Look at this Darling," she said as she passed me a shiny leaflet, "It's got everything you could want."

I looked at the front of the leaflet and the words 'Bainbridge Boarding School for Boys' took up most of it. Inside there were pictures of gothic buildings and school playing grounds, with bright young schoolboys and juvenile rugby players smiling out from them. The words, 'clean and comfortable boarding accommodation with traditional British catering', seemed to crystallise my thinking and I looked into my mother's face.

"Will I have to stay there?"

"It's for the best sweetheart, all this hopping from school to school can't be good for you."

"But what about you? Where will you be?"

"I'll be just down the road at your uncle's house. I'm going to stay with him for a while, at least until your father comes back from the Far East."

So that was that, I became a Bainbridge boy, and went walking through their doors a week after my birthday. I was nervous but also strangely excited.

Rob clicked on 'save' with a flourish. He then opened Outlook and penned a quick email to LHR, explaining that chapter two was well in hand, and that he hoped to finish it in a couple of days.

His memory was stretched now and, in need of a break, he put on his walking boots and a Gortex jacket, snatched a silver hip flask from the array of whisky bottles on one of his bookcases, and set off for a walk in the hills behind the cottage.

-+-

Chapter Five

Francis Rafferty sat back in a big leather armchair and cradled his gin and tonic before looking at his watch. The Dragoon Club, just off Piccadilly, was always a good place to meet his contemporaries. It was discreet, quiet, and the service was exemplary. Originally set up for returning cavalry officers from the Crimea, licking their wounds after Sevastopol and other disasters, the club embraced people from across the services nowadays. As long as they had once held a commission, they could apply for membership.

He saw the familiar figure of Sir Archibald Findlayson lumbering across the smoking room, his portly girth stretching the holding powers of his dark blue waistcoat, and making his jacket flap outwards like two untrimmed, pinstriped sails. He plonked himself in the matching armchair at right angles to Rafferty's, with a grunt and a "Frank." He got the reply "Archie," from his old friend, who proceeded to hold up two fingers in the direction of the bar.

Two gin and tonics were promptly delivered to the small table between the men and, now suitably equipped for conversation, they enquired about each other's health and made other small talk about the publishing world and life at the Foreign and Commonwealth Office. After a suitable refill, Frank leaned forward and said, "Cat's book project is up and running. Early signs are promising."

"Good show," replied Archie, "Discretion assured old boy?"

"Oh yes, pen name sorted and got him tucked out of the way where the journo's can't get at him."

"What is it?"

"Sorry Archie?"

"What's his bloody nom-de-plume?"

Frank shuffled a little on the chair, "It's Chancellor... Robin D. Chancellor."

"Sorry, 'Robin D. Chancellor', you must be joking?"

"Cat chose it, always was an irreverent fucker."

"Oh well, it will be fun if a copy ever turns up at number 11 Downing Street! And this will be promoted as purely a work of fiction, yes?"

"Absolutely Archie, we will use Cat's... Robin's stories but not identify anyone that could cause problems for HMG."

"Ok Frank, how about going through for lunch now and talking bollocks about the good old days in the regiment."

"Sounds perfect."

After a long and liquid lunch, Frank got a cab back to Riveting Read LLP and beamed his flushed face at Carla as he went in. Having established from her that LHR was there, he let himself into Lydia's office and sat down opposite her desk, without an invitation.

"Good lunch Francis?" she asked.

"Splendid... the tournedos were sublime."

"As was the wine, by the look of it."

"Never mind that, how's our boy doing."

"If you mean Cat...or rather, RDC, he's promised me the next chapter by first thing, Friday."

"That's tomorrow. Good work Lydia, sounds like you're getting him into a productive groove. The good news from my chum at the FCO is that if we do it the way we said we would, there'll be no repercussions from them. Update before the weekend please?"

"Sure thing... Boss."

After Frank left, it was getting on for 5pm and Lydia was just about to turn off the screen when a new email popped up in the bottom right of her screen. It was from Rob and had an attachment headed: AONAG - C2. The email reminded Lydia that this was now the second chapter to be delivered in less than a week, and it also declared that this was 'not bad for a beginner'.

Lydia opened up the attachment and she appreciated the story of Rob's sailing experiences as a young boy and how he had ended up having to go to boarding school. As she read on, it became clear that the seeming vulnerability of those infant years started to drop off the youngster, as he came to grips with his new environment and tackled it head on.

His descriptions of the school and how it worked were insightful, especially the sub-culture surrounding the way the senior boys treated the new juniors. Bullying seemed to be part of the fabric of Bainbridge School society, but what came from Cat's words was not self-pity, but the sense that this was not going to be tolerated by him and that he would find a way to oppose it.

One passage, that followed pages outlining some ferocious bullying by one of the senior boys on the youngster in his second year, caught Lydia's eye in particular:

Fletcher laughed again, while swinging his boot at me on the opposite side of the scrum to the referee. I laughed back at him to show that I didn't care. And, in fact, I really didn't care, as I had already put in place the measures that were going to finish Fletcher off for good. His love of pies was legendary and would be his downfall.

The day prior to the rugby match, I had made myself throw up in assembly with copious sweets after breakfast and a finger down my throat. I had been sent to matron and was left on a sickroom bed for the morning, as matron went about her other duties. While she was gone, I picked up the dispensary cupboard key from her desk and helped myself to a strip of laxative tablets and a morphine injector syrette. I relocked the cupboard and, by lunchtime, I told matron that I thought I was ok to go back to the dormitory for the rest of the day and do some maths revision.

Back in the dorm, within my locker, I had a steak and kidney pie that had been delivered by my mother the previous weekend. I very carefully crushed the laxatives (all 14 tablets) with two spoons and, through a small incision, fed the powder into the pie, before wrapping it back in its greaseproof paper and returning it to my locker for the right opportunity.

My chance came the very next day. In the evening after the rugby match, where Fletcher had fouled me innumerable times, I was, with my fellow juniors, in the study room along the corridor from our dorm. Fletcher's dorm was on the other side of the wide staircase where the lavatories were also situated. He had a habit of looking in on us, either to get jobs done like cleaning his boots, or just 'on the scrounge' for treats.

I got the pie, still wrapped and resting on a plate, and told my dorm-pals that I wasn't going to touch it until I'd finished a particularly difficult set of maths questions. It was to be my reward. The study period was almost over when finally Fletcher made his appearance at the door. "Did you enjoy the game Gorny?" (this was a nickname I had acquired).

"Not much, Fletcher. Someone kept kicking me."

"You shouldn't get in the way of your seniors, should you? What's that you're trying to hide, you little shit?"

"Nothing Fletcher, honest," I said as I made a show of sliding the plate and pie under the table onto my knees.

"Let's have a look," he said diving towards the table and putting both hands underneath.

He emerged triumphantly holding the pie and tossing the plate back on the table. He started to unwrap it in front of us and asked with a leer, "Got any ketchup, urchins?"

"Come on Fletcher," I said plaintively, "My Mum made that."

"It should be delicious then... Shouldn't it Gorny?"

With that, he took a huge exaggerated bite and crumbs of pastry dropped onto his shirt, followed by a narrow rivulet of gravy. He said no more until it was finished, then licked his lips, burped, and strolled out rubbing his belly appreciatively.

I made my way to the toilets and sat in the middle one of three stalls and waited, my maths book on my knee. I studied the equations and tried mental arithmetic to pass the time. One or two other boys came and went, then after nearly half an hour, a groaning Fletcher banged the toilet door then the cubicle door open in succession and I could hear his heavy breathing as he managed to get his trousers down, before sinking onto the seat.

The pleasurable gasps as his bowels opened were heartfelt, but it seemed that just as he thought he had finished, nature reminded him that it wasn't over yet. By then I'd got onto the floor and, trying not to gag on the smell, put my head level with the floor so that I could see Fletcher's legs from the back. Just above where his trousers were bunched around his ankles, was my target. The fleshy left calf of my antagonist was open to attack. I didn't hesitate but plunged the morphine injector straight into Fletcher's leg. I could feel the pulsing of the liquid into the target as Fletcher roared and swore but couldn't move from his position. I withdrew the injector, put it in my pocket, then fled the toilets back to the dorm and jumped on my bed.

It wasn't long before a crowd of boys gathered and, after a few minutes, the Housemaster arrived in the toilets. "Make way you boys, there's nothing to see here." Clearly not a boy in the area believed that for a moment and stayed hovering, while listening to Fletcher continuing to groan and gasp through the door of the left hand cubicle.

"Fletcher! What on Earth is going on in there?"

"Aaaarrggghhh, ooooh, aaaaaawwwrrrrrr, God Almighty."

"What is the matter with you boy?"

"Siiirrrrrrrr, sorry.......siiirrrr, aaaarrggghhh, siiirrrr...... Ooooooohhh, no, no, no."

"This is most alarming," said the Housemaster, "You boy,

go and fetch the Headmaster at once," pointing to one of the seniors. "Can any of you boys throw any light on this?" By this time I had gone back to the toilets and squirmed my way through the throng. "Sir...", I said, "I don't know if this helps, but when I came in here about 15 minutes ago, I could hear Fletcher... Well, Sir, he was... singing in there... And there was an awful smell, Sir."

"Singing! Fletcher, are you drunk boy?"

"Dunno Siiiirrr... Don't really, weally, know-dee-ooh-doh... Siiirrrr."

Eventually, the Head arrived and Fletcher was still locked inside, sounding delirious.

"We'll have to break the door down," said the Head.

"But Sir, might that be dangerous for poor Fletcher, Sir?" I suggested. "If I may Sir, perhaps I could squeeze under the side of the cubicle and unlock the door from the inside. Then we can get Fletcher to matron for help, Sir?"

"Excellent, get to it lad."

The sight that faced teachers and students as the door slowly opened, and they looked over my shoulders, was not pleasant. James Fletcher was slumped on a toilet where excrement had splashed in every direction. He was almost unconscious but not enough to stop him uttering low animal-like moans. His pupils were totally dilated and the two teachers looked at each other knowingly. My coup de grace, was to, in all innocence, look at the Head and pass him the empty morphine syrette. "I found this on the floor next to Fletcher Sir, I don't know what it is, but it might be important."

We never found out exactly what happened to Fletcher,

just a brief announcement at the next Assembly, that he had left the school to 'save any further embarrassment' and would not be returning. Until now, I've never told the truth to anyone but, somehow, almost by the instinct of 300 boys, bullying never seemed to be a problem for the rest of my time at Bainbridge.

"Wow," said Lydia to no one in particular, still sat at the screen soaking in what she'd read. She needed to communicate her thinking now while it was fresh. She went to her emails and sent a message:

From: Lydia@rivetingread.co.uk

To: Robindc58@gmail.com

Sent: Thu 16/10/14 18:19

Subject: AONAG - Second Chapter

Rob,

Just been through chapter two and really enjoyed it. You are hitting the spot my friend!

Big strong man like you upset by a bit of seasickness...bit of a surprise!

I see relationship problems coming up, especially with your Dad?

I must say that being capable of such deviousness and single minded actions at little over nine years old is extraordinary. Was Fletcher really such a bad person? Did he deserve what he got? Is he one of those whose name we need to change, or have you already done that?

Alternatively, you've made it all up! But, as they say,

never let the truth get in the way of a good story!!

Either way, you are on a roll, don't stop!

Love,

Lydia.

-+-

Chapter Six

Rob stretched out his arms and legs from within his study chair and enjoyed the way his muscles responded to the flexing. He had done a twelve mile walk yesterday, which on top of the trekking he'd done on Tuesday, had left his joints a bit sore. It was now Friday morning and he was up early, beating the sun. He had read LHR's email of yesterday evening, and its message of encouragement. He was keen to make a start and get some words done before breakfast. The laptop screensaver, a landscape photograph featuring many luxuriant green hills, dotted with small, randomly placed houses, stared out at Rob as if egging him on.

He looked at his notes for chapter three and frowned. After lots of chewing the end of his ballpoint pen, he scribbled a few things down, crossed a few things out, then started typing:

This part of my story takes me to the end of my time at Bainbridge when, at the age of thirteen, I killed my mother. More of that later but, before that, I was to discover the satisfaction of soldiering. Well, the nearest thing that you can get at a British boarding school, the Combined Cadet Force.

You could join at age twelve and one of the housemasters, Ogilvy, was the Officer Commanding. He was apparently ex Coldstream Guards and was always impeccably turned out. He was also strict on the parade ground and when doing inspections of the Cadets. Many of us would have to do press ups with packs on our backs, for sloppy turnout, or be hosed in the showers with a powerful stream of cold water for more serious misdemeanours.

We'd have two parades a week and an exercise every

month. I loved it, once I'd mastered the steps and routines of the drilling, it gave me a real sense of pride to perform in time and as near to perfect as I could. The exercises, which could be anything from orienteering through the woods near the school, to caving or low level mountaineering on the Pennine crags a short drive away, were pure excitement as far as I was concerned. I didn't seem to get scared by anything we did and found out that I had a very steady hand when it came to shooting on the firing range.

So, while I was enjoying school life, I'm not sure that I was very good at making friends. I remember being quick to criticise if one of my peers did something wrong. This didn't endear me to them, and the way some of the boys kept their distance ever since the Fletcher incident, probably contributed to my isolation. There was also a fair bit of inherited snobbery and I hadn't pretended to be anything I wasn't. The other boys knew by my tatty school uniform that we had little money, and the fact that I was good at studies, sports, and a star of the Cadet Force made me a natural target. They knew better than to bully me, but the ways they found not to engage with me, seemed somehow worse.

The highlight of my first year in the Cadets, my fourth in the school, was the annual War Games weekend against Aysgarth School. This was the self-proclaimed 'Best school in the North', and Bainbridge had always lived in their shadow. Aysgarth had won the war game on the previous six occasions and, by their attitude when we met them at the start near High Force waterfall, they seemed to assume that this would be a repeat.

Effectively, the contest consisted of the two competing teams ("A" and "B") dividing into two groups or platoons each ("1" and "2"). The two number 1 platoons were placed over twenty miles away, at a wooded location between the two schools, each guarding their own "headquarters". The two number 2 platoons each had a flag that had to be delivered safely to their own HQ. The winners were the first team to deliver the flag to their HQ, entitling them to fire a coloured flare declaring their victory.

All the combatants were equipped with a firearm, a small supply of blank ammunition, compass, map, torch, combat rations, sleeping bag, uniform, and different coloured armbands with their school's letter and platoon number on it. There were at least half a dozen rivers between the start and the HQs so each platoon was equipped with one inflatable dinghy and a foot pump. They also had three walkie-talkies in each platoon but, with a range of less than one mile, communication was difficult.

Accompanying each platoon was a senior teacher to ensure fair play. The main issue for them was deciding whether a cadet who was fired upon by the other side (using their blanks) had been disabled from further involvement, something they showed by lifting a red flag to identify casualties.

The starting gun echoed around the gorge at 0900 on the Saturday morning, and the two platoons, set about half a mile apart on the south bank of the river Tees, started the mission. The game had a closing time of sunset on the following day. If neither team had won by Sunday night, it was declared a draw. As the game was always played at the end of the summer term this allowed for plenty of time and a draw had only happened once in the twenty years of the competition.

The seniors on both sides were in platoons A2 and B2, and the rest, including me, were in the number 1 platoons, guarding the HQs. Over the years the number 1 platoons had tried different tactics to help bring victory to their teams. The quandary was that if you deployed too many troops to try and slow down the opposition aiming to find their HQ, you were left with an insufficient force to support your own second platoon bringing the flag.

Presumably because I'd done well in the Cadet force and was a Corporal, I had been appointed second-in-command of platoon B1. I spoke to the Sergeant in charge, a weaselly-faced, skinny boy called Melville and asked him what we should do. After a discussion involving a high degree of uncertainty on his part, he told me that I should take two sections (16 boys) and stop the Aysgarth rabble from getting through. We knew roughly the route that our B2 platoon were intending to use and we agreed that we would patrol to the east of that, broadly across the direct route from A2's start point to their HQ. We were told to communicate any contact with the enemy to Melville at our remaining HQ section, without fail.

After a whole day searching we found absolutely no enemy forces. The boys were grumbling and as the sun touched the top of the hills to the west, I decided we should make camp for the night. The weather was kind to us and the moon was almost on the full as we settled down, in a clearing by a river, to cold rations. Some of the boys climbed into their sleeping bags and I kept one section on guard, to prevent us being surprised by the Aysgarth team. Our assigned referee, Ogilvy, also decided this was a good time for him to sleep, as did I, and we both took to our bags.

When it got to midnight without incident, I awoke, swapped the sections around - taking care not to wake Ogilvy - then came to a decision. We had to do something more positive and a plan had been germinating in my mind. I told two of the section to stay on guard and pass on a note I had scribbled down. The rest of the section (now six of us) were to bring their kit and come with me.

We went a safe distance from the camp and launched the dinghy, which we'd used to cross the river going north earlier, to go back to the southern side. I gathered everyone around me then, using the torch, I reviewed the map and aligned it with the compass.

"Right, team," I said with as much confidence as I could muster, "We know where we are, but we don't know where our number 2 platoon is, nor theirs. I've left Beasley a note to take the others back to our HQ, when they wake up. If they've got past us, some of Aysgarth 2 will be on the way to block our HQ, and Beasley's section's help will be needed to attack them."

"What about us?" asked one of the boys, "Where are we going now?"

"We're going here," I replied pointing at a spot on the map, "And we're going to stop Aysgarth winning. The rest is out of our hands. Come on, this is going to be a hard march and we're going to have to be quick."

It was a hard march, by moonlight, with constant checking of map and compass. Over four hours later, as the dawn light started to edge into our vision, we estimated that we were half way to our destination. I let the section have a two hour sleep in a dense thicket and stood watch, while going over the map again to be sure of our bearings.

I woke them at around 0630 and took them south-east. It was important to the plan that we didn't bump into any other platoons, and if that meant walking extra miles then it was worth it. Many hours, and more river crossings later, we got to a small wooded ridge about a mile to the south of where the enemy HQ was meant to be. Lying on my belly and using some binoculars from my pack, I was able to look north and see the green tents in a clearing that made up the Aysgarth HQ. There wasn't much sign of activity, apart from two cadets standing guard, with their backs to me, looking towards the expected threat.

I reckoned that we might just be in range of our own HQ, so tried the walkie-talkie, "B1, Section 1, to BHQ, over... B1, Section 1, to BHQ, over".

After much crackling, a faint change of note, then Melville's reedy voice came through, "Section 1, where the hell are you? Over."

"We're safe, what's happening there? Over."

"Had a runner from B2 to say they got lost and their ETA is now this evening. According to the referees, the men you left behind have all been 'killed' by A2 in an ambush, and A2 must now be on their way to their HQ, with only eight of us here to try and intercept them. I think you'd better get back here and we can plan an attack. Over."

"No time for planning, Melville, suggest place your section north of AHQ to delay A2 advance, we'll see what we can do to help. Over."

"I order you to return to BHQ, over."

I clicked the button a few times but did not reply. An enraged Melville came back on, "Come in, Section 1... Come in, damn you..."

I turned the device off, then turned to the others, "We haven't got much time, we need two long straight branches from these trees, use your knives." I then explained the final part of the plan to, at first, bemused faces, then knowing nods from the boys in my section.

When all was ready, I gave the order to lift, and a makeshift stretcher consisting of two battledress jackets, with wooden poles threaded through the sleeves and me lying on it, was lifted by four boys. Before putting me on the stretcher, they had rolled me in dirt and rubbed some into my face and hands. With practiced fearful frowns on their faces, my bearers set off tentatively down the slope towards the enemy HQ.

Due to their concentration on looking north, we were less than thirty yards from the AHQ guards, before we were noticed. As soon as they saw us, their rifles were levelled and we continued to move forward. "Stop, and drop your weapons," commanded the first guard. My bearers, who had their rifles slung over their shoulders, complied and the remaining member of our party went forward.

"We need your help, our Corporal is badly hurt."

"Aargh," sneered the Aysgarth boy, "Has one of you Bainbridge girls twisted their ankle then."

"We think he's got a broken leg, he fell out of a tree while observing you, and..." With that I groaned loudly and spouted some gibberish ramblings and swear words. "And, we think he must have hit his head on the way down."

"Wait here, watch them," instructed the guard to his colleague, as he ran into the largest of the tents. Within moments, half a dozen cadets came out of the tent along with a referee, who took charge.

"You boys, pick up those weapons and put them somewhere safe. Bainbridge team, get your man inside and lay him down at the back of the tent."

"Sir," said an Aysgarth cadet, "It could a trick, Sir?"

Another blast of foul gibberish came forth from the

stretcher as the referee bent over me and looked at my legs and face.

"He looks and sounds like a mess, Jennings. Carry on here and try to make him comfortable, I'm taking the car to get to a phone box and call an ambulance."

Jennings mumbled, "Can't we just shoot him?" But the referee was already on his way to the dirt track at the side of the tents to get his car.

Back in charge, Jennings then ordered all my squad into the smallest of the three tents and put two guards on the outside. It was at that point we heard the crackle of gunfire coming from north of the site. Clearly some of our team had found some of theirs. I knew that we didn't have much time but I hadn't reckoned on the referee going for help. There were many more enemies than friends here, but we had to give it a try.

Then the odds evened up, Jennings' blood was clearly in combat mode and he shouted at the two guards by the small tent to keep an eye on the Bainbridge scum. He then told one cadet to, "Watch the cripple", before ordering, "Rest of you, on me, let's charge to the sound of the guns". With that, the twelve other cadets picked up their rifles and followed their leader with a ragged cheer.

The gunfire seemed to be getting closer and, without the referee, my plan had to change. I called deliriously for water, and the young cadet who brought me some seemed genuinely concerned for my welfare. When he leaned forward to bring the mug to my lips, my right hand that had been behind me brought my revolver out of the waistband of my battledress and into the face of the cadet.

"I know these are only blanks, but this close it would really hurt if my finger were to twitch," I told him quietly, "Just

don't move or say anything." Then, slipping back into delirium, I started to sing the Bainbridge School song at the top of my voice. With that, my five fellows burst out of the prisoner tent, through gashes cut by a penknife, and overpowered the guards. They ignored the fact that one of the guards shot at least two of them in the struggle - the lack of referee worked both ways. We tied up all three of the Aysgarth cadets and gagged them, leaving them on the floor of the main tent. We then ran to the stores tent, glad that the layout of their HQ was similar to ours, and found what we were looking for. We then retrieved our weapons and ran hard to the west.

Ten minutes later, so we heard afterwards, it was a jolly 'band of brothers' who emerged into the clearing of the Aysgarth HQ, laughing about another victory over Bainbridge. Jennings and the leader of their number 2 platoon (carrying a big Aysgarth flag) marched towards the stores tent before the absence of their team-mates registered. At that point the referee returned and intercepted Jennings with the news that an ambulance was on its way. All this came together and, with growing panic in his voice, Jennings called to his cadets, "Where is everybody?"

They searched the camp and found their trussed colleagues, and the rip in the prisoner tent. Of the Bainbridge contingent, only the stretcher poles remained. It was with major trepidation that the two senior cadets went into the stores tent. Amongst the bottles of water, sleeping bags, and backpacks, there was a metal ammunition box about half the size of a briefcase. They lifted the lid and, resting on the indented shapes of where two fat pistols would normally sit, the only thing inside was a leaflet with 'Bainbridge Boarding School for Boys' on the front.

The referee would not back down. "I know your team got

the flag home Jennings, I can see it," he said patiently, "But the winner can only be declared after the recognised signal is given. No flare, no win."

The Aysgarth boys spent the next hour searching for the missing flare guns and those who had run off with them, swearing bitter vengeance should they be successful. At about 1930 hours that Sunday evening, a flare flew up from the Bainbridge camp and burst over the valley. Our lost platoon had finally made it to camp having gone far to the west and only had to fight through the somewhat dispirited attempts at intervention, from the Aysgarth force, at the very end of their mission.

I was congratulated for my initiative and promoted to Sergeant by Ogilvy, even though he dressed me down for my unorthodox methods. He thought them somewhat 'unsporting' and even 'French', which for him was the ultimate insult. Having won the day, and finally got the Aysgarth monkey off our backs, I was turned into some sort of hero. Strangely, my schoolfellows seemed even more wary of me than before. I didn't know why.

After re-reading and editing, Rob saved the latest version then looked at his watch. It showed a quarter to twelve so what had started as a bit of pre-breakfast warm up, had become a full on, pre-lunch writing session. He went to the kitchen and got some blue cheese out of the fridge, an uncut loaf from the bread bin, and a plate from the cupboard. Rob warmed the cheese slightly in the microwave and cut some chunks off the loaf. He returned to his desk with the lunch and a tall glass of pineapple juice.

The screensaver cleared as Rob touched the mousepad, and he lifted the glass to his mouth. As he did so, his eyes darted to the left of his field of vision and he put the glass down, reaching instead for the binoculars on the side table.

He quickly focused on the road as it came around the edge of the hill, and on it saw a tall, slim, young man walking, while looking to his left and right, towards the cottage. He got as far as the gravel track that led up the slope behind Water Cottage and the man stopped, looked up the hill, then carried on until going out of sight behind the slope. He re-emerged as the slope ended and looked to his right, straight up at Rob's window. Through the binoculars, he saw the man clearly. He had a smooth, soft caramel coloured face, with short cropped dark brown hair. He was clean shaven and handsome, with full features. Dressed incongruously for Harris, in an open black raincoat, light blue suit, with a dark blue tie over a white shirt, he also carried a leather suitcase.

The young man must have seen Rob looking at him and, nervously, put up his hand, smiling in greeting. Rob quickly put down the bins and waved back, as if it was perfectly normal seeing Africans dressed as bible salesmen on the byways of the Outer Hebrides. He waved again from the window but this time by pushing his open palms forward as if saying 'wait there'. Rob went out onto the slope at the front and got to the edge over the road. He looked down at the stranger who had waited as asked, and said, "Good Morning, or possibly Good Afternoon."

"Greetings", replied the stranger in a clear, high voice and a trace of an African accent.

"Perhaps I can help you? I've only lived here a month myself, but Crawnish is very small, if you're looking for anyone in particular?"

"Yes."

"Yes... What?"

"Yes... Sir... I am looking for somebody in particular."

"You don't have to...never mind... Who are you looking for?"

"I need to find a gentleman called, 'Carter Aragorn Talbot'... Do you know him?"

Rob looked left and right then back at the youthful, expectant face below him. Sighing under his breath, he said to the stranger, "I... I may be able to help. Why not come in for coffee? Those clouds look like turning to rain fairly soon anyway," he added as he waved out to sea.

"Thank you for your kindness, Sir," said the stranger, with a slight bow from the neck.

-+-

Chapter Seven

The shadows grew immense over the ranch as the setting sun went behind Mount Elgon and, in the lee of the extinct volcano, bright day became comparative twilight. The house backed onto the green lower slopes, as if it has been herded to the end of a gully and couldn't go any further. A long, red dirt track followed the contours of the gully and snaked its way westward from a distant made road between Kitale and the Ugandan border. A sluggish stream, showing with its wide banks that it knew what it was like to behave as a full flowing river, ran down from north of the house along the neighbouring crease in the mountain's fringes.

Milton Kwizera drove his white Toyota Prado Land Cruiser along the dirt road towards the mountain. Next to him was his, much older, driver who ventured, "Shouldn't I be doing the driving Bwana? You must be tired?"

"No need Joseph, I enjoy it."

Joseph, sensing the finality of the young man's words, kept his tongue quiet and his eyes on the dusty track ahead. He could see the white outline of the house as they progressed through the late afternoon gloom. It was built as a sprawling array of wide, low, flat roofed blocks, which must have been considered the finest European style when constructed in the 1990's. Plenty of glass so that the occupants could enjoy the views and only the central ranch house having more than one storey, as if to show that economical use of land was of no concern to the owner.

Milton slowed the car as they crested a small rise and levelled out to approach an imposing set of black steel gates set in heavy concrete block work, also painted black. To the left and right of the gates, as far as the eye could see, stretched an eight foot high heavy steel mesh fence, topped by endless coils of razor wire. Joseph lowered his window as the car pulled up and shouted, "Askari, open up."

The gates opened inwards and a guard in a soldier's uniform saluted the car as it drove through. About half a mile ahead, the various buildings that made up the ranch house complex became clear. Between the gates and the house was a low barracks style building with many small windows set in bare concrete block walls. Up a small slope and a gravel drive was the main ranch house entrance. This was made of several marble pillars supporting a white rendered concrete porch dressed with luxuriant trees in black ceramic pots. Between the pillars were heavy, metal studded doors in gleaming ebony wood. From the centre piece of the entrance, single story wings stretched out left and right in the same rendered finish as the porch. Above the entrance was a smaller second storey in similar style, graced with large double glazed windows and no sign of any openings.

From a small white bungalow beyond the left wing of the house, two young girls in matching long blue dresses came running up to the car. One carried a pitcher and towels, the other a tray with glasses and bottles. After moving to the passenger's side they realised their mistake and rushed around to the driver's door, curtsying as Milton got out. After splashing his face with cupped hands and towelling it dry, he took a cold bottle of beer and, ignoring the proffered glass, opened it with his teeth. He took a long swig and gave a satisfied sigh, before finishing the bottle and striding towards the front door.

Milton didn't dwell in the cool, quiet entrance hall, but went straight through towards the rear of the central block through a Swahili style door. An enormous lounge scattered with large soft-looking leather couches in cream and brown, led onto a complete glass wall with big sliding doors in the open position. Beyond the glass panels, arrayed like an oasis, was a kidney shaped, blue tiled, swimming pool, fringed by a terrace on three sides, with an open view of the mountain - now in deep shade - to the rear.

Milton called out in the direction of one of the many padded sun-beds, on which a woman wrapped in a white towelling robe with a smaller towel turbaned on her head, was reading a book.

"Mother, it's me."

The woman didn't lift her eyes, but waved a casual hand towards the interruption with a calling motion.

Milton went through and sat on the bed next to his mother.

"No one else around, Mama?"

"Just me, Milton. I think Jane is within calling distance if you need a drink or something?"

"Nothing for me... And Papa?"

"He's probably in the Jacuzzi upstairs... Two new 'friends' arrived today. How was Nairobi?"

Glad of the change of subject, Milton launched into a description of the long weekend of partying he had enjoyed in the fleshpots of the capital, censoring some of the more lurid details involving drug taking and orgies, to spare his mother's blushes. He watched her face as she pretended to listen, it was the colour of milky coffee, oval shaped and still beautiful at forty five, with full bright hazel eyes and only the barest hint of crow's feet at the edges. He glanced at her trussed up in the robe, and thought how well she had kept her figure. Nothing is his tale seemed to prompt a genuine smile so he asked her outright.

"What's wrong Mama?"

"Nothing... I'm... No, nothing."

"Come on Mama, perhaps I can help."

"I'm not sure you can... I'm worried about your brother."

He was unable to keep all the sarcasm out of his reply, "What's the 'Professor' done now?"

"It's what he hasn't done... He finished his first year at Edinburgh months ago and said he was going to take a couple of weeks to tour around Britain while he was there, then come home before the second year. Here we are in October, he never came back and the last I heard from him he said he was taking a gap year."

"Good for him, perhaps he's learned to get his nose out of his books for a change and live a bit. It'll do him the world of good."

"But it's so not like him, he's always been the quiet one. I thought that university would be perfect for him... and good for you, for that matter."

He sensed the accusatory tone and bristled, "I'm too busy to be wasting times with boring studies. Too busy being an entrepreneur, networking, looking for deals, that sort of thing."

"Milton, you're nineteen. Getting drunk with your ex high school mates and second rate Kenyan celebrities is hardly the same as building a business empire, is it?"

"Some of my friends are very well connected, we are on the brink of some great property developments."

"Are these friends from the same families that grabbed so much land after independence? I'd imagine that it's not too difficult to make money, developing land that was stolen from someone else."

"You don't understand, Mama."

"That's probably just as well."

Milton bit his tongue then called out for Jane to bring him a cold Tusker while he stewed in silence. She arrived and opened the bottle then went to pour it into a glass. He snatched it from her then threw it down on the tiled terrace floor where it exploded. "I said COLD you stupid bitch, fucking BARIDI."

The house-girl scuttled off at speed to get what was required and Milton, instantly calm again, turned to his mother and enquired, "So when exactly did you last hear from my illustrious twin?"

"About two weeks ago, end of September, he called and said he was in Edinburgh and was about to go on a trip to explore the islands."

"What did Papa say?"

She smiled ironically, "You know your father's temper... He was furious. Said that he hadn't spent all that money on a British education so that his son could roam around looking at landscapes. He tried to call him and order him to come home, but your brother seems to have turned his phone off."

"Not for you, I'll bet", said Milton as he snatched his mother's mobile up from the side table between the sun-beds. He quickly scanned the list and pressed a name. After some delay, Milton heard a ring tone and then the voice of his twin brother, "Hello Mum."

"Not 'Mum'... Milton... You are in so much trouble Brother. Papa has been trying to call you and you've ignored him. He wants you home, now, no excuses."

The phone went quiet, then softly, "I'm sorry Milton... I don't want to come home at the moment. I'm... I... There are things I need to do first."

"Perhaps I'm not making myself clear, Brother. You will come home, right now, or we'll come and bring you home."

There was a long pause, then a simple, "No Milton, that's not going to happen", then a beep as the call was terminated.

Milton threw the phone down on the sun-bed and grabbed the bottle of cold Tusker, that had arrived while he had been talking. He tipped it to his mouth and drank most of it in one go, before wiping his mouth with the back of his hand and looking intently at his mother, "He has no respect for this family, Mama, he needs to be taught a lesson. One that all his lecturers and teachers can't give him. I'm going to talk to Father."

Before his mother could answer him, he stood up and went back into the house and headed for the wide circular staircase that led up to his father's suite of rooms on the second storey of the building.

His mother watched him go, with tears in her eyes. She dabbed at them with the sleeve of her robe, then picked up the phone and composed a text before pressing 'send'.

-+-

Chapter Eight

By boiling some eggs, slicing some tomatoes, and unwrapping some ham from the fridge, Rob had turned his bread and cheese late breakfast into lunch for him and his African guest. They sat in the two overstuffed armchairs in the lounge and picked at the buffet on the coffee table, while sipping tea. Rob smiled as the other man poured half the contents of the milk jug into his mug, then added four heaped spoonfuls of sugar.

"You like your tea African style, young man?"

The visitor looked mortified, "I'm sorry Sir... You said help yourself."

"And I meant it, please tuck in. I just had a flashback."

"You know Africa?"

"You could say that."

"Where have you been?"

"Plenty of time for that later. First things first. Why don't you tell me about you, and what you're doing so far from home?"

The visitor lifted some ham and bread onto his plate, and took a long draught of his tea.

"My name is Shakespeare Kwizera, and I'm from Kenya. I've been at the University of..."

"Did you say Kwizera?" asked Rob, anxiously leaning forward in his chair.

"Yes, K, w, i, z, e, r, a. Why?"

"It's....it's ok, I interrupted, sorry. Please finish your story." With that Rob sank back but he looked intently at the young man while he continued. Close up, Rob could see that Shakespeare had grey green eyes that seemed to shine as he spoke.

"Yes, so I've done my first year at Edinburgh, reading modern history. This is not my first time in the United Kingdom. I spent two years at Marlborough school and sat my A-levels there. English, French, history, and geography."

"I thought your English was very good", encouraged Rob, "but shouldn't you be back at Edinburgh for your second year?"

"Something came up...as you British say."

Rob waited for more insight, but Shakespeare took a hard-boiled egg and, after removing its shell quickly, took a big bite and chewed slowly.

"You said you were looking for a man, someone called 'Carter' was it?"

"I did, I am, and it is, but I thought that, in your culture, you had to both make introductions before much talking took place?"

"Yes, sorry...of course. My name's Rob... Robin Chancellor."

Shakespeare leaned forward, brushed the last of the eggshell from his fingers, and held out his hand towards Rob's chair. "Delighted to meet you... Rob," he said with a broad grin. "What's your story?"

"I'm here writing a book actually. Only just started it, but my agent seems to like the early bits. I needed somewhere quiet. And Crawnish is about as quiet as it gets, the road to the west stops here and the next land out there is Canada, about 2,000 miles." The last words said with a wave at the broad picture window behind Shakespeare's chair.

"What's it about? The book, I mean?"

"Sort of my memoirs really, possibly juiced up a bit? The phrase, 'inspired by real events' would seem to cover it. It's not going to change the world or anything."

"Not like 1984 then?"

"Sorry, Shakespeare. I don't follow."

"Well that was written by an Englishman on a Scottish island wasn't it? Jura I think. George Orwell... But that wasn't his real name. He was named Eric Blair." Rob felt the bright eyes of his guest looking closely into his face.

"I do believe you're right...although he did die of consumption as a result...anyway, more tea?"

As Rob busied himself in the kitchen brewing fresh tea and digging out a box of biscuits, Shakespeare looked around the small lounge and out to sea. The clouds had turned to rain, as Rob had predicted earlier, and the wind had increased in intensity. It was blowing sizeable waves onto the rocks at the water's edge, and softly rattling the window pane in front of him. He felt his mobile phone vibrate in his inside pocket, before he heard it ring. He extracted it and touched the screen. He spoke, then Rob came back in holding a tray, and heard "...not going to happen", before seeing Shakespeare put a phone into his jacket.

"You're lucky to get a signal, the network here is far from perfect," he said as he saw the worry on the African's face.

"Have some fresh tea."

They settled down again and were lifting their mugs when Shakespeare felt inside his jacket and again retrieved his phone. He scanned and touched the screen, then put it back.

"You look worried Shakespeare, can I help?"

"I need to find Mr Talbot, I'm sure he'll help."

"Who is he...to you, I mean?"

"I've never met him, nor even seen a photograph, but he was a good friend of my mother. They lost touch many years ago but she said that if I ever needed help, I should track him down. She said that if Carter Talbot was alive, he would be there for me, and for her."

Rob had been inadvertently holding his breath and now exhaled slowly, his eyes never leaving the face opposite. "What was your mother's name, Shakespeare?"

"It is Nicole."

Rob tensed and sighed, then softly asked, "How old are you?"

"Nineteen, twenty in January. Why?"

Rob ignored the question and did some mental arithmetic. "It can't be," he said. Then another thought seemed to strike him and he cried out, "You said 'it is' Nicole. Surely you meant 'it was'..? The Nicole Kwizera I knew was killed in the Rwandan genocide, in 1994. You must have been born in 1995, well after the end of that nightmare."

"Well, my mother is very much alive, I've just had a text

from her! Anyway, you said you knew that name but you also said you are Robin Chancellor."

"Let's just say, for now, that you might be right about the George Orwell analogy. More important, do you have a photo of your mother?"

Out came Shakespeare's mobile again, and he pressed the screen a few times before handing the device over. A sharply defined, full length photograph of a slim woman leaning back against a thick white pillar, with a swimming pool behind her, filled the screen. She had a milky brown complexion and this contrasted well with the loose white linen dress that fell from her shoulders and brushed against her breasts, hips and knees.

Rob looked for a long time at the smooth, elegant face and closed in on it by pinching at the centre of the screen and splaying his fingers out. He felt himself gulping hard, his pulse racing, and stomach churning as he took in the big hazel eyes and the classic features. Eventually he handed back the phone and said, with a faltering voice, "It's been over twenty years, and I can hardly believe it... I grieved for so long...and now...now she's... Oh my God! This is... incredible... shattering... news. Forgive me, Shakespeare, you don't even know me, and I'm going on about your mother like this... It's almost too much to take in."

"Can I get you a whisky...Rob? That might help?"

"Good man, yes, in the study. Just grab the first bottle you come to, and two glasses. We need to really talk. And...erm...Shakespeare, sorry about earlier. I am, Carter Aragorn Talbot, and very pleased indeed to meet you. My friends call me Cat. Now, go and get the whisky!"

-+-

Chapter Nine

Milton awoke in the middle of his king-sized bed and stretched across the lithe young body on his left, reaching for a bottle of water on the bedside table. The girl mumbled and pulled the lightweight quilt around her. In the breaking light of the morning sun streaking through the edges of the drapes, he saw the pale face of the girl on his right. She lay on her back, thin lips slightly open, breathing deeply. Her blonde hair tousled and spreading, like unbundled straw on the white cotton pillow.

He swigged at the water bottle as he cupped his testicles with his other hand. He threw the empty plastic bottle across the room and, as it clattered across the wooden floor, the noise seemed to disturb the girl on his left. A black face with a sleepy expression emerged from under the quilt and stared at Milton. He moved his now free left hand to her tight curled hair and pulled her face to his.

"I need your mouth," he said as he guided her under the quilt to his groin. He felt her mouth engulf him and start sucking. With his right hand he reached for the still sleeping blonde and put his hand, palm down, between her legs. He started stroking, as his hips began thrusting gently in time with the attention he was getting from the black girl.

After some minutes of arousal, he turned them both onto all fours next to each other in the middle of the bed. He got into position, then mounted them in turn, swapping between them every so often. His climax was noisy and strong, but without much fluid. As he drained the residue over their buttocks he said, "I think you took too much out of me last night girls," then flopped onto his back to recover his breath.

The girls came up cuddling on each side and thanked him, saying how they loved powerful men like him and his father. "I think that maybe you love the money more, but you were good, and unusual that one of you is a mzungu."

The white girl clearly knew he was talking about her and said simply, "Russka!" while pointing at herself. The black girl told Milton that the Russian girl had only been in Kenya for two weeks, but was already proving popular with their favourite clients.

"Right girls, I've got things to do. Get your stuff and go back to my father, he may want you this morning."

As the prostitutes got dressed, Milton walked into the shower and quickly felt the powerful jets cleanse him. When he stepped back into the bedroom wrapped in a bath towel, the girls had gone. He put bush clothes on, with high boots and a wide brimmed hat. He then went into a wardrobe and opened a safe in the back wall. He strapped a revolver belt around his hips. He put a handful of rounds into the pouch pockets of his safari jacket, then stuffed a bundle of banknotes into his back pocket. He picked up his phone and made his way along the corridor from his quarters to the central ranch house area, then up the stairs.

"Father," he called, after knocking on the door at the centre of the first floor landing, "It's me... Milton."

A deep baritone voice came through the timber, "Come."

Milton looked at the imposing figure of his father, standing beside a massive mahogany desk in just a bright green silk robe, towelling his completely bald head. He was the colour of fresh charcoal and stood like an old solid tree stump that remains rooted after the top fifty feet have been chopped down. His muscular shoulders extended his width, the bull chest and prominent paunch at the waist, serving to accentuate his bunker-like build. His flabby jowls wobbled as he spoke from a mouth with fat lips and bright white teeth.

"Milton my boy... Did you enjoy my presents... The black and white assortment?" His wide nose and big black eyes moved with the rest of his face as he laughed throatily at his joke.

"I thought they'd come back to you this morning?"

"They did, but...I'm not as young as I was, Kijana. I'll have some more fun later, then Joseph can take them back to Nairobi tomorrow."

"I'm not sure I'm a boy any more Papa."

"You still have so much to learn, Milton."

"As does Shakespeare, Father."

Alphonse Kwizera frowned at his son and said, "He's so different to you, very disobedient, but very clever."

"He shows you no respect, Papa. I spoke to him yesterday."

Alphonse sucked in his breath, "I did not know this."

"I came to tell you, but your... friends were with you I think, and you didn't answer the door."

"Yes, we were partying in the Jacuzzi."

"I called him on Mama's phone, told him to obey you and come home immediately."

"And...?"

"He....he...ehm...he...hung up on me...saying it wasn't going to happen."

"So what do you recommend... Kijana?"

Milton blushed, then, throwing his shoulders back, replied firmly, "Let me go and find him... And bring him back to you. Prove I'm not a boy."

"Are you serious?"

"I can do it Papa, cousin Pascal is in London. He can help me. I can leave tomorrow."

Milton's father looked long and hard at him before nodding and, speaking unusually quietly, "I will think on the matter and let you know. It is most important not to bring any unnecessary attention to our home. By the way, why are you dressed for the bush?"

"I understand, Father. According to our pet Ranger, an exceptionally old bull has been seen less than a kilometre from our fence, in the Elgon National Park. We're going to go for him today, while the Ranger diverts his colleagues to the south of the park with poacher reports. The tusks are immense and could fetch us more than a quarter of a million dollars."

Alphonse's eyes sparkled as his son's voice registered the excitement of the planned killing. "Well done, my Son," he said and walked over to pat him on the back. "And good hunting!"

-+-

Chapter Ten

Shakespeare had returned from the study to the lounge holding a two-thirds empty bottle of whisky and two crystal tumblers.

"Which one have you picked?" asked Cat.

"The label says 'Glenmorangie, 15 years old, matured in Port Wood', wherever that is?"

"It's a type of barrel, not a place," grinned Cat, at the puzzled looking face in the doorway. "A cask that used to have Port wine in it, is then used to store the whisky for the last years of its maturing process. It makes the whisky very dark, rich to taste, and smooth to drink."

"Well, I chose it because you obviously like it," teased Shakespeare lifting the mainly empty bottle to the fading light from the window.

"Good shout, my friend, let's get comfortable." Cat then got up, went over to the multi-fuel stove and, adding kindling from a basket at the side, got a fire started with a gas firefighter. He placed some small logs on top, then a lump of peat, and closed the fire's door. He flicked on two wall lamps which gave the room a soft peach-coloured glow.

Shakespeare had poured whisky into both glasses and placed them on the table that still hosted the remains of their lunch. Cat took the plates, mugs, and remains of the food into the kitchen and returned with a small jug which he put down next to the drinks.

"Water, for the whisky," he said.

"In Kenya, my father and brother drink whisky, but they have it neat."

"What about you, Shakespeare?"

"I've tried it, but just don't like the taste."

"Perhaps it's the brand they drink? Have a taste of this, you might change your mind?" With that, Cat added the barest drop of water, from the little jug, to each tumbler. "That's to release the flavour and make it perfect, like the dew on the petals of a rose." he said, as he passed one glass to his guest and lifted the other to his nose.

"Smell it first," he suggested, "The flavours are sublime."

Shakespeare sniffed, tentatively at first, then with more effort as his mouth shaped into a grin. "Can we taste now?" He asked, already tilting the rim towards his lips.

"Why not!" replied his host, and they both took generous sips.

They looked at each other without a word, then both took larger draws on their glasses, swirling the whisky around their mouths, before settling back into their armchairs and swallowing with matching sighs.

"I think, I'm a convert," said Shakespeare breathily, "That tastes so good. Nothing like the Johnnie Walker they drink at home."

"Glad you like it," said Cat, with genuine pleasure in his face. "Now, we need to talk."

And talk they did, as the early arrival of autumn darkness in these latitudes, turned a Friday afternoon gradually into a Friday night. Cat prompted Shakespeare to take his time and tell his story. He started to tell him about his studies, but Cat stopped him and asked him to go further back, to childhood.

"You just want to hear more about my Mum," he challenged him.

"Not just that, I'd like to understand more about you, what motivates you, what has brought you from the African savannah to the last windswept outpost in Europe?"

So, guided by Carter Talbot and the rest of the Glenmorangie, Shakespeare Kwizera went through the story of his life so far. His first memory was falling into the swimming pool at the Mount Elgon house. He had been fished out by a house-girl, and his mother had hugged him for a very long time.

The family background, told to him, his brother, and any visitors to the house, was that his mother and father were Rwandans, who had left Kigali in 1992, and moved to Kenya. His mother was half Belgian and half Tutsi. His father had been a well-connected senior civil servant and, after the ceasefire in the country's civil war that year, he took the chance to leave. His connections extended to the family of President Moi of Kenya, and he was granted a house in the President's tribal area, in return for the capital he brought with him and a share of future farming profits.

After settling in the Kenyan ranch, and adding improvements and new structures to the site over time, they had been blessed by twin boys in 1995. Shakespeare and his brother had not gone to school. They had been kept on the ranch and tutors would come in to teach them. As they grew they displayed very different interests. Milton loved daring things like going out with the farming manager, learning to ride and shoot. Shakespeare, by his own admission, considered himself boring as he did not enjoy those type of activities and grew up buried in the world of books and studying. He even used to insist that the tutor never left until he had read his work and marked it.

Family life was somewhat strained with his mother and father not spending much time together. His father had his own quarters at the top of the house with lavish bedroom, luxury bathroom and plush office. He was usually there when he wasn't out on the estate. His mother had her own suite of rooms in the southern wing and spent much of her time there, in and around the pool, or in the small gymnasium. Shakespeare got the feeling that his mother would sooner be anywhere else than at home, but that her husband used the continued safety and security of her sons as a way to keep her cocooned at the ranch.

When they reached sixteen, their parents had agreed that they could go to England so that they could get qualifications suitable for university entry in the First World. Shakespeare was sure that his mother was behind this and that Milton, with his father's indulgence, would have been quite happy not to leave his cosseted lifestyle. But, Nicole must have prevailed and so it was that, armed with a five year UK visa each, the twins arrived at Marlborough school to do their A-levels.

By way of encouragement, Cat interjected at this point saying, briefly, "I went to Marlborough, must have mentioned it to your mother... Anyway, please carry on... Sorry."

Shakespeare went on to explain how Milton had only lasted about six months at the school before being expelled, for experimenting with drugs, and went home to Kenya. He continued to relate how he himself had embraced the academic disciplines and opportunities for learning, on offer. How he had worked hard and ended up with four A+ grades, but no real friends. He wasn't used to being surrounded by anyone beside family and servants. He had gone home in the late spring of 2013, having submitted his university applications, and spent the summer resting at the ranch.

Being accepted at Edinburgh made his mother very proud and his father ambivalent. His brother tired of teasing his 'bookworm' twin, and spent his time in the pursuit of hedonism. Shakespeare set off in September with high hopes of success and some scanty details of Carter, that his mother could remember, scribbled in his notebook.

He had moved into part of the university set aside for 'freshers' and ended up rooming with a rather chubby, spotty, youth from Sunderland. Terry had a great love of Sunderland Football Club and what he introduced to Shakespeare as, 'Real Ale'. They were both doing a modern history module and while Terry chose the 'Pre-World War One arms race and rise of the Dreadnoughts', Shakespeare wanted to learn so much more of the country of his background and was doing 'Central Africa since Independence'.

He threw himself into the course and his independent studies. Every day, it seemed, he found out new facts about where he came from. How the Belgians had wanted the administration of Rwanda to be easy, so they introduced tribal identification papers and appointed the Tutsi minority to perform the roles of control and management of the country. The Hutu majority became second class citizens and years of resentment against the ruling Tutsi's built up. Shakespeare learned how, when the Belgians finally pulled out, they left their former colony to the upheaval of independence, without any genuine transitional support.

As the months went by, he got more and more intrigued by

the Rwandan civil war that started at the end of the 1980's and gradually went out of control, in fits and starts, until the almost inevitable genocide in 1994.

Then, Shakespeare revealed how, around the end of his first year at the university, he had been shocked to his core. He was reviewing a raft of old online United Nations reports written by the UN Commander in Kigali and there was a a reference to a group of Hutu officers forming the link between the government forces, and the militias who were carrying out most of the Hutu genocide of Tutsis. By following the online references, he found a photograph of this small group, dated 17th June 1994. The names were all unfamiliar to him, but one of the officers was not. There, with the name tab 'Portier Gatanazi' was, without any doubt in his mind, an image of his father. Somewhat slimmer than now, but still running to fat, his peaked cap on his lap, and his round, dark face, unmistakeable.

"So the whole story about getting out of Rwanda before the genocide started was pure fabrication?" asked Cat.

"I couldn't think of any realistic alternative. My whole background was a tale of my father's, to protect him in his new life. Worse, to think of my own father involved in the senseless slaughter of over 800,000 people, was just beyond comprehension."

"So, Shakespeare, what did you do?"

"I took the exams, then did some more digging in the summer, to find what I could about my father's 'alter ego'. I found references to him in some of the roadblock massacres, interaction with the Interahamwe thugs who went from house to house, murdering Tutsis. Also, he made a call over the radio to 'Defend Kigali to the last man', in the closing days of the genocide as the rebel forces moved in to finish the war. The last reference I could find was when the remnants of the government Hutu forces were on the run into Eastern Zaire. He is mentioned under the Gatanazi name as one of those officers in liaison with French peacekeepers, at a refugee camp in Goma, who were trying to help their former stooges in Rwanda with their escapes."

"Are you Ok?" asked Cat, as he saw the tears welling in Shakespeare's eyes. "We've finished that whisky, but I can get more."

"Perhaps a cup of tea?"

"I'll put the kettle on and...here's an idea... Let's have some fish and chips? As today's Friday, Crawnish gets visited by the fish frying van... It's called 'The Frying Scotsman' for God's sake!" Cat looked at his watch. "Not too late, I'll jog along and be back in a few minutes. Ok?"

Shakespeare nodded and sat back in his chair, his eyes heavy with tears which he wiped with a handkerchief. While Cat went for the fish suppers, he looked again at the text from his mother, earlier that day: 'S. I think they will come for you. Mum X'.

-+-

Chapter Eleven

Carter didn't stand on ceremony when he returned with two bundles of creamy coloured paper, spattered with dark spots where some of the oil was leeching through the wrapping. He threw one gently to Shakespeare saying, "This will make you feel better on a cold night. Straight out of the sea today, and cooked by the trawler man himself. He even put the salt and vinegar on for us!"

Shakespeare opened his package eagerly and grabbed at some chips then, as he chewed, he started pulling apart the crispy batter and, taking a big piece of flaky white fish, in his hand asked, "What is it?"

"No idea, my friend. There's no option at the 'Frying Scotsman'. You just get whatever he's caught today, deep fried in batter. Probably best not to ask on some days!"

After they finished and wiped their greasy hands clean, Cat got more tea and they sat back, almost scared to go back to their earlier conversation.

Cat suggested that, if it was too painful, perhaps they could leave it until tomorrow? He said that Shakespeare had to stay, the hamlet of Crawnish not being favoured with readily available accommodation. His study settee converted into a bed, he told his guest.

"Thanks, Cat," he responded, "That's kind of you. I'd like to keep talking... If that's Ok with you?"

"Sure, I suppose you're curious about how I know your mum? Of course you are, and I'll tell you all about it. But first, how did you find me? I'm meant to be incognito up here and a teenager, albeit a very intelligent teenager, tracks me down as if I'd left muddy footprints all the way from London!"

"Simple really Cat, I didn't find you... I paid someone else to do it! Whatever else my father is, he's always been generous with my allowance. After what I'd discovered, I couldn't go home and didn't want to upset my mum by telling her about what I now knew. So, I told the family, and the university, that I was going to take a gap year. The next thing, remembering what she'd said about you, was to find you. I Googled 'finding a lost friend', went to 'missingpersons.co.uk', gave them your name, the few details about you that my mum gave me, and paid a deposit. That was in August. Here I am, seven weeks later."

"As simple as that... But what information did you give these people?"

"I knew your full name, birthday, that you were born in Yorkshire, you were an orphan, had a British army background, mainly in the parachute regiment, worked for the Foreign and Commonwealth Office since leaving the forces, lived in London when not on assignment overseas, loved the western isles of Scotland, and was a member of the Dragon Club."

"That's 'Dragoon Club' but otherwise your mum's memory was very good. I must have made a strong impression on her..."

"Really Cat, you should have seen the light in her eyes when she spoke to me about you. I can't remember seeing such emotion in her before."

"Did your contact say what it was that led them to knowing I was here, in Crawnish."

"They're quite protective about their sources, but I get the impression that word was out in the Club about you going off to the Isles to write a book. Perhaps they then homed in on properties being newly leased in the Hebrides?"

"I did have a very boozy send off with a handful of members," said Cat, with a hand to his head as if the memory itself would provoke a hangover. "The main thing is, that you're here now. Although you almost walked right past?"

"The address given to me was 'Water Cottage', Crawnish. Your board down by the road says something completely different, so after the taxi from Tarbert dropped me off at the edge of the village, I walked past your entrance after seeing your house sign."

"Uisge Bothan," said Cat, "it's Gaelic for Water Cottage".

"Will I have to learn any of the language here?"

"Only if you upset the locals... If they like you, they'll talk in English!"

"So... You and my mum. What's the story Cat?"

Cat sat still for a few moments, took a deep breath and told how his boss at the FCO had broken the news of his new assignment to Kigali, at the department Christmas party in 1993. He was informed that it was all going to 'kick off' and how the French were helping to arm the Rwandan government forces. His job, in the absence of a British embassy, was to go into Country and see what could be done to help protect British interests and the hundred or so British residents, even if meant evacuation. He had two main points of contact, the non-resident Ambassador to Rwanda, who doubled as the British High Commissioner in Uganda, and the British Honorary Consul in Rwanda, who tended to live on his coffee plantation, rather than spend time in Kigali. He had also been assured of the 'friendly co-operation' of the Belgian Embassy who would help out with logistics 'on the ground'.

He had arrived in pleasant sunny weather in the middle of January and, as it was his first ever visit, he took in the approach to Kigali from the aircraft window with interest, likening the wide spread of luxuriant hills to a, 'very green Sheffield', to the stranger in the seat beside him. He was assigned a room in a small cottage just down the road from the Belgian embassy, sharing with a Flemish, English-speaking, trade and industry attaché called Jules, who he thought immediately was 'as gay as Christmas'.

Shakespeare giggled at this, so Cat looked at him quizzically. "Sorry Cat, I've not heard that expression before."

"It's not meant unkindly... He was gay, and happy about it... It was through him that I met your mum."

"Do carry on."

Cat told Shakespeare about how he had agreed a plan with the British Ambassador in Kampala. Cat would go to Kigali as a guest of the Belgians and would, with the help of the Honorary Consul, establish the whereabouts of all the Brits. He would then send a report to Kampala and the Ambassador would decide whether an official visit, by him, was, 'appropriate'.

"Does that mean 'safe' for him?" asked Shakespeare.

"Safe for him, and to make it look to London as if he was in control of the situation."

Cat explained how the first few weeks flew by and was spent trying to get information, often with frustrating outcomes. It took him a week to even get to see the HC and then only because he got one of the Belgian drivers to take him up country to his coffee plantation. The database of UK citizens resident in Rwanda consisted simply of an old battered box file in the Honorary Consul's farmhouse kitchen, half full of tatty notes and business cards, with not even a pretence of any order. He had been very pleased to pass this over to Cat, who turned the scraps into a list while he was there. He then, through questioning the coffee farmer, filled in some of the gaps in terms of contact details, where they existed.

He then spent the next three weeks back in Kigali, where the majority of the names on his list were thought to be. By finding those he could and asking each Brit to corroborate his information, where possible, he gradually built up a location list of about 90 missionaries, charity workers, business people, and other UK passport holders. To everyone on the list, he allocated two other Brits from the list, ideally close by. The idea being that if things really did 'kick off', word would get around the British community quickly and instructions could be distributed. He pointed out to Shakespeare that this was in the days before reliable mobile phones.

By the end of February, Cat had done what he could and his 'signal system' had been tested effectively. He then compiled his report for Ambassador Collins in Kampala and, over a cold Primus beer with Jules in the cottage, told the Belgian that he was as ready as he could be. Jules had been keeping him up to date with the developing political situation and it seems as if it was slipping out of control, with increasing numbers of reports from rural areas of random tribal murders.

Shakespeare volunteered his views, "In my studies on this, by early March 1994, the repeated attempts to put together a transitional government of all sides following the civil war and subsequent peace accords, kept failing. If you added to that the rather toothless token peacekeeping force put in by the UN to try and steer the parties to a mutual agreement, and the energetic arming of the militias by the Hutu-led government forces, helped by the French; it seemed clear that there were all the ingredients for a disaster."

"Spot on. Even while those in power were talking about the importance of 'continuing the dialogue' and other diplomatic phrases, the tools and attitudes of the genocide to come were being shared out and embraced, sometimes by the very same people! Anyway, sorry Shakespeare, I didn't mean to give you a history lesson... You probably know more about this than me. Let me get to the point. While chatting to Jules that day, he invited me to a cocktail party at his embassy. That's where I met your mum."

Shakespeare said nothing but looked intently at Cat, waiting for him to continue.

"I thought I knew about women. I'd had a string of girlfriends but never settled down with any of them. I was very single minded about my career, while in the Army and afterwards. Often I was involved with more than one woman at the same time, and didn't care much about their own circumstances. As long as they were available for me, when I wanted them, that suited me fine.

Nicole though, now that was so different. I can still remember how I didn't want to let go of her hand when Jules introduced her, as his 'colleague from administration'. That whole evening, I couldn't stop my eyes following her around the room, searching the gaps between the various diplomats and other guests, for just a glimpse of her face. Nor could I help feeling anxious when, it seemed from my scanning, that she wasn't in the room.

I found that my usual easy approach was completely undermined, each time I tried to talk to her. She spoke much better English than I did French, but my tongue felt too big in my mouth whenever I tried to discuss anything meaningful, and I felt like the sort of boy who always hides in the kitchen at parties, to avoid embarrassing discussions or (perish the thought) dances, with girls."

"What happened?"

"Armed with a flute of champagne, late in the evening, I waited until she left one group of guests to approach another, then intercepted her with what, on the football pitch would be thought of as a 'late tackle'. In other words she almost got to the next group before I grabbed her shoulder too enthusiastically with my spare hand and managed to slop bubbly onto her arm with the other."

"Good effort, Cat!" hooted Shakespeare.

"Her response was brilliant... 'If you want to give me a champagne bath, could you please have the subtlety to arrange it somewhere more private?' I blushed like a lobster with sunburn while trying to mumble apologies then, thankfully, after a quick look at my embarrassment she said, 'I'm joking Monsieur.' I laughed, the ice was broken, and we must have spent what was left of the evening talking. I don't remember much of what we said, I was too busy counting my blessings. The important thing was that she agreed to dinner with me the next night...and the next...and the next."

"And she's definitely the woman in my photograph?"

"There's absolutely no doubt, that's my...that's Nicole Kwizera."

"And, perhaps we can assume that my dad, as part of his efforts to take a new identity on his way to Kenya, decided that he would take my mum's name for the future. Has a kind of irony too, the name Kwizera being Kinyarwanda for 'hope'."

"Yes, your mother told me that. Shall we call it a night?"

"Sure," yawned Shakespeare, "It's almost midnight and has been a long day."

"One of the longest, and strangest, and...most surprising...ever, I'd say. I'll make up your bed. Thanks Shakespeare, you've made a great effort to find me and I won't let you down."

"Good night, Cat."

-+-

Chapter Twelve

Olelenko eased the cramp in his right leg by stretching it out while taking more of his weight on his left arm. He didn't want to rustle the bush he was sheltering behind, as this might reveal his position to the patrol of Rangers who were walking towards their ramshackle old Bedford truck about a quarter of a mile away.

He had been contacted on Friday morning and told about the big ndovu that had been seen near the edge of the park. As a Masai he had spent a lifetime tracking game and, after many years in Tsavo, before moving north to escape two troublesome wives, he had an instinct for the habits of elephants. He had taken up position between the two water holes nearest to the location of the sighting and stayed there for a night and a day with just his blanket, a water bottle, some dried meat, and his Kalashnikov for company.

Once the Kenyan Wildlife Service patrol had boarded their lorry and headed south-east in a cloud of dust, he turned on his mobile phone and called back the last number used.

"Habari yako, Josphat. They're gone."

"Sawa, Ole. We'll be there soon. Have you seen it yet, my brother?"

"Only at a distance, it should be at the northern waterhole."

"We'll see you there."

"Hapana, Jos. Your dust will scare him off. Come along the fence track from your gate and I'll stop you. We'll continue on foot."

"Sawa, we know how you Masai like to walk!"

Olelenko then picked up his rifle and, with the grace of someone much younger than his thin, wizened body would suggest, glided noiselessly through the light brush towards the perimeter fence of the Kwizera ranch estate.

From the sun's position, Olelenko knew it was around midday when he saw clouds of red dust rising along the fence to the south-west. He stepped out into the track and waved as a Land Cruiser and an Isuzu truck arrived. A round black head stuck out of the car's front passenger window, "Where shall we leave these?"

"Follow me, Bwana," said Olelenko, waving both drivers towards a small copse of trees, behind which there was a slight depression where the vehicles would be shielded from casual observers.

The party was now eight strong, Olelenko and three other men had AK47s. Three had axes and pangas, and their leader, Milton Kwizera, his holstered revolver. They walked along the fence, following Olelenko who, after half a mile, took them at a tangent to the right and the ground level started to slope downwards as they walked. After another half a mile the dusty scrub had given way to greener surroundings and they hunched down at Olelenko's hand signals. "Wait here, I'll see if he's at the waterhole," he whispered.

The rest of the party sat and drank from their water bottles. Milton took the opportunity to remind those with the automatic rifles, "Remember, if we have to bring him down on the move, only fire at the back legs. This will cripple him without damaging the tusks. If any of you ignore this, you get nothing for the work, understood?" A slow nodding of heads implied consent.

While they waited, Milton got out his revolver and ensured that each chamber had a 45 calibre round in it. He spun the chamber on the Colt and replaced the heavy gun in his holster. By the time Olelenko returned, they had started to worry that he couldn't find the bull. The smile on his face told them otherwise.

"He's deep in the shade of some jacarandas, on the other side of the waterhole. On his own, no family. Too old."

"Right," said Milton, "Let's go, follow me."

Olelenko laid the barest of touches on the young man's safari jacket sleeve, "Bwana, I'm sure that you'd like us to split into two groups, with two guns in each? Then we can go both ways around the waterhole, and stop him if he goes in either direction?"

"Yes... I was just about to say that. Josphat and you two, with me," he said, pointing at the three men who had travelled in the car with him. "The rest of you, with the tracker. You go on the west side, we'll go east. Remember, if you get to him first, only cripple him until I arrive."

Fuelled by adrenalin, they set off hastily in the two opposing directions. Milton's group soon found the going tough and they had to cut their way through some of the moist foliage near the waterhole. After half an hour, Milton tried Olelenko's phone, only to find it was switched off. Irritated, he urged his colleagues on, "Come on boys, extra bonus if we get to the ndovu first!"

The western group were first to see the rustling high in the lush green trees, fifty yards beyond the waterhole, and crouched down as they watched, waiting for a clearer view. As the elephant turned to get to the leaves on even higher branches, his enormous back legs came briefly into view but were soon swallowed up as the bushes closed around him. The tracker and his team kept low, and went slowly along the edge of the waterhole towards the bushes. Olelenko knew that elephants have poor eyesight but a great sense of smell and was glad that he felt, what little breeze there was, in his face.

The tree branches still churned as the old bull plucked big chunks of leaves from within their shade, and Olelenko's party took position behind a chunky baobab about thirty yards from the copse. They would wait until he came for a drink, or they got a clear field of fire.

On the other side of the waterhole, unseen by the other group, Milton's team were about two hundred yards from the clump of trees shading their target, but still hadn't seen him. They were now on a rocky outcrop which formed a small cliff above the water to their left and the foliage had thinned out. Milton squinted in the bright sunlight at the trees ahead and was sure he could see rustling within them. It was as he turned to tell his men, that his mouth dropped open and he screamed... "Simba!"

Olelenko heard the scream from his baobab, followed by a loud roar, and quickly brought his rifle to his shoulder, as did his colleague. They couldn't see the other group but the noise had come from the other side of the small cliff that obscured their view. "Stay still," he commanded, "and watch for the ndovu."

Milton struggled with his studded holster strap as the lioness - enraged at the threat to her cubs in the bushes near to where the men had cut through the undergrowth - who had followed them until they were in the open, pounced high. She sank her powerful jaws into the neck and left shoulder of the rearmost man and twisted him to the ground in one fluid movement. His rifle flew from his grip into the bushes to the right and the nearest man to the victim dropped his axe and panga, then fled in the direction they'd been travelling.

The other man, Josphat, ran forward, then turned and tried to take a bead on the lioness as she clawed at the man she had brought down. Milton, panicking, couldn't get his revolver out of the holster and screamed at Josphat to, "Shoot the fucking thing!"

"I can't Bwana, I'll hit my friend."

With that, Milton finally got his Colt out into his hand and didn't hesitate to fire two shots at the lioness. They both missed her, and the man underneath jerked twice. The lioness, no doubt alarmed by the loudness of the shots from the heavy calibre weapon, leapt quickly into the bushes and vanished from sight.

The bull elephant was over sixty years old and had always been alert to danger. When he heard voices, smelt man and lion, then heard two explosions in close succession, he turned away from the source and started to run. He burst out of the trees heading west, at the same time as the terrified poacher from Milton's group ran level with the copse. His last feeling on this earth was the complete emptying of all his breath, with no chance of drawing another one, as the left foot of the enraged elephant pushed him to the ground and squashed the life out of him in one movement.

The ndovu didn't break step and kept running towards what he saw as safety, right towards the tree shielding Olelenko and his men. Taking Ole's lead they stood straight and flat behind the trunk. "Safety catches off," he called to the other armed man. As soon as the old bull had careered past the tree, the AK47s were aimed and fired. The men kept their fingers on the triggers and sprayed the back legs and rump of the elephant, until both magazines were empty. The momentum of the bull took it forward another twenty yards or so, then it's back legs crumpled and it slid forward to the ground, bellowing horrific cries that pierced the ears and brains of the men watching.

Olelenko's group moved slowly along the right flank of the beast, keeping well back, until they got level with its head. Its right eye looked at them through a half shut, wrinkled eyelid, and long curly eyelashes. It was a warm brown colour with flecks of yellow and still shining brightly. Olelenko pointed his Kalashnikov at the eye, while his group looked at the body of the trampled man, confirming that he was beyond any help.

Milton then arrived, with Josphat who was nursing a deep cut on his face, where his master had pistol whipped him. "Ole, don't shoot, he's mine," ordered the young man, as he looked appreciatively at the immensely long and fat tusks sitting on the ground, astride the trunk that was curling feebly at the tip.

"Excellent, and they're undamaged. Well worth two askaris"

"Two, Bwana?"

"Yes, the simba got one and it looks like the ndovu got the other. Isn't that right Josphat?"

Josphat's head dropped as he muttered, "That's right, Bwana."

"Our boy could have been saved if Jos had shot the lion when I told him to. Still, can't be helped."

Milton then walked next to Olelenko at the side of the now heavily gasping elephant. His revolver was still in his hand and he pointed it at the eye.

"Behind the eye, and above... Bwana."

"I know Ole, this isn't my first ndovu you know."

He cocked the weapon and noticed how wide the elephant's eye went when he pulled the trigger, and sent a heavy calibre round into its brain area. He fired three more rounds just to make sure, then holstered his now empty gun. The blood spurted weakly from the head wounds and the magnificent old elephant rattled quietly as it died.

"Josphat, take one man and get the vehicles. The rest of you, start cutting those tusks out. Let's get back while there's still daylight."

-+-

Chapter Thirteen

The wind and rain had died away overnight in the Western Isles and Shakespeare Kwizera looked out at a sun kissed North Atlantic, through Carter Talbot's study window, on Saturday morning. He had risen early, his head still full of yesterday's discussions and revelations. When going to sleep on the bed/settee in the study the previous night, Carter's laptop had been left on and was in sleep mode. With some movement of the keypad, Cat's screensaver now came to life and Shakespeare noticed what he was sure was a landscape of the verdant hills of Kigali. He had seen similar shots in his studies although he had never visited the country of his heritage. The photograph made the place look so peaceful, not at all like the images brought to mind when reading about the terrible events of 1994.

"Morning Shakespeare," he heard from the doorway as Cat came in with the barest knock, "Everything Ok? I thought you'd like some tea to wake you up?"

"Thanks Cat... Your laptop was on, is that Kigali?" asked Shakespeare, pointing at the screen.

"Yes. I've always thought of it as a beautiful place, the whole country in fact, not just Kigali. I went to see the mountain gorillas...with your mum...just before the horror started in earnest. The word 'idyllic' is overused nowadays, I think, but that really was the most idyllic weekend of my life. Within a week, everything had changed, and I believed she was dead. My heart was well and truly broken."

"Wow Cat, I don't know what to say."

Cat smiled grimly, "Sorry...I just...well I...not on an empty stomach eh? Fancy a bacon sandwich?"

Over bacon sandwiches and HP sauce, in the lounge, they discussed practical matters. How long did Shakespeare want to stay? Did he have any other plans? Should he talk to anyone at home? Cat said how much he enjoyed the young man's company and that he was welcome to stay as long as he wanted, provided that he didn't get in the way of the book writing. Cat didn't want a nagging Lydia on the phone.

Shakespeare kept the potential threat of his twin to himself. He didn't want to be asked to leave and still liked to think that it was just Milton playing the big man. The thought of his indolent brother going to the effort of tracking him down and getting him to go back to Kenya with him just didn't seem feasible. He told Cat he felt safe in the cottage and would love to get to know more of the scenery and perhaps do some hill walking if the weather allowed. He promised that he wouldn't be a burden and could even help do some chores, while Cat concentrated on his work.

"That sounds like a plan," said Cat enthusiastically. "Let me begin by showing you around this part of Harris. We'll go for a walk this morning and end up in Crawnish at lunchtime. You can find out where the shop is and the little pub. That's just about all you'll need. I've got a spare pair of walking boots and, I'm assuming in that suitcase of yours, there are some casual clothes?"

Shakespeare nodded sheepishly in his dressing gown, borrowed from Cat and, finding his case against the wall, pulled out a pair of yellow corduroy trousers, a brown checked shirt and a sleeveless grey sweater.

"That'll do," said Cat, "No time like the present, get dressed and we'll go exploring."

Ten minutes later, they went out into the sunshine and set off up the hills to the back of the cottage. Cat began at what he called 'light infantry pace' which Shakespeare, although fit, found it difficult to keep up with, so they had to slow down after a while. They took a circuitous route of around ten miles, had some stops for photographs and enjoyed the cold, but welcome, sun on their faces.

Three hours later they were in the village, approaching from the northern path that joined the end of the actual road where it ran out of land going west. Village was too big a word for Crawnish, hamlet seemed to fit better the three or four dozen houses scattered around the edge of the bay and clinging to the slopes of the hills.

As they walked closer to the houses and cottages, Shakespeare commented on the large grey two storey building in a prominent position, "Is that the pub?" he asked.

"Sort of," replied Cat as they headed towards it.

When Shakespeare saw the boarded up windows he queried further, "It looks completely shut down."

"It is, some American guy apparently dreamed of building a golf resort and this was going to be the hotel part. He ran out of money before it ever opened, and went back to Arizona. Mad as a box of frogs, they say. Anyway, the pub is round the back, and the village shop - which is also a post office - is on the way home. Don't forget, Shakespeare, that to the people here, I'm Rob."

They went into the pub and Shakespeare asked what 'Dion' meant. Before Cat could reply, Finn, rising off his stool, told him it was Gaelic for 'Shelter'.

"Thank you Sir," bowed Shakespeare, "May I buy my friend Rob here, a drink please?"

"Certainly you may," smiled Finn, "Perhaps you can give this Englishman a few lessons in politeness, while you're about it?"

"I notice your 'Yes' sign is still up, by the way," offered Cat. "Flogging that particular dead horse must get tiring, even for a big lad like you Finn?"

"Bollocks...two pints is it?"

"Aye, go on, give us the heavy."

"Heavy?" queried Shakespeare.

"Keg bitter, nearest thing Finn's got to the sort of beer your Uni friend Terry likes."

"Sounds good."

"Anyone else been in, Finn?"

"That retired German couple had an early one then left, otherwise quiet for a Saturday."

The reddish brown pints were put on the counter and drunk with enthusiasm by the thirsty walkers. They were refilled by the big barman and the drinkers went and sat by the fire, carrying bags of crisps as well as the full glasses. Seeing that Finn had put on a large set of padded headphones and was gently rocking on his stool, Cat started up a conversation.

"So, with what you learnt about your dad and what I've been able to tell you about your mum, how do you feel?"

Shakespeare thought for a while, then replied, "Well, I'm still the same person. My passport says I'm Kenyan but I've always known my parents were from Rwanda, and that hasn't changed. I don't know exactly where I was born now, but I don't think that matters very much. Clearly my Dad played a part in the genocide and that makes me feel sick, but I can understand why he had to create a false history to protect himself and his family."

"If it makes you feel any better, your situation is far from unique," said Cat, "A lot of the perpetrators were brought to justice since Paul Kagame became president, after his Rwandan Patriotic Front beat the Hutu's in July '94 and finally stopped the slaughter. But the world knew that many had escaped. West to Zaire, South to Zimbabwe, East to Kenya, and North to the Middle East and Europe, the killers fled, funded by the loot taken from their victims."

"One key part in all this, that has been playing on my mind all morning is, if you and my mum were so close at that time, why did she suddenly end up with my dad? And, frankly, why did you abandon her?"

"In your boots, I'd be asking the same questions. Let me tell you all I can remember, see if it makes sense. I told you about the gorillas didn't I? Well, we got back to Kigali, after that long weekend, on Wednesday 6th April 1994. She dropped me off at Jules' place and went back to the Embassy. That was the last time I saw her. Tensions were high and you could hear the odd gunshot in the near distance. Later that night, the aircraft carrying the Rwandan president into Kigali airport, was shot down by a surface to air missile and everyone on board was killed.

The telephone service was erratic at best but word got around and, from the news coming into Jules and I, it was obvious that this was the trigger for violence. The gunfire outside was now virtually constant and, when people could get through on the phone, it was to plead for help or tell you of murders they had just witnessed.

My first thought, perhaps selfishly, was for Nicole. The Belgian embassy switchboard was jammed with calls so I told Jules that I was going to try and get there on foot. Even a few hundred yards in the middle of the night, was probably a mad thing to do when murderous gangs are wandering the streets, but Jules couldn't talk me out of it, so I put my sidearm in my pocket and went out of the door.

It must have been around 03:00 and I could see a truck of armed men going into a nearby house as I walked on the opposite side of the road. Within less than a minute, I could see orange flashes through the windows of that house and hear bursts of automatic fire. I hurried on and, although some roadblocks were being assembled by wildly excited militias, none had yet been finished between the cottage and the embassy. I got there and showed my credentials to a Belgian paratrooper behind a sandbagged machine gun post. He waved me towards a side door and, with a feeling of relief, I went inside.

That relief soon turned to fear as I quickly discovered that Nicole had taken an embassy car and gone to collect her parents who lived on the other side of the city. I could understand that, as her mother was a Tutsi and therefore a target of the killers, but it didn't stop my growing feeling of panic. A friendly secretary gave me a large brandy to calm my nerves and I must have drifted into a fitful sleep on a bench in reception.

I woke up as light started coming through the partly sandbagged window, and noticed that a worried looking Jules was bending over me. He had a bruise the size and colour of half a plum on his forehead. He told me that the armed militia had called and demanded to know if there were any Tutsi's in the house. When he had told them to get out, one of the men had hit him with the rifle butt and asked again at gunpoint. Having found no-one but the Belgian and our Hutu house-girl, they had gone to the next house.

There was still no news of Nicole, and a call to her parents' house had gone unanswered. Jules agreed to help and we decided to go and search for her. There were two obvious routes to her parents' house and so we split up, with each tracking one of those routes in small embassy cars, and each accompanied by one paratrooper, which was all that could be spared. Before setting off, I made sure that the British alert system was working, with a couple of calls that got through.

Within less than half a mile from the embassy, my car was stopped at a solid looking roadblock. A burnt out bus on its side took centre stage, with sandbag walls on one side, and a timber and barbed wire moveable barrier on the other, behind which were brightly dressed militia. They were waving a few French automatic rifles and plenty of pangas. At the side of the roadblock there was shouting going on, in French, between the only man with a uniform and a well-dressed family who had been removed from their car. Half a dozen machete wielding men surrounded the family and were pointing into a ditch, as they joined in the shouting. The family's voices took on a tone of pleading now, the desperation in their words transcending any language barrier.

Nobody had yet taken any notice of us, but the paratrooper corporal said he would see if he could help. I said we should go together but he wouldn't have it, saying I was a civilian and carried more weight sitting there looking important. He left his rifle in the car and approached the road block with arms raised, asking to speak to the officer in charge.

The tempo of the shouting changed and seemed calmer for a while, as the corporal and the militia officer conversed. All at once, one of the two children in the family, a boy of about seven, turned towards my car and started to sprint towards it. He only covered about ten little strides, before the crack of a rifle, and a sudden red flowering in the middle of his chest, brought him down. Back at the roadblock, weapons were now pointed at the paratrooper and the shouting intensified again. The wailing parents of the boy and his sister were manhandled behind the bus and the corporal, with arms returned to the air walked backwards to me.

The Belgian got into the car with his eyes still on the roadblock, and was just about to speak, when three shots rang out in quick succession from behind the bus. Then, before we could react, a short burst of fire was aimed at the front wheels of our car, shredding the tyres. All noise seemed to die away then, until we heard raucous laughing from those manning the roadblock which, from their pointing and panga waving, was clearly aimed at us. We had no real choice. We got out of the car and trudged back towards the embassy.

On the way, Corporal Modave told me something that I still struggle to believe to this day. The well-dressed family were Tutsi, as shown on their identity cards, and they were given a choice by the officer. They could buy a bullet each to be shot in the head. This would cost them all they were carrying. Alternatively, if they resisted or had no money, they would be butchered by machete, as had happened to some of those bodies in the ditch. The corporal told me that when the father had seen his young son killed, he had handed over the money and resigned himself to their fate. They shot out the tyres to, so the officer said, 'stop us being a nuisance'.

We had no choice back at the embassy, but to wait for Jules to get back. There were no more cars, they were all being used to rescue Belgian citizens. The time went by and we heard nothing. I passed the time by trying to call all the Brits on my list who had so far been unaccounted for, there were many. I also spoke to the UN HQ to see if any of them had turned up there. All the calls coming in, and the responses of those who answered our calls out, left the same impression. The situation was already out of control after less than one day. As the sun set over the hills to the west, there was still no sign of Jules and his escort, and I was frantic about Nicole.

That night was as hectic as the night before, with the tattoo of gunfire as a background to the intermittent sound of telephones and people desperately trying to keep their voices calm. I kept on updating my list of Brits accounted for and some even came into the Belgian embassy, due to the influence of a relative or a friend. Ten Belgian paratroopers who were detailed to guard the home of Tutsi Prime Minister Agathe, had gone missing and forceful attempts to get information about her, her family, and the protection force were fruitless.

Again, I dozed on the reception area bench, and must have looked a mess the next morning when the friendly secretary brought me some strong black coffee. At about 09:30 Jules and his escort finally arrived in the compound and ran indoors to see me. Their news was bad. Catastrophically bad, as far as I was concerned.

They had made very slow progress on the previous morning, being held up by a number of roadblocks and having to bribe and cajole their way through after elongated negotiations each time. It had been early afternoon before they'd got to Nicole's parents' house in the suburbs. There had been no answer to their knocking so they tried the door and walked in. There, on the living room carpet, was the crumpled body of the Belgian banker, Francois Wauters, your grandfather. He was still holding a small handgun, so Jules had assumed he had tried to resist whoever had come into his house. He had been shot twice in the chest and once in the head. There was no sign of anybody else there."

"But you said my mother's name was Kwizera, and that was the name taken by my father when we ran away?" commented an awestruck Shakespeare, who had been listening with rapt attention to Cat's story.

"Nicole was born well before her mother married her father, so was given her mother's surname and stuck with it. Shall I go on?"

"Please... Do you want another drink?"

Cat shook his empty pint glass, "Thanks," he replied.

Cat went on to tell Shakespeare about how Jules had then backtracked their route towards the embassy and had to negotiate their way through the same barricades a second time that day, just as slowly as the morning. As it got to late afternoon, they'd come to a corner and saw a group of around thirty women and children being herded by some uniformed soldiers. At the front of the group, Jules clearly recognised Nicole and shouted at his escort to stop the car. Without thinking, he had jumped out and strode purposefully over to the group asking who was in charge. A burly officer moved in front of him and said, in French, that he was.

Jules then explained that he was a Belgian diplomat and that within this group was one of his colleagues and, he suspected, her mother. The officer told him that he had rescued them from a gang of 'militia thugs' and was taking them to a nearby church for the evening. Here, his men would protect them and process their distribution tomorrow. Jules was partially relieved until Nicole spoke up, in English, perhaps to confuse the soldiers, 'Don't listen Jules, his men killed my father.' At that point, the officer shouted her down and said quietly to Jules, in perfect English, "Do listen Jules, you had better leave here right now unless you want the same fate to befall you." then, louder and back in French, "Tutsi ladies and children, no harm will come to you if you show no resistance to my men. We are going to a sanctuary and you have my word that all will be sorted out properly tomorrow." He then turned on his heels and with a few sharp orders, the group continued to the church that overlooked the corner of the main road. Noticeably three soldiers stood as a rearguard across the pavement, weapons at the ready, and Jules with his escort returned to the car.

Jules had told Cat that he and his paratrooper had spent the night at the nearby UN compound. They failed to get anyone to act, as the officer commanding confirmed that they had no mandate to use force to intervene. They returned to the church at first light. It was a smell like sweet roast pork that they noticed first, before that of burnt timber and petrol. They found a way into the smoking ruin and were both violently sick at the sight of the burnt skeletons, clad with melted flesh, skin, and vague tatters of burnt clothing. They tried to count the bodies but there was no way of identifying anyone in that charnel house. They returned to the embassy and Jules broke the news to Cat.

"I couldn't believe that the love I'd found had been cut off so brutally. Jules was sure that the whole group had been slaughtered and burnt. It made sense, if anything made sense in that place, at that time. Clearly, somehow she escaped, and went on to meet your dad. The rest is history."

"Did you look for her?"

"I didn't see the point, she was half Tutsi, she was with a group of Tutsi's who were wiped out and Jules had not only seen them go in, he'd seen their bodies the next morning in the same place. I knew that she was as dead as her parents."

"What happened next?"

"It was all a bit of a blur really. We heard the next day that the paratroopers sent to guard the Prime Minister were shot dead - along with her and her family - and their bodies mutilated, all ten of them. That was enough for the Belgians, they announced a complete withdrawal at the earliest possible moment. I spoke to Ambassador Collins in Kampala, tried to give him a coherent report from the scanty and rapidly changing information coming in, and waited for him to respond. Within a couple of days, as the mass murders continued, Kampala confirmed that an RAF Hercules would be coming in at first light the next morning to evacuate every Briton who could make it to the airport. All my remaining efforts went in trying to fill that plane."

"Did your efforts work?"

"One thing you need to know about the British, Shakespeare, is that when it comes to an evacuation from a place of danger, we're the world's best! Think Dunkirk, Gallipoli, American War of Independence. Nobody gets away after a defeat as efficiently as we do. Seriously, with the help of the UN, who provided some much needed road transport, we had 84 UK passport holders waiting by the runway as the plane came in, just before sunrise. So I left Rwanda that day, and have never been back."

"And the genocide went on for three more months," mused Shakespeare, "And the rest of the world did nothing, until it was too late."

"I'm afraid that's true. But, in the tradition of every cloud having a silver lining, your mum did somehow survive it all, and you are the living proof of that. It would be good to hear her side of the story one day."

"Yes, I... We need to."

They stopped talking for a while. Cat noticed that Neil had come into the Dion while they were busy and was standing at the bar. Cat nodded to him and finished his pint. Shakespeare drained his glass and, in silence, they left the pub. After a stop at the village shop for supplies, they walked home in silence.

-+-

Chapter Fourteen

"M'zee says come now please," said the house-girl at Milton's bedroom door, with her head bowed. Milton, who was towelling himself dry after showering off the rigours of the day's hunt, replied with what sounded like an unnatural cheerfulness, "What does the Old Man want?"

"I don't know, Bwana. He just says you must come."

Milton quickly put some shorts, a tee shirt, and some slippers on, then went upstairs and knocked gingerly at his father's door. Invited to enter, he stood before the giant desk while his father leaned back in a generously upholstered leather swivel chair, and fixed his son with a fearsome stare.

"How much, did you say, we'll get for those tusks, Kijana?" Alphonse asked quietly.

"At least $250,000 Father, although they're heavier than we thought, so maybe more..."

"That's just as well, isn't it Milton?"

"Father?"

Alphonse leaned forward and banged both of his fists hard into the centre of the desk. "Because, you imbecile," his voice louder, "I'm going to need plenty of money to clear up your fucking mess... aren't I?"

"But, we got the tusks, undamaged, and the KWS know nothing about it."

"Yet, you clown. They know nothing, yet. With two dead local men, how long will it be before questions are asked, at my fucking door? What were you thinking of? Olelenko's the best tracker for hundreds of miles, why didn't you let him be in charge?"

"Because..."

"Shut up, I'm not interested. What I know is, that while you were acting the big game hunter and bungling it so badly, two men died. This is going to mean me having to pay hush money to all your team, the families of the dead men, the KWS, and the local police. God knows what will happen if they want to question you. It's a total fucking nightmare."

"I'm sorry Father."

"You being sorry, doesn't help me at all does it? You need to get away, somewhere you can't be found or questioned."

"Like I said yesterday, I could go to find Shakespeare, and bring him home?"

"I'd thought about that and was going to say no. But now... While the idea of you going on any sort of hunting trip fills me with dread, perhaps you can do less damage to the family while in Britain, than when you're here. At least Pascal has got some sense, thank God. But I don't want anyone here, except me, to know where you're going, even your mother. That way nobody can track you down and ask you embarrassing questions. Go quickly, alone, get to Nairobi tonight and take the first flight tomorrow. Now, get out of my sight."

"What sha...."

"I said, get out of my fucking sight, Kijana, and try not to screw up again."

Milton, with hot cheeks, turned from the desk, bunched his hands into fists and strode out of the door.

As he angrily packed a suitcase in his bedroom, he heard a knock and his mother's voice, "Milton...are you Ok? I heard shouting...can I come in?"

"If you must," sighed Milton.

"I heard that things went badly today?"

"It depends on your point of view, Mama."

"What's your 'point of view' my son?"

He stopped his packing for a moment and looked at his mother, "Mama, I know you don't approve of hunting elephants, but what I did today will bring lots of money into the house. I made it happen, and all he can do," his eyes looked upwards for a split second, "is find fault."

"Two men died Milton."

"Sometimes there are accidents, they weren't my fault, I was just trying my best to do a good job for us."

She looked at the suitcase, "Where are you going?"

"Father wants me to lie low for a while, so I'll go and stay with friends."

"Where?"

"I...er...I haven't decided yet."

"You know it's already dark out there? Why not go tomorrow?"

"I can't Mama, I really need to get away... I'll be Ok."

"If you must...well take care and stay out of trouble."

Nicole went forward to embrace her son, but he turned back to his pile of clothes, and she ended up lightly hugging his shoulder as his body stiffened. She noticed his passport lying on the bed with some loose banknotes, before leaving him to his sulking.

Later that night, Milton had driven his Land Cruiser only as far as Eldoret, when a wave of tiredness from the long day's events washed over him. In the centre of the town he found a big whitewashed hotel and got himself a room. He went down to the bar and ordered a large Johnnie Walker on the rocks. He couldn't see any obvious hookers in the bar, so after downing his whisky, he found the concierge. While slipping him a thousand shilling note, Milton said he needed a girl quickly and told him his room number.

Ten minutes later he answered a knock by opening the door to his room. The most noticeable thing about the black girl standing there, was her bright red, and very full lips. Milton did not stand on ceremony. He ushered her in and got her sideways in front of the full length mirror by the bed. He gave her a couple of banknotes, then said, "Get on your knees." She complied as Milton hurriedly undid his belt and jeans. He was already hard and grabbed the back of her head to pull her mouth onto his erection. He bucked his hips for about a minute before groaning with relief as he emptied himself into her soft mouth.

The concierge was rather surprised to see the girl back downstairs so soon and asked her if she'd got the right room. One glance at her well smudged lipstick told him all he needed to know and she just winked at him, before walking out in search of more - and better - business.

In Milton's room, light snoring was already coming from the bed as he surrendered to his body's need for rest and recovery.

-+-

Chapter Fifteen

Outside her apartment, it was a blustery autumn Sunday in Hampstead with leaves blowing in every direction, and it occurred to Lydia Hockley-Roberts that perhaps a stroll on the Heath that morning might not be such a good idea. She turned from the window and pulled her dressing gown more tightly around her, before putting on the kettle. She sat at the scrubbed oak kitchen table and looked through some emails on her laptop. Nothing of great interest, and nothing from Cat. Although it had only been three days since she'd last had any contact, she wondered what progress he was making with chapter three. She picked up her phone then, frowning, put it back down.

She reached forward to the keyboard and prepared an email:

From: Lydia@rivetingread.co.uk

To: Robindc58@gmail.com

Date: Sun 19/10/14 09:33

Subject: AONAG - Third Chapter

Good Morning,

It's a cold morning here in civilisation, although no doubt it's worse where you are!

Just thought I'd check to see whether you're Ok? I was going to ring but thought better of it. Who knows, you might have found a buxom Scottish fisherman's wife to keep you company after a Saturday night of whisky and haggis... Or something!

Anyway, how's chapter three coming along? I'm impatient for the next instalment.

I'm trying to convince myself that a healthy walk would be a good idea, although I may delay that until the pubs are open.

Lots of Love,

LHR.

She clicked on 'send' and made herself some coffee. The pile of unopened post on the table had grown that week and she set about it without enthusiasm. She sorted it into 'junk mail' and 'other' before throwing all the first pile into a basket for the fire. In the 'other' pile there was a window envelope from Her Majesty's Revenue and Customs, one each from her bank and credit card provider, and one from her solicitor. She opened that one and read the letter, plus the attachment.

There wasn't that much to read and she reread slowly before letting them drop to the table and resting her lower jaw on her propped hands. She sat like that and started blinking. The tears soon became too much for her eyelids to contain and ran down her face, over her hands, and fell at random onto the Decree Absolute in front of her.

Before she could find a tissue, her phone rang and the screen showed 'RDC'. She hesitated a moment then picked it up and touched 'answer'.

"Hello Cat," she squeaked.

"Lydia? Is that you? Are you Ok?"

"You pick your moments, don't you?"

"What's happened?"

"I've just read that my divorce has been finalised."

"But why the upset, you told me you were well rid of him?"

"Yes Cat, women say that, but you can't help somehow feeling that you've failed. It just... I can't really explain it, but I felt very emotional... Then you called, and I don't know whether that makes me feel better or worse."

"Ouch! I could call back?"

"No, no, I'm only kidding, go on."

"About your email this morning. So you think I'm having fun with a fishwife?"

"Are you?"

"Of course not, you're the only one for me Lids... But I do have a guest, the son of an old friend of mine. He's staying for a while. But don't worry, the work goes on. I'm halfway through chapter three..."

"Look Cat/Rob, whatever, I've got nothing much to do today. Why not send me what you've already done and I'll review it straight away."

"Ok, I'll send it shortly. Speak soon."

Lydia got back to her, now lukewarm, coffee and thought that some breakfast might be in order. She felt that she needed to keep busy today, not to dwell on the past, or on the fact that she was in her forties and single.

Five minutes later, her laptop beeped and within moments

she had the embryo of Cat's chapter three in front of her. She read the start, then reread the first paragraph a couple more times, before going through the rest. She made one or two notes on a legal pad as she went through it, and muttered "What the fuck?" to herself a couple of times.

She reached for the phone.

-+-

Chapter Sixteen

Carter and Shakespeare had woken up that Sunday morning to weather that was more than a bit blustery. Cat had not yet seen one of the severe winter storms for which the Hebrides were well known but, as he looked out to sea at first light, the crashing waves in the bay and diagonal rain battering the cottage suggested that this might be the building up of an autumn one. He took tea into the study and Shakespeare was already awake, lying on the sofa bed with a biography of the First Duke of Marlborough in his hands.

"One of my heroes," volunteered Cat. "Fought the French time and time again, usually with inferior numbers of troops, and never lost a battle. An absolute legend."

"I looked at the weather and thought that we wouldn't be venturing out much today," said Shakespeare, "And as a former pupil at the school of the same name, I was attracted to this book. Hope you don't mind?"

"Of course not, and yes, we could get the car out, but I think you're right. Batten down the hatches today, we got the shopping yesterday, so plenty of food and whisky to keep us warm. I'll get the fire stoked up then do us a full, if a bit late, Scottish breakfast."

After a fine feast of fried bacon, sausage, black pudding, haggis, eggs, and baked beans, taken at the small breakfast bar in the kitchen, they nursed large mugs of tea. They were both quiet, as if the discussions of yesterday in the Dion had drained them of emotion.

Finally, Cat said, "I think I'll go and check my emails, you Ok hanging out with the Duke in the lounge?"

Shakespeare smiled, said that was fine with him, carried the large book into the living room and settled down in one of the armchairs to find out more about the European wars of the early eighteenth century.

Cat turned on the laptop and went to his emails. On reading Lydia's from earlier that morning he picked up the phone. Discovering that she was upset, he kept the call short and agreed to send her the work he'd done on chapter three.

He sent her the Word document without checking it then, sensing someone behind him, turned to see Shakespeare, book in hand, looking over his shoulder at the screen.

"Sorry Cat, I was curious about your book, what does 'AONAG' mean?"

"It's the acronym of the supposedly humorous title that the agents want to use for my story. 'An Officer, Not A Gentleman'...

"I'm not sure I get it...?"

"The received thinking that all British officers are, by definition, gentlemen, therefore gets turned on its head."

"Suggesting that you are, or have been, somewhat unorthodox?"

"Nicely put, Shakespeare, can you do the PR in future? 'Carter Talbot - somewhat unorthodox,' it sounds superb!"

"Will I be able to read the story, as you are building it?"

"I'll need to think about that. The literary agents don't want anyone seeing it but them, before it's finished. There will be one or two sensitive matters involved. Let's see how it goes and perhaps I could accidentally leave the screen on one night...by mistake?"

"Anyway, on a different topic, what do your friends call you? Shakespeare can be a bit of a mouthful in conversation? You must have had a nickname at home, or at school?"

"Not at home really, my brother called me the 'Professor' but in an insulting way, and our father used to call us both 'Kijana' - 'Boy' in English. Terry used to call me 'Shaky'."

Shakespeare's face then lifted as he glanced at the book he was holding, and a memory struck him, "At Marlborough some of the boys called me 'Bardy'...which I thought was Ok."

"Splendid, 'Bardy' it will be! Anyway, I'd better get on, I need to draft the rest of chapter three while awaiting my agent's response."

"Right, I'll get back to John Churchill's exploits then."

"Thanks Bardy...and perhaps you can do some coffee later?"

"Yes...Bwana," replied Shakespeare, bowing flamboyantly to tease his friend.

About an hour later Carter, still seated at his desk and sipping coffee supplied by Bardy, answered a call from Lydia. She seemed to have shrugged off her earlier upset, if her animated voice was anything to go by.

"Cat, you remain full of surprises don't you?"

"Hello Lids... What do you mean?"

"Well, interesting and exciting as your story of war games

at school is, it gets rather overshadowed by the very first sentence. Don't you think?"

"Sorry Lydia, I didn't check it before sending. Let me get it on screen."

Lydia, carried on without pause, "Bearing in mind that this is meant to be your memoirs Cat, however we disguise your identity, do you think that it's wise to admit a murder in print?"

"I've got it up now... hold on... I think you'll find that I didn't make that admission, I just said that I killed my mother. It was an accident."

"But the reader doesn't know that and it diverts attention away from the narrative that follows. I, and they, will think that you're rather downplaying the importance of matricide and going on at length about playing soldiers."

"I wanted to keep readers interested."

"Which is a good thing, but this is a real sledgehammer of a tactic. Could I suggest that you take it out of chapter three, finish that - all about your time at Bainbridge - then do a separate chapter about your mother's accident? Honestly Carter, it reads well enough without that, and we want the reader to like you... A loveable rogue, remember?"

"Yes, that's the angle your boss likes isn't it?"

"Francis wants people who read your book to be desperate to find out your identity, and to fail in those efforts. The potential publicity it could create would be epic."

"Book signings in some sort of Ninja disguise...that sort of thing?"

"Now you're taking the piss... Mind you, perhaps... Anyway, I'll think about it."

"You're the boss Lydia. I'll edit chapter three and send a new version, with its last few pages, in a day or two."

"Thanks Cat. By the way, how's your new friend?"

"Makes good coffee."

"Won't your neighbours think it odd that you've got a young man in the house? I'm sure that the God-fearing folk of Harris would frown on two single men living together!"

"Don't be such a dinosaur, you know how 'not Gay' I am, Darling."

"Yes, but they don't, do they?"

"Goodbye Lydia."

" 'Bye Cat."

-+-

Chapter Seventeen

After a refreshing night's sleep, a reasonable breakfast at the Boma Inn, and a few phone calls, Milton Kwizera left Eldoret around mid-morning. The drive south was easier than most days due to light Sunday traffic and, after a refuelling break in Nakuru, he got to the outskirts of Nairobi just as the sun was going down over the western escarpment of the Rift Valley.

He went to the house of a friend in the elegant suburb of Runda to pick up his air ticket, dropped off for him, along with a boarding pass, earlier in the day by his travel agent. They shared some wine and a couple of lines of cocaine, before going to a nearby restaurant for an early dinner.

Milton was feeling a lot better than he had on the previous night, and gladly accepted a lift from his friend to Nairobi's main airport. It saved him the hassle of parking in the limited space resulting from the devastating airport fire the previous year. Milton told his friend that he couldn't say where he was going. However, it wasn't that difficult to work out when Milton asked to be dropped at the terminal which served British Airways. Everyone knew that they only had one direct route, and one flight a day on that route, to London Heathrow.

He dropped his suitcase off at a BA desk and made his way, through the usual bureaucracy, to the First Class Lounge. His platinum credit card had still worked when he'd booked the ticket and he didn't hesitate to use his father's money lavishly. Milton helped himself to champagne as he settled down to wait. The flight to London always left at around midnight and he thought he deserved to drink his way to a decent sleep on board. He'd seen off a whole bottle by the time the public address system announced the departure of BA 65 to London

Heathrow, from gate number 9.

The cabin crew were more than generous with the whisky in First Class when Milton settled into his flatbed seat. Half an hour after take-off he must have had four already, when he told the steward not to wake him for food, and he slept for the next three thousand miles.

It was a turbulent landing the next morning as the Boeing 777 approached Heathrow, still in darkness, and with thick layers of stormy clouds swathed across the area. Milton felt a little queasy by the time the wheels hit the runway hard and bounced along, making his discomfort worse.

His welcome into Britain was perfunctory, as the border agency officer reviewing his old entry visa asked him if he was here for business or pleasure, and he replied, "A bit of both." His smile was not returned, but his passport was. Waiting for him in arrivals was his cousin Pascal, who he hadn't seen since he was last in England, and then only briefly while he in the process of being expelled from school.

Pascal Muwera was in his mid-thirties and looked almost scholarly, with frameless spectacles on a round coal black face and curly hair, longer than neat. He was wearing a baggy brown leather jacket over a thin body, and wore an expression of tiredness and puzzlement.

"Hello Milton," he said with little enthusiasm, "Welcome to a cold damp England."

"Thank you Cousin...it's good to see you."

Pascal limply shook the hand offered then said, "Come on, the car's close by. Eric, take his bag." A mixed race man in a charcoal suit behind him stepped briskly forward to take Milton's suitcase.

The cousins settled into the back of a dark blue Range Rover Sport, while Eric eased their way out of the airport and onto the M25 going north and then east, clockwise around the capital. During the drive, the early morning traffic started building up and Pascal pressed a button which made a dark glass screen slide up, isolating the front from the back seats.

"You didn't make much sense yesterday on the phone," observed Pascal, "So I checked with your father."

"And...?"

"And, he said you need to lie low for a few weeks, but at the same time look for your brother? He also asked me to keep a close eye on you, wherever you go."

"I can fend for myself, cousin."

"From what I hear, that isn't always true, Milton. Either way, I owe your Dad and will do whatever's best. Business is going well at the moment, the club is thriving, so perhaps I can take a bit of time off and make sure you don't get into any trouble."

"Thanks Pascal, I think that Shakespeare is in Scotland."

"Big country, Cousin."

"The last time he spoke to mother, he said he was in Edinburgh and going to 'explore the islands'. On Google maps it seems that most Scottish islands are off the west coast, but perhaps we could find his friends at the university and see if they know any more?"

"Perhaps. We'll get prepared today and leave late tonight or very early tomorrow."

"Pascal, you said you 'owe' my father. What for?"

"He helped us out, after my mother, his sister, died when I was a teenager. He got documents so that my father could get to Britain and start his business here. He died a few years ago, and I've been running things ever since. Uncle Alphonse was always at the end of the phone with good advice. I greatly respect his strength."

"Yes, he's certainly strong."

They went quiet for a while and Milton tried to work out where they were. They seemed to have turned off the M25 and we're heading along a road signed as the M11. In the gloomy distance, he could make out skyscrapers and the big signs were starting to say 'City' while smaller signs were saying 'Stratford'. Just as Milton saw an enormous round sports stadium, Eric eventually turned off at one of these signs and they negotiated several corners in urban streets before coming to the end of a street. It was closed off by a modern red brick house with wings to either side, high cast iron railings, and a large triple garage behind a double gate. Through the gaps at either side of the house, Milton could see a very sluggish looking river, or maybe a canal, behind the structure.

Eric pressed a small device in the ashtray and the gates started to swing outwards towards the car. He then drove up the gravel drive to the front of the house and jumped out to open the car doors for Pascal and Milton, who went up the steps to the large timber entrance.

The interior was very modern with expensive electronic equipment in almost every room but nothing to soften the clinical appearance. Milton could see no family photographs, no mess anywhere to suggest the presence of children, and nothing alive - like flowers - indicating a human touch. Eric, carrying Milton's case, led him to a big bedroom with ensuite shower room, a big curved TV at the end of the bed, and a glass fronted fridge with a wide variety of bottles visible through the door.

Pascal popped his head into the room briefly and asked if everything was Ok. He then told Milton to make himself comfortable in his room and they would call him down for a late lunch. He also asked him not to wander about, as he had various guests coming and going over the next few hours, and they were wary of strangers. Milton knew better than to argue so got himself a beer and lay on the bed, flicking through the hundreds of TV channels. He wondered which ones had porn.

At one point, he got up and looked out of the bedroom window which overlooked the rear of the house and confirmed his earlier view that the stretch of water behind the house was a slow running river. Tied up securely on bollards, at the end of a path leading from the rear of the property, was a modern motor cruiser. According to the blue writing on its white fibreglass superstructure, it was a 'Fairline 42' and its name on the bow was 'Just a Drop'.

After a couple of beers, he nodded off for a while then watched some football highlights on one of the sports channels. Eventually, at around 3pm, Eric knocked and told him to come down for lunch. The large mahogany table was far too big for just Pascal and Milton but it was laid with a wide selection of meat, fish, salads and bread. There was chilled German wine and a Somali looking maid to pour it. Milton enjoyed the food and Pascal was very attentive.

"I guess that this morning's business went well, with your visitors?" proposed Milton.

"Why do you say that?" bristled Pascal.

"Sorry Cousin, you just seem in a good mood."

"Well...as I'm going to be away for a while, there were one or two important things to sort out...with the business. All is now in order."

"I'm intrigued by the name of your boat. What's that about?"

Pascal's reply sounded almost rehearsed it was delivered so smoothly: "I was trying to show off to the salesman when I was looking to buy a cruiser. So when I asked him how much and he gave me some astronomical price, my 'too flash' reply was 'It's just a drop in the ocean' and the name stuck."

"Good one," replied Milton, only half convinced.

After lunch was cleared away, Pascal got serious and said that they had better make sure they had all the equipment they needed for winter in rural Scotland. Eric was ordered to load up the boot with blankets, a shovel, food, walking boots, water, torches and batteries. Each of them also put a holdall with spare clothes in the Range Rover. Pascal then took Milton to the safe in his study and, to his clear surprise, got out three automatic pistols, still in protective plastic wrapping. He fished in the safe further and got some boxes of 9mm rounds then put weapons and bullets in a small airline style bag.

Milton tried joking, "We're going to Scotland, not Syria, Pascal. Are those really necessary?"

"You never know what you might need, especially if some persuasion is called for. 'Be prepared' is the right motto, I believe? Anyway, we'll keep them locked in the glove compartment...just in case."

"Right," continued Pascal, "Get some rest, we'll be leaving at around midnight, so that we get to Edinburgh in time for some breakfast."

-+-

Chapter Eighteen

The winds screaming over Harris, from far out in the Atlantic, whipped the bay at Crawnish into a frenzy of waves and spray. What had been building from a gale to a storm was now, on Tuesday morning, the real thing with a solid wall of horizontal rain blasting against everything in its path. Although now after ten o'clock, the daylight was a feeble dark grey shadow coming from behind the mountains to the east.

In Uisge Bothan, Bardy had settled down again in the lounge and was ploughing through the Duke of Marlborough's battle of Blenheim while Cat was back at his desk pondering the start of chapter four. He had sent the edited chapter three back to Lydia late the previous night, having made the change she had suggested and added more memories of his schooldays. This took his story to when he was fifteen and his uncertainty would have been clear to anyone watching him as he scribbled in his pad, crossed the scribbles out vigorously, hovered his hands over the laptop, and scratched different parts of his head.

He called out to Shakespeare to, "Get the kettle on, Bardy, my brain needs a kick start... Strong black coffee should do the trick!"

Minutes later, he stared out at the storm as he nursed the big mug and took a few swigs of the powerful brew. He closed his eyes for a few moments then put down the mug and started typing:

Chapter Four

After seven eventful years at Bainbridge, I had every intention of staying there until I could join the army.

That's what I had determined my career path to be and Ogilvy had told me that he would put in a good word to try and get me into the military academy at Sandhurst. 'You've definitely got real officer potential' he had imparted on more than one occasion.

It was a parent's day that changed all that. My father had some leave and had joined my mother at Uncle Hugo's. Some years before, Hugo had suggested that she take the empty gatekeeper's lodge and use that as a home. She would have her independence and often on Sundays I would travel from school to spend the afternoon in the cosy parlour of the lodge, playing Monopoly and eating cake with my mum.

The plan was that my parents would come to the parent's day on the Saturday then take me back to the lodge for the rest of a bank holiday weekend. As soon as I saw them, I knew that something was wrong. My mother had on very big sunglasses, which although fashionable in the early seventies, weren't the type of accessory I'd seen my mum wearing before. The way she walked, almost hesitantly, slightly behind my father, also seemed out of place. I was used to my mum almost gliding from place to place, without appearing ruffled by anything.

We did the rounds of the masters, and the conversations seemed stilted while the comments appeared to be in code. A code which my father took great delight in cracking at every opportunity. So if a master said that I was 'Relaxed' about a certain subject, Dad would say 'You mean lazy'. 'Independent of spirit' became 'Rebellious', 'Leadership qualities' meant 'Likes to bully others' and, most distressing to my mum, 'Doesn't suffer fools gladly' to my father clearly suggested, 'He's got no friends'.

After the embarrassment of meeting the teachers was over, we joined the gaggle of parents for high tea in the dining hall and my father became very insistent that he wanted something stronger than the large urns of tea that were placed on a long table at one end, next to huge plates of sandwiches and bowls of crisps.

My mother tried to mollify him and suggested that when we left, we could go to the pub. This wasn't enough for my Dad who grabbed a housemaster by the lapels and, in no uncertain terms, demanded some whisky. I didn't know what had got into him but I was squirming with embarrassment and, in the end, Mum and I left the event in the hope that Dad would follow us out of the building.

As we hovered by our old car, eventually he showed up, arms waving about and curses coming from his agitated mouth. He couldn't stop, and I noticed that Mum cowered when he came near to her. 'I can't fucking believe it,' he grunted to nobody in particular, 'I've given my life to the Navy, and this is how they repay me... They take my fucking ship, then... when I want a drink at somewhere we pay a fortune to... I'm offered a nice cup of fucking tea. It's an absolute disgrace. Margaret, get me to the pub...right now.'

In the car, the journey was quiet, except when Dad berated Mum for grating the gears. After a few minutes, I summoned up the courage to ask, 'Dad, what do you mean when you say the Navy have taken your ship, I thought you were on leave?' All we could hear was the whining growl of the engine before my Dad half turned from the front seat and said quietly, 'Cutbacks son... The Admiralty say they've got too many captains and not enough ships. Some have to go, I'm one of them. Bastards!'

I knew better than to speak further but my Mum tried to help, 'They'll be other ships, John Darling.' she offered. 'No, you stupid bitch, there won't.' he said more viciously than I could ever remember, 'That's me on the fucking scrap heap.' Mum then went silent and pulled into a pub car park about a mile short of the lodge. 'I don't want a drink.' she said, taking off her sunglasses for the first time that day. I saw her reflection in the rear view mirror and was shocked at the dark blue and purple bruising around her eyes. Before I could speak, Dad grabbed the keys, out of the ignition in the middle of the dashboard, and said, 'Well you two can fuck off then, but I'm keeping the car... A man needs a drink at times like this.'

Mum and I got out and I hugged her as we walked down the lane towards the lodge. I had really shot up in the last two years and was now her height. I could feel her silently sobbing in my grasp and didn't know what to say. She stayed quiet until we got indoors then, over mugs of hot chocolate, she talked. And she kept on talking, telling me how her happiness had gradually eroded over the years. How she had started to dread my father coming home, how he had turned all the frustrations of an unfulfilled career into anger at her. She'd always tried to see his side and sympathise with him, but he had started hitting her a few years ago and admitting having other women in the midst of his rages. The worst of it, she said, was not having anyone to turn to. She knew that Uncle Hugo was cut from similar cloth as my father and would expect her to 'Get on with it old girl.' She had been glad that I was at boarding school so I was spared the dreadful scenes when Dad was home, but this meant her sacrificing seeing me as much as she would have liked.

For the first time in my life, that I could remember, I felt genuine guilt. I should have looked after her, stood up to Father, been her support in all the troubled times she'd had. I should have taken action, like when I was being bullied or when leading the cadets. I told her as much, to which she smiled for the first time that day and said that while she appreciated the gesture, it was her problem.

But to me, it was far more than an empty gesture, I had never been close to my father and had sensed the growing tension between him and Mum over the years, but this was different. I was now aware of a totally different situation, one in which my father John had to be stopped. And I was the one to do it. I made an excuse and went to my room.

I lay back on the single bed in the tiny box room, that saw service as a bedroom when I stayed at the lodge, and tried to formulate a plan. In the absence of any real friends I had become a voracious reader at that age and I tried to remember ways to get revenge that I'd read about. Revenge with little chance of being found out, obviously.

As I pondered the options, I heard my mum - through the box room door - tell me that she was going for a lay down. This triggered me into movement and I quietly went to the shed behind the lodge and rummaged amongst the tools. Light was falling as I left the shed and made my way back towards the pub, uphill along the darkening lane. I could see the lights on through the pub windows and could hear some juke box music. There were about a dozen cars in the car park, including one each side of our old Ford Cortina. This was useful cover as I ducked down and slid under the car.

I'd had a look at a specific part of the Haynes maintenance guide to the Cortina Mark 1 in the shed before leaving, and shone my torch underneath the front axle until I could see something that looked similar to what I'd seen in the book. I reached into my anorak pocket and pulled out some heavy duty pliers. After a few minutes fiddly work, I slid over to the other side of the car and repeated what I'd done.

After putting my torch and tools away, I slid out on the side of the cars away from the lights of the pub and, zipping my anorak against some light drizzle, made my way back down to the lodge, via the shed. I looked in at my mum and saw that she was fast asleep under her blankets. I was feeling grimly pleased with myself and, on retiring to my room, wasn't long in bed before sleep took me.

I woke early the next morning, just as the rising May sun sent shafts of light through the trees that surrounded the lodge. The house was quiet and I got dressed in jeans and a rugby shirt before leaving the box room. My mum's door was slightly ajar so I stepped lightly towards it and peered into the gloom. The small double bed was ruffled but empty, so I called out to see where my Mum was. No reply came, so I then explored the bathroom and the other rooms of the lodge, without success.

Of my father there was also no sign but then, I hadn't really expected there to be. I put on some training shoes and went outside. There was nobody in the small walled garden or shed, so I started to retrace my steps of the previous night. I'd been walking for less than five minutes and was halfway around an uphill bend when I saw the effect of flashing blue lights reflecting off the trees to my left. I continued around the bend and saw the source of the lights being a police car, parked on the inward, my right hand, side of the curving, sloping road, facing down the hill. To its passenger's side there was plenty of yellow and black stripy tape joining the trees together where they were set back off the road. A male officer was sitting in the car, and a female officer was standing by to direct what little traffic there might be.

As I got closer, I looked down to my right past the tape and my heart jumped as I saw a blackened yellow Cortina, our yellow Cortina, with faint pillars of smoke rising from its windows, and other cavities exposed by the fire that had clearly raged here. Its boot rose up out of the shallow ditch that edged the road, and the front wheels almost hugged a large tree which had clearly taken the main impact of the front of the car.

'Can I help you... Sir?' asked the policewoman.

'I... Yes... Er... That's my...that's our car,' I replied, pointing at the wreck in the trees.

'Where do you live, sir?'

'What?, uhm, normally Bainbridge school but here, with my mum sometimes. Down there at the gatekeeper's lodge.'

The policewoman then, unexpectedly, put her arm around my shoulders and said gently, 'I think you'd better come with me.'

At the nearest police station, I discovered what seemed, to the emergency services, to have happened. According to the pub landlord, my dad had been the last customer to leave the Dog and Duck, and was particularly the worse for drink. He said he was going to walk home. Clearly he thought better of it, and he must have tried to drive. Five minutes after Dad left the bar, a motorist coming up the hill saw flames coming from the trees to his right. As he slowed to investigate, he almost ran over a crumpled body lying in the middle of the road. He'd jumped out of the car and tried the pulse of the body to no avail. He then ran to the wreck and found Dad half out of the driver's door with orange flames licking at him. He grabbed his arms and wrenched him free, rolling him along the ditch as he cried out and mumbled drunkenly. The motorist got him a safe distance and threw his jacket over Dad before what was left in the fuel tank exploded with a crump. He then ran to the pub and raised the alarm.

While a fire tender was extinguishing the burning wreck,

an ambulance took my father to hospital, along with the shattered body of the unidentified female pedestrian. The pit of my stomach was churning as I told the policewoman that I didn't know where my mum was. I explained that she'd been in bed at around ten o'clock the previous night but wasn't there this morning.

There were huddled discussions in the interview room between several officers and eventually WPC Toomey sat down in front of me. She said that the dead woman had still to be identified as she'd had no bag or documents on her when, as they assumed, the car had hit her on the side of the road and thrown her body into the centre of it. She then asked me if, purely for the purposes of elimination, I could go with them to the hospital and make sure that the woman wasn't my mum.

Of course, I knew. I thought of my loving mother, waking up after I'd gone to bed and thinking, 'Best go and get John, after all he's been through. I can drive him home and once he's slept it off, we can have a proper chat tomorrow. Won't take long to walk up to the pub.' But, one look at the sliding body tray in the morgue was enough to confirm that she'd never made it to the pub. My dad had either been too drunk to see her, or more probably, had tried to brake and the lack of hydraulic fluid caused by my actions in the car park had made the car unstoppable on that hill. He'd hit the tree full on but, it seemed, not hard enough to kill him straight away. He had broken his back, most of his ribs and both arms, had numerous soft tissue injuries, and some brain damage, but was just alive in an intensive care unit.

The police investigation determined that John had been over six times the legal limit for alcohol in his bloodstream, and that his wife had been killed by his dangerous driving. They were puzzled that there had been no skid marks on the road, just before the two impacts, but put it down to the total intoxication of the driver and the light rain on the road surface. He would be charged, when he recovered enough to stand trial.

I remember feeling terrible remorse about my mother. I'd killed her, even though I hadn't intended to. For my father, I felt no pity and couldn't bring myself to go and see him straight away. Then it occurred to me that if I didn't visit him, people would get suspicious, so made a point of going and gazing at him in his induced coma.

Weeks went by during which the doctors tried several times to bring Father out of his drug driven unconsciousness. Each time his vital signs showed rapid deterioration, and they put him back under. Eventually, I think, his body and mind just got used to being asleep and stimulation was increasingly pointless as his coma became permanent.

A day came in the autumn of that year when his brother, Uncle Hugo, stood by Dad's bed while I watched, and signed forms confirming that the use of life support could be terminated. Three days later my father was dead, and I was glad. I'd hated him for what he put my mum through but, if nothing else, my father had achieved something to earn my gratitude. He had made me tough and hardened my emotions more than he could have ever imagined. It was time to get on with life.

It was only in writing these words that Carter, for the first time in a long while, actually thought about his parents. He sometimes missed his Mum but, in all honesty, had gone cold when it came to what others thought of as normal family interaction. He also remembered how Uncle Hugo had stepped into the breach after the tragedy and arranged for him to finish his education, via Marlborough school, and get him ready for Sandhurst.

Cat noticed that what little light there had been outside was now fading in the west as the storm continued its relentless lashing of the coast and threatened to damage anything that wasn't securely anchored to the rocky ground in these parts.

He emailed the file to Lydia and then went to see Bardy, who was nearing the end of the Marlborough book and looked up from his armchair.

"Another chapter done, my friend?"

"Yes... It was tough but I'm pleased to get that one finished."

"Looks like another quiet night in, Cat?" said Bardy with a nod toward the window.

"Indeed," agreed Cat, "You can cook if you like? Give us one of your student specialities!"

"Right, tinned tuna and baked beans it is..."

"I'll get the whisky, sounds like we'll need it."

-+-

Chapter Nineteen

That same Tuesday, on the other side of Scotland, the morning sun had not yet shown itself when a dark blue Range Rover cruised into the environs of the University of Edinburgh. It stopped, idled, then moved off again, sometimes turning round as the occupants followed the instructions given by the car's satellite navigation system. The SatNav was convinced that Eric the driver and his passengers, Pascal and Milton, had 'arrived at your destination' and repeatedly told them so. The fact that the rugby pitch in front of them looked nothing like the student flat address they had programmed it with, didn't deter the system at all.

"Milton, are you sure about this address?" asked Pascal, irritable from the long drive north.

"Pollock Halls of Residence, EH16 5AY. I've sent him stuff there, John Burdett House, Apartment C17. Let's turn off the SatNav and try on the other side of the park."

The modern row of four storey buildings across the green looked a lot more like a campus and when they got closer and consulted an early morning jogger, she confirmed that they were indeed at John Burdett House. Pascal told Eric to wait in the car, while he and Milton loitered by the front door of block C. Soon another student jogger emerged from the security protected door and Pascal grabbed the door before it could lock itself. They went inside and found Apartment 17.

Terry Arnott was in a world of dreams, inspired by the six pints of 'Bitter & Twisted' he'd enjoyed at the student bar the previous night. Why on Earth was someone using a steam hammer when it was still dark? The banging continued and some sense of reality started breaking through Terry's subconscious. It was the door, somebody was knocking at his door. With his eyes still closed, he grabbed at a dressing gown from the floor and shrugged himself into it, then staggered to the door.

"Hoozit," he mumbled.

"Is that you Terry?"

"Hoowanztoono?"

"It's Milton... Shakespeare's brother... Can we talk?"

"Shaky's broother? Aye, coom in, man."

Terry unlocked the door and pulled it open. He hadn't expected to see more than one African at his door, but held out his hand as they walked into the twin bedded student room. Milton shook his hand first, then introduced his cousin. The visitors sat on the unused bed, opposite Terry on his.

"Hang on a minute," queried Terry, "You and Shaky are meant to be twins, yeah?"

"That's right."

"But...forgive me, you don't look anything like him. He's so much ligh...he has a different skin tone than you."

"Nevertheless, we are twins... Here's my passport."

Terry looked at the document and handed it back. "So, what's he bin up to then, my mate Shaky?"

"We were hoping that you'd know," interrupted Pascal, "He seems to have gone missing and we are...worried about him."

"Well let's try and ring him eh...where's me phone?"

"His is turned off, we need to see him...face to face. Please... Terry, where do you think he is? Should we look through his stuff?"

Through his beer fogged brain, Terry sensed, through the possible menace, the need to help and thought back to the summer.

"The Hebrides. Shaky said he was looking up an old friend of his mother, didn't give a name."

Pascal smiled and replied, "We need you to be more specific, Terry. The Hebrides is a big area."

"Right... yeah... let me think. Do you guys want coffee? There's no breakfast I'm afraid, I go to the canteen usually."

Milton sighed and said, "We're in a hurry, so n..."

"Coffee would be good, Terry, thanks," interrupted Pascal, nodding at Milton and shuffling towards Terry's bedside table, as the student went into the ensuite bathroom to fill the kettle.

"Milk and sugar, lads?"

"Yes please."

"Just like Shaky eh?"

They settled down with the coffee, Pascal now back on the spare bed.

"I'm sure Shaky said Harris," volunteered Terry as the

caffeine flowed through him.

"Is that an island?" asked Milton.

"Yes, and no."

"Explain," ordered Pascal.

"Well, it's called the Isle of Harris, but it's part of the bigger Isle of Lewis. Outer Hebrides."

"Do you have an address on the island, where we should look for my cousin?"

"No...really, that's all he told me and he didn't leave anything but clothes here. He kept personal stuff on his iPad."

"Mentioning clothes... What was he wearing, when he left?"

"He always liked to be smart, did Shaky, even for lectures. He'd have bin wearin' his blue suit."

"Thanks Terry, we are sorry to have disturbed you. Perhaps you can go back to bed now?"

"That's a cracking good shout, lads, I will."

While Terry settled back down to sleep off his hangover, assuring himself that he would ring his friend at a more civilised hour, the Range Rover pulled up at a cafe and the occupants went inside for breakfast. In between mouthfuls of bacon sandwich, Milton was Googling 'Harris' on his iPad.

"The thing is, Pascal, Shakespeare's phone may not be turned off and Terry might call to say that we're searching for him?"

"That will be difficult without this," he replied, holding up a mobile phone from his pocket. "I picked it up as Terry was making coffee."

"He might have backed it up."

"Yes, but he'll still have to discover he's lost it, and get another phone. Which gives us a bit of a head start, wouldn't you say?"

"Right, yes. Anyway... looking at this," Milton nodded down at his screen, "Harris is best accessible via ferry from the Isle of Skye, which we can get to over a bridge. That's about five hours from here. The next ferry we could possibly make is at 2 o'clock this afternoon."

"Let's get going then," urged Pascal, "And you can continue our geography lesson on the way. Eric, are you still Ok to drive? We can't stop."

"If one of you can do the next hour, Boss, and let me sleep in the back, I'll be fine after that. What's the postcode of the ferry terminal?"

The threesome set off and quickly got to the motorway and over the Forth Bridge, feeling the high winds that were affecting all of Scotland to some extent or another. They cruised north at high speed along the M90 then A9, with Pascal at the wheel, for about an hour and a half. They then woke Eric and he took over while Milton imparted further information about their destination.

"Harris is quite a size, but with a small population, less than 2,000 people. The only place of any size is Tarbert, where the ferry comes in. Not many roads, a few villages, lots of hills and sheep. Some fishing. No airport. A lot of ground to cover, to find one man, especially if he's gone to Lewis, to the north? Bigger place with lots more people."

"But," responded Pascal, "Terry was pretty definite about Harris, and how many Kenyans, or black people of any nationality, do you think are on the island right now?"

"I'm guessing hardly any, sounds like it's too cold!"

"Exactly. Your brother will stand out a mile."

In spite of the increasingly bad weather as they journeyed north-west towards Skye, including snow being blown into drifts across the road near Invergary, the Range Rover made good time. They eventually pulled into the ferry terminal at Uig, in the north of Skye, at 1:40 pm and, through the driving rain, saw the red and white Caledonian MacBrayne ferry lashed to its moorings at the end of an elevated concrete pier.

Pascal volunteered to brave the elements and get the tickets. When the others, watching from the car, saw how much he had to bend forward to make headway into the wind, they were glad he'd gone. He was back in a couple of minutes and bundled himself back into the car.

"Well, I've got tickets," he said, "But the 2 o'clock is cancelled and they don't know when they'll be sailing. Could be tonight, but more likely will be tomorrow. It all depends when this storm eases up. They recommended going to the Uig Hotel and checking back every couple of hours by phone."

"I saw that hotel as we came into Uig, it overlooks the terminal," observed Eric.

"Ok, at least we can get a hot bath, food, and sleep," added Milton.

"We don't seem to have much choice, gentlemen," said Pascal, "To the hotel it is then."

-+-

Chapter Twenty

Nicole Kwizera sat on one of the cream leather couches in her lounge and looked out onto the swimming pool. In the glow from the patio lights, the surface seemed to boil as the sheets of rain crashed down into it. The November rains had come early to north-west Kenya and this was second night of torrential downpours. She picked up her mobile phone and tried to call Shakespeare. The ringing signal kept repeating until it eventually stopped. This was the third time she'd tried to call him, so she composed a text:

'Darling, I've been trying to ring you today but no luck. Milton left 3 nights ago and didn't say where he was going. I think he's trying to find you. Please take care. Mum XX'

She then tried to phone Milton but with the same lack of success. With a sigh, she got off the settee and headed for the stairs. Her husband looked up from his desk as she entered his study and seemed flustered. Nicole heard climactic groaning from the computer on Alphonse's desk, before his hand darted out to the keyboard and killed the volume. He brought his other hand from under the desk and glared at her.

"You know you should knock, before coming in here." he growled.

"I'm worried about the boys Alf, and I shouldn't need permission to talk to my husband in our house!"

"I'm sure the twins are Ok. Milton's probably with his friends in Nairobi, laying low for a while after Saturday's situation. Shakespeare will come home when he's bored."

"By your tone of voice, you haven't even convinced

yourself."

"My sons will be fine."

"Our sons, Alf... Our sons. What are you goin..."

"SILENCE! Woman. I won't be nagged by you. When it comes down to it, they will always come back because they fear what I'd do to you, if they didn't. It has always been that way."

"You can't hurt me any more than you have, over the last twenty years!"

"Hurt! You live in luxury and want for nothing. I have always provided well for you."

"You say I want for nothing, it's not true... I want freedom, and self-respect. Freedom from your bullying, from being confronted with your procession of whores, from being ashamed in my own house, bought with what you took from your Tutsi victims."

"We agreed, we would NEVER speak of that time again. DO NOT PROVOKE ME FURTHER Nicole!"

"I despise you...and one day I'll make you squirm. Then I'll leave this place for ever."

"You won't leave, bitch, because you know I'd make your son's lives a misery, beyond what a mother could bear."

As Nicole went to her bedroom and cried herself to sleep, Alphonse tried to call Milton with the same lack of success as his wife. He pressed the SMS icon next to Milton's name on the screen and wrote:

'When you find S, tell him he must come home with you.

If he does not, your mother will suffer badly.'

Alphonse sent the text, then went back to 'groupsexfun.com' on his desktop computer.

+

In the Pollock Halls, University of Edinburgh, Terry Arnott pulled on a can of Federation Bitter that he'd just removed from his fridge. He savoured the hoppy taste as the cool beer went down his throat and he sat down at his study desk to open a black box.

He hadn't discovered that his phone was missing until after lunchtime, when he finally arose from his interrupted sleep. He had tried to work it out, why would Shaky's brother want his phone? He didn't look hard up, and nor did the other guy. His list of contacts would be of little interest to anyone outside his family, and his circle of Sunderland-supporting, beer-drinking friends.

Whatever the reason, he'd had to brave the gales outside to go and get a new Windows phone. Luckily he still had a bit of credit left on his Visa card and so here he was, early in the evening, unpacking the new device. He plugged the handset into the charger and opened his laptop to find his saved list of contacts.

Within ten minutes he was trying to call Shaky, but got no response. A text seemed a good idea so he composed:

'Shaky, I had visitors today, your bro Milton and his cuz. Dey were looking for U and I told em re Harris. Don' know Y but dey stole my phone! Be gud, Tez.'

Having sent the text, Terry settled down to finish his beer and flicked on the TV. After last night's indulgence and today's strange events, a quiet evening in was the best bet.

+

Lydia Hockley-Roberts was staring hard at the screen on her laptop. It was a gloomy Tuesday evening in Hampstead, cold winds gusting outside her house. She'd left the office early to avoid the worst of the rush hour and had sat down with some tea and crumpets at the big kitchen table. She had been delighted to get another email from Cat and was reading the attachment for the second time. Her tea went cold as she went slowly through the words and her eyes widened in shock.

She had to call him and held the phone tight to her ear as she muttered, "Pick up, pick up." The rings finally stopped, so she sent a text which read:

'Rob, WTF, your latest piece is sensational, and could probably get you arrested! We must talk, call me as soon as you get this. LHR."

-+-

Chapter Twenty One

Cat reached over the table to spoon out the last of a very passable tuna and pasta bake that Shakespeare had concocted, from a casserole dish onto his plate.

"Very good Bardy, you can come again."

"Thanks, what do you English say... Not bad for a beginner?"

"Exactly, storm doesn't look like calming down yet. Pass the whisky please."

Shakespeare passed the bottle of Ardbeg 12 year old across the table, and the little jug of water. Cat poured some of each into his tumbler and took a good mouthful, which he swallowed with a satisfied sigh.

"Peaty, but I'm sure you can taste roast chestnuts in that," he said.

"It just tastes smoky to me, like the smell after a barbecue," replied Shakespeare.

"Have you spoken to your mum, since you got here, Bardy?"

Shakespeare hesitated, then said, "No... I've thought about it, but... I...it could cause trouble for her."

"In what way?"

"If my dad saw that she'd been in touch with me, he could get angry with her. I refused to obey him when he told me...well, told my brother to tell me, to come home."

"But you're a grown man, Bardy, he can't order you around like a servant."

"But he does, Cat. He still treats Milton and me like little boys. Sometimes he will indulge us but he knows that we...no, I, would do anything to protect my mum. Milton is more like a junior version of dad. I'm afraid that they both think I'm a bit of a mummy's boy."

"Perhaps you ended up with all the good qualities from your mother and Milton inherited more of your father's blood?"

"Kind of you to say, Cat. There's some... Something else... You remember on Friday when we were taking about Mum and I told you I'd just had a text from her. Well, you'd better see it."

Shakespeare found the text on his phone and passed it to Cat. He read it and handed it back. "I think they will come for you... Who's 'they' and how serious is this, Bardy?"

"My dad doesn't like to leave the ranch. I think she means my brother, perhaps with some help? My dad has personal security staff. He likes to get his own way."

"I think we should call your mum? Ask her for news? If she is worried, you can tell her you've found me. Obviously, if she wants to talk to me, then... I'd like that."

Shakespeare fiddled with his phone for a moment, then passed it back to Cat. "Network must be down?" he asked.

Cat pulled his phone from his pocket and confirmed that yes, the network must be down and he couldn't get any working alternative. "It must be the storm, perhaps it wrecked the local network mast or something," he added, with a real note of regret.

"We can try again tomorrow Cat?" said Bardy, in an attempt to cheer up his friend.

"Yeah, and anyway, even if your mum's right... Nobody's going anywhere in this storm."

"I'm sure you're right, and there's plenty of whisky in that bottle!"

"Do you play chess?" asked Cat, "I've got a nice set in the study."

"I do, learned at school, no one to play with at home."

"Well, what better way to spend a stormy evening than a few games of chess by the fire? I'll get the set."

So, as the storm blew itself out on that long Tuesday night, the Englishman and the African played chess. Cat quickly built a two game to nil lead over the youngster but then, as Shakespeare got into the swing of the game, he started to see further ahead than he had in the early games. The third game was a titanic struggle with a lot of pieces captured and counter captured. By the end, they each had a rook and two pawns left, but through sheer dogged determination, and helped by Cat having had more of the Ardbeg than his opponent, Shakespeare managed to get one of his pawns to Cat's back line. As soon as he picked up a fresh queen, Cat laid down his king and shook Bardy's hand. "Well played, you deserved that."

Shakespeare went to bed happy, and determined to speak to his mum as soon as the network was back. It was surely time, he told himself, for him to stand up to his father and, perhaps with Cat's help, he might even be able to somehow get his mother out from under his father's dominance, so that she could be happy too.

On the way to his bedroom, Cat also had thoughts of Nicole Kwizera, although his were more linked to memories of a damp canvas tent in the mountains of Rwanda, and nights in a shared sleeping bag, dreaming of gorillas. Something about the conversation earlier that evening stayed in his mind however, and purely from an instinct born of many years in the service of Her Majesty, he made a point of locking and bolting the main and side doors of the cottage. Something he had never thought of doing before.

-+-

Chapter Twenty Two

Milton, Pascal, and Eric sat around the breakfast table at the Uig Hotel, and looked out of the picture window towards the CalMac ferry, bobbing against its mooring ropes on the jetty across the small bay. Their landline phone calls the previous evening had confirmed that the first sailing to Harris would now be the 09:40, provided that the storm had abated by then. Although they could still see a big swell in the waters beyond the harbour, the wind had dropped down to no more than a strong breeze.

They finished their breakfast, and their rough planning for the day ahead, then paid the bill and got into the Range Rover. They were at the jetty before nine o'clock and nursing coffees in the ferry's lounge, before the on-time departure. In spite of the ship accommodating the passengers stranded by the previous night's cancellation, the three men had noticed that the car deck wasn't even half full. Pascal was firmly of the opinion that this still showed that too many people wanted to go to such cold places and that nobody with any sense should ever willingly go to where civilisation ran out. His opinions became stronger as the ferry rounded the end of the bay and was fully exposed to the rolling waves in the Minch.

+

Terry Arnott woke up, for the second morning running, with a beer-induced headache. His planned 'quiet night in' had become a 'noisy night out', when two friends had called at his apartment and invited him out for a 'livener'. He peered at his new mobile, to discover that it was nearly 10am. Looking at the screen reminded him vaguely of a conversation with his mates last night. Something about the theft of his old phone, and he'd agreed to do something unusual today. What the hell was it? He took a big swig of the pint mug of water on his bedside cabinet and his brain slowly started to focus.

That was it... They'd been sitting in the student bar watching the BBC news about storms hitting power and phone networks, especially in Scotland. His mate Adrian had seen his new phone and asked him about it. When he told them the story about his early morning visitors, they were outraged at the 'Fucking cheek of some people'. Adrian said that he should tell the police, or 'Grass them up to Plod' as he called it. When he explained that he had no details in terms of what car they were in, their full names (apart from Milton - who didn't live in Britain), or any other contact details, Adrian went quiet. Colin, however, pointed out that what Terry did know, was where the phone thieves were going. Terry therefore promised to 'Get down the cop shop in the morning and tell them what happened'. Colin observed that, if nothing else, reporting it to the police would make an insurance claim much more likely to succeed. They had then got stuck into the generously discounted ale on offer by the faculty to 'Help the social interaction between students', and got seriously drunk.

Terry reluctantly got out of bed and threw himself into the shower. The power setting generally added to his throbbing headache, but he had begun to feel human again after he got dried, dressed, and drinking coffee.

He was at the local police station by around eleven o'clock, filling in a theft report form. The form didn't seem to have a question along the lines of, 'Where do you think the perpetrators might be now?' So Terry spoke to the rather old looking duty sergeant as he handed him the completed form, "I'm pretty sure that I know where the thieves are... If that's any help?"

Sergeant Wallace, looked at the form and drawled, "Reeaally? Do share that with us then... Sherlock."

"Harris... They were looking for my flatmate, his name and description's on the back of the form. I knew he'd headed for Harris about a week ago. They said that they needed to find him. Now, if they were giving him a good surprise, they wouldn't have stolen my phone...would they? So perhaps they mean him harm, I don't know?"

Something in Terry's tone made Wallace take notice, "Did they threaten you?"

"Not threaten, no. But they seemed...sort of...menacing, if you know what I mean."

"Have you made contact with your flatmate?"

"Tried, with my new phone, but no answer. Sent a text but don't know if he got it. There was stuff on TV about the Western Isles having storms and power cuts."

"And this was yesterday morning?"

"Yes."

"Address of your flatmate?"

"Don't know, just Harris. I'm guessing they'd get the ferry, if the storms allow?"

"Thanks, Mr Arnott, we'll take it from here. I don't imagine it will do any good but I'll share this with the police office on Harris and leave it to them. Running around looking for stolen phones is unlikely to be a top priority, even for the sleepy sheep-sha... The fine men and women of the Highland constabulary, but you never know. Good day, Mr Arnott."

+

At Water Cottage, Carter and Shakespeare sat down for a late breakfast of steaming bowls of freshly made porridge, dressed with honey and whisky.

"We'll need this...out there, Bardy."

"Out there, Cat? What are you thinking?"

"Fishing."

"It looks a bit cold for that sort of thing."

"Nonsense, the storm's just about blown itself out now and the sun will be breaking through the remaining clouds in an hour or so. I know a great little beach, with rocks to each side that we can cast from. It's only a ten minute drive, so we'll get the jeep out and get up that track on the other side of the village. I'll get the fishing stuff together, you grab some food for a packed lunch, and wrap up warm!"

So, by around eleven o'clock, suitably attired and packed, they were due to leave on their fishing expedition. Cat dived into his study just before they left, unlocked his filing cabinet and put something from it in the poachers pocket of his Gortex jacket. They then carefully locked up, got the Suzuki jeep from the garage at the side of the cottage, and set off on the road to the village, then the dirt track to the north.

"Have you got any network, Bardy? I still can't use my phone."

"Same with me, still, we're used to erratic networks in Kenya! By the way Cat, I've never fished in my life," explained Shakespeare, as they bounced along the track, "Will we catch much?"

"Probably not, but that's not the point, it's all about relaxation and enjoying the surroundings, as much as hoping to bring anything home for supper."

So they set up, on the boulders to the southern edge of a beautiful beach with sand the colour of Dijon mustard, and Carter showed his willing pupil how to cast their long lines into the area just beyond the surf, as it broke gently on the shoreline rocks. The rhythms of the gentle routine of casting and recasting, as the sun broke through in line with Cat's prediction, relaxed the men and they started to talk.

Shakespeare found himself telling Cat about his home in Kenya, about life with his parents and brother. The scrapes that his brother got into, and how his dad turned a blind eye. The beauty of the Mount Elgon national park and the sadness of his mother, trapped by a shared past with his father, that was only now beginning to come to light to him.

Cat in turn, told Shakespeare about how his childhood had been pretty much friendless and that he had found real fulfilment in the Army, and later the foreign office. How he had been all over the world, trying to sort out problems that were nothing to do with him personally. He didn't want to cause embarrassment to either of them, so didn't mention Nicole. He did confirm that he had never got married and that his only possible regret was not having children.

Neither of them got a bite and the time went on until it was time to rest the rods and take some coffee from a flask that Shakespeare had prepared, plus nibble at a couple of small pork pies that he had put in a bag. Over this sumptuous feast, Shakespeare asked Cat if he minded a personal question. "Ask away," he replied.

"Carter Aragorn Talbot? Everyone at school read 'Lord of the Rings' and of course Aragorn is a great character, but I don't know anyone else with that name."

"It was my mum," he said, with a sad look in his eyes. "She was a real bookworm and read it way before it became popular, while she was expecting me in 1958. I think she really wanted me to be a hero too. Perhaps to make up for the disappointment she had in my father?"

"What does she think now?"

"Both my parents died in a car accident... When I was fifteen."

"Sorry Cat... you never said."

"Long time ago now... Aragorn, it was the source of my nickname at Bainbridge, by the way. They called me 'Gorny'. Anyway, let's try for another hour, then we can call it a day and perhaps have a pint on the way home, with our big haul of sea trout!" He nodded at the empty keep net resting on the side of a rock, then picked up the rods. They went back to the rhythms of the casting and the waves.

+

Pascal seemed to be the most pleased of all the passengers on the 'MV Hebrides', as the ferry lunged into the small inlet and ferry terminal that surrounded the very small town of Tarbert on Harris, almost on schedule at 11:25. His greyish pallor behind the African complexion, seemed to dissipate as quickly as the roll-on, roll-off ramp came down with the bow of the vessel.

He and his colleagues hurried down to the car deck and got ready to drive off. They needed to talk to any taxi drivers here before ferry passengers without cars jumped into any cabs, and disappeared to the far flung reaches of this mountainous island.

Eric turned the engine on and, as soon as the couple of vans in front of them edged forward, he skirted to the side of them and bore down on the ramp, ignoring the shaken fists of the drivers he had inconvenienced. A nod of apology to the crewman on the ramp, a touch of Eric's right foot, and the Range Rover was on Harris.

They quickly found an excuse for a taxi rank, with two silver Toyota estate cars - embellished with white taxi signs on their roofs - waiting fifty yards from the ferry ramp. Pascal jumped out and went to the front car. The driver's window was down as he finished a cigarette. Pascal leaned in and spoke.

"Excuse me, I need some help, we're looking for a young Kenyan, who arrived on the island about a week ago. Do you remember him, he's black and was wearing a blue suit?"

"Aye, well, now my memory's not what it was," said the driver who, from the lines on his face, looked as if he should have given up taxi driving many years before. "It needs nudging now and then... If ye ken what I mean?"

Pascal reached in his pocket and thrust a twenty pound note in the drivers face. "Don't make me 'nudge' you again old man," he grunted.

"Ye see, I do remember a young smart black laddie last week... But he didn't use my cab."

"And?"

"And, he used wee Alec, the driver behind me there," he

said with a backward jerk of his right thumb.

Pascal immediately turned his attention to the rear cab, which was just having the doors opened by two mature ladies in hiking boots, oilskin jackets, and backpacks. "Alec," he shouted, "Hold on." He went to the driver's door, found another twenty and banged on the driver's window. As it part opened he stuffed the money through the gap and made a sign to lower the glass fully. "Sorry Ladies," he said to the ramblers who were now settling into the rear seats. "Alec, the black guy you picked up last week, where did you take him please? There's a family emergency and we've got to find him fast."

"Black guy, you say..? Mmm... Can't say I remember too clearly..."

"Alec," he hissed close to the driver's ear, "No more messing about, if you don't mind. Tell me now, or face the consequences."

Alec Millar had been driving taxis for long enough to recognise trouble when it confronted him. "Oh, er... Yes, I remember now. Crawnish, he wanted to go to Crawnish and just be dropped at the edge of the village, by the sign. It's about 20 miles, along the B887."

"Thanks Alec, thanks Ladies," he said breezily and jumped back into the Range Rover. He selected the SatNav on the dashboard display and entered 'Crawnish, Harris'. They were soon driving north out of Tarbert and, as the sun broke through the clouds ahead, took in a breath-taking view.

+

Sergeant Roddy MacLeod was proud that he achieved that rank and still, just, be in his twenties. He was also frustrated that caring for his widowed mother meant he couldn't leave the Isle of Harris and enjoy the exciting police work that he knew was awaiting him in Glasgow or Edinburgh, or even Inverness. The most exciting things that happened in Tarbert police office, usually involved letting drunken teenagers sleep it off in that station's one cell.

Getting an email from Edinburgh, as happened that Wednesday just as he was about to tuck into his lunchtime sandwiches, was therefore not something to be ignored. It mentioned two African's and there were descriptions on the scanned copy theft report. Apparently they had stolen a student's phone from his flat and were on their way to Harris, probably by ferry. Roddy looked at the office clock from which he knew that the ferry had not only arrived, but by then left for its return to Skye, and all the passengers would be well away. So, in spite of the fact that he clearly (so his instinct told him) had two international drug dealers running wild on his island, he could at least finish his rounds of corned beef and mustard before commencing his enquiries.

+

The Range Rover pulled up briefly at the village sign saying 'Crawnish' and Milton turned off the CD player which had been, rather incongruously, belting out strong drum and bass dance music as they glided along the twisting road through the mountains of West Harris.

"What now, Cousin?" he asked.

Pascal - from the back seat - replied, "Eric, just drive slowly into the village and look for any sign of life."

They saw no-one as they cruised down the one street and, when the road ran out, they ignored the track to the north and went back the way they'd come. As they passed the post office, Pascal told Eric to stop and wait, while he and Milton asked a few questions in the shop.

As they went into 'MacArthur's Stores and Post Office' the door triggered a tinny bell to ring. This, in turn, prompted a middle aged woman from a room at the rear to come through a doorway, pulling her cardigan around her. "Good afternoon Gentlemen, Moira MacArthur, at your service," the woman said.

"Good afternoon... Moira. We wondered if you could help us?"

Moira waved her hands around the shelves, stocked mainly with canned and bottled goods, plus a rumbling, glass fronted fridge to one side, full of dairy produce and wine. "I'm sure I can," she replied.

"We don't really need to buy anything today, but we'd like some information please? The thing is, my cousin here is looking for his brother, Shakespeare, and we're fairly sure he's around here somewhere. We can't seem to contact him on his phone, and there's a bit of a family emergency... You know how it is?"

"Well...now I'm not one for gossip, no matter what you may have heard...but I think I can help. There is a young bla... African looking gentleman, staying with Rob, the Englishman, up at Water Cottage. It's the last house on the left as you go back towards Tarbert."

"An Englishman, you say?" queried Milton.

"Thank you, Mrs MacArthur, you've been very kind, we'll not trouble you anymore," interrupted Pascal, "Come on Cuz."

They quickly drove up to the entrance to Rob's cottage and stopped on the road. Pascal was now in the front and opened the glove box. "Better safe than sorry, boys," he said as he unwrapped the three handguns and distributed them, along with nine millimetre ammunition for each. "Fill the magazines," he ordered, "You just never know what could happen."

Milton had been handed a small Sig Sauer and he commented that the clip only took seven rounds. "Thinking of needing more?" Pascal sneered, "I thought you were a hunter?"

Milton blushed and said nothing.

Pascal had a Beretta in polymer, with Eric wielding a neat Walther PPK, and they all tucked them into their jacket pockets. Eric then drove slowly up the drive and stopped when they were level with the main door, in the middle of the rear wall of the cottage.

"You go first Milton, and see if you can have a friendly chat with your Bro."

Milton didn't argue, just got out and knocked on the door. He tried again then looked through one of the windows to the side. He walked around the whole cottage peering through every window, then came back to the car, with his arms outstretched sideways.

"Nobody home and both doors are locked," he confirmed through the car window.

"Any sign of life?" Pascal asked.

"The wood burning stove is alight."

"So they've gone out, but expect to be back. We'll wait,

but need to hide this," Pascal tapped the dashboard for emphasis. "Milton, try the garage door."

It was open, so they squeezed the big 4x4 into the restricted space then closed the door again. Instructed by Pascal, the three of them took up waiting positions. Eric to the left end of the cottage, so only visible to someone coming near to the top of the drive. Pascal to the right end, behind the corner by the rear door with a part view of the road coming from the village. Meanwhile, Milton was perched behind a boulder on the overhang to the front of the house. That way he could see down onto the road in either direction but stay hidden if needed. The sun was shining, but the breeze was cold and the boys gradually chilled as they waited in silence.

+

About an hour after their coffee break, Carter and Shakespeare were getting cold and had failed, in spite of sterling casting efforts, to catch anything for the pot. They agreed that a pint in the Dion, being warmed by the fire, would be the best thing to do. They quickly stowed away their rods and tackle in the jeep and Cat drove it back down the track to the village. They hopped out into the pub and rubbed their purple hands together, occasionally turning their palms towards the blazing peat fire as they stood and waited for Finn to deliver the beer to the bar top.

No sooner had they had their first mouthfuls of heavy, than Neil walked in and sat at the bar. He sipped at a pint then half turned and said, "Someone was looking for you Shakespeare."

"Sorry, where? When?"

"I just popped into Moira's for some cigarettes and she told me that there were a couple of African lads asking after you. Some sort of family emergency or something?"

"Neil?" Cat interrupted, "Did Moira say how long ago this was?"

"She wasn't specific but mentioned it being after lunch. So not long ago I guess...is there a problem Rob?"

"What did she tell them?"

"I got the impression that she told them where your house is."

"Thanks Neil," he said to the fisherman then, under his breath, "Bardy, we need to finish these, then quietly get outside."

When outside, Cat told Shakespeare that they would be best leaving the car at the pub and climbing up the slopes behind the cottage to approach from an unexpected direction.

"Look Cat, I know you're trying to help, but this is my problem. I can't keep avoiding my brother forever and perhaps if I can talk to him, he will understand why going home would be so difficult for me?"

"You're assuming he'll be reasonable."

"But he can't literally force me to go all the way to Kenya, if I don't agree to it, can he?"

"What if he threatens your mum?"

"Cat, if it makes you feel better, why don't you go the back way to the cottage, as a sort of back up, while I walk up the road as if it's the most normal thing in the world? Assuming he's at the cottage, I'll try and talk to him and you can come to the rescue if it gets awkward?"

"Ok, but give me ten minutes to get into position, then carry your rod to the house as if you've come back early and alone. Any trouble, and I'll be there in a flash."

+

Comforted after his lunch, Roddy MacLeod strolled the short journey from his police office to the Tarbert ferry terminal. He went into the ticket office and asked if anyone had seen any Africans get off the ferry. The two administrators behind the desk confirmed that they hadn't seen anyone, as they only served those people departing not arriving.

Roddy next went to the taxi rank and asked the same question of Alec Millar, who had returned to Tarbert after dropping his two hikers at Amhuinnsuidhe Castle.

"Hello Sergeant," said the driver through his open window. "As it happens, there was a black lad off today's ferry, looking for another black lad, who I took to Crawnish about a week ago."

"What was he driving?"

"Navy Range Rover."

"How many in the car?"

"I couldn't tell, Sergeant, the windows were smoked glass. But... I think he said 'We've got to find him,' so at least two of them."

"Thanks Alec, and, by the way... I see you're still showing an out of date tax disc. I'll assume you're on the new system?" added Roddy, nodding towards the errant item in the windscreen, before walking away.

Sergeant MacLeod returned to the police office and told his civilian assistant that he was going to take a trip to Crawnish and would be back later.

"Don't forget it's my early finish today Roddy?" she replied.

"Aye, Morag, not a bother, you put the answerphone on and lock up when you go. See you tomorrow."

With that, Roddy took the keys to Tarbert's only police car and strolled out to the small car park where the white Vauxhall Astra, with blue chequered livery, was sitting. It made him smile as he cruised gently through the narrow streets towards the north and west, thinking how surprised the foreign visitors would be when he confronted them with their misdemeanour. Who knows, he thought, this could be just the tip of the iceberg. They could really be up to something, and he was the very fellow to stop them in their tracks.

+

Cat quickly scrambled up the slope behind the pub and turned towards the right, keeping the higher reaches of the hill to his left. Well within ten minutes, he was behind a couple of boulders about thirty yards from his own back door, where he could see the back of a man peering around the corner of the cottage, towards the front. He stayed hidden and looked towards the bend in the road, where Shakespeare would be coming from.

The first thing that any of the watchers saw, was the tip of a fishing rod waving about and getting larger over the rise in the road. Soon the rod took full form, sloped across the shoulder of Shakespeare Kwizera, as he ambled towards the cottage, a canvas bag in his other hand. He was clearly alone and seemingly oblivious to the discreet attention he was attracting. He went past the overhang at the front of the cottage and lazily strolled to his left to go up the drive.

Milton waited until his twin was halfway up the drive then stood up from behind his rock calling, "Good afternoon, Brother." Shakespeare stopped and turned to his left, "Milton?"

"Yes. Where's your boyfriend?"

"Sorry?"

"The Englishman you've been living with... Where is he?"

"Oh... He's, uhm, still fishing. I'd had enough, thought I'd come back for a hot bath. Anyway, what the hell are you doing here and how did you find me?"

"As to, what I'm doing here, I could ask you the same question. It's like living on the edge of the world! How we found you is not important."

"We? Who else is with you?"

"Me," called Pascal, motioning Eric to stay put and emerging from behind the cottage, "Your favourite cousin."

"I'd say it's nice to see you, but I'd be lying, Pascal."

"A charming welcome. Perhaps you won't be so disrespectful, when you get back in front of your father? We are here to make sure you obey him and go home."

"And what if I won't co-operate?"

In a fluid movement, Pascal drew his Beretta from this jacket and pointed it, two-handed, at Shakespeare. "Oh, I think you'll find it in yourself to be co-operative. Now, no more talk, we need to get out of here."

Carter had seen and heard enough. He pulled the Glock 19 from his coat and ran down the short slope to the front of the cottage, pointing it straight at Pascal.

"There is no need for guns in this conversation, Gentlemen. Bardy, please relieve your cousin of his weapon."

As Shakespeare moved slowly towards Pascal, Eric reacted and sprung from the other side of the house, also with a handgun in his hand, aiming intermittently between the Englishman and Shakespeare.

None of the people in this tableaux had noticed the white Vauxhall cruising slowly along the road towards the cottage, and were astonished to suddenly hear a tannoy magnified voice crackling, "WHAT THE BLOODY HELL IS GOING ON HERE?"

The bodies of all five men on the rough grass froze, but they all turned their heads towards the source of the noise. They could see a uniformed man holding a handset in the driver's seat of a police car, then heard, "ALL OF YOU, DROP THOSE WEAPONS." The men stayed frozen and Sergeant MacLeod repeated his command, adding, "DO IT NOW, HELICOPTER BACK UP WILL BE HERE IN MINUTES."

Roddy MacLeod had opened his window and heard the white man of the group say, "Come on guys, there's no need for any more trouble, let's do as the officer says. After three?"

"One," said Cat, as Pascal gave a slight turn of his head and winked quickly at Milton.

"Two," Pascal nodded affirmatively to Cat and Eric.

"Three," all three guns were on the ground.

"THANK YOU GENTLEMEN, NOW PLEASE STEP BACK AWAY FROM THE WEAPONS... A BIT FURTHER. THANKS, YOU KNOW IT MAKES SENSE."

It was a very relieved Sergeant MacLeod who got out of his car and walked quickly towards the handguns. He knew he'd taken a massive risk, but by nature he was a brave man and hadn't thought twice. This was going to look great on a report, armed men arrested single-handedly, and a blood bath averted. Queens Medal surely! He had almost reached the firearms, when Milton pulled his Sig Sauer from his pocket and shot the policeman in the chest. His momentum took him one step further, then he crumpled forward, with a surprised cry. Milton stepped forward and, without hesitation, fired a second round into the back of the prone officer's head, which jerked at the impact.

Pascal, Eric, and Cat, all dived for their own guns at the same time, while Shakespeare jumped down onto the drive, twisting his ankle on the rough gravel. Cat rolled as his hand grasped the polymer handle of the Glock and from lying on his left side, he loosed off four rapid shots at Pascal and Eric who were trying to get up. One missed, one hit Eric in the throat, and two took Pascal back down from their impacts in his midriff.

As Cat tried to turn and look for Milton, he felt a shuddering pain in his right shoulder blade as it fractured with a shot from behind by the Kenyan. He lost control of his hand and the gun dropped to the grass. As he gasped for air and tried again to turn, he felt another shot slam into his left hip, leaving him flat and helpless on his back.

Cat could see Pascal groaning loudly and clutching at his abdomen in a half sitting position, and Eric on his side, his neck spurting jets of blood in an arc, as he tried to stem the flow with his crimson hand. Cat was finding it hard to breathe and he lay there as Milton walked over, standing above him, the little pistol in his hand pointing at Cat's face.

Slow motion seemed to take over the run of events for Cat, as he gasped for some words that wouldn't come. Bizarrely, he heard the bleeping of mobile phone messages being received. He saw the boy's fingers stiffen slowly on the gun, and heard Shakespeare's voice, loud and pleading. The last sensation he had was an explosion, then all was darkness.

-+-

******

Part Two

Chapter Twenty Three

It was still dark in Hampstead when Lydia Hockley-Roberts sat down with a mug of coffee at home and pressed the channel 1 button on her TV remote control.

The reassuring colours and faces of the early morning programme came onto the screen and Lydia sipped her coffee. "This is BBC Breakfast on Thursday 23rd October..." Her early morning routine seemed to get her in the right frame of mind for the journey to central London, equipped with caffeine and a smattering of current affairs knowledge.

After some random sports news, including another win for Chelsea the previous night, she leaned slightly forward as she heard the anchor say, "And now over to James Neill on the Isle of Harris."

A young man in a windproof coat was holding a fat microphone close to his face and the camera panned around over his shoulder as he made gestures with his other arm.

"It was yesterday afternoon when the peace of this tiny hamlet in the Outer Hebrides was shattered by gunfire, in what the police are describing as a 'sudden and violent gun battle'. It took place in the front garden of this cottage behind me, in the village of Crawnish on Harris."

Lydia couldn't believe her eyes. When she had helped find Cat his 'place by the sea' she had personally visited the short list of properties and this was, quite definitely, the one she had chosen. She wouldn't have necessarily described the space at the front of Water Cottage as a 'garden' but it hardly seemed relevant compared to what the reporter was saying.

"...Police went on to say that there had been three male fatalities, currently unidentified, and another unidentified male was unconscious and in intensive care at Stornoway hospital. They are conducting enquiries in the village and surrounding area to try and establish the series of events that led to this tragedy. No officer is currently available for an interview."

The camera continued to roam around the scene and picked up a white police car in the drive, with stripy tape around it, plus two people in white zipped suits bending over in the 'garden', stroking the grass with their gloved fingers.

"No theories as to just what happened have yet been put forward and the cottage is currently unoccupied. The local residents we spoke to described this as a genuine shock and one said, 'We never have any trouble here, nobody even bothers to lock their doors, it's a true community spirit.' As we get more news, we'll bring it to you. This is James Neill for BBC News, at Crawnish, on the Isle of Harris."

Lydia just sat staring at the screen as the presenters on the couch moved to interview the Education Minister about the quality of school meals. She picked up her phone and found Cat's number. She hesitated, hovering her finger over the screen, then scrolled it down to find a different number. She pressed this one without hesitation and got an almost immediate answer.

"You've seen the news then?" said the rather sharp male voice on the phone. "I was wondering when you'd call."

"Francis, what the hell has been going on?"

"Something I'd very much like to know. I've had Archie

beating me up on the phone late last night and again this morning."

"Archie?"

"Findlayson...MI6. He can't believe that your boy has caused such an uproar."

"MY boy? My boy... Frank, you asked me to babysit Cat, was he involved?"

"I just don't know. The police have been ordered, probably by Archie's pals in the Home Office, to release no names to anyone until further instructions. That includes me. I've tried ringing Talbot, no luck."

"I was about to try him but thought I'd speak to you first."

"His phone is turned off."

"Fraaaank?"

"Why are you putting on your girly, 'Can I have a favour' voice?"

"I need to go...to Harris. Find out what's happened, if h... If Cat is Ok?"

"Alright Lydia...make it a long weekend. But I want a full briefing from you on Monday morning, my office! Ok?"

Within two hours, Lydia was at Heathrow sorting out connecting flights to Stornoway, via Glasgow. She picked up a copy of the Independent to read on the plane and the report from their Scotland correspondent didn't throw much more light on the Crawnish incident than the BBC man earlier. One resident of the hamlet had apparently commented on Twitter that 'It was strange that there seemed no sign of the young African boy who had been staying at the cottage.'

She pondered that, and so much more, as the Glasgow flight boarded.

-+-

Chapter Twenty Four

The Friday morning sun rose in a cloudless sky, bathing the eastern slopes of Mount Elgon in bright light and highlighting the multitude of green and brown shades in the furrowed landscape. Nicole Kwizera, in a cream-coloured chiffon nightdress, took in the view standing at the French windows of her bedroom and sipped some chilled passion fruit juice brought earlier by one of the house-girls.

She picked up her phone and, in an absent-minded gesture, pressed the screen, barely glanced at it, and threw it onto the bed. It had been nearly a week since Milton left the house and longer than that since she'd heard from her other son. Her phone calls and text messages to both of them had gone unanswered.

Way beyond the Kwizera's main gate and estate fence, she could just make out a small bubble of red dust, gradually growing as it came up the track from the direction of Kitale. It was clearly heading towards the gate and she watched as it bounced along the track. Although heavily encrusted with red dust, Nicole could see that within the speeding cloud was a white Land Cruiser, just like Milton's... Exactly like Milton's, she realised with a start.

She pulled the nightdress over her head and reached into her wardrobe for some shorts and a top. Throwing them on, with some sandals, and tying her hair with a headscarf, she hurried to the main lounge. She called the house-girls and ordered them to prepare cold drinks, coffee and breakfast. Nicole then went to the front doors and threw them open, just as her two sons stepped onto the front porch.

"Boys," she beamed, "You're home!"

"As you can see, Mama, I have found my errant twin," Milton boasted, as he wrapped his arm around the stiffening shoulders of his brother. Shakespeare shrugged him off and limped forward, throwing his arms tightly around Nicole and squeezing her for much longer than he had ever done before. "I love you Mum. Are you Ok?"

With an imperceptible glance at Milton, she quietly whispered into his chest, "Of course...you mustn't worry." Then, louder as she pulled back, "Why are you limping?"

A voice boomed from the staircase, "Welcome home boys!" Alphonse Kwizera wearing a brightly coloured pink and white kikoi over white linen trousers, stepped briskly down to the hallway and moved towards the group. "Why didn't you call?" he said casually, but looking firmly at Milton.

"We hav... We lost our phones, Papa," Milton answered with his head angled towards the white marble floor. Nobody spoke until Alphonse broke his puzzled look with a forced smile and said, "Never mind that, you can tell me all about it later... Now, let's have some breakfast."

At the dining room table, the Kwizera family tucked into the steaks, eggs, tomatoes, and bread that had been quickly prepared for them and Alphonse insisted on opening a bottle of champagne to 'celebrate their homecoming'. The conversation was stilted, in the extreme, and all four concentrated on eating to avoid having to talk.

Once they were full, avoiding discussion became harder, and Nicole tried to lighten the mood with an innocent question, "How is Cousin Pascal?"

The twins looked quickly at each other, and before Shakespeare could say anything, Milton replied, "He was fine," before taking a big swallow out of his champagne flute, and adding no further comment.

"We didn't expect you back so soon, Milton." smiled his father, pointedly. "People are still asking about the elephant fiasco."

Milton quickly reached again for his glass and kept his eyes off his father, as he finished the wine, then called for more. A house-girl poured the last of the bottle into Milton's glass and Shakespeare could sense his brother steeling himself before he replied, "I'm sure that the money from the tusks will help shorten people's memories, Papa."

Alphonse picked up his coffee cup, and drained it in one big gulp then half turned to Nicole. "I think," he said, "That I need time with the boys alone... Darling, could you leave us, please?"

Shakespeare hated seeing the wounded look on his mother's face and caught her eyes as she silently left the table, they were glistening already.

As the door closed, Alphonse dismissed the house-girls, put his elbows on the table and his chin on his clenched fists. "Right, you two, I want to know what the fuck has been going on? I've heard nothing from you in a week, I couldn't get hold of Pascal, or either of you. The next thing, you turn up here, out of the blue. Where, Milton, I specifically told you to stay away from until things had calmed down."

"Have you seen any news from Britain in the last two days, Papa?" Milton asked.

"No, I don't usually bother, your mother sometimes does, but not me."

"We...there was...we had some trouble. It got a bit...out of hand."

"OUT OF HAND!" Shakespeare shouted, "Milton, you shot two men...'out of hand' doesn't really cover it. One of them was a policeman, for God's sake!"

Alphonse couldn't remember ever seeing Shakespeare show such a temper and urged him to calm down. He then demanded that Milton tell the full story, from the moment he left the house the previous weekend.

As Milton recounted his journey to Harris, Shakespeare sat still and noted how, at every opportunity, Milton assigned credit to himself while showing Pascal and Eric in an unfavourable light. Milton reasoned that by the time they got to the island, the police had probably been alerted by Shakespeare's friend Terry, omitting to tell his father that this bit of reasoning had come from his brother on the way home.

The confrontation at the cottage was described by Milton as a situation where he, and his cousin, and Eric had been ambushed by armed police, in uniform and plain clothes. All they had done was defend themselves. After the firing had stopped, Milton had (according to Milton) taken charge and, realising that they would be blamed for the whole thing, decided to flee the scene. He helped - an allegedly panic stricken - Shakespeare to get his passport and case from the cottage, and collected all the guns, mobiles and wallets from the bodies on the ground. Milton had then taken his bag from the Range Rover - thinking that was too risky to use - and helped a limping Shakespeare down to where the Suzuki was parked near the pub. They had then driven away, before those villagers alerted by the gunfire had been bold enough to emerge from their homes.

"Was that how it was, Son?" Alphonse asked Shakespeare.

He said nothing immediately, remembering the groaning men covered in blood at the front of the cottage, and Milton's threats if Shakespeare didn't come with him, and support his story. "That's about right, Papa," he said, looking down at the table.

"How did you get home?"

Milton was especially proud of this chapter in his tale and related how he had decided to drive to Stornoway and exit the island from there. On the way, they had stopped on a bridge over a steep inlet, where a sea loch cut into the land, and dumped all the guns and phones, including their own, plus the redundant IDs. Continuing to the capital of Lewis, they then parked near the ferry terminal and got a taxi to the airport. Milton explained his logic in that if anyone had seen them drive away, and the car was traced, the police would think that they were waiting somewhere for the early morning ferry.

At the airport, the last flight of the day was to Glasgow so they took it, getting the late connection to Heathrow, where they hung around in the terminal until the morning Kenya Airways flight to Nairobi. Having seen some news items about the incident on the airport TV screens, of course, confirmed Milton, they were worried when they went through check in and security, thinking that somehow the police might have found out their identities. Nothing out of the ordinary happened and, when back in Kenya, a taxi to Milton's friend's house to pick up the Prado and a drive through the night. Home.

"Home indeed," Alphonse pondered, "We should check out the latest online news for an update. Are Pascal and his man dead? Can you be sure?"

Ignoring a sneering glance from Shakespeare, Milton confirmed that they had seemed dead when they left.

"Right," said Alphonse, in his most business-like tone, "You two are confined to the house until further notice. You are not to go anywhere or talk to anyone over the phone. You'll have to do without mobiles for a few weeks until we're sure that any trail to you two has gone cold and that there will be no repercussions, from what you've done."

"From what HE's done, Father... Not me!"

"Just do as I say please Shakespeare, keep the peace and no harm will come...to anyone."

-+-

Chapter Twenty Five

Lydia was mooching about in the shopping zone at Glasgow airport, looking optimistically at some overpriced and flimsy underwear, when Francis Rafferty's name came onto her telephone screen as she responded to its persistent ringing.

"Hello Francis, I've got as far as Glasgow."

"Fast work Lydia...listen, at Stornoway, someone will meet you. I'll send you a number shortly, just text it with your flight details and they'll pick you up. One of Archie's chaps."

"What's the latest news?"

"Fuck all, at this stage old girl. There's talk of a press conference tomorrow but they're keeping their cards close to their chests so far. All in the interests of National Security, of course...'possible terrorist connections' are being mentioned to muddy the waters. There's a rumour in *The Sun* that a policeman is one of the dead. 'Hero Bobby dies in hail of bullets!' is their online version."

"Anything else you can tell me?"

"Uhm... No. You'll think me callous."

"More than I already do Francis? Unlikely."

"Only thinking that it's true what they say about, 'no such thing as bad publicity'. If we do get a book out of this, surely it'll sell so much better now, than it would have before?"

"You really are such a shit, aren't you?" Lydia observed,

then pressed 'End Call' before walking directly to her departure gate.

The Embraer took about an hour to get from the gloomy grey skies of Glasgow to the surprisingly sun-drenched strip of concrete that is Stornoway airport. She could tell, from some of the banter between rows of seats, that some journalists were on board and she made a specific point of not talking to any of them.

Coming though arrivals with just her walk-on luggage, Lydia was immediately confronted by a stocky young man in a dark navy suit, holding a sign with the printed words 'Ms Hockley-Roberts' stretched across his ample chest. Once she acknowledge her identity, she was ushered outside by the man, who'd announced his name as 'Davie'.

Right outside the automatic terminal doors, in the area where parking was 'Strictly Forbidden', there was a new looking Ford SUV in black, looking abandoned. Davie clicked at his keys and its side lights lit up, to the accompaniment of loud beeping.

Davie, pointedly, held open the rear door and as Lydia settled in with her wheeled case on the seat next to her, she asked Davie where they were going.

"I'm not at liberty to say, Miss."

"Well, is it far?"

"I'm not at liberty to say, Miss."

"Can you... Oh, never mind." Lydia looked around the suburban road they were on, and it seemed from the sun that they were going west towards Stornoway. They skirted the middle of the town to the north-west and came within a few minutes to an NHS sign. Here, Davie turned right and manoeuvred around a car park until he was at a disabled parking space, adjacent to an 'Accident and Emergency' fascia above the canopied entrance to the Western Isles Hospital. A police car with two officers was parked there.

Davie locked the car and escorted Lydia along various corridors and up in a lift until they arrived at a small open office with a plain white desk and two white plastic chairs. The handwritten sign on a locked door behind the desk said 'ICU - Authorised Personnel Only', in black felt pen. Perched on one of the chairs was a ginger haired young nurse, with a freckled face, filling in a clipboard mounted form. On the other chair sat a very slim, angular faced man in a similar suit to Davie. He had a thick mop of collar length brown hair and he got up to offer Lydia his hand. In cut glass, aristocratic English, he drawled, "Ms Hockley-Roberts, delighted to meet you. Toby Crabbe." They shook hands. "Shall we endeavour to take tea?" He continued, "I say, Nurse Sconser, could you do the honours, perhaps?"

The nurse blushed as she went to do Crabbe's bidding and Lydia could see that although he was several years younger than her, he was awash with either the charisma of an older and wiser man, or the affectation of one. He made small talk until the tea arrived, asking about her flight, explaining that he'd only got up here late the previous night from Edinburgh, as the news broke. The nurse collected her clipboard and headed through the door with the makeshift sign.

When they were alone, Crabbe took a delicate sip of his tea and leaned forward.

"I'll come straight to the point Lydia. This has been a bad show. We had Talbot on our database, obviously. We do that for anyone who's been 'on the firm' as it were. Keep an eye out for them, that sort of thing. Anyway, when our regular scanning of police communications revealed reports of a gunfight yesterday afternoon, outside Talbot's cottage, we had to move fast. We blanketed any details from being released until we knew more, but finding out what occurred is proving very challenging. There were no direct witnesses, and for all we knew, all the combatants were either dead, or not far from it. We have since heard about a young African who we think was at the cottage, staying with Talbot, but who has since vanished."

"He said he had the son of an old friend staying, but didn't mention a name."

"Well, we'll have to talk to neighbours and trawl through stuff at the cottage, to see if any ID comes to light. In the meantime, you may have noticed some police outside, keeping reporters at bay?"

"Yes, I saw them. Toby, look... I'm afraid to ask, but... What about Carter? Is he alri... Is he...alive?"

"Let's have a look shall we?" Crabbe responded as he rose from his chair and steered Lydia towards the door. As he keyed the number pad and pushed to allow entry, he said, "They don't actually have a full ICU here, but this is the nearest they've got!"

Inside, there was a noticeable difference in the air, somehow it felt more difficult to breathe. Behind Nurse Sconser and her clipboard, was a wide, high bed surrounded by monitors connected to mechanical and electronic machines. Running from the bank of machines at the head of the bed, were a number of different coloured tubes, pipes and wires. The business ends of each of these conduits were, in various places, attached to a body lying on its back underneath a blue and cream striped blanket. The left leg of the patient was raised up out of the side of the blanket by a cord linked to some plastic scaffolding, and the right arm was folded across the chest and strapped into place. The head was mostly covered by a huge array of bandages, some going around the top and some circumnavigating the face from temple down to chin and up to the other temple then beneath the top dressing. The identifiable parts of the face were mainly underneath a large translucent oxygen mask through which the body's chest was inflating and deflating slowly.

Although the face was puffy in parts and the eyes were closed, Lydia knew the shape of this man and she shuddered, partly in shock and partly in relief. "How is he?" she asked. "Sorry, Nurse, stupid question. What I meant to say was, can you tell me about his injuries please?"

Nurse Sconser looked quickly at Crabbe and got a nod back. She described how the man had arrived by air ambulance in a critical condition. He was unconscious due to a head wound, his right lung had collapsed, his right shoulder and his left hip were bleeding profusely. They didn't think he would survive the night.

"And now?"

"Well, it's still only about 24 hours since admission, so far too early to tell. The bullets are out of his shoulder and hip, and the head wound has been stitched. We've given him significant volumes of blood. His lung, which was punctured by bone pieces from his shoulder, has been drained and is gradually reflating. He remains unconscious."

"Was he shot in the head?" Lydia asked, with a horrified look on her face.

"Not that we can see, we did retrieve some fragments of

rock from the temple and there is severe bruising, but the skull seems intact."

"Is he in a coma?"

"Not as such, we had to sedate him heavily for all the surgery, and he's still carrying a lot of drugs, but he should be able to come round naturally in a few hours."

"Lydia?" Crabbe queried, "Shall we leave Nurse Sconser to get on with her work?" He moved to the door and held it open for her and they went back to the little desk. "Just for the sake of good order, as I've never met this chap before, can you confirm his identity please?"

"Oh yes," Lydia replied, "That is most definitely Carter Talbot, lately retired from Her Majesty's service, but still managing to get into serious trouble, it would seem. Have you any idea what this was all about?"

"As I said, that is proving difficult and only Talbot can really give us the answers. I'm hoping that he'll be... Ok to talk..."

"That he's not sustained brain damage you mean?"

"Quite so, Lydia. Where are you staying?"

"The Royal, by the harbour."

"As am I, there didn't seem too much choice here. Perhaps dinner later?"

"I have no plans."

"Davie will drive you there now. In the meantime, I'll let you know, if there are any...developments."

"Thanks Toby."

Within twenty minutes, Lydia had checked into the hotel and was sitting in the lounge bar, sipping at some chilled Pouilly Fuisse. She had been surprised and pleased to see it on their wine list, and now savoured the cool fluid in her mouth, before swallowing gratefully.

She sent Francis a text from her place at the bar, saying that she'd arrived, that Cat was alive but unconscious, and that MI6 were treating her to dinner that night.

"Cheers," she whispered to herself, while lifting the misted glass to her lips.

-+-

Chapter Twenty Six

Detective Inspector William Keilloh adjusted his reading glasses and stroked his moustache, while he pondered the thin manilla file of papers in front of him on a desk in the police office at Tarbert. He twisted his head towards the middle aged woman at the next desk. "Morag, isn't it?"

"Aye...sir, that's me, right enough," she replied as she patted at her eyes with a tartan handkerchief and sniffed at the sandy-haired, chubby man in his fifties, opposite.

In his most gentle voice, Keilloh said, "What was he like Morag?...Roddy I mean."

"Oh Sir, he was...he was...Roddy was... Good, Sir. A good man in a world where that doesn't seem to count for much these days. He loved his job and he loved the people here. He would try and help them, before he would do anything else. I'd say that Roddy saw arresting people as a last resort, Sir. I'll really miss him...and so will his mother. I've heard that she's completely devastated."

"I can see how upset you are Morag. Would you be better off at home?"

"I'd like to help Sir, if that's alright with you?"

"Aye, of course. Although we aren't being allowed to do much at the moment. The intelligence service are still insisting on a news clampdown and we've been instructed to keep away from the survivor for the moment. I think that's one of the reasons they sent me down here from Stornoway today, to stop me asking awkward questions at the hospital. There's talk of a press conference tomorrow some time, and then we'll be passed copies of the 'relevant papers', whatever that means."

"That file has copies of notes that were left here by the first officers on the scene from Lewis, Sir. They are mainly interviews with the villagers at Crawnish. The originals had to be given to MI6, but I...made sure I tucked copies away. Hope that was Ok?"

"Yes, that's fine, our little secret, eh Morag?"

"What do you make of them, Sir?"

"Not much to go on, I'm afraid. The guy that lived at the cottage," Keilloh opened the folder and looked down, "...Rob Chancellor, was a writer, apparently. Kept himself to himself, hadn't lived there long. Likeable bloke, so they seem to think. He'd had a visitor staying but there's no sign of him. The two other victims...apart from Roddy of course...were a couple of complete strangers who had only arrived in the village that day. The descriptions are not strong, two black men were seen by the shopkeeper, who also said that they spoke English. She wasn't sure about their ages, said she'd not seen many black men in the flesh. That sort of matches the bodies except that, from the photographs, I wouldn't have said they were both black. One looks distinctly mixed race. But people use language in different ways don't they?"

"Aye, what about ID, Sir?"

"No identification was found on either of the dead strangers, nor any phones. And there were no guns found on the scene. Therefore, someone must have done a clean-up job."

"What next then, Inspector Keilloh?"

"Next, Morag, I will drive on up to Crawnish and see what I can see for myself. Can't sit around here all day! Please ring me with any messages, you might get a ballistics report emailed through on the bullets used. I'll be back later this evening and..." DI Keilloh looked at his watch, "...I'll see you tomorrow."

Keilloh knew the roads of Lewis and Harris well. He therefore didn't need his SatNav to steer his Ford Focus along the route to Crawnish as the sun went down behind the stubby mountains to the west. He could see clouds bubbling up on the breeze, out where the sun left the last of its glow, and got to Crawnish with his headlights piercing the growing dusk.

A uniformed police office got out of his car parked on the drive of Uisge Bothan and waved a torch in the direction of the man crunching his way up the gravel.

"This is a crime scene, nobody's allowed in," he called out.

"Yes Danny, I know."

"Oh, it's you, Mr Keilloh, Sir...sorry about that."

"No bother Laddie, could I borrow your torch?"

"Aye Sir, though the intelligence boys locked up the cottage and took the keys."

"Righto Danny, I'll just have a wee mooch around."

DI Keilloh took the torch and methodically walked up and down the ground at the front of the cottage, illuminating the rocky grass with the powerful flashlight. He paused at several points where bloodstains had browned, since the events of the previous day. He shone the light up and down the road from his vantage point in the garden, then walked over to the cottage. He looked into every window, then turned towards the large timber shed at the rear of the building. The double doors seemed unlocked but had a strip of crime scene tape across them telling him, 'Do Not Cross'. Keilloh tore it off and opened the doors.

A Range Rover filled the entire space within the shed, like the filling in one of his wife's overstuffed bridies, thought Keilloh. He scribbled the registration number down and made a mental note to check the file when he got back to Tarbert. He could remember no mention of the car in those documents. He tried the tailgate of the vehicle and it opened to reveal an empty boot. He got the same result from squeezing though to each of the doors, the car appeared to have been cleaned out. He closed the garage doors, then pulled a roll of crime scene tape from his overcoat pocket and reapplied it to the exterior where they joined together.

Although it was now dark in Crawnish, and the moon was hidden by the growing banks of clouds from the west, it was still early. As he returned the torch, DI Keilloh asked the young constable if there was a pub in the village. Having got the affirmative he bid him good night and drove west to locate the 'Dion'.

The little bar was much busier than a normal Thursday night. DI Keilloh had to manoeuvre his way through at least two dozen people to get to the counter. He showed his warrant card to Finn and announced himself quietly. Not quietly enough it transpired, and the crowd turned towards him. He felt he needed to say something. It was clear that the villagers had gathered together to cope better with yesterday's shocks, and he didn't want to intrude on that process.

"Good Evening," he said, "I'm Detective Inspector Billy Keilloh. I can imagine what you're going through, I'm a Lewis man, from the north, Port of Ness. I know how small island communities can be hard hit by tragedy, and

I'm not here to pry. I've just been to Water Cottage and thought I could do with a drink. If anyone wants to share any thoughts with me, that would be fine, but otherwise, all the best to you. Barman, a pint of heavy please."

The first people to approach Keilloh were a small clutch of journalists from the corner. There was a BBC man and three from national newspapers. They corralled him at the bar and started their questions. Before they could get into their stride, Billy said, after a hefty sip of his beer, "You know, I'm only going to say 'no comment' to everything you ask. So why bother? There's a home office imposed news blackout anyway. I believe that the news conference will be in Stornoway early tomorrow morning. I'd save my energy for that, if I were you."

As the journos finished their drinks and left, mumbling amongst themselves, Neil Mackenzie sat on a stool at the bar and lifted his glass to Billy, "That seemed to get rid of them, they've been asking questions since opening time. Is it true about the press conference...early tomorrow in Stornoway?"

"I've no idea...there might be. Cheers!"

"Nice one. By the way, Rob seemed like a good guy, I hope he's Ok. And his friend, Shakespeare, young African lad, very well spoken, polite you know? They seemed close, in here talking at great length the other day, something about Rwanda, I think."

After an hour or so, and reluctantly refusing the offers of further pints, DI Keilloh bade good night to the good people of Crawnish and drove back to Tarbert, stopping briefly at the cottage to find that Danny had been relieved by another Lewis PC for the night shift.

Back in the police office, Billy went through his emails

and found one from ballistics that had arrived after Morag would have gone home. Without the guns to match, the results were inconclusive in terms of the specific weapons used. However, they did show that the 9mm rounds removed from Sergeant MacLeod matched those extracted from the survivor, while the three found in the two dead men were all from another weapon.

There was nothing more that Billy could do, so he set out for a long lonely drive home to Stornoway, hoping that his wife might have baked some of her special bridies for a late supper.

-+-

Chapter Twenty Seven

When Lydia woke from her afternoon nap, it was already dark and her mouth felt dry. She reached for a bottle of water on the bedside table, thoughtfully provided by the Royal Hotel, and took a long drink. She laid back down again, having moved too quickly for her wine-soaked head to catch its bearings. As the wave of dizziness calmed down she got up more slowly, stripped off her clothes and got quickly into the walk-in shower, having got it to an uncomfortable heat first.

She was soon sitting back on the bed, swathed in a generously fitting white towelling robe plus complimentary slippers, and a smaller towel in a turban style around her head. She sipped at instant coffee made from the tray on the other bedside table and glanced at her mobile. She was surprised to see that she'd been asleep for nearly three hours and disappointed that she'd had no calls. There was one text, with the somewhat curt message, '20:00, Bistro Bar, Toby.' That gave her less than an hour to get ready and she only had the casual clothes she'd thrown in her bag that morning before rushing out to Heathrow.

Forty-five minutes later, perched on a bar stool, scrubbed up in light make-up, curly hair dried naturally, a loose yellow woollen top, and a pair of jeans tucked into some ankle boots, she glanced casually round as Toby Crabbe entered the bar. He looked exactly the same as earlier, but had removed his tie.

"What's that Lydia?" Crabbe asked, nodding towards her glass.

"Tomato juice," she replied while lifting it to her lips.

"Barmaid? I'll join Ms Hockley-Roberts but make mine a Bloody Mary, could you?"

"Any news, Toby?" asked Lydia.

"Yes...and No, I suppose."

"Go on."

"Well, your friend Talbot came round about two hours ago, but it didn't last long. He didn't seem to be too clear about who he was, where he was, or why he was there. He was mumbling something about Shakespeare."

"Is he in a lot of pain?"

"Unlikely Lydia, not with the huge amount of barbiturates they're dripping into him. High as a kite, I'd imagine."

"Anything else?"

"He's clearly having morphine induced dreams about literature, as he also mentioned Milton once or twice. Oh, and he kept berating himself, 'How could I have been so stupid?' he grunted to himself, repeatedly."

"What do the doctors say?"

"The consultant is very pleased that he's been awake, even if it was for only half an hour. He said they will reduce the dosage overnight and hope that he wakes up in better form tomorrow."

"Can I see him in the morning?"

"No...and Yes, Lydia."

"What?"

"That is to say, I will need a private chat with him first thing, confidential stuff, you know? Then you can see him, it will cheer him up I'm sure."

"Thanks, could I..."

"Let's order shall we?" Crabbe's question sounded more like a statement to Lydia than a question, "Then you can tell me all you know about, ex-Major, Talbot, over dinner."

They conversed over Scotch broth, well hung venison, and Cranachan, lubricated by some very passable Malbec Mendoza from Argentina. The tone was light and relaxed and Carter Talbot was a main topic of discussion.

As they sat down in aged leather armchairs after dinner, nursing a Caol Ila each, Toby turned to Lydia and said softly, "You've slept with him, haven't you?"

Her blush told Crabbe all he needed to know, and the denial froze in her throat. "Crystal clear, my dear," Toby affirmed. "No problem, he's a charming chap."

"Yes... He is," was all she could say.

"Look Lydia, I'm hoping that Talbot will be able to tell us about these dead chaps tomorrow. You've already said that he hadn't mentioned any trouble brewing up here, but I can't help thinking that this involves some enemies of his from the past. People that he'd hurt badly in a former 'operation' of some kind. He's been involved in some hair-raising stuff, according to his file."

"I think that's the very reason that he was seen as such a good prospect for a 'warts and all' biography."

"Quite. One more as a nightcap?" Queried Crabbe, waving his whisky tumbler in Lydia's direction.

"Just the one then."

"Barmaid!" Toby called out, "Two more, if you please... And make then doubles, there's a good girl." Then, in an aside to Lydia, "After all, Her Majesty is paying."

As she awoke on Friday morning, Lydia thought that it had arrived far too quickly for her liking, but then she and Toby had seen off the best part of a bottle of Caol Ila and not turned in until well past two o'clock. She could still taste the smoky flavour of the Islay malt at the back of her throat, and the effect of the 45% alcohol content, on her head. It had been good to be in the company of someone so charming and, even though he'd been the perfect gentleman with no overtures towards his bedroom, she'd enjoyed laughing with a man and had slept well.

There was a text message on her phone, from Toby. 'Hope you're Ok? I'm at the hospital. Come here at 10:30. Press conference at noon, hotel function suite.' Looking at her watch she then called reception and asked for coffee and fruit to be sent to her room. She then went to run a bath. When Cat saw her, she wanted to be at her best.

Toby met her outside the makeshift ICU at the hospital and had what Lydia took for a perplexed expression on his face.

"What's the story?" she asked him, "Is he alright?"

"He's lucid... But not able to throw too much light on things... Apparently."

"And?"

"We'll have a story for the press conference that will sound plausible but, between you and me, Cat's holding back. Tells me he doesn't know anything about the men he killed, only that they fired first, killing the policeman, and it was self-defence."

"What about the young African guy who was staying with him, and seems to have disappeared?"

"Talbot isn't giving much away there, said it was just the friend of a friend who looked him up as he was in the area. I don't believe a fucking word of it, frankly Lydia. You don't just happen to be in Crawnish, its one step away from the edge of the world."

"Can I see him Toby?"

"Of course, you might get more out of him than me...you will share it... Won't you?"

"After that lovely dinner last night, I think it would be churlish not to."

As Lydia went through to sit by Carter's bed, a suited, middle aged man with a moustache came up to the desk and addressed Toby.

"Commander Crabbe?" he said, "DI Keilloh, Stornoway Police." and thrust forward his right hand.

"Detective Inspector, a pleasure I'm sure. How can I help you?"

"I think, I may be able to help you, as it happens."

"Do tell... Please?"

Keilloh explained that late the previous night he had done

a search on the registration details of the Range Rover he'd seen in the garage and found it was registered to one Pascal Muwera of Stratford, London E15. He'd spoken to an old friend in the Met that morning and established that Mr Muwera was, on the face of it, a night club owner. However, he also had significant links with key players in the East London drug trade.

Crabbe listened and asked a few questions. He thanked Keilloh for his input and escorted him to the hospital corridor. With a brief, 'See you at the press conference' they parted company and Toby got on his phone to London.

Meanwhile, Lydia hovered over Carter's bed and tried not to make too much of a womanly fuss. He was conscious and smiling, in spite of the tubes hanging out of his arms, and looking at her with sparkling eyes.

"I can't believe you Talbot, I find you the most peaceful place to do your work in the whole of the United Kingdom, and you turn it into some kind of 'Die Hard' film set. What on Earth have you been up to?"

"Sorry Lydia, not my fault. Some guys turned up, making trouble, what's a man to do?"

"Well...kill them obviously...you lunatic!"

"I was...off my guard, Lids."

"What do you mean?"

"We knew they were coming. By the way, this is for your ears only, yeah?"

"Sure thing, Cat"

"But I was slapdash, didn't think to look right round the fire zone, thought there were only two of them. Got caught out, big time. Retirement has made me sluggish."

"Crabbe thinks you're holding a lot back about this, Cat."

"I can't help that Lydia, this is a serious business and one that won't be helped by MI6 sticking their oars in."

"But they're on your side, surely?"

"You've obviously been swayed by, the ever-so-handsome, Commander Crabbe haven't you Darling?"

"He knows how to treat a Lady, if that's what you mean."

"Mmm, the point is Lids, I won't be lying here forever and when I'm patched up there are things I need to do. Things that need to be done outside the blanket of the official security forces."

"Patched up! Your body is pretty much fucked as I understand it. Broken shoulder, punctured lung, fractured hip. You're going nowhere for quite a few months Carter."

"Flesh wounds only, Lydia. I'll be up and about in no time."

"Bollocks will you! Anyway, I've got to get off to this press conference. See what spin is being put on this whole sorry business."

"Ok...look Lydia, thanks for coming. I'm really grateful. For a moment I thought I'd had it back there. It was Shakespeare, he saved me. Will you be around for a while?"

"Back to London for Monday morning. But I can come

back Carter...if that's what you'd like?"

"I'd like that," Cat said, as he slumped his head back onto the pillows.

The main comments by Commander Crabbe at the press conference summed up proceedings, to the extent that the fourth estate seemed satisfied. He declared that two men with strong links to the trade in class 'A' drugs in the United Kingdom had tracked down a retired Intelligence Service agent, who had caused them severe problems in the past, and tried to kill him. Sadly in the events that immediately followed, a local police officer had bravely tried to control the situation and been murdered in cold blood by the criminals. Due to the superb training and instinct of the nameless security agent and in spite of life-threatening wounds sustained by him, both criminals had been shot and killed in the ongoing action. Nobody else was a being considered a suspect and the thoughts of the security forces are very much with the family of Sergeant MacLeod at this difficult time. In view of the sensitive nature of the involvement of the Intelligence Service, it was thought by the Home Office that no value would be gained by allowing further questions on the incident. This could prejudice future operational integrity.

Lydia had a brief chat with Toby after the conference and apologised that she was unable to throw any further light on Carter Talbot's experience. He was keeping his own counsel on the matter, she told him. She did, however, confide in him that she fully intended to help Cat through his convalescence, whether he liked the idea or not.

-+-

Chapter Twenty Eight

Shakespeare Kwizera had always been close to his mother, and it pained him greatly to see her drained and miserable. It was Friday evening and, since they'd got back that morning, he'd kept himself in his room, away from any chance of bumping into his father or brother. Now though, after some well needed sleep, he felt the need to see his mum and comfort her while seeking comfort himself.

He slipped out of his room, a couple of doors down from Milton's, and walked to his mother's room. He knocked gently on the white door and heard a soft, "Who's there?"

"Mum... It's me, Shakespeare."

He heard the lock turning and the salt streaked cheeks of his mother's soft face, came into view at the level of his chest. She looked up at him with puffy, red veined eyes and, wiping her face with her slim hand, whispered, "Son... Come in."

Nicole stepped back and they moved towards the upright armchairs by the window. "Do you want a drink?" she asked him.

"No thanks, Mum. I just couldn't stand the thought of you being in here on your own." Shakespeare replied while enveloping his mother in his arms, and giving her a bear-like hug. "I've been so worried about you, more so than ever, over the last few weeks," he said, speaking above the top of her right ear, nestled next to his neck.

"That's completely mutual, Darling. I hope... I'd like it if... Could you just tell me what's been happening... Please?"

"I don't know where to start...shall we sit down?"

"Ok." They took a chair each. "What about, why you didn't come home when term finished at Edinburgh?"

"Before I begin, can we agree that we are completely honest with each other? Both of us? There's been too many lies in this house, and there can't be any more...not between us."

"I don't know what to say... But, yes, we need to stop hiding things, my son."

Shakespeare took a deep breath then, rather haltingly, he told his mother about how he had discovered the truth of his father's background through his studies. How he knew that he'd been involved at high level in the genocide, and how he had escaped after the defeat of the Hutu's and changed his name to take a new identity in Kenya.

"I think he was ashamed, your father."

"Not too ashamed to hand himself in, to those searching for the war criminals involved in the massacres, clearly. I think he was pleased to get away with it and quite happy to live a lie, along with his family. How can he live with himself, let alone us, after what he did?"

"Perhaps it's me who's ashamed, Shakespeare? I've known for all these years, and deliberately buried the truth, thinking that the important thing was to see my boys grow up and be better men than their father."

"So, I couldn't face the thought of coming home and seeing Dad. Not with what I knew. I couldn't see the best way forward so I thought I'd try and talk to someone who might help. Who, you'd told me, would help."

Nicole scrunched together her eyebrows, "Someone, I'd

mentioned?"

"Yes, I set out to track down Carter Talbot."

"Oh my God... You found Carter?"

"Well, some experts in the field of finding people, found him for me. He had retired to write a book, some island in Scotland, called Harris...I went to see him. He made me very welcome. Everything was fine, until Milton and Pascal, plus one of his thugs, turned up."

"So you found him...and Milton found you?" Nicole looked puzzled for a moment and rubbed her eyes. "Was it him? On the news...there was a story from Harris about a gunfight. It mentioned an 'Intelligence Agent' who had to remain nameless for security reasons... Was that... Carter?"

"Yes Mum, it was Carter Talbot...and....and..."

"And what?"

"He told me all about... You and him, in Rwanda, just before it all started there."

"Shakespeare, we said no secrets, so I'm proud to tell you that I loved him...then and probably for years afterwards, even though he abandoned me in the horror."

"He thought you were dead Mum."

"What?"

"His friend had seen you forced into a church, that was then burned out. He saw all the charred bodies and assumed that you were one of them."

Tears sprung into Nicole's eyes and she put her hand to her mouth, while giving a high pitched choking sound.

"Sorry Mum, I don't want to upset you...but that's what Carter told me. He was devastated, but in his mind there was nothing he could do. So he finished his duties and flew out with the rest of the British contingent on a Hercules."

Nicole had gone very quiet and looked at her son from the chair that she was now sitting forward on. In a very quiet voice she said, "I never did try and contact him again, I thought he'd be cold to me, that I was just some fling. I couldn't help strong feelings towards him even though by then...your father...was...let's say, 'in my life'."

"You told me you were good friends, that's why I tried to find him."

"We were...good friends...and so much more... What really happened then...on Harris? And why weren't you better prepared? I tried to warn you with text messages when you didn't answer your phone."

"There was a massive storm which knocked out all the mobile networks. In terms of what happened, in a nutshell, Milton and Pascal wanted me to come home and I didn't."

"But how did it turn so violent?"

"Guns were pulled out and it was a bit of a stand-off. Then, this policeman arrived and tried to calm things down. He would have succeeded too, but for Milton. He shot him dead, in cold blood, then all hell let loose. Carter shot Pascal and his man, but was hit twice by Milton and went down. Milton went to finish him off, but I shouted him to stop. I said I'd come home with him if he spared

Carter."

"What did your brother do?"

"He still fired and I thought he'd killed him anyway, I ran over and Carter seemed to be unconscious but still breathing. I think Milton had moved his aim and some sort of ricochet had knocked Carter out."

"And then?"

"Honestly Mum, Milton seemed to be in his element. He was organised and focused on getting us out of there as quickly and safely as possible. Our cousin was dying and his pet tough had already haemorrhaged the life blood from his neck onto the grass. We left and I was in a bit of a blur until we got to the airport. Milton made it clear that if I tried to disrupt our return home, you'd be the one that suffered. I was in such shock, I just went along with whatever he said."

"I can't believe that your own brother can be so callous, it's as if you've got all the good blood from me and he's only got his father in him. You said that he didn't even wait with Pascal, or try to get him some help. To think that I gave birth to...that."

"There's not much to add to the story. We got home without incident, I just feel physically sick whenever I'm with Father. Sorry Mum but that's what overwhelms me, if I'm even in the same room as him."

"I don't know what we can do, Son. But please promise me... Don't do anything rash. Just keep out of his way...and Milton's for that matter. Let things calm down and then we can see about the future."

"Ok, I'll not do anything to put you in danger anyway."

"About Carter," asked Nicole, keen to change the subject, "How badly is he hurt? The BBC said he had been seriously wounded but was out of danger."

"It all happened so fast, but I think Milton shot him in the shoulder and the hip, plus the wound to his head."

Nicole looked out of the window for a few seconds, seemingly focused on the horizon, hazy in the afternoon sun. "I'd love to speak to him again," she confided in her son, "Even after all these years..."

"Do you know what? From what I know of Carter Aragorn Talbot, he would love that."

"Perhaps, it's something we can explore... As long as your father and brother don't know about it."

"It will need some research. I put his number on my phone but Milton dumped all the phones while we were quitting the island, he said it would be harder to pin anything on us if we were stopped."

"I'm sure we can find a way. Anyway, no urgency, he'll be convalescing for quite a while, I'd imagine."

"Mum, we need to look out for each other over the next few weeks."

"Don't look so worried Shakespeare. You forget, I've survived with your father for this long and I have learned to be patient. And do you knew the best thing? It upsets him much more when I'm calm and thoughtful, than if I argue with him. Take the tip and stay cool."

"Right... I love you Mum."

After another long hug, Shakespeare returned to his room and went online with his laptop to search for any more news about the astonishing recent events on Harris.

-+-

Chapter Twenty Nine

Mention of the previous week's happenings in the Hebrides seemed to have faded from the news when Lydia watched the Monday morning bulletin with her early morning coffee. The people in the studio were now interested in the early positioning of the parties, in advance of the build up to next year's General Election.

It was a cold, but still, day on the tree lined streets of Hampstead as she walked purposefully towards the underground station. She knew she had to brief Francis this morning on what she had found out on her trip to Stornoway, and remembered her last discussion with Cat on Saturday evening. Finding Toby Crabbe on the same flight back to London had been both a pleasant surprise and the cause of some consternation, as he had quizzed her forensically regarding Talbot.

Carla's greeting at the office seemed overly respectful to Lydia, who asked her what was going on.

"Well," said the receptionist conspiratorially, "It's not every day that one of our writers, in particular - one of yours - turns out to be a hero?"

"Carla, whatever you think you know, it isn't public knowledge and I suspect we'd rather keep it that way."

"But, Ms Hockley-Roberts, if it's not public knowledge, what's all this about," Carla asked while brandishing the editorial page of that morning's *Sun*.

'COP-KILLER'S KILLER NAMED' screamed the headline. Lydia grabbed it and read the editorial; '*In spite of attempts by the security forces to keep it a secret, The Sun can reveal that the brave unidentified agent who gunned down*

the brutal murderers of Sergeant Roddy MacLeod, on Harris last week, was Robin Chancellor. We tell the British people this, not to 'cock a snook' at authority, but to give credit where credit is due. Retired Agent Chancellor, in his fifties, stood up to the terrorists without any thought for his own safety, and now lies seriously wounded in hospital. Local sources on the Island say that he was a quiet character who kept himself to himself. The Sun says, he is a Hero and, along with Sergeant MacLeod, deserves the unqualified thanks of a grateful Nation.'

"Oh bollocks," Lydia grunted, "Is Francis in yet?"

"Frank's in his office, if you want to go straight in."

"Thanks Carla."

Frank looked up at his colleague and his smile reminded Lydia of a hyena, sniffing fresh carrion on the breeze. "Low profile doesn't seem to quite cover today's events...wouldn't you agree, Lydia?"

"I thought that MI6 had put a D-notice across the whole press?" she answered, with a trace of belligerence.

"They did, and everyone else has stuck to it. *The Sun*, however, have proved to be a law unto themselves again. And they've been pretty clever too. They've tried to look as if they've published this as comment, rather than news, there are no actual correspondent reports. And, of course, how bad would the government look, taking action against the self-proclaimed supporters of a true British hero?"

"And, that action could all unravel anyway, as it's not even his real name," added Lydia.

"Of course. Anyway, how is the old bastard?"

"Mr Talbot is as well as can be expected, in the circumstances. His body's in bits but he's not lost that sharpness, which you can't help liking. He's talking, in the physical sense, but probably holding back. He somehow seems 'deeper' than before, if that makes any sense?"

"Not really, tell me more."

"Well, I spent a couple of hours with him on Saturday night and he was unusually guarded in what he was saying. He wouldn't tell me any more details about last Thursday, saying he didn't remember any more than he'd already explained, 'because of his head wound'. He downplayed the role of this Shakespeare character, confirming that he had nothing to do with the shooting and suggesting that he'd run off after the event, being scared that he might get blamed for it."

"But you think there's more to it?"

"It's strange, but when we spoke on Friday morning, he said that Shakespeare had 'saved him', but when - on Saturday - I reminded him of that and asked him what he meant, he claimed that he must have been confused and that the mysterious African had done nothing."

"Perhaps he needs some 'professional' interrogation?" Rafferty suggested, with a bit too much relish for Lydia.

"Not much point, Toby Crabbe from MI6 was with him for most of Saturday, and he didn't say any more to him than me, apparently. We exchanged notes on the flight back."

"So what now, old girl?"

Lydia chewed gently on her lower lip then, gathering a deep breath, she launched into something of a mentally prepared statement.

"Ok Frank, number one, let's let sleeping dogs lie. All the police and MI6 can be sure of is that our Cat killed two suspected drug dealers, no bad thing in my view. One of them shot dead a policeman, so just desserts were served. There was at least one other person involved but, in the absence of any evidence, he's not suspected of anything. There are no other witnesses and no guns or phones to study.

Number two, Crabbe told me that the police will be investigating the accomplices of the two dead men in London, to see if the impact of the deaths will flush out more drug dealers from the network of the deceased.

And, number three, we've got a book to write! It's already got the makings of a belter. Carter is flat out on a bed at the moment and probably will be for a while, but I can do the donkey work while he lies back and dictates. Imagine the marketing build up for this one? It was always planned as a memoir and that doesn't need to change. People will be clamouring to buy it, especially if we can get it done over the next two or three months, while the hero effect continues to be a factor."

"So what are you telling me?"

"I wouldn't dream of 'telling' you anything Frank. What I'm 'suggesting', in the strongest possible terms, is that you'll have to do without me for the next ten weeks or so, while I sit in Scotland and urge Cat to produce a virtually guaranteed best seller."

"Just like that?"

"Very much, 'just like that', Francis."

"What does Cat think?"

Lydia's confidence slipped just a notch, before she replied softly, "I haven't actually told him yet... But he'll be fine...honestly."

"Good God, you still fancy him don't you?"

"That, Frank, is a low blow and I am surprised at you," she smiled.

"I suppose you want me to make sure that MI6 and Plod keep clear of your fancy man, while all this is going on?"

"If you could have a word with Archie, it would be a great help, Frank Darling."

"Ok, I'll treat him to a boozy lunch today, weave my persuasive magic."

"You're an Angel. I'll spend the next couple of days passing out my workload to other partners, and aim to be back with Cat by the end of the week."

"We won't ramp the marketing up just yet but over the next few weeks, once Cat is 'in the groove', we might do some teasers through the website and social media, saying that Robin D. Chancellor is slowly recovering and eager to finish the book he went to Harris to write in the first place."

"Brilliant Francis, this is going to be a great success."

"It had fucking better be, Lydia."

-+-

Chapter Thirty

Western Isles Hospital patient, Robin D. Chancellor, sat up in bed and greedily munched some toast that Nurse Sconser had brought him a few moments before. He was in the same bed that he'd first occupied just over a week before, when he was oblivious to his surroundings. After finishing the two, somewhat dry, bits of toast he slurped the black coffee from a straight white mug held in his left hand, and lay back against the stack of firm pillows supporting his back and neck.

"Nurse Sconser?"

"Yes, Sir?"

"I never realised how much I'd enjoy National Health Service burnt toast and muddy-pond coffee."

"We aim to please, Sir," she grinned in his direction.

"Yes, it has to be said, that eating and drinking the old fashioned way is a lot better than all those tubes and drips. Even feeling the pain, instead of floating on all those drugs, is kind of... Well, it makes you feel grateful that you're still alive."

Nurse Sconser went to the foot of the bed and picked up a silvery clipboard and looked at it with a pen in her hand. "How's your breathing today?" She asked him.

He took a series of deep breaths and winced at each peak of inhalation. "Still sore, but doesn't double me up like a few days ago."

"Good..." She marked the chart, "Right arm?"

"Can bend at the elbow without much grief, but all this strapping keeps the shoulder as tight as a drum."

"Ok. Left leg?"

"You know I can't move it, with all this plaster," he said.

"Of course... I was talking about the pain."

"If I don't try to wriggle, it's calm enough. But whenever I try to ease the numbness, or scratch an itch, it hurts like buggery."

"Well, Mr Chancellor, there I'll have to bow to your greater knowledge in such matters!"

"Nice one Nurse, you got me...but you're contractually not allowed to make me laugh. I've had a punctured lung you know... I'll report you to Matron!"

She made a point of looking at the chart studiously, then said, "Righto... Rob...progress is reasonably good, for a man of your age. Doctor will be along later, to do a proper assessment. In the meantime, you've got a visitor."

"Male or female?"

"Female... Nice female, if that helps?"

"Nurse?"

"Yes."

"I feel a bit...sort of...grubby. Do you still do bed baths these days?"

"If you were mobile, I'd think you were just a pervert but, in the circumstances, don't move and I'm get some stuff."

So, it was a relatively clean and sweet smelling Robin D. Chancellor that welcomed Lydia Hockley-Roberts to his bedside some ten minutes later.

"How are you... Rob?" Lydia asked, noting that Nurse Sconser had yet to withdraw.

"Good, thanks Lids. Thanks again Nurse, I think I can be trusted on my own now."

The nurse nodded at them both and left the room.

"She's just given me a bed bath, the saucy minx," chuckled Cat. "I'm glad to see you Lydia, thought that once you'd gone back to London last weekend, it would have taken wild horses to drag you back."

"Any other visitors?"

"Nobody I liked really. Local Plod popped in, told them pretty much the same as I told Crabbe. They've laid off since. Some journos have been trying to visit but they soon got bored with being turned away by the police at the hospital doors. So very quiet, I'd say."

"What's the latest prognosis?"

"Not sure yet, the Doc is seeing me this afternoon and perhaps he'll give me some idea of when I can get out."

"Surely you won't be allowed home yet?"

"Lydia, that sounded like you were excited about the prospect, what's going on?"

"I've...erm, got you a present... Two presents actually. I thought grapes and flowers would be dull, but this, on the other hand might cheer you up."

She reached into her cavernous handbag and withdrew a bottle shaped parcel in black and gold paper. She handed it over, taking care to put it near his left hand. He manoeuvred the package until he could unwrap it without dropping it onto the floor, and quickly revealed a black tinted bottle with the words 'Lagavulin - Distillers Edition, aged 30 years in sherry casks', prominent on the label.

"That's a real cracker Lids," Cat said softly, turning the bottle over in his hands and luxuriating in the descriptive tasting notes on the back. "Top marks, Darling!"

"And," she said, reaching back into her bag, "There's this."

A much smaller parcel, wrapped in the same paper and not looking much bigger than a cigarette box, emerged and was, slightly more sheepishly, passed over to Cat. He unwrapped it and a glossy white printed box ended up in his left hand, being scrutinised.

"It says, 'Philips MemoMate' Lydia. I'm thinking there must be a motive here?"

Lydia's usual self-control, developed through many years of dealing with unreasonable authors and self-important publishers, seemed to desert her, just when it would have been particularly useful. She blushed and stammered a little, then stopped and said, with a nervous smile, "Perhaps I need some of what's in that bottle."

Cat went to start removing the metal seal on the top of the bottle but Lydia shook her head vigorously and waved her hand. "Only kidding...you lunatic," she gasped. "Perhaps I'd better tell you about my discussion with Francis?"

"If you could Lids, that might be helpful, especially as I'm thinking it was all about me?"

So Lydia recounted her discussion at the Riveting Read offices the previous Monday and outlined the next three months that she had imagined with Carter. How she would make sure that he was comfortable, while his body healed. And how he would be productive while she, and the MemoMate, gave him all the necessary assistance.

"So you'll be, effectively, a combination of nurse and secretary, in my cottage?" Carter asked, with a broad grin.

"Yes, for as long as it takes, to get you better and finish your book."

"Have you got the right outfits for those two roles?" he smirked.

"If you mean the nurse and secretary outfits as depicted on countless pornographic films, then, no."

"And you'll be living with me? You know there's only one proper bed?"

"I can stay on the put-me-up, no problem...frankly, the thought of banging into your plaster cast as you roll over in the night, doesn't excite me, Carter."

"Fair comment... How's your cooking?"

"Pretty good, given access to the right ingredients. But, presumably, Crawnish isn't exactly awash with farmer's markets and suchlike?"

"Not really, Lydia, but you can sometimes get lovely fish and lobsters straight off the boats."

"So, do we have a deal then? Although your body can

relax, I will be pumping your mind hard, if we're going to finish on schedule."

"I can imagine that you'll be tough on me, but why not? What else am I going to do?" explained Carter, as he nodded towards the strapping on his shoulder and the plaster on his hip and leg.

"So the next thing is to stop your malingering here, cease you being a drain on the NHS, and put you to work! I think I'd better be here when your Doctor arrives, so there's no talk of 'We should keep him in for few more days, just in case,' or similar nonsense. Best to let me do the talking on this Cat, Ok?"

"Ok Lydia, you're - quite clearly - in charge."

-+-

Chapter Thirty One

Commander Toby Crabbe glanced at the electronic calendar on his highly polished, smoked glass, office desk top. Saturday 1st November 2014 reminded him of two things. That it was now over a week since the unpleasantness on Harris, and that he was, unusually, in the MI6 office building on a Saturday. He thought briefly of his regular golf partners and how they would probably be glad of his absence. He'd been in a good streak of form lately and had therefore lunched at their expense on the last three occasions they'd ventured out as a fourball.

His musings on the events at Kings Ferrers golf club were interrupted by the desk phone beeping with a slight vibrating tone against the glass surface. He picked it up and in a voice that was meant to convey a sense of brisk, business-like activity, barked, "Crabbe."

"Er...hello Commander, it's DI Keilloh...from Stornoway."

Toby quickly switched into smooth friendly mode, "Morning Billy, thanks for calling, wasn't expecting you for an hour or two."

"I arrived last night, stayed with my daughter in Enfield. Thought I'd come into town first thing. I'm at the gates now...there seems to be a wee problem, Sir."

"Oh, bugger it, I was going to sort out your clearance later this morning...you've caught me on the hop Inspector. I'll come down."

Four hours later, Crabbe and Keilloh completed a diligent thirty minute inspection of a navy blue Range Rover, in the basement workshop of the MI6 headquarters on the South Bank of the Thames. It had been in the hands of the

Covert Technical Team all morning, and Toby expressed his satisfaction that there was no sign whatsoever of the work the CTT had done on the vehicle.

"Aye," said DI Keilloh, "They've done a grand job. You've got some fine experts there Commander. But now comes the really hard part."

Crabbe nodded, "Are you still OK doing this Keilloh? We could still hand it over to the Met?"

"No... As you said on the phone, a boring Scottish local copper would be more convincing than someone from the London force, who might know the targets."

"Right then, you saw in the briefing room earlier the mug shots of who you might meet and some other background from SOCA, but essentially just play your part as the simple policeman, tidying up the pieces."

"This really isn't MI6 business, is it Commander?"

"Not normally, no. This is very much on the turf of the Serious Organised Crime Agency, as you're aware. However, now that the identity of our ex-agent has been leaked in the press, we have a vested interest in 'keeping our hand in', as it were. And, as we'd met, I thought you'd be ideal for this job."

"Where does it go from here?"

"You do your bit, today, and just email me and SOCA with a brief report on how it went, who you met, etcetera. SOCA will do the rest from there, and you can fly back to Lewis."

"Righto, Sir. Anything else?"

"There is one thing, Billy, that I'd be extremely grateful for."

"And that would be...?"

"Keep an eye on Ca... Rob for us, would you old chap? Pop round now and again, see if any suspicious characters are nosing about, that sort of thing? Everything seems to have died down, but there are still the Procurator Fiscal's inquiries to come, which will stir it all up again. Plus the fact that the two dead civilians, by all accounts, have some nasty friends. It just leaves me somewhat uneasy, that's all."

"Aye Sir, I'll make sure that we keep an eye on Crawnish for the immediate future. No worries."

"Thanks Billy, most helpful. Good luck this afternoon."

It was late afternoon and the sky was already dimming, by the time DI Keilloh negotiated the central and east London traffic courtesy of the Range Rover's satellite navigation system, and arrived at the house in Stratford E15 previously occupied by one Pascal Muwera. He had stopped two streets away and alerted the SOCA surveillance team, via his mobile, that he was close to the drop off.

Billy was dressed in casual clothes to give the impression that this was an off duty task and he thrust his leather jacketed arm out of the car window, to press the intercom panel on the gatepost. He got no answer and pressed it again. After three more attempts and no voice of welcome, Keilloh was prepared to turn away and leave. Just as he selected reverse, the electronic gates gave a whirring noise and began to open. He drove up to the steps below the front door and got out.

There was still no obvious sign of life, so Billy climbed the steps to the front door and pressed a large button. He heard chimes sounding faintly through the solid double doors and waited. A single leaf of the door opened and a large, black, dreadlocked head stuck out of the gap. "Yeah?" it said.

Billy feigned fumbling in the pocket of his jeans, and pulled out his warrant card. "I'm Detective Inspector Keilloh, Highland Police. This vehicle," he waved at the Range Rover, "Is registered at this address. I've come to return it. Who might you be, please?"

"I might be anyone, man, but I ain't telling no filth, my name. You'll need to see Mr Muwera. Wait there." The door shut.

Around a minute later, the door opened again and Dreadlocks appeared again. "He says you can come in." Keilloh walked cautiously through the open door and followed the huge dreadlocked man down the hall. They went into a lounge with lots of leather furniture, including a pale blue armchair in which sat a young looking, tall, black man with a completely shaved head. He was wearing a tight, white tee shirt that displayed the muscles of his upper body, and the sleeves seemed to cut off some indistinct red and green tattoos on his dark biceps. His dark brown colouring reminded Keilloh of the water filling one of the heavily peated inland lochs on Lewis. Billy also saw some facial resemblance to the photos of the dead Pascal that he'd seen.

"Mr Muwera, I presume?" DI Keilloh asked, still standing.

"Frisk him, Joshua. Oh sorry, er, Mister, or rather, Inspector, Keilloh. I hope you don't mind? Standard procedure at this house."

Before the words, "Carry on," left Billy's mouth, the man with the dreadlocks started, very precisely, stroking his hands all over Billy's body. He even felt inside his jacket and shirt.

"No weapons, no wires," grunted Joshua.

"I'm Georgie...Georges Muwera. I saw on the monitor, you've got my brother's car," replied the man on the sofa, who showed no sign of getting up.

"Yes, I..."

"Were you part of it?"

"Sorry, part of what?"

"The killing of my brother."

"I was not, I don't know much more than you. I wasn't involved in the incident and I'm very sorry for your loss. I have some idea of what you're feeling, I also lost a friend. Roddy MacLeod and I used to go fishing together."

Georgie leaned forward on the settee, "The papers are saying that Pascal and Eric were drug dealers. That's all bollocks, of course."

"I know that no evidence of drugs was found at the scene, perhaps they just got into the wrong crowd around here," replied Keilloh glancing around the sumptuous sitting room. "Perhaps we'll find out more when the inquiries are done?"

"What 'inquiries' do you mean?"

"By the Procurator Fiscal. We don't have inquests in Scotland, but the Procurator's department conduct inquiries into unusual deaths, and publish their findings."

"Do you want to know what I think?"

Billy ignored the temptation to declare that he didn't give a fuck about Georgie's opinion and responded, quietly, "Please."

"This bloke, who the papers are saying is some sort of secret agent, borrowed some money from Pascal and did a runner. My Bro and Eric tracked him down and asked for it back, then he shot them in cold blood to keep the cash."

Keilloh couldn't resist the urge this time and asked, "Where does the shooting of Sergeant MacLeod fit into this theory?"

Georgie shrugged, "I dunno, wrong place, wrong time? What is it the American's call it... 'collateral damage'? Anyway, if I'm right, I won't let it rest. I'll have that 'James Bond' bastard. People have fucked with the Muwera's before, and not lived to regret it."

"I don't know about any of that Mr Muwera, I'm just here to do a job."

"And what 'job' is that, Inspector?"

"Your brother's car was at the scene of the crime. We've examined it for evidence and have no more use for it. I'm just trying to return it to Pascal's next of kin. I couldn't find a record of a wife or children so I thought I'd come here. Would you be the next of kin, Sir?"

"I'm his only brother, so yes, that would be me. But... Why would a busy inspector get involved with a simple car delivery?"

"No mysterious secret, I volunteered to drive it down here. I have a sister in London and thought it would be a good chance to see my nephews for the weekend, then fly back."

"How fucking sweet! What about Pascal and Eric's stuff?"

"There are two holdalls in the boot of the car, with what looks like a change of clothes and personal effects in each. They've been searched for drugs, but otherwise untouched."

Georges voiced nothing for a few moments, as if weighing the words of the policeman against his own thoughts, then held out his hand and said curtly, "Keys!"

DI Keilloh pulled them from his jacket pocket and dropped them into the palm of the seated man. "If you could just sign this discharge form, Sir, to complete formalities?" Billy added, removing a sheet of A4 and a pen from inside his jacket and holding them forward. He returned the signed form and the pen, into his pocket, a few moments later.

Georges Muwera's comment to Joshua, as the departing back of Keilloh left the room, was clearly intended for the Inspector as well. "J, make sure you check that car for anything dodgy, before I drive it." He then shouted out, "Do have a safe journey back home, Officer. You can usually get a cab at the end of the road, head for the Olympic Stadium."

Back at his sister's house, Billy sent a short email to his contact at the SOCA and cc'd Toby Crabbe. In it, he confirmed delivery and that the target was going to search the vehicle for anything untoward. He knew that it was unlikely that any of the varying array of devices would be detected and, even if one were found, not all would be.

The future, inasmuch as it involved the Muwera family, was now out of his hands and he could enjoy an evening on the Play Station, with his two young nephews.

-+-

Chapter Thirty Two

In the end, the very forceful Lydia Hockley-Roberts and the very professional doctor, Angus MacInnon, had compromised. LHR wanted Robin Chancellor released on the same day that she first met the doctor, while the doctor said that the patient needed another week's supervision. So it was that Talbot found himself being manhandled through the door of his cottage by two paramedics from the Western Isles Ambulance Service, with Lydia carrying his overnight bag, at lunchtime on Wednesday 5th November.

They laid him on his bed then rigged up some apparatus to keep his left leg raised, and the self-dispensing morphine drip close at hand. Lydia had firm instructions from Mr MacInnon on medication, warning signs of any deterioration in Rob's condition, and physiotherapy routines for the shoulder and leg. Rob's new hip, that MacInnon had fitted after taking the plaster cast off him a couple of days before, needed to get moving on a daily basis. The shoulder strapping should be kept tight apart from daily exercises with the right arm, then re-strapped to allow the fractured parts, held together with metal pins, to fuse together in the right way.

Overall, MacInnon had insisted that total rest, with controlled exercises, was the only way the patient's body could properly heal. No sudden movements, or strain, was to be placed on the injured parts. Best to just lay on his back and let nature do her thing, was the strong advice from the consultant. If Lydia was determined to take him out of hospital early, she would have to help Rob with toilet functions, involving as little movement as possible for the patient, MacInnon had added, with no little relish.

Once the ambulance and crew had left, LHR sat next to

Carter's bed and took his left hand in hers. "Fair play to you Cat, I thought all men were pathetic when they got sick or injured. But you haven't moaned once in the last few days... Very impressive. You look pretty knackered now though!"

"Thanks, I love you too!"

"Want a cup of tea?"

"Please Lids, and a whole box of shortbread... I'm sick of those cardboard tasting Rich Tea the NHS serve!"

Lydia returned from the kitchen less than five minutes later, with a loaded tea tray, to find Carter fast asleep. His open mouth gently vibrating with soft snoring and his left hand flopped out of the bed. She took the tray away and let him sleep, then went into the study and looked for something she might enjoy reading. Talbot's book collection was not particularly aimed at women, but she eventually settled for something about the Falkland's War by Max Hastings. She knew that Carter had been in that conflict and thought some background stuff might be useful, when they got to that part of his story.

Relaxing in the study chair, with the big book resting on the desk, and the vista of the North Atlantic under a grey sky through the window, Lydia also fell asleep. It was dark by the time she woke up and she immediately jumped out of the chair and went into Cat's bedroom.

Talbot's head slowly turned towards her and he said gently, "Thought you'd gone for some tea, Lydia?"

"Sorry Cat, I made some, then we both fell asleep. Let me do some fresh."

They drank their tea together a few minutes later, staring

out of the window at the dark and munching shortbread biscuits.

"Do you think this is going to work, Lids?"

"Carter, we will make it work. After the tea, it will be time for your evening exercises, then I can run you a nice bath and help you into it. I haven't done any shopping yet, so dinner will be whatever I can rustle up from your cupboards. Then a couple of nice whiskies and a good night's sleep. Tomorrow you'll be fresh as a daisy, and ready to get stuck into the next chapter of your book. What do you think?"

"You make it sound an absolute doddle. Let's hope you're right... And no taking advantage of an invalid when he can't fight you off."

"Sounds like you're getting better already, Mr Talbot!"

Lydia's optimistic prediction seemed right when, at around 9am the next morning, the sluggish winter sun beamed brightly from behind the cottage onto the sea, and Carter welcomed his secretary cum nurse into his bedroom, with a smile almost as gleaming.

"Why are you so pleased with yourself?"

"With the help of those rather ugly looking crutches," he said, nodding at the wall to the side of the bed, "I managed to get to the bathroom and back early this morning."

"But MacInnon said..."

"Never mind what he said, Lids, I did it... Fucking painful, but I did it. Now I want breakfast in bed, then we can start work."

"Right, I'll see what I can do, you stubborn old twat!"

Without fresh milk, the porridge that Lydia produced for breakfast was markedly less creamy than Carter was used to, but at least, he thought, she'd had the sense to add a generous slug of single malt and he ate the lot.

"Thanks Lydia, the village store is just down the road and if you need anything different, you can use the jeep to get into Tarbert. The police dropped it off for me while I was in hospital. Thank God eh, we don't want another day of watery porridge, do we?"

"Cheeky sod! Think yourself lucky, I don't make porridge for any other authors you know."

"Fair enough Lids. Now where are we, in the book I mean?"

"You've finished chapter four, where, you say, you sabotaged the family car to get at your cruel dad, but ended up killing your mum as well."

"Right, so where should I pick up the story?"

"Hold on Cat, I'm not sure you really want to admit to that. I don't think I want to know the reality but, true or not, it doesn't help the average reader to feel sympathy for the writer. It could even get you into trouble."

"But you said it was to be sold as a work of fiction."

"And it will be, but after what happened a fortnight ago, you are well known now, we've got to take the readers with us, willingly, on your journey. Controversy sells in the short term, but I have to think of protecting you for the future too."

"I'm not sure I'm as convincing, when I write lies though."

"We can, perhaps, just leave a critical aspect out and make the rest ring true. Along the lines of *'I hated my father for how he treated my mother and although I was devastated when the car accident took her from me, frankly, I was glad to see the back of him.'* Why don't you let me play around with that part of chapter four and show it to you later? In the meantime you can use the MemoMate and make a start on chapter five. What will we be looking at there?"

"Ok Lids, you're the expert. Chapter five is going to tell how my Uncle Hugo stepped into the breach when I was orphaned. About going to Marlborough for my A-levels and life at the Sandhurst Military Academy. And about discovering girls!"

"So you didn't save yourself for me then? I'm sure you told me that you did, during our fortnight's fling at the Savoy?"

"As we agreed earlier, this is being sold purely as a work of fiction."

"By the way Cat, I've polished your rough chapter plan... The one in your notebook, so that we can both know where we are and where the story is heading. Some of your scribbles didn't make much sense but we've got a professional framework now."

They worked well doing different parts of Carter's story. After editing the controversial aspect of chapter four to leave out Cat's crucial role in the accident that killed his parents, Lydia sat in with Cat as he dictated the next chapter. She didn't interrupt but let his voice flow into the machine. She got some soft drinks from the fridge to help keep Cat's throat lubricated and popped down to Mrs

MacArthur's for supplies, while Carter carried on teasing the memories from the recesses of his mind.

Lydia noticed that if Carter had a correcting thought about a previous sentence, he would rewind the machine and try to put it right, then navigate his way back to his present place. This clearly caused him frustration so she advised him to not think about editing at this stage, just get the story down and she would turn it into manuscript for him. Then he could edit to his heart's content, once he could sit up properly with two working arms and address a screen comfortably. By the time the sun had settled, in their sight from the bedroom window, on the western horizon and the light faded, Cat had finished his verbal draft of chapter five and lobbed the MemoMate gently at Lydia.

She caught it and smiled at him, "Great effort Mr Talbot," she said.

He turned his tired eyes towards her face and replied, "I know I probably shouldn't, lying on my back all day, but I feel completely knackered."

"I kept wanting to stop you, but your face looked so alive when you were remembering all those adventures, like you were still there in some way. I couldn't spoil the moment, not even for lunch. Although once or twice, you had me blushing...especially the seduction of the Colonel's daughter...bloody hell Cat, there was a time when you'd have been whipped out of the college, surely?"

"Happy days, Lydia, but think on, I had nothing else but the army in my life. I was, if you remember the tape, according to Staff Sergeant Milligan, 'the most focused potential officer in all my years at Sandhurst, but the one with the fewest friends'. 'Focused and friendless', summed up my early life pretty well, I reckon."

"I'll start writing that up tomorrow. But now, I'm going to get you a lovely gin and tonic, then make you a fantastic supper."

"Fantastic is a strong word, bearing in mind the culinary limitations of MacArthur's Stores."

"You'd better believe it, one of the fishermen brought Moira in some fresh scallops to sell. Flamed in whisky, they'll be sensational. We shall dine like kings tonight, Carter."

Carter laid back on his pillows and smiled as he heard the food preparation noises coming from the galley. This wasn't working out too bad, he thought.

-+-

Chapter Thirty Three

Georges Muwera sat at his dining room table and watched his two associates finish off the last of what had been a mountainous pile of chicken wings. He put a cold bottle of Carlsberg to his lips and drank, then wiped his mouth with the back of his hand. The two muscle bound, crew cut, white men, both in their late thirties, threw down the chicken bones onto big plates and leaned back in their chairs, to belch and fart respectively.

"Right, Boys, we need to arrange a bit of a set up."

"How do you mean Georgie?" the oldest of the two 'boys' replied through his last mouthful of barbecued chicken.

"We've got to make sure that Pascal's Range Rover is clean. Josh has been over it and found nothing, but you can never really trust Plod. The thing is, it's a great motor and I want to use it, but not if every fucking computer nerd in the Met is listening in."

"So what are you thinking, Boss?" asked the largest of the men.

"What I'm thinking, Tim...and Tom," Georgie said, looking at both of them in turn, "Is that we need to play a little game with them, and if the car is bent, we can catch the fuckers out. It's been nearly a week since the Jock guy dropped it off. So it's time for some fun."

"What's the plan, Boss?" Tom enquired.

"Right, listen good, you two..."

+

"Any plans for the weekend?" asked one scruffy looking young man without headphones to another scruffy young man, wearing a large padded pair of them. When he got no response to his question, he reached over from his computer monitor, lifted the pad over his colleagues left ear and said, more loudly, "What are you doing at the weekend? Our shift is over at eight tonight."

The man with the headphones relaxed them around his neck, while keeping an eye on the dials of his laptop screen. "I think some excessive online combat, in the wonderful world of Warhammer 40,000, might be in order," he replied.

"You sad twat," said the first young man, "Not only should your thoughts be turning to beer and sex late on a Friday afternoon, like any single Londoner, but Warhammer 40,000 is so out of date."

"I guess then, that we are both seeking mindless fun when off duty, it's just that we find it in markedly different ways," responded Young Man Two, while putting his headphones back on. "You're still a sad twat," was the somewhat feeble retort of Young Man One.

No sooner were the headphones back on than YM2 sat forward in his chair and lifted his hand towards his colleague to draw his attention. "Matt... I think we've got something, put your cans on."

Matthew grabbed his own set of headphones and positioned them quickly on his ears. They both sat forward and Dominic touched the record button on his screen. They both increased the volume to maximum. They could hear what sounded like gravel faintly crunching then the sound of car doors slamming, twice quickly, then one deeper single noise, then a pause, and another, lighter, single noise. The faint sound of an engine starting and then a gentle hum told the story.

"Sounds like the targets are on the move," volunteered Dominic.

"Bloody typical Dom, we've heard nothing all week, then just as our last shift of the week is nearly over, they decide to go out. Bollocks!"

"Ours not to reason why, my friend. Ours but to record all this and pass on any information. Have they used the SatNav yet?"

"Just getting that now... The postcode is showing up as somewhere in Rainham, Essex...actually Rainham Marshes, near the RSPB Nature Reserve, of all places."

"Right Matt, get Seagram down here, they've started talking."

As Matt called the officer in charge of their unit, some ten floors above their basement post in New Scotland Yard, Dom could hear three different voices from the microphone device, which was intertwined with the overhead courtesy light in the target vehicle.

A strong cockney accent; 'Nice motor, Boss.'

A slightly French accent: 'Not too shabby is it? And Josh screened it for bugs, so it's safe to use.'

Dominic, who had been partly trained by the MI6 Covert Technical Team, grinned to himself before hearing a different cockney accent, 'Are we expecting any trouble tonight, Guv?'

'I don't think so, regular customer, two 'undred K to collect, for that bag of gear you put in the boot. Should be fine.'

'What then?'

'Well they wanted to meet near the bird sanctuary, if you two wanted to do some twitching?'

'Are you taking the piss, Boss?' asked a frustrated cockney accent.

'Only fucking slightly.' French accent replied.

'What I meant Guv, is are we gonna go clubbin' or anyfink. You know what these Essex girls are like?'

'Tim and Tom, you are, without doubt, total animals... But I suppose we could spend some of the proceeds on a night out, while we're in Slagland.'

'Cheers, Boss.'

'Yeah, fuckin' nice one, Guv.'

With that, Detective Superintendent Seagram came into the surveillance centre and asked for an update. Matt went through what they had so far and played back the conversation, while Dom continued to listen to the targets 'live'.

"What have we got in place here?" Seagram asked.

"Listening device in the roof, back-up behind the central air con blower, SatNav relay, and a sniffer in the boot, Sir." Matthew replied confidently.

"The drug detector in the boot, what's it saying?"

Matt and Dom both looked at their screens, then Matt replied, "Negative activation, Sir."

"So this 'bag of gear' they've mentioned, isn't drugs?"

"Impossible to say, Sir," continued Matt, "They may have vacuum packed it, and/or masked the drug aroma with another stronger smelling substance."

"But why would they do that, Farrell?"

"It may have come into Britain like that, Sir, to protect the carrier from sniffer dogs at the airport. Basically, that boot could be stuffed with loads of class 'A'. But, without a reading, we can't be sure."

"Ok, let me have a listen," said Seagram, placing a spare set of headphones over his neat police officer haircut. His introduction to the conversation was a loud blaring single note, as the driver hit the horn and held it. The inspector screwed up his face with the shock, then heard someone he assumed to be the driver shouting, 'You fucking dozy cunt, get out of my lane you wanker!'

"Mmm, poor timing on my part I think, Farrell."

"Sorry, Sir."

They continued to listen and, when the target vehicle was about halfway to the destination given to the SatNav, Superintendent Seagram took off the headphones and turned to Matt and Dom.

"Apart from Tim and Tom, and we can guess that the Boss is Gorgeous Georges Muwera, I'm not hearing any names that we recognise. Mind you, they're not talking much about business. They seem more concerned about where they'll get the best chance of getting their legs over tonight. But look, better safe than sorry, I'm sending a SOCA welcome party, get me DI Johnson at Barking, please Mr

Farrell. With any luck we can catch dealers and recipients here."

+

The blue Range Rover glided gently along the unlit, single track Tarmac road, with a variety of trees over a fence to their left and wide open marshland to their right. The sun had just set and the industrial lights of south Essex industry were flickering in the near distance. The car came to a stop and the headlights were relegated to sidelights, with the engine still humming.

The sixteen eyes watching through the trees at the side of the car, could see three men in the yellow interior light passing around a flask, the contents of which could be seen to be steaming as it was poured into white cups. The owner of one pair of eyes had a wire coming out of his suede jacket pocket and into his left ear. The surveillance team had patched through the live talking from within the car to his mobile phone and he listened intently. Three other officers from SOCA were in plain clothes and they were supported by four uniformed police. One with stripes on his arm was breathing heavily as he manoeuvred his large frame into a more comfortable crouch behind a bush, next to the officer in charge. "What's the plan, Sir?" he asked, his breathlessness making this question louder than he had intended.

"Keep it quiet, eh Sergeant," whispered the Inspector. "As far as I can tell, their customers haven't arrived yet, even though they're on time themselves. We will wait for orders from Scotland Yard. Don't forget, Sergeant, if we get the green light, your team are in support. My squad will take the lead."

"Yes, Sir... Inspector Johnson?"

"What is it now Sergeant?"

"What if they're armed, Sir? The dealers, I mean."

"That's why you must leave it to my men. Now, let me listen."

Twenty minutes went by, and the only thing that seemed to happen in the Range Rover was that they finished their coffee and one of them put on a strange looking black helmet with protruding horns over the eyes. As the wearer turned his head to scan into the direction of the eight police officers, Johnson realised what the helmet was and, in a stage whisper, hissed, "Everybody down flat, NOW."

The police, as one, threw themselves into nettles, thorns, muddy pools, and dead branches fallen off autumnal trees. The man in the night vision goggles kept looking and passing comment, the sound of which still came into DI Johnson's ear. 'Can't see any Boss,' said the wearer down the wire. 'Let's give it five more minutes, and if our friends haven't come, we'll get into Romford for that night out,' the voice went on.

There was some crackling noise next on the line, then, "Johnson, can you hear me?" DI Johnson pressed the tiny pad on the wire then whispered, "Yes, Sir."

"I think I've heard enough, Johnson. Looks like their customers have got cold feet tonight, but at least we can get that gang in front of you. Move in now and let me listen in, would you."

"Righto Sir." Johnson said, with obvious pleasure. He then turned to the nearest men and whispered, "Superintendent says Go. Thirty seconds, on my signal, pass it on."

During that half a minute, DI Johnson thought about which signal he would use. He would have loved an old fashioned police whistle, but didn't have one. He thought about firing a round from his handgun, but that might prove provocative if the targets were armed, as he suspected. So, when the second hand of his watch swept to the right luminous digit he contented himself with a very loud, "GO, GO, GO!"

He ran to the driver's door and his officers all took a door each. They all held their weapons in both hands and at arm's length aiming at their respective windows. The uniformed police, armed with strong flashlights, put two officers in front of the car and two behind it, to deter the suspects from driving away.

"Window down driver, NOW," barked Johnson, gesturing up and down with the gun to make the point. Tom complied and stared at the DI. "What seems to be the tr..."

"Shut up and turn the engine off... DO IT." Tom complied again. "Now get out of the vehicle and turn around against the door, keep your hands where I can see them."

Soon, all three of the Range Rover's occupants were standing to the side of the car, with their hands cuffed behind their backs. They were read their rights and told that they were suspected of trafficking in class 'A' drugs, in contravention of the Dangerous Drugs Act.

Loud enough for Georges and his minders to hear, DI Johnson called out smugly to his team, "Let's get this car searched, please gentlemen."

In a matter of seconds, one of the officers emerged from his rummage in the tailgate of the car, just managing to hold a very large green plastic sack, such as would be used to line a council wheelie bin. "I think this might be what we are looking for, Sir." said the officer.

"Well, Georgie, what do we have here?" Johnson asked as he gestured Georges to him and pointed to the sack in one fluid movement.

"Quite simple Inspector, it's shit."

"So you admit it? You're going to go down for a long time for this, there must be 40 kilos of the stuff."

"I told you... It's shit."

"Bring it here, Mason," ordered Johnson. "Constable, get that light on this bag."

"Open it, Mason."

Everyone watched, as Detective Sergeant Mason struggled to open the metal wire clasp at the top of the sack. When he did so he pulled the top apart, only to reveal another sack and another clasp. This was repeated twice more until finally, Mason pulled back the fourth sack top and sunk his face towards the opening to look inside. He recoiled upwards as if he had encountered a spring loaded jack-in-the-box and put a hand to his face.

"Fuck me," said the detective, "It really is shit Sir!"

"Don't be fooled Mason, everyone know that's only there to prevent the sniffer de... Er, to disguise the drugs. Tip the whole lot out. They'll be packets of cocaine at the bottom of the sack, don't you worry."

"Ok, Sir, if you're sure."

Mason took a huge breath then lifted the bag from the bottom and held the opening away from him. He tilted the whole lot at the roadway and shook it as best he could, until he was forced to take another breath, when he threw the empty bag onto the ground.

DI Johnson grabbed a stick from the side of the woods and started to poke about in the stinking, brown, wet pile at their feet. It was clear to everyone by the time Johnson gave voice to the common thought, "This is shit, and not in a drug slang sense. But we were told it was worth two hun... never mind. Our intelligence was that you were carrying drugs tonight Mr Muwera. I'm sure you won't mind if we search your car thoroughly." He didn't wait for an answer before instructing his team to 'carry on'.

"In the meantime, Mr Muwera, what were you doing in this lonely spot, in the dark, with your two 'companions'?"

Georgie could just about suppress the laughter in his throat but could do nothing to prevent his joyful smile. "We were bird watching, Mr Johnson. We're especially keen on the nocturnal species, owls and suchlike. That's why we got ourselves a set of night vision goggles, the one's that Tim over there is wearing."

DI Johnson was fully aware by now that he had been 'done like a kipper', as his colleagues would say when news of this got out, but he had to go through the motions.

"Were you planning to meet with anyone?"

"Not particularly, although some other ‘twitchers’ do come out from time to time, when we come here."

"And the bag of... manure, in your car?"

"Oh, that's for Tom's mum, to fertilise her Roses, got it from a mate who owns horses."

Mason returned from the car. "No drugs, no guns, nothing... Sir."

"Thank you Mason, please release the cuffs from these men, and gather the team. We'll get back to the station."

"Er, Inspector, what about Tom's mum?" Georges asked. "Her roses will go short... The manure?"

Johnson seethed through gritted teeth as he most reluctantly ordered two of the uniformed boys to re-bag the offending fertiliser and put it back in the Range Rover.

"Are you sure you don't want this for evidence, Inspector?" Muwera queried with fake concern.

"Are you sure you don't want to have your head stuck in that sack, you smug bastard?" Then much closer, "Don't push your luck, Georgie. One day, I'll be the one laughing." DI Johnson then stood back a little and said loudly, "On behalf of the Metropolitan Police, I would like to apologise for the inconvenience caused to you and your colleagues. You are, of course, free to go."

The rather muddy and bedraggled looking police contingent made their way back to the two cars that they had parked behind the trees. As they settled into the cars and drove back along the same track, it was no surprise to see a flash of brake lights 200 yards ahead, followed by a lifting tailgate, then a disappearing Range Rover. When they drew level to what they had seen, there in the middle of the road was the big green sack, its contents partly spilled across the tarmac.

Detective Superintendent Seagram did not, as some of the junior officers at Barking did, take DI Johnson to task for the failure of the operation. He had made the high level decision to try and arrest the gang and took full responsibility for the embarrassment that followed. Matthew and Dominic were assigned other targets but maintained access to the Muwera devices, just in case. This was a pretty forlorn hope, underlined by the last message they got on 'Bag of Shit' day, as it came to be known. Five minutes after Tim had jettisoned the green sack from the car, they picked up a final transmission which was Georges saying to Tim, "Tomorrow, get this car to Jimmy Daly, I want it sold, immediately."

-+-

Chapter Thirty Four

Lydia couldn't quite believe how short the days were getting, now that December had arrived. It was Sunday the 7th and she sat nursing a morning coffee in the study which she was using as a bedroom, looking out onto the still dark sky. She could just make out the leaden black clouds in the feeble, slightly grey emanations from the streaks of thinner cloud as they were constantly re-shaped by the wind. The only points of reference she could make out lower down was an even darker block, of the island in the bay, and the occasional dull white fleck from the top of a wave breaking on the boulders at the shore.

The wind didn't look like it was going to clear the clouds anytime soon and Lydia doubted whether they were going to see any sun that day. There was every chance of rain, she thought, but then she had thought that on most days in the month since she had moved in with Carter Talbot.

"Knock, knock," came Cat's voice through the door, disturbing her reflective mood, "Fancy a brew?"

"I've already got one, thanks."

"And you didn't make me one... cheers..."

"I looked in on you and you were dead to the world... and at half past nine in the morning!"

"Fair enough... Let me get myself one, and we'll have a chat." She heard his uneven footsteps and pictured him limping into the kitchen.

Cat was in her room a couple of minutes later with a large white mug in his hand. He sat down on the bed/settee, currently in bed mode, while Lydia stayed in the swivel chair.

"Are we still on for that walk today?" Carter asked, looking knowingly at the less than encouraging weather outside the window.

"I know you're keen Cat, but it is only a couple of days since you stopped using the crutches. You've not been outside for six weeks. Do you think it's sensible?"

"Won't know, unless we try, will we?"

"Ok, but can't we wait for a sunny day?"

"This is the Outer Hebrides Lydia, the next sunny day might be next June! Come on let's have a go... I promise I won't try and overdo it...and I'll cook lunch for you, when we're back."

"Your stubborn streak can get a bit wearing at times Carter, but you've convinced me this time. And, of course, we've got to stick to our 'no writing on Sunday' rule. Clearing our heads ready for the week ahead, and all that. No long distance stuff or hills though, pottering about on the beach and in the village will be fine, thank you."

After a light breakfast of fruit and yogurt, the friends got wrapped up to face the grim December weather. Cat had found an old fur lined leather helmet in his wardrobe, very much in the Russian Red Army style. Lydia immediately referred to him as Vladimir but secretly wished she had one too. She made do with a huge woollen scarf wrapped around her neck three times and an old football bobble hat of Carter's in the colours and badge of Sunderland AFC.

"I didn't know Sunderland were your team Cat?"

"They're not really, but Shakespeare left it here, gift from his Uni flat mate apparently, and you said you needed a hat."

"I think you miss him."

"You sound very sure of that opinion, Lydia."

"Well?"

"Well, what?"

"Tell me you don't miss him."

"I... Well I do miss him a bit, he was, is, a really nice guy. We sort of...bonded...a bit."

"Was he involved?... You know...in the shooting."

"I've told you, I'm keeping my own counsel on that, for good reasons. You'll have to trust me, Darling."

"Ok, Ok, come on then Vlad, assuming you've got a hip flask of vodka to keep the elements at bay, we can get going."

"Come on then," replied Cat, "Race you to the Village Shop."

It wasn't as cold as they had expected, the cloud acting like a fat blanket on the bleak earth of Harris, and the usual south westerly wind being mercifully gentle that day. Their pottering about in the village and on the sandy beach at the village end of the bay, took the rest of the morning.

Carter was breathing heavily as he limped around the beach going in seemingly random directions, and dragging the heel of his good leg through the sand for long intervals. "Stand up there," he called to Lydia who had been peering into the rock pools along the shore, pointing at the higher land between the beach and the scattered houses. Lydia humoured him and climbed up the boulders to the flat path, then turned. Facing her in letters at least ten yards tall, carved out of the beach, was the word: 'LYDIA'.

"Very artistic," she called, "Can I have a go?"

"Be my guest."

Lydia giggled like a schoolgirl as she hopped back down to the beach, and Cat could see her sticking her tongue out in concentration, as she copied his writing style and dug her boots repeatedly into the soft sand. Eventually she had dragged the word 'ROBIN' from the damp grains, lined up roughly next to his offering, and stood back proudly.

"Stand between them, Lids," Carter asked her, "We need some photos of this." With that he removed his mobile from his jacket, went up to the path, and took a few snaps, Lydia posing as best she could in the bulky outfit and Sunderland bobble hat. They reversed positions and Carter even lay down in the sand with his arms and legs spread, making for a memorable tableau.

"That's quite enough of your showing off," shouted Lydia from the path, "Come on up, you're buying me a drink."

Sunday lunchtime at the Dion was a strange affair. Some people, who went to church, still felt the need to wear a suit or their best dress, and you could almost taste the guilt in the air emanating from the handful of locals so attired, as they stood in the small bar sipping drinks. Cat and Lydia got a pint and a gin and tonic and squeezed into the corner near the more casually dressed of the patrons.

Carter spoke in a low tone, "The thing is, Lids, it wasn't so long ago that all pubs in Harris and Lewis were closed all day on the Sabbath. Going for a drink after church is very much a new thing here. Introduced, no doubt, by heathen

English like us!"

"So I see Ca... Rob, this is the first time we've been here together on a Sunday. Presumably there are many who still stick to the old ways and go home straight after church?"

"Not just go home Lydia, but go home and spend the rest of the day reading their bibles."

"Seriously, in 2014?"

"It will probably be another generation before these habits die out."

A middle-aged couple by the fire finished their drinks and rose to leave, freeing the small table which Rob and Lydia slid into.

"Good to get the weight off," Rob grunted, as he perched on the small chair.

"How's it feeling?"

"Like it needs the soothing effect of some painkillers when we get home."

"Does Finn do wine here?" Lydia ventured.

"He can probably dig out a bottle of Algerian Belly Wash, or something. Want me to ask?"

"I'll go, you take it easy."

After some glass clanking noises from behind the bar, Lydia returned clutching a bottle of red and two wine goblets. "When it comes to painkillers, this is something we can share," she said as she unscrewed the top off the

Chilean Merlot and poured.

"Cheers," they said in unison as they half lifted the glasses in the air then took a decent slurp each. "Not bad," said Robin. "Agreed," replied Lydia, "Glad to see that your right arm is functioning so much better now!"

"I think it's fair to say, Lids, that I'm very much 'on the mend'. And, so much of that is down to you." Rob lifted his glass in her direction and gave her his best smile.

She acknowledged the toast with a half lift of her glass and then took a sip to hide her blushes before responding. "For someone who seems, if what we're discovering in your book so far is even halfway true, to be such a cold hearted bastard, I'd say you're showing your soft underbelly there... Mr Chancellor!"

"Fair point, well made, Madam," he replied, while topping up both their glasses. "Speaking about the book. Are you happy with progress so far?"

Lydia went quietly pensive for a few moments, took another sip, then said, "Well, we've got ten chapters written and edited, and that's good. I'd say we're about a third of the way through it, but the speed has been erratic. Your memory seems to dwell on those moments of greatest excitement, but you slow down and get bored when it comes to the rest of it. We're trying to tell a life story here, not just a serious of anecdotes."

"But surely people read for excitement, not stories about battalion administration in a boring army camp, in the middle of nowhere?"

"People also read for illumination, understanding, education, and escapism. They want to empathise and identify with some of the characters, put themselves in their shoes. I would like the more human side of you to come out, get the reader to have some sympathy for you, the warm you, that I know is in there somewhere."

"But, in my mind, those early years after school were just focused on one thing, my success. I knew, especially after Sandhurst, that I was born to be a military leader of men, and the best chances of progress were to be seen to be the best. Being all fluffy and light-hearted wasn't my cup of tea at all. Ruthlessness was all, to me."

"What about love, Robin? And I don't mean all your successful conquests of officer's wives and daughters. Was there nobody to care for, or that cared for you?"

It was Cat's turn to look pensive, then very softly he said, "That came later...later than chapter ten anyway." He looked back at the table then put his wine to his lips, as if to close that particular subject.

Lydia got the message and quickly changed the topic. "Ok, so we've got through Sandhurst. We then went to the parachute regiment armed with your commission, and sailed gloriously through some of the toughest training in the world. Chapter seven took us to Germany with endless battlefield training to keep the Warsaw Pact forces contained. This also involved you experimenting with several West German women, who were most grateful to you personally for keeping the Soviets at bay! Right so far?"

"Yes, fair summary, I suppose."

"Chapter eight involved some Arctic training in Norway and some leave at Uncle Hugo's, where you seduced his housekeeper. In chapters nine and ten, you rotated to and from Northern Ireland, successfully commanding a company of paratroopers, in the one place in the world where they were despised. Your main claim to fame, on those tours, was that you never lost a man, in all the IRA bandit actions you were involved in. In addition, not only did you enjoy the close attention of random Belfast girls, but had an affair, that you described as purely physical, with the wife of your brigade commander."

The man that Lydia had got used to calling Robin Chancellor, when they were in public, now sat opposite her looking as sheepish as she had ever seen him. Through his blushes, he responded, "I was just doing my job."

"Not always, Rob. Her Majesty paid you for fighting, or learning to fight, not for fucking. That was meant to be in your off duty moments, but you didn't make that distinction, clearly."

"I'm not ashamed, you know?"

"I know, really I do. Sociopaths don't usually have any shame or guilt. That's part of their make-up. Anyway, here we are on the brink of chapter eleven. Where are we off to next?"

"It's now coming to the end of 1981, the eve of the Falklands War."

"One of the finest hours of the parachute regiment, I believe?" said Lydia encouragingly, feeling that she may have been a bit tough on him.

"Yes, I was still a Captain then, and starting to feel frustrated at the lack of real fighting opportunities in the peacekeeping drudgery of Germany and Ulster. The next thing I knew, I was on the deck of the Canberra, heading for the South Atlantic."

Lydia's face and insides were glowing with a combination of the red wine and the deep strong feelings she had for Carter. They finished the bottle, and she could see that he looked tired.

"Come on Rob," she said, "You've already had too much fun today. Let's get you home for a nap, in what's left of the afternoon, before the Hebridean darkness sets in for another long shift."

-+-

Chapter Thirty Five

Lydia busied herself in Carter's kitchen putting together some late lunch, while he soaked in a hot bath, easing the muscles stretched by being used again. The idea was to have a Sunday afternoon nap after their exertions on the beach and the welcome wine in the Dion. She had suggested that he would sleep better if he had something to eat and got clean. He seemed too tired to argue and gratefully slipped into the tub of bubbly, steaming water which she ran for him.

She put the finishing touches to two plates, both with layered towers of potato cakes, and big roundels of black pudding, topped with fluffy scrambled eggs. "Carter," she called out, "Lunch is ready." She got no reply, so called again... Still no response from the bathroom, so she put the plates in the top part of the range to keep warm and went down the hallway.

She pushed open the bathroom door and made her way through into the still steamy room. Looking down into the bath she saw that Cat's eyes were closed and his head lolled back against the curved top end of the bath. "Come on Talbot," she said softly, "I've made your favourite." He didn't move or speak, so she crouched down by the side of the tub and reached out her hand towards his shoulders, while looking at his body. She stayed her hand for a moment as she noticed that Carter's own right hand was wrapped around his penis. It seemed to have emerged from the soapy depths and was swollen if not fully erect. She smiled at the sight, turned her face back towards his head, and gently touched his shoulder.

"Cat," she said, louder this time, "Time for lunch."

His eyes flickered open, and blinked in different directions as he woke up. They settled on Lydia and he said, somewhat obviously, "I think I nodded off."

"Yes you did, Carter. But not before a bit of special physiotherapy for that right arm of yours... Eh?"

Cat looked down, and he moved his hand away from his groin, as he blushed at Lydia. "You have to keep things active, Lids! I didn't... I mean, I fell asleep before any... 'conclusion'."

"Come on, big boy, here's a towel, and your dressing gown's on the back of the door. Lunch is in the lounge in two minutes."

They enjoyed lunch and Carter poured them both a whisky to wash it down. "Stornoway black pudding, Lydia. The very best in the world, cheers!"

"Glad you liked it," she replied, joining his toast.

"Now, it's bed time for you... with a special present from me."

"Present?"

"Come on," she held out a hand and helped him, even though he didn't need her to, to his bedroom. She pulled back the duvet on his big solid bed, then turned and untied his dressing gown. She deftly slipped it off him and she guided him into the bed. As he pulled the duvet over his naked body, she stepped back and started to take off her clothes.

"Lydia?" Carter said, "What's going on?"

"Cat, you have done so well, to make so much progress with your recovery. But, I've been thinking of you too much as a patient and not enough as a man. It's quite obvious from the bathroom what you need, and your old friend Lydia, is just the woman to provide it."

Lydia removed her knickers last of all and, lifting the duvet for access, she climbed in next to Carter. She reached across his chest and cuddled close to him, then trailed her hand down his body to feel a once familiar stiffening in her palm.

"Let me do the work Cat," she whispered. "I want you to just relax and enjoy the pleasure, the sheer satisfaction of relief, after all these weeks."

Carter's hands instinctively went behind his head, and his right shoulder caused him to wince, as he felt Lydia slide her face down his body to engulf his bulging erection.

After she had him fully aroused, she threw back the covers and mounted him wantonly, wrapping her firm thighs around his hips, working up and down on him, gasping as each thrust went deep. Carter moved his arms forward to grasp her waist as the momentum built further. She grabbed his hands and held them tightly in front of her as they both groaned with the delight of the unleashed feelings. Lydia could feel the extra stiffening within her and knew he was about to come. She forced her body down his shaft as deeply as she could and stopped moving, just as Carter let out a growling moan and exploded inside her. They did not move for some time, just luxuriated in his continuing spasms as he emptied himself completely and sighed with each subsiding pulse.

They were still holding hands and Carter looked into Lydia's eyes with such gratitude it was almost physical. "Of course, now I feel really guilty," he said, "You didn't even come."

"Today wasn't about me, Carter. But trust me, I truly enjoyed it, giving you that much pleasure, which you so desperately needed. I feel fantastic, and...who knows, you might get a chance to pay me back? But, now it's sleep time, do you want me to go?"

He helped her down onto the mattress, and wrapped his arm around her shoulders. "No. Please stay here, next to me. Thank you Lydia, thank you."

They slept for three hours, waking in the deep dark evening, and seeing a magnificent array of stars through the bedroom window. The heavy clouds had all drifted away and the complete lack of light from the earth gave total clarity to every pinprick of light, right around the horizon. Carter and Lydia lay there without speaking, just enjoying the view and the comforting warmth of each other.

Later they had tea and toast and took the modest supper back to bed, to continue watching the night sky.

"Cat?" Lydia ventured, over the rim of her mug of tea, "This doesn't have to change anything, you know?"

"Sure Lids, I know. Tomorrow we'll get back to the book, but...?"

"But, what?"

"It's just that I like having you here and, now that I can pretty much fend for myself, I'm worried that you might want to get back to London."

"Sometimes Carter, you can be a complete arse, can't you? I like being here, and we make so much better progress by working together, I wouldn't dream of going back until the job is done."

"So, living at the edge of the known world isn't a problem to you, then?"

"Not if you're with me... Cat. Now, about that orgasm you owe me...?"

"Consider it done..." Carter replied as he reached for her body.

+

The next morning, they were up early, having spent the first night together in Carter's bed since Lydia had been at the cottage. They made coffee together, him in his dressing gown, her in one of his old army tee shirts, then took it to the study. There was an air of playful confidence between them and they smiled at each other often.

"Lids," Carter said, "I think I'll get back to using the laptop today. Dictating is all very well but harder for me to edit, and it can interrupt the flow, when I mess about with the MemoMate. I really fancy getting back to actually writing."

"Well, I think I can vouch for the improvements in your right arm, Cat! So go for it. I'll carry on editing the previous chapter on my laptop."

So the tone of the day's work was set and, with scarcely a glance at the developing daylight through the window, Carter started tapping away at his keyboard. Lydia snuggled down on the settee with her laptop, having earlier folded the bed parts away, and casually began re-reading chapter ten, polishing it with odd revisions as she went.

With a break for a sandwich brunch around noon, they continued in similar vein right through to the early evening, when Lydia declared that she was done and was going for a shower. Declining her invitation to 'scrub her back', Cat said he had about another hour to go on his first draft for chapter eleven.

She returned two hours later having showered, caught up with emails from London, and watched the TV news. Carter triumphantly punched the air gingerly with his right arm, swivelled his chair, and stepped out of it. "It's all yours, Lids." He then limped out of the study in the direction of the bedroom, sat on the rowing machine in the corner and began thirty minutes physio for his hip and shoulder.

Lydia slipped into Cat's very warm chair and looked at the screen. She scrolled back to the chapter eleven start point and began to read. She was immediately reminded of being an eight year old girl when she read Carter's descriptions of the great sense of energy that seemed to grip Britain in the spring of 1982. The flag waving, the TV pictures of the warships and passenger ships heading out of Portsmouth, to the sound of military bands. She could just remember the grave voices of politicians on the radio news, as Britain flexed the last of its Imperial muscles.

She laughed out loud at the unruly cheeriness and banter that Carter described as 3rd Battalion, the Parachute Regiment (or 3 Para, as the newspapers loved to call it), enjoyed the tropics on the great P&O cruise liner SS Canberra. She remembered the tune, although at the time she had not understood the words, sung by Cat's colleagues on the news and which he had now written on the screen. She murmured the song to herself, to Cliff Richard's melody of 'Summer Holiday'... "We're all going to the, Malvinas. We're all going to kill a, Spic or two. Fun and laughter on our, Summer Holiday... For Me-ee and You-oo-oo... For Me and You." Typical British soldiers, on the eve of battle, she thought. It was interesting to read that for the officers, according to Carter, they still didn't think it would come to a fight. They thought that in the modern world, diplomacy would prevail, but clearly that was not to be.

Carter didn't dwell on the wider conflict in his words, just tended to focus on himself and his surroundings, similar to much of the rest of the book so far, she thought. In spite of that, he did have a good way of making the key issues relevant, and she was pleased to see examples of how the mood of everyone in his battalion changed after the sinking of the Belgrano (joy of success) then the sinking of HMS Sheffield (realisation that they were in for a real scrap).

She enjoyed the way he tried to keep his men motivated, ignoring his own limitations at mixing with people and relying on the trained sense of disciplined professionalism that his men had. He constantly appealed to their competitive nature, especially against other troop contingents on board, and sharpened their appetite for, what was increasingly looking like, a tough fight ahead.

When the Canberra arrived at San Carlos, on the west coast of East Falkland, they were about sixty miles west of their objective, Port Stanley. Cat related how he had briefed his men and diffused their moaning about going in at, what they saw as, the back door. *'Yes Gentlemen,'* he had written, *'We could, of course, have just steamed into Port Stanley, taken heavy fire and loads of casualties, and watched as our bombardment killed hundreds of civilians. But, we are not Americans, we will therefore adopt a degree of subtlety. Plus the fact that you boys get the chance for a lovely nature ramble across the moors, before the punch up at the end!'*

There had been much chaos at the disembarkation of the

battalion into San Carlos. Being paratroopers, they had never trained for an amphibious assault, and were teased mercilessly by the Royal Marines to whom this was a walk in the park. The best thing was that the Argentinians had left this part of the coast virtually undefended and, apart from a series of air attacks on the ships, the troops got safely onto the bridgehead ashore.

She read how the troops who had landed were chronically short of much heavy equipment and even some basic supplies, although bizarrely the battalion's case of condoms had arrived safe and sound - for the sheep or the penguins - Cat assumed. The days went on without any movement forward and the weather got continually colder and wetter. Lydia read how, eventually, the Lieutenant Colonel in charge of the battalion had called Carter to him late one evening, and read intently from there on.

"How are things, Captain Talbot?"

"As well as can be expected, Sir."

"Men Ok?"

"May I speak freely Sir?"

"Of course, Talbot, you know me."

"Thank you Sir. The men are cold, wet and worst of all, bored, Sir."

"As are we all, Talbot. But look here, I've been talking to Major Brindle and he's agreed to release you, and one hand picked platoon from his company, if you fancy a special mission?"

"Whatever it is Sir, I'll do it. Anything's to be preferred to sitting around in the cold here for another moment."

"Good man, Talbot. Let's look at the map."

Lieutenant Colonel Baxter explained that once the equipment was up to scratch, and they got the green light from the Task Force Commander, the whole battalion was going to march across the island towards Stanley, meet up with reinforcements from the Welsh Guards shortly landing at Bluff Cove, and tackle the main Argentinian Force currently spread between the hills around the capital. In the meantime, 2 Para were going to neutralise the Argie contingent at Goose Green to the south, then join in at Stanley later.

"But what about the north of the island, Sir."

"That's where you come in Talbot. We didn't think there were any Argies up there. The only settlement of any kind is at Seal Inlet, diagonally north-east of here. A real dead and alive place, with barely a handful of farm buildings. No phone contact but naval intelligence say that they picked up a radar signal of something about the size of a large trawler going in there yesterday. One of the Harriers has flown over, a fishing boat is moored there, but the pilot couldn't see much sign of life. I want you to check it out, please Talbot. Better safe than sorry, eh? If there are any Argies, then please deal with them, before joining us to what will then be your south-east, on the push to Stanley."

"When you say 'deal with them' Sir, what do you have in mind?"

"Use your initiative Talbot, that's what her Majesty pays you for. Carry on."

I immediately went to the officer in charge of number two platoon and told him that I was taking his team on a special mission leaving at 0400 the next morning. Lieutenant Donoghue's first reaction was to complain that he hadn't been consulted, to which I explained that I was consulting him now. We had a twenty-five mile yomp ahead of us and he should get the whole team to take some sleep now, while they had the chance. I told him that we must take whatever we needed with us, as HQ would be busy with every helicopter and every gun for the main assault. I added that I would brief him further on the march, then went to my tent and climbed into my sleeping bag.

The rain at 03:45 next morning, as the platoon assembled in flashlight order, was virtually horizontal but, heavily laden with kit, weapons, and ammunition, we set off on time. I shared our objective with Donoghue and we cross checked our compass heading regularly until a grey half-light enabled us to take visual compass bearings. In case of any Argentine air intervention, I ordered the men to spread out widely while all staying in view of each other. I sent one section of six men forward to act as scouts with a rendezvous every hour.

Even though the rain stopped by mid-morning, the going was tough with the peaty ground very boggy and there was no chance of normal infantry pace being maintained, let alone the light infantry pace that was preferred. It was therefore not until around 15:00, with the light already fading, that two of our scouts hurried back towards the main body of the platoon with news that the settlement was in sight over the next ridge of moorland. They reported no sign of the enemy, or anyone else.

On top of the ridge, I viewed the half a dozen farm buildings through binoculars, as did Lieutenant Donoghue. "I reckon we've got half an hour of daylight, Sir," he said.

"Agreed. No time for fannying about then! I think skirmishing order Mr Donoghue, and an assault with me using the right wing as the lead with one section, followed by the centre, with two sections and the heavy machine gun for support. You can go left with the scouting section and cut them off from the boat, if they are here and try to make a run for it. If I was in charge of defending this position I'd be on their left in what looks like concrete sheep sheds. Exactly where I'll be heading. Be ready to move in two minutes please."

120 seconds later, six men and I, with weapons cocked, started to fan out to the right of the ridge and headed towards the outside wall of the sheep sheds, where there appeared to be no openings. A glance to my left showed the two support sections spread out and walking, crouched, towards the large corrugated iron barn in the centre of the buildings. It was getting too gloomy to see Donoghue and his section away to the left, circling towards the shore line.

We were about 75 yards from the sheds when I saw a tiny flash seeming to come from within their timber roof. The cry from the man to my left, as he was hit in the chest by a bullet, coincided with the sound of the gunshot as it reached me. Immediately there were more rifle shots and another man went down, further to my left. "Get to the wall!" I screamed and sprinted for the solid concrete as more shots thudded into the soft ground I was trying to sprint through. As I ran, I could see that the defenders had cut small holes in the soft timber apex end of the roof and were sniping through them. By the time I successfully threw myself against the wall, I had only two comrades left standing and we all tried to regain our breath from the dash through the treacly ground.

By now, our support section had found a semblance of cover for their heavy machine gun and were pouring fire at the roof. I could hear the splintering of wood above me as the heavy rounds burst through the timber, hopefully putting an end to the threat from up there.

I signalled to the two men next to me, Lance Corporal Leaver and Private Webb, that we were going to move to the right, along the wall. I led the way and moved the 40 yards or so along the rough concrete wall, then peered around the corner. I couldn't see much in the gloom but the firing had now stopped and I could hear muffled voices to my left. I strained to hear and although I didn't understand the words, could make out that they were Spanish and close, possibly in the first or second open bay of the sheds. This would give them a sideways view to the middle of the settlement and they could therefore ambush our support team as they came forward.

I looked back at Leaver and Webb, pointed to a grenade on my webbing, then around the corner, and raised three gloved fingers, before pointing back at myself. The men understood and quickly passed a grenade each to me while I unclipped my own. I slung my automatic rifle across my chest, then slid forward along the solid end wall crouching as I got to the front corner. I was slightly below the level of the sheep bay walls and could just see the gun barrel ends resting on the top. I had already removed the pins from the grenades and gently lobbed them over the wall where the guns were visible, then moved quickly back behind the end wall, gesturing to my men to get down. As our chests thudded to the ground, three explosions in rapid succession came from behind the wall. We leapt up and around the corner, brandishing our weapons and taking the first three bays as our targets, ran through the openings in the low wall and sprayed long bursts around the smoking interiors.

The scene in the first bay, when I eased my finger off the trigger, was of smoke, blood and concrete dust, all conspiring with the growing darkness, to mask the dead and injured men within. There were two of each, and one of the injured raised one arm towards me. I levelled my gun at him and fired a shorter burst around the bay to finish them off. I then went into Webb's bay and did the same, before reloading and going into the third bay, where Leaver, his drooping SLR still smoking, was holding a man by the arm. His three companions were lying in unnatural poses and clearly dead while Leaver was shouting into his captive's face. "How many here? Which buildings?" The man was spluttering words we couldn't understand. I looked towards the other buildings in what little light was left and made a decision. I told Leaver to let him go and gestured to him with my rifle, towards the back of the bay. The pitch and volume of his voice increased and he kept shouting, "Me rindo, Me rindo". I shot him quickly, and he slumped to the straw lined floor. Webb had joined us as Leaver asked me what 'Me rindo' meant. "I surrender, I think, Lance Corporal... Right, where are those support sections?"

Ten minutes later the sporadic sounds of gunfire had ceased and Sergeant McEvoy ran up in the dark to report that the barn and farmhouse had been cleared of the enemy by the support sections and that his team had suffered only two casualties killed with minor wounds to three more. He estimated enemy dead at fifteen with no survivors. I made sure he checked the roof space above the sheep sheds and they had found four dead snipers up there. Leaver had gone to check on the three men hit during the attack on the sheds and reported that they had all died.

The combined platoon now swept towards the shore and in their flashlights could make out the fishing boat at mooring just off a tiny timber jetty. On the landward side was a small timber hut and there they found Donoghue's section, sheltering from the bitter wind blowing in from the

South Atlantic. There were also two Argie conscripts sat on the floor in a corner of the hut. "Report please Lieutenant?" I asked.

"We swept the shore side of the settlement as ordered and met no resistance. The farmer and his family, according to Pedro here, went to Port Stanley at the time of the invasion. These two were guarding the boat and didn't put up a fight. We took up covering positions and waited until you showed up, Sir."

"Thank you Mr Donoghue. As your team haven't had much to do, you can dig graves for the five men we lost, and clear any enemy bodies from the farmhouse. We'll squeeze in there tonight and rejoin the battalion tomorrow."

"And what about the prisoners Sir? One speaks some English, might be useful?"

"I'll deal with them Lieutenant. Carry on."

Later in the farmhouse, Corporal Bunce - the radio operator - got me connected to Baxter at Battalion HQ on a scrambled net. I told him what had happened at the farm including casualty details for both sides and about our two prisoners. I passed on what little the English speaker had told us. That they'd been ordered to take the boat from Stanley and wait at the farm until the British attack started, then act against their northern flank and harass their advance. He had also confirmed that during our attack on the farm, they'd had no time to send a radio message.

The Lieutenant Colonel informed me that the advance was starting early tomorrow and that we should rendezvous with them asap by heading due south from our position at first light. He made it clear that we mustn't be late, the attack was going to need every man. It was, he said, important that the Argies didn't know what had happened to their recon force at Seal Inlet. The more uncertainty and confusion the better.

"Roger that, Sir. See you tomorrow. And, Sir, what shall I do with the prisoners? Over."

"I think you know well enough, Talbot. Roger and Out."

I needed to act quickly, before doubt and sentiment clouded my thinking. I gave Bunce the mouthpiece and left the farmhouse, heading for the hut in the light of a torch and bent almost double in the gale force wind. Two Privates were guarding the prisoners inside the hut and I dismissed them both. As they grabbed their gear and weapons and went to join their mates in the farmhouse, I noticed that the Argies were both asleep on the floor with a couple of greatcoats over them. I withdrew my sidearm from its holster and held it inches from the first ones forehead. I fired, a red hole flowered instantly, then I moved my aim, pulling the trigger again, just as the second one's eyes opened. His head jerked back, some spatters of blood sprayed my hand, and both men were no more.

Lydia sat back in the swivel chair and rubbed her eyes, they felt damp. She blinked a few times then went back to the screen. There were a few more pages of how Cat's platoon had completed their mission by joining their colleagues and taking part in the battle for Mount Longdon. Then there was the liberation of Stanley and the Argentinian surrender.

It was only as the chapter closed, with Captain Carter Talbot in reflective mood on the journey home from the Falklands, that he even tried to analyse his actions at Seal Inlet. His commander had stressed what was important, he had no choice that wouldn't have risked the lives of his comrades, and he'd had the courage to make the tough decision and carry it out himself, rather than order someone else to do the dirty work. His overall professional approach had earned him praise from Baxter and the likelihood of promotion. But, his reputation as a cold, hard, bastard was now a legend; even in a regiment full of cold, hard, bastards.

Lydia finished the chapter and turned off the laptop. She needed a drink, so grabbed a bottle from the whisky shelf and put a splash in a tumbler then drank it in one gulp. She knew she couldn't discuss this chapter with Cat at the moment, she also knew that there was some editing to do tomorrow. What she needed, was to let her mind settle. She went into the bedroom and saw that Cat was already asleep. She climbed in on the window side of the bed and looked out into the dark sky, only a few stars were peeping through tonight and she kept her back to Carter as she sought sleep, by looking at them all in turn.

-+-

Chapter Thirty Six

Matthew and Dominic cringed over their pizza in the New Scotland Yard civilian canteen, where a tinsel draped speaker was pumping out the festive spirit to the poor suffering patrons. They stopped trying to converse, as Wizard declared their undying wish that 'It Could be Christmas Everyday', and grimly munched at the pepperoni and chilli, 15 inch special. They had plastic bottles of Coke Zero to help lubricate this feast and kept swigging at them in between wiping their hands on paper napkins.

The softer tones of 'The Little Drummer Boy' gave them a chance to hear each other and Matt volunteered the opinion that, although it was a bummer to get the whole weekend's surveillance shift that Friday before Christmas, it meant that they were off duty for the whole of Yuletide and right into the New Year.

"Doesn't matter much to me, I'm not into all that partying stuff."

"Fucking hell Dom, don't you ever just let yourself go? It's Christmas! Are your parents as boring as you? Do the Turner family just treat the whole holiday as some kind of 'Geekathon'? Sitting around in dreadful jumpers, setting computer riddles to each other, over mugs of Ovaltine in your haunted Suffolk village?"

"We certainly don't embrace all that fake jollity and rank commercialism. It's more a time to relax for us. Most people eat and drink too much, and spend money they don't have, constantly telling themselves what a great time they're having. We go for walks, read books, take it in turns cooking, and have plenty of time to ourselves. For me, it's the only time of year when I don't turn on any computers...and it's all the better for that."

"All the best with that Dommo, I'm gonna be doing some big time drinking. Me and some of the lads are on a great Christmas Eve pub crawl in Islington, chase some birds, hopefully get a shag, pass out, then wake up just in time for turkey and all the trimmings at me Mum's the next day."

Further discussion was prevented by Wham coming on the canteen stereo with 'Last Christmas', prompting the young men to leave the last two slices of lunch and move towards the lifts. Back in their basement they donned their big headphones and started scanning the various devices for all the live cases that they were looking after.

When Dominic had started in the department about 18 months before, he had been genuinely surprised at the sheer number of surveillance operations that were going on at the same time. He had done a spell in the phone tapping team, along the corridor, but preferred this part of the basement. Much of it was automated, in terms of digital recording and filtering for key words by the integral programmed software. But many of the remote devices might sit in place for days, weeks, or even months before the voice activated switches would turn them 'live'. It was then that the boys would need their instincts to see if this was something important or just more nondescript chatter of no import to the SOCA, whose very expensive baby, their basement control room happened to be. On a weekend shift like this they had access to a small bedroom, through a door at the back, to get some sleep while still being near their equipment for three days.

By around 3.30pm, all their checking routines had been completed and Matt started 'dipping'. This meant he would flick from one device input to another seeing when they were last activated or checking if they had become redundant. Without transmitting, the devices could last up to a year, just waiting for someone to talk near enough to start them up. After that, the tiny battery would fail. That failure would come much earlier, in line with the more talking, and therefore the more transmitting, that was done.

All this was displayed in a matrix on Matt and Dom's screens. The live devices, with code numbers linked to electronic case files, showed up as green. The devices that were potentially active but not used since installation, glowed yellow, and the 'dead' ones that had no power remaining, appeared in red. There were a few white squares for the addition of new devices. Dominic reviewed the overall grid while Matt continued his dipping and updated the case file records with transcripts, where appropriate. Near the middle of the 72 coloured squares, Dom saw a yellow square start flashing green. He immediately touched the screen and the flashing green became solid. Out of habit, he adjusted his headphones around his ears, and turned up their volume while waving to Matt and telling him, "We've got a bite!" over his screen.

They slipped into a seamless procedure where the 'spotter', in this case Dominic, focused on the conversation, while the 'recorder', Matthew, did the background checks so that they were listening, armed with the right context. Matt clicked on the new green square twice and the case file came up on screen, neatly indexed and automatically directed to a device log. Matt went straight to the case summary notes page and started smiling broadly as he scanned the headlines of the case.

Dom enquired, "What are you grinning at, mate?"

Matt completed his early scan then responded, "Do you remember that attempted drug bust, down at Rainham Marshes a few weeks ago?"

"The sack full of cocaine, that turned out to be horse shit! How could I forget?"

"It's the same case."

"Hold on though, I remember, we had that car wired stiff, but the suspect had rumbled the fact that there were bugs all over it and sold it. We spent much of the next couple of weeks listening to some Bengali restaurant owners from Hackney discussing the price of onions, in their own language, as they drove around their East End curry house empire."

"According to the notes, apart from the car bugs, there were two portable voice activated transmitters, and they have never gone live... Until now."

"So what? Are you telling me that we're now going to get another fascinating recipe for Lamb Dhansakh?"

"Let's listen and find out."

The boys stopped talking and listened intently. All they heard initially was mumbling and a occasional wooden banging sound. Then, the unmistakable sound of a long metal zip being operated, followed by, "We can get rid of all this crap, but the bag is sound, I'll use it for the trip, Josh."

Dom threw his hands wide and asked Matt, "What's the story?"

"This is a special one Dom, the file is coded 'SIS' so it's got an MI6 connection. You'd better let Seagram know about it."

Using his cursor at the edge of the screen, Dom clicked on

a phone icon, then on the strip of blue with the white letters spelling out 'Det. Supt. Seagram'.

"Seagram," blustered the voice in Dom's ear.

"Good afternoon Sir, Turner here...in surveillance Sir. We've got a new chat link open in the Muwera file. Thought we should er...let you know, Sir."

"Thanks Turner, anything unusual?"

"Not sure Sir, sounds like the talkers are planning a trip."

"Voice recognition checked out yet?"

"Mat... I mean Collins is on it Sir..." Dom lifted his head, "Matt, voice rec?"

Matthew immediately finished running the disk check against the earlier recordings in the file, and called out, "Yes, it's deffo Georges Muwera."

"Positive ID Sir, Muwera junior."

"Hang on though Turner, I thought all that went cold when he disposed of the car?"

"Indeed Sir, the car bugs have no value now, but according to the file, MI6 also put a P-VAT in the lining of each of the two dead guys' holdalls."

"I'll be down."

Twenty minutes later, it was clear to Seagram that Georges Muwera still held a massive grudge against Robin Chancellor. He had, in sometimes clear and sometimes muffled speech, explained to his henchman Joshua, while he put some clothes and other items into the soft leather holdall housing the department's transmitter, that it was about time Pascal was avenged.

Joshua had queried the wisdom of going only a couple of months after the gunfight, pointing out that as an ex MI6 guy, Chancellor was bound to be guarded, or at least watched. Georges had, impatiently, said that's why they were going at Christmas, when there was more chance of any security being slack. And anyway, he had added, that so-called inquiry by the Procurator Fiscal had been carried out in secret, according to the press, because of 'National Security'. The verdict had been unsurprising, one unlawful killing, of the policeman, and two lawful killings, of his brother and Eric. 'No further action would be taken' had been the official published conclusion. This was something that Georges was determined to put right, as he put it, 'Fucking further action would very much be fucking taken!'

The noises from the 'Portable - Voice Activated Transmitter' quietened and, eventually, Seagram got bored with listening to nothing but the vaguest hissing. "This is dynamite boys, keep listening," he ordered them, "We need to know the timings. I'm going to get some foot soldiers deployed."

With that he went to the lift and with mobile phone in hand started calling his team together. In a Spartan meeting room back on the tenth floor, with little more than a large table and chairs plus a rickety old flip chart, the Detective Superintendent instructed two shifts of stake-out on the Muwera house. One of his officers had been involved in keeping the historic case files up-to-date and shared the details of the car that had replaced the blue Range Rover in the Muwera driveway. Now they all knew that they should be on the lookout for a Black Hummer with blacked out windows.

As the first stake-out team headed for Stratford E15, Seagram went back to the basement, stopping on the way at one of the clerical officer's desks in the general administration office and picked something up. He got out of the lift and handed a box of mince pies to Collins and Turner. Before they could say, 'Thank you Sir,' he asked them, "Anything new, lads?"

"Sorry, Detective Superintendent, complete blank," replied Matthew.

"Well apart from the other P-VAT Sir," added Dominic, "The one in the other holdall, it’s gone red Sir."

"What the hell does that mean?"

"It's deactivated Sir, we checked it and got no voice input, then it went red on the screen. The battery can't be exhausted, so it's probably been destroyed, or possibly malfunctioned. We can't tell."

"Do you mean that Muwera has found it?"

"Not necessarily Sir, the bag could have just been thrown away, and crushed or burnt."

"Ok, so we've just got the remaining one to go on, eh boys?"

"Yes Sir."

"And remind me, can we track the P-VAT location."

"Not this model Sir. There is a new one out with built in GPS signalling, but this is a plain old voice transmitter. When the bugging was done on this case a SatNav relay was fitted to the vehicle, so we could track it through that."

"But that was the car that got sold... Never mind, lesson learnt I think. Let me see that file, please Collins."

Matthew flicked the file effortlessly with a touch of his mouse, to a spare terminal on a corner desk and Seagram sat in the chair behind the desk to scan the electronic paperwork.

After a few minutes, he reached for his mobile phone and pressed a few icons before Dom noticed and reminded him that they shouldn't use them down here. Sheepishly remembering the rule that was meant to prevent mobile signals from interfering with the equipment, the Detective Superintendent lifted the desk phone and, using information from his mobile, called a number.

Matt could see their boss listen for a few moments, then he said, "Hello Crabbe, just thought we'd let you know, we've picked up news that Georges Muwera is planning to pay a little Christmas visit on your man in Harris, and I don't think he'll be taking any frankincense or myrrh." There was a break while Seagram nodded pointlessly into the phone, then he finished with, "No definite time or date Commander, we'll keep you posted if we hear anything more. Best regards of the Season."

At the other end of the phone, Toby Crabbe hung up the receiver and immediately looked up Billy Keilloh's number. When he got through to D I Keilloh, Crabbe asked him how the 'discreet guarding' of ex-agent Chancellor had been going. Keilloh explained that it was a pretty straightforward process. As Crawnish was at the end of the only road in those parts, they had a car permanently stationed at the Eastern end of that road where it joined the main road, between Stornoway in Lewis and Tarbert in Harris. There was no other practical way to get there, so the officer on watch only had to check the registration number of any vehicle he didn't recognise over the radio, and take action if that check threw up anything suspicious. The almost complete absence of any tourist traffic at this time of year made the job even easier, if staggeringly boring, finished the Inspector.

"Ok, thanks Billy. We've got it on good authority that our man may expect an unwelcome visitor, sometime over Christmas. I've yet to speak to him. After I have, I'll email you with more details and what we're thinking of doing. Just keep your boys on their toes, could you old chap? Thanks again."

Toby's next call was to Carter Talbot. "Merry Christmas Talbot," he said after hearing the ring tone end, "Crabbe here."

"Hello Toby, and Season's Greetings to you too." came the somewhat feminine voice answer down the phone.

"Oh, hello Lydia, wasn't expecting you to pick up."

"Cat's on the rowing machine again," she laughed, "I'll get him."

Once Crabbe had shared the news, Carter's immediate reaction was, "Bring it on Toby, he'll get the same as his brother got, as will any two-bit thugs he brings along for the ride."

"Yes, Major. That's what I thought you'd say..."

"Not a Major any more, sadly. Otherwise I'd get some mines laid and prepare a platoon defence to make sure that nobody got more than a yard or two over my perimeter."

"Indeed, Talbot. But, and this is a big 'but', there's to be no more disturbances of that sort. The Service can't let the Hebrides be turned into a kind of Scottish Kosovo, where there are shootouts every few weeks. I'm afraid you'll need to get away for a while, take the delightful Lydia somewhere romantic, come to London for Christmas, whatever. You're just not staying anywhere near Harris until this threat has been...dealt with. Clear?"

"What will you do?"

"Need to know basis Talbot, best you aren't in the loop."

"I suppose that's your last word on the subject, Commander?"

"Correct."

"Roger that, we'll pack tonight and leave tomorrow."

-+-

Chapter Thirty Seven

It was the next morning, Saturday 20th December 2014, and over three thousand miles away, when Nicole and Shakespeare Kwizera sat down for breakfast by their swimming pool as the early sunlight worked its way down the windows and walls towards the water. Since Shakespeare's return to the house, the mornings had assumed something of a pattern. He and his mother would always be up at dawn and enjoy fruit, coffee and pastries by the pool on their own. They could talk without fear for at least a couple of hours before Alphonse and Milton even thought of getting up, and be out of their way by the time they did make an appearance.

The house had become something of a prison for the family. Alphonse had demanded that none of them was to be allowed to leave their home until he deemed it was safe. He had enforced this by openly arming the askaris and locking away the keys for all the estate vehicles. He had forbidden any of them to have mobile phones, disabled the landlines except for the one in his study, and taken away their laptops. He let Nicole and Shakespeare retain their Kindles so that they could read without any risk of sending messages, but would not allow them any other hand held electronic devices. He made a point of having the house-girls searched for messages whenever they left the house.

Nicole and Shakespeare were, of course, fully aware that this was nothing to do with their security, but all about curtailing their freedom. Over the weeks since the family had been reunited, Alphonse had clearly sensed Shakespeare's antipathy towards him, and had lived with Nicole's for many years. His main fear was that they would abandon him and escape their gilded cage. Milton was allowed more flexibility but even he would always be accompanied by one of Alphonse's loyal and armed guards if he went onto the estate, and not allowed further.

The paranoid behaviour of Mr Kwizera Senior had even resulted in a reduction in the number of comfort visits to the house, by selected prostitutes. In fact, the two who had stayed last night were only the second pair since the new regime had begun, and Milton had not been allowed to share their skills.

Shakespeare poured himself some more pineapple juice from a glass jug and, in a low voice, asked his mother, "Is it safe to talk?"

Nicole gazed casually around and saw that the two kitchen house-girls were sitting on the other side of the pool, in the shade. "Yes," she replied.

"Have you done it?"

"I have... Here." Nicole slid a newspaper across to her son and he opened the front page as if glancing at a story on page 3. There he saw a blue airmail letter with a single word on it. He re-folded the newspaper and went back to his juice.

"I have mine, and an envelope still open, in my dressing gown. I'll put yours inside it" he told her, before asking, "When do think will be a good time...to get the help?"

"Well, he usually lets them have some breakfast, so wait around here and you should get a chance."

Shakespeare let his breakfast settle, had an invigorating swim in the biting cold water then settled down on a sun bed, in his big towelling robe, to enjoy an eBook. Nicole stayed with him for an hour or so, then retired to her room, mainly to avoid her husband and other son if they decided to make an appearance.

The Persian hordes were giving the Spartans a tough time of it, in the book on Thermopylae which Shakespeare was reading, by the time two very tall, bikini clad girls in their early twenties sauntered out to the pool on high heels and holding robes. One was very black, like an Ethiopian, the other also African but much lighter, as if some European content had played a historic part in her ancestry. They were both gorgeous and Shakespeare would have been aroused had it not been for the thought that his father had been inside both of them the night before, and probably this morning as well. Nevertheless, he had a task to perform and for that he must talk to them.

"Good morning Ladies," he smiled from behind his book, "Are you well?"

The Ethiopian looking one adjusted the sunglasses on her head and settled back on a sun bed without reply. Her colleague smiled back and said, "We're fine, thanks. I'm Monique," she added, coming over and holding out her beautifully manicured hand.

Shakespeare took her hand in his and gestured to the next sun bed. "Why don't you sit here?" As she settled her shapely bottom on the bed, Shakespeare gestured to one of the house-girls to bring drinks.

Over juice and coffee, he made small talk with the hooker and tried to put her at her ease. She clearly knew how to talk to men and complimented him on how handsome he was while making sure her bulging breasts did some of the talking too. After half an hour, he dropped his voice so that the Ethiopian couldn't hear him, and whispered to Monique, "Would you like to earn some extra money this morning?"

She seemed to shy away at this question and replied, also

in a whisper, "The thing is... We're both really sore this morning, Alphonse is big and strong and has pumped us both hard... I could use my mouth on you, if you'd like that?"

Shakespeare smiled at her and held his hand up to stop her saying any more, then whispered again, "Another time perhaps. No, this is for another job, and payment comes in two parts. Come with me," he added, motioning her towards the bathroom adjacent to the pool, and taking her inside. "I've got a secret letter which must remain secret from everyone here. I'll give you 50,000 shillings now if you'll smuggle it out and post it for me. And another 50,000 bob, the next time you're here, once I know it's been safely received."

Monique looked into his eyes and saw a genuine need for help. She silently held out her hand and fixed her gaze on him. He pulled out a pale blue envelope with writing on it and passed it to her. In a flash it was down the front of her bikini, and her hand was out again. Shakespeare felt in his robe pocket and passed her fifty notes in a bundle, which she put in the pocket of the robe over her arm. "One of those will be more than enough for the postage," he said, "Thanks Monique."

"It will be my pleasure, Mister Shakespeare. Now, are you sure I can't give you pleasure, it would be on the house?" Monique grinned as sank down to her haunches in front of him.

-+-

Chapter Thirty Eight

The sun that was already warming the Kwizera home in north-west Kenya was nowhere to be seen at the Muwera residence in Stratford E15, being three hours behind East Africa, that same Saturday morning. It was still dark when the inhabitants began stirring. Tim had already opened the heavy double garage doors to the left flank of the house, reversed the new Hummer inside and re-secured the doors from the inside. The SOCA stake-out team, watching sleepily from an unmarked car halfway down the street, took notice of this and called Seagram at the Yard. He had been dozing at his office desk and, in turn, went to the basement and told the duty operator, Dominic.

Matt and Dom had taken it in turns to use the sleeping quarters in their basement during the night, and Dom quickly woke his colleague up with the news that there might be developments in the Muwera case. They quickly checked that the holdall based P-VAT was still active, and listened carefully for any clues as to what might be happening.

It wasn't long before the faint hissing of the live device was silenced by a grumbling voice growing louder as if it was getting nearer the bag, "Don't know why we have to leave so fuckin' early," the boys heard through their headphones.

"You're always bloody moaning, Tom, ain't yer?" another voice replied, then continued, "Look on the bright side, they'll be no bleedin' Christmas shoppers out this early. Traffic will be a doddle. Come on, let's get this lot into 'The Tank', 'e wants us to go before it gets light. Just time for a bacon sarnie, then we can get going."

Dominic and Matthew then heard little more than some

doors opening and closing, some sort of electronic double beep, and some dull thuds, followed by a heavy thud, presumably as the holdall was thrown somewhere with a solid base. The final sound was the distinctive clunk of a car door or boot lid closing.

"Sounds like the trip they mentioned is getting underway, Mr Seagram Sir."

"I think you're right, Turner. Tell the 'Watchers' to follow discreetly, please."

Twenty minutes later, the garage doors opened again and the Hummer emerged. The doors closed behind it automatically, and the front gates of the drive silently opened to allow the ungainly looking vehicle to take to the roads of London. The stake-out pair had already turned their car around and called in as the Hummer went past them, "Target vehicle mobile, number of occupants unknown as windows blacked out. We are following as instructed. Will report heading as we go."

+

In Crawnish, Lydia woke up to the faint snoring sound coming from Carter who had slipped onto his back in the night. She had shared his bed for the last two weeks and it had been, to her, a very satisfying fortnight. His rehabilitation had continued and, although he retained a slight limp from adjusting to the new hip, his mental strength and determined approach to exercise had got him in good shape. She smiled as her hand found that he was erect and she stroked him very gently, knowing that he enjoyed waking up to sex.

The snoring stopped, as the use of her hand had the desired effect, and he turned his body towards her. She opened her legs as he manoeuvred on top of her and entered her effortlessly. His pelvis moved in a steady rhythm and she put her hands around his back, holding him as he brought her to an orgasm, just before he froze in his own. He relaxed his body on hers and she enjoyed the comforting weight.

"Good Morning Lids," he whispered in her right ear, "How are you?"

"An awful lot better than I was five minutes ago...thanks for asking, Mr Talbot."

He rolled off her and lay on his back again. "Glad to have been of service, Ms Hockley-Roberts."

"So, we packed last night, remind me of the plan?"

"Well, Crabbe insists that we are too big a risk to the peaceful security of the islands if we stay here and, after a couple of whiskies last night, you invited me to stay at your house for Christmas. Apparently, my idea of a trip to the Caribbean for the festivities wasn't a good one as 'we'd get too distracted from the book' and you are insisting on continued progress, Christmas or not."

"Correct, we're over halfway through, but mustn't slacken the pace. And now you're fit again, you've got no excuse for malingering."

"Understood. Right, there's a lunchtime flight to Glasgow and we'll be in London by tonight. You make breakfast and I'll just lie here, recovering from being woken up by a sex-crazed literary agent."

The hurled pillow from Lydia made, to her, a satisfying contact with Carter's face and she donned a bathrobe to go and put the kettle on.

+

Ten minutes after his Hummer had left the house, Georges Muwera finished getting dressed and walked along the first floor landing to knock on Joshua's door. "Come on Josh, I want get away at first light," he called through the panelling. "Ok Boss," came a muffled reply.

Georges was nursing a cup of black coffee in the kitchen when a barely awake Joshua arrived, his dreadlocks looking way beyond tousled and wearing a bizarre combination of a multi coloured jacket over two white tee shirts, with tight trousers in a completely different rainbow of psychedelic hues. The whole outfit set off with a blue and white Millwall FC scarf.

"Determined not to get noticed today then Josh?" Georges observed.

"Low profile, that's me boss!" Josh replied, "Did the boy's get safely away?"

"They did, and I could see the Filth following from my bedroom window."

"How did you know, Boss, that they would be watching?"

"They regularly keep an eye on us Josh, more so since what happened to Pascal and Eric. Even if I hadn't recognised the car in the street, why would two blokes be sitting in the car all evening in December? We're never going to avoid it. We just have to try and box clever sometimes. Right, are you ready?"

"Yes Boss."

"Come on then," said Georges as he went through the kitchen door into the back garden with Joshua following. As they walked quietly across the lawn they could see the first streaks of a watery sun hitting the low clouds from just below the eastern horizon in front of them. They fiddled with the padlock before going through the secluded wooden gate in the rear hedged wall, along a path, and down a few shallow steps to a concrete jetty abutting the River Lee Navigation. 'Just A Drop' was riding high and making no noise as her mooring ropes held her gently to the rubber cladding of the jetty wall. Her bow was facing south and the men clambered aboard, the only baggage being the leather man bag on a strap over Georges' shoulder. His dark jeans, thick navy jumper and heavy black suede clothes contrasting distinctly with Joshua's calypso explosion.

Georges started the twin engines with one turn of the ignition key and kept the throttle on idle while Josh leaned over the bow and then the stern to loosen the ropes and bring them on board. Once he was back in the cockpit, Georges eased the throttle gently forward by less than an inch and they were under way. Their breath frosted on the air in the early sunlight and the engines softly purred, as the cruiser glided downstream with only the smallest of ripples that washed both banks, showing any sign of their passing.

As the river snaked its course southwards and gradually widened, the view of the banks went from residential and light industrial units to larger warehouses and factories. They increased speed the further they went and were cruising modestly at around ten knots when, after about half an hour, they rounded a starboard bend and came to a small area of greenery on the east bank. They could see half a mile ahead, the junction of the creek with the River Thames and Josh dropped speed to manoeuvre towards the stretch of derelict parkland on the port side. Georges dropped four balloon shaped fenders over the port side and adjusted their lines until they were protecting the protruding part of the hull.

At a dead slow pace, Josh bumped the cushioned cruiser against the broken brickwork of the bank and Georges reached out for an iron ladder that was set into the masonry. As he did so, a roaring notice above them made them look up and they saw the fuselage of a twin-engined jet going from east to west as the undercarriage was retracting into its body.

Georges concentrated on his handhold of the ladder and climbed to the top, while Joshua kept the boat steady, then called out, "Don't forget your bag," and hurled it, by the strap, up towards the grassy area above. Georges caught it and called out, "Cheers Josh. Get off home and remember, don't answer the door or phone to anyone if you can help it. Keep that low profile you're so proud about, yeah?"

"You know me Boss," smiled the big Jamaican as he gunned the engine and took a wide turn to starboard, to head back up river.

Georges looked around the familiar weed and rubbish strewn ground and graffiti daubed walls. They had used this place before for discreet pick-ups and drop offs and he knew that a short walk would bring him to some streets and alleyways that, for all the gentrification of London's East End, had been little changed for decades.

He'd been walking for fifteen minutes when he saw a black taxi with its yellow light on. He waved and it slowed to a stop. He leaned in on the passenger side and said, "City Airport, please mate."

"Hop in Guv. Although you could probably walk it from 'ere."

"I was, but couldn't resist seeing a taxi so early on a Saturday. You been out all night?"

"Yeah, so tired I forgot to turn the effin' light off. London City Airport it is."

+

According to the article Georges' assistants had read in *Top Gear*, The General Motors Hummer H2 is the 'must have' vehicle for any high profile club owner/drug dealer. *'It provides the sturdy protection essential in an urban environment where the occupiers can feel safe from external assault. It also gives a clear message that says, 'Don't even think of messing with me, if you know what's good for you.' Apart from this mobile ego trip, what this car also has, is an unquenchable thirst for fuel.'* So it was that after Tim and Tom had completed a full clockwise circuit of the M25, they had to pull into the services on the north side of the Dartford Bridge to refill their petrol tank, at a cost of nearly £200.

Under strict instructions never to leave the vehicle unattended, they took it in turns to go into the services for bathroom visits and return with drinks and snacks. They set off again and the large, SOCA manned Vauxhall faithfully followed. Its crew reported into HQ that they had been given a sightseeing tour of the London Orbital Motorway and, after one lap, were setting off again. They could only confirm two people in the vehicle so far but couldn't be sure of other occupants. They had also topped up their fuel tank, picked up some Coke and chocolate, and asked for advice. "Standby," squawked the radio in reply.

Being a Saturday morning the traffic on the motorway, often horrendous on weekdays, was light and easy to negotiate. The second lap of the M25 took about the same time as the first one at just under two hours. The SOCA officers had received instructions to continue surveillance until further notice and carried on. It was around 12:30 when the Hummer and their, by now reluctant, 'shadows' pulled into the Dartford services for the second time that day.

The tank filling, washroom visiting, and snack buying routine was repeated again and the Hummer sat unmoving for a few minutes. The SOCA officers contacted Seagram and asked for advice over their radio.

"I don't know what to tell you lads. We can't get a peep out of the bag in the boot. The bulkhead must be armoured or something, so no clues from that quarter. They are clearly giving us the run around, but why take the bag unless Georges is with them?"

"Perhaps they know it's bugged Sir?" suggested one of the mobile officers.

"Mm, I just don't know. Can you stop them and see if Muwera is in the car?"

"On what pretext Sir."

"I don't fucking know, just think of something and give me a call back when you've checked them out."

"Right, Sir."

"You heard the officer. Off you go Connell, we might as well do it now."

"But Sarge..."

"Quickly please!"

Detective Constable Connell got grumpily out of the passenger door and set off slowly towards the Hummer, parked about 70 yards away. He was still pondering what to say once he had knocked on the target's window, when, as he squeezed between a van and an estate car about five yards from the Hummer, it suddenly roared into life, lurched forward in a squeal of tyres and a whining growl from the six litre engine.

He jumped towards the monster, as if he could somehow curtail its progress then, as it turned sharply right and raced across the car park, he realised what had happened and turned to run back to his own car. His Sergeant had the window down and was screaming encouragement as he reversed out of the parking space and turned towards Connell. By the time he had thrown himself through the open passenger door, the Hummer was lost from view behind the services buildings, but there was only one direction it could have gone and the SOCA lads followed the exit sign. They got quickly to the roundabout beneath the motorway and then had four choices: M25 South, M25 North, A13 East, or A13 West. It was at that point they realised their chances of picking up the trail weren't good. After a couple of roundabout circuits, they decided that A13 West would be their best chance of picking up the Hummer again, as it was the way back to Stratford. They took that exit and Connell picked up the radio receiver to break the news.

Ten minutes later, a black Hummer was seen emerging from between a couple of parked container trucks in the holding area just before the HGV fuelling station at Dartford Services and it followed the M25 North sign at the exit roundabout. A few miles further on, it took to the A1 northbound and the driver put his foot down.

-+-

Chapter Thirty Nine

Carter and Lydia got to Stornoway airport in plenty of time for the 12:55 flight to Glasgow and, after the usual (to Talbot somewhat ludicrous) security procedures, they settled in the tiny departures bar to pass the time. A couple of gin and tonics each later, they were dipping into a big bowl of salted peanuts and staring out of the window overlooking the terminal apron. A turbo prop plane had started taxiing at the western end of the runway and was creeping steadily towards the buildings. The intermittent sun glinted occasionally off the blue and white livery of the Flybe aircraft and within a few minutes it was pulling up and stopping a stone's throw from the window at which Cat and LHR were sitting.

"I do believe that is our plane, you know," volunteered Carter.

"It certainly seems to be wearing the right colours," agreed Lydia.

"Once the passengers are off, they turn these around so quickly nowadays, we might even get off a bit early? Should be in Hampstead in time for you to take me out for dinner, Lids."

"I suppose, as the host, I should do the decent thing?"

"Completely correct on the etiquette front, Lydia."

They carried on chatting and enjoying each other's company as the aircraft's own internal steps were folded out by a windswept stewardess and the passengers began to disembark. Carter sipped at his icy glass and gazed casually at the line of bag carrying strangers heading quickly towards the arrivals gate into the building, eager to escape the Hebridean wind swirling across the concrete surface.

To Lydia, who was much more interested in her lover than in the freshly arrived visitors from Glasgow, the transformation that she next witnessed in Cat's face was remarkable. From the easy smiling and relaxed demeanour, to slit-eyed, wrinkle-framed, sniper's face in a millisecond. As she followed his gaze to the line of passengers it was clear that his focus of attention was on the round faced, young, black man in dark clothing who was now slipping out of view as he entered the terminal.

"Cat," she said as she grabbed at his arm, "What is it...or rather, who is it?"

Carter said nothing but got out his new Windows Phone, touched various parts of it and scrolled through some images. "Here, Crabbe sent me this, just in case," he said, "A fair likeness, wouldn't you say?" Lydia took the proffered device and looked at the head and shoulders photo. "It certainly looks like the guy in the queue off the plane out there," she confirmed. "But who is it?"

"That, Darling, is none other than Georges Muwera, the younger brother of the main guy I shot and killed two months ago. The bloke that Toby warned us off the island to avoid. He's already here."

"Did he recognise you, do you think?"

"I don't think so, he didn't even glance in my direction."

"So what do we do?"

"I know what I'd like to do."

+

Tim and Tom left the A1(M) near Stilton and, after following a minor road, turned the Hummer down a farm track until it was obscured by a small copse. They both got out and opened the boot from which they withdrew two clean number plates and some tools. With one of them at each end of the car, they changed the plates quickly, replaced the tools, and got back on the motorway, continuing north.

As they cruised along, Tom asked Tim if he thought they had a tail. His colleague answered from the driving seat in the negative upon which Tom got out his mobile and called Georges. "Hello Boss, it's Tom," he said into the phone a few moments later. "How are you getting on?" There were a few seconds of nodding by Tom then he continued, "We did what you told us Boss, gave Plod a right runaround before losing them at Dartford. No sign of them since, and we've just changed the plates. Copies of those on that Hummer we saw in Chelsea last week." More affirmative head movements, then, "SatNav is saying ten hours, Boss. Ferry tomorrow morning, be with you at lunchtime." Nod, nod, nod. "Ok, see you there." Tom touched the end call button.

"Well?" Tim asked.

"The Boss has just landed in Stornoway. The flight connections went great, so 'e sez. We're meeting him at some hotel there tomorrow."

"Right, well we'd better get a move on then, it's still a fucking long way. Oh, and by the way," continued Tim glancing down again at the dashboard, "We're gonna need some more petrol soon."

+

At their screens, Matt and Dom had become marginally excited when they'd heard a change in the noise from the holdall mounted P-VAT. The few moments of boot opening, metallic clinking and scraping noises, boot closing, then a repeat a few minutes later, gave them hope that they might hear something of interest. The fact that they heard no talking meant they had no clue as to where the Hummer might now be.

"Any ideas boys?" Seagram asked.

"Possibly changing a wheel, Sir?" Dom suggested.

"Unlikely, unless they've hit a land-mine on the M25! Have you seen the tyres on those things? What about number plate recognition, lads?"

"We've circulated the number to all forces north of London Sir, but heard nothing back yet," replied Matt.

"Ok gents, keep listening, I'm going for a shower and a very late breakfast. And, speaking of number plates, I'd suggest that you advise all northern forces to look out for any Hummer heading for Scotland, irrespective of the plates, they might have changed them."

+

"Don't do it Cat, you know what Toby said," pleaded Lydia.

"I can't just fly away and leave someone else to clear this up Lids. If I follow him now, at least I can find out where he'll be and pass that on to the local police."

"When do you stop, Carter?"

"What do you mean?"

"When do you stop being the ruthless killer and hero? We've not discussed your Falklands exploits. I've kept quiet and got on with the editing. You killed people in cold blood for God's sake."

"I was doing my job Lydia... Just doing my job."

"But it's not your job any more...is it? You actually enjoy it."

"There's no time for this now, he'll be through arrivals any moment. I've got to follow him, then I promise I'll get the next flight...unless you want to wait for me?"

"I'll expect you when I see you, you've got my address... Bye Carter." With her eyes starting to mist, Lydia Hockley-Roberts turned her back quickly and walked to the end of the hall right next to the departure gate. When she did turn to see if Talbot had reconsidered, he was nowhere to be seen.

Cat had already gone back through security, citing an emergency and advising the checker that he wouldn't be taking the flight after all. He spotted Muwera standing at the 'Carhire Hebrides' desk putting his mobile in his shoulder bag, and stood at the bookstall browsing through paperbacks, as he kept him in sight over the top of titles such as '50 Great Walks in Lewis and Harris'.

As Georges headed out of the main doors, car key in hand, Cat followed discreetly and ambled to his own jeep in the car park, close to the hire car bays. He noticed the double flash of lights and the accompanying beeps from a gold-coloured Honda Civic as Muwera pointed a key at random, then got into his old Suzuki.

It wasn't a long journey to the harbour part of the town and the very light traffic enabled Talbot to hang back and tail the Honda from a less than suspicious distance. After about ten minutes the Honda turned into a side street then the car park at the rear of the Royal Hotel. Cat saw it go in and drove straight past to park a few hundred yards away, outside one of the harbour front pubs.

Carter pulled his mobile from his jacket and opened up his contacts. He hovered a finger over the name Toby Crabbe and pressed it. He hovered again over the options of a mobile number or an SMS, and kept his finger suspended as he gritted his teeth and sucked a deep breath through them. The words of LHR went through his head repeatedly and still he didn't move his finger down. Eventually, Cat moved the finger of his other hand to the master button on the side of the phone and clicked out of the contacts list, pocketing the phone and getting out of the car, in one easy movement.

He limped his way along the harbour, looking at the collection of scruffy fishing boats bobbing slightly on their moorings, and the steam coming from the red funnel of the big CalMac ferry getting ready for its last trip of the day. He reached the main entrance of the Royal and went inside. The dark, timber panelled bar was empty apart from a barmaid and a huge Christmas Tree, superbly lit and decorated, which took up much of the space between the bar tables and reception. He didn't stop at reception but followed the sign on the lintel above the Christmas tree that pointed to 'Car Park'. As he emerged into the daylight he quickly scanned the area and then did it again, more carefully. After a few seconds, one word left his lips, "Bollocks!" before he turned around and retraced his steps.

-+-

Chapter Forty

Having checked into the Royal under a false name and paid cash in advance for his room. Georges Muwera had immediately gone back to the car park and driven off in his rented Honda. He was thinking that, as Tim and Tom wouldn't be arriving until the next day, he could do a bit of scouting to check the lie of the land and make a plan. He had taken a TomTom with the hire car and put 'Crawnish' into the device. It guided him south along the A859 for about three quarters of an hour, then told him to 'turn right in 400 yards'.

As he slowed for the turn, Georges noted a police car parked on the intersection, near the signpost pointing to the right, labelled 'B887 Crawnish'. He took the turn and drove without hesitation along the new, thinner road. Another signpost saying 'Single track road, Use passing places' was on the verge to his left and Muwera cruised sensibly.

The new young PC in the police car, carried out his usual routine and called in the registration number on the radio for a driver check. A few minutes later the message came back that this was a ‘Carhire Hebrides’ vehicle, currently rented to a Mr Nelson Lloyd. This wasn't a name that he had been briefed on, so he logged it, sat back, pulled his standard issue greatcoat around him, and returned to his *Top Gear* magazine.

George continued on the bendy and mountainous road, at one point going through the grounds of an old castle by the sea, before getting into the bleaker countryside beyond. To his left, constant views across the machair scrub to the beaches or rocks abutting the choppy sea. To his right the grey, boulder strewn slopes with no consistent signs of life to adorn them. The weather had worsened to match the lunar type landscape, with any whiteness in the clouds rapidly turning dark as the sun went lower and the wind picked up.

As Muwera rounded yet another bend, he could see faintly in the distance, some buildings scattered along the south side of some small hills. He carried on and eventually got to the village sign 'Crawnish'. He'd checked plenty of news archive and YouTube footage online showing the scene of his brother's shooting, so he changed down into first gear and very slowly drove on from the sign looking for a familiar sight.

Before too long he saw Uisge Bothan to his right and stopped. He took in the high sloping front 'garden' area and the squat solid stone cottage set back in the lee of the hill behind it. This was the place, no doubt in his mind. There was no car in the driveway and just too early for lights in the windows. He didn't really want to advertise his presence by asking in the village and so settled down to watch the house for a while. Until it got dark he told himself, then, if no lights came on, he could risk a quick look around the house to get a feel for it before returning to the hotel for the night. Tomorrow, with muscle and weapons arriving, would come the reckoning.

+

Carter Talbot raced the small jeep as fast as he could on the twisting road south from Stornoway. He realised that if Muwera wasn't in the hotel, then the probable place to find him would be in or near Crawnish.

The little Suzuki engine whined a lot and struggled to gain any uphill momentum, as the relatively flat parts of Lewis gave way to the increasingly hilly Isle of Harris. When he got to the junction with the B887, he pulled over to the police car still sitting there, so that his door was adjacent to the PC's door, and lowered his window, motioning the driver of the police car to do the same.

"Good Afternoon Officer," he said, "Busy afternoon?"

"Not really Mr Chancellor," he replied, "I thought you were away for Christmas Sir?"

"I am, that is, I will be... but I left the presents behind so had to come back for them."

"Bad luck Sir."

"Archie... Can I ask if there's been any Honda's going up the Crawnish road in the last half an hour or so."

"There was a gold Civic about 20 minutes ago, hire car I think. Why Sir?"

"Doesn't matter, an old friend said he might be dropping me off a bottle of his special single malt, as he was on the island for a day or two. Doesn't drive a Civic though, a White CR-V, I think."

"I'll look out for it Mr Chancellor. Although I'm off shift at four, so that's less than an hour away."

"Thanks Archie... I'd better go and get those presents. Merry Christmas."

"And to you Sir."

Talbot revved the engine hard to get off the soft bank and headed along the Crawnish road, as his mind worked on the plan that had been formulating since he left the Royal Hotel. He drove on and occasionally a sunbeam would break through the windswept gloom, low on the horizon ahead. The place he was heading for was not much more than a couple of miles west of Crawnish where the road was straight in each direction, and there was a small freshwater loch, on the seaward side of the single track carriageway with passing places.

+

Georges turned on the engine of his car to warm himself up, just as Neil Mackenzie was walking around the bend towards the Honda. He was vainly trying to hold back his two lively West Highland terriers on their leads, from romping too quickly up the hill from the village. He walked up to the gap between the steep slope to Rob's garden and the driver's side of the car, then waved at the black face behind the wheel.

Neil leaned forward and mouthed to the driver, 'Are you Ok?'

Muwera dropped his window and relied, "Yes, thanks, I'm fine."

Perhaps conscious of the fact that his little hamlet had, for a while, been under the scrutiny of all manner of ghoulish visitors and other strangers, the fisherman ventured further, "Are you looking for somebody? Perhaps I can help?"

There was an audible, resigned sounding sigh that came out of the car next, followed by, "Do you happen to know where Robin Chancellor lives?"

Neil felt sure that the questioner already knew the answer and therefore took modest pleasure in replying, "Well, yes, this is his house," jerking his thumb up the slope, "But I happen to know he's not there. He's gone away for Christmas, I believe."

Georges thought he could detect rank smugness in the villager's comments, but also realised that sitting here any longer was just going to draw attention to himself. "Ok, thanks," he said, "I'll come back another day." With that, he released the handbrake and Neil plus his dogs had to leap smartly out of the Honda's path as Georges turned the wheel hard and executed a hasty three point turn. He headed back past the village sign and thought about what he would do to Robin Chancellor if he, and Tim, and Tom, ever did get their hands on him.

He was only two miles out of the village when the road straightened out and at the same time seemed to narrow, with the upward edge of a hill to his left. Muwera noticed the black rippled surface of a loch down below the road to his right, and ahead a small jeep that had been in a passing place, but had now moved forward into the road. He expected it to reverse back into the passing place, as presumably the driver hadn't seen him coming. However, it continued to advance and after a few dozen yards, both drivers stopped, their front bumpers only a few inches apart.

Talbot had seen the gold Honda in the dying light and had moved to intercept, knowing that Muwera's only immediate choices were to hit his car, go into the side of the hill, or into the loch. He sat behind the Suzuki steering wheel and waited. He didn't need to wait for long, as the muscle rich African threw open his door and stomped furiously around the front, so that he was level with Cat's window, that was already wound down.

"What the fuck do you think you're doing, you shit-for-brains arsehole?" Georges screamed.

"I'm very pleased to meet you too... Mr Muwera," said Cat with his right hand firmly holding the door handle open.

He'd never seen a photo of Robin Chancellor, but a sudden look of realisation adorned Muwera's face and he threw back his right arm to launch a punch through the open window. As his weight had transferred, in that split second, mainly to his heels it was perfect timing when Talbot threw his entire body weight at the driver's door and sent Georges spinning backwards to land, with the wind briefly knocked out him, on the rocky verge by the hill side of the road.

Carter immediately followed up by jumping on Muwera's chest and pinning his arms down with a combination of his knees and hands. "Listen Georges, I can guess what you're here for, and it's not going to happen. You're big and strong, but I've been trained by the best. Your brother thought he knew better, and look what happened to him. So why don't you just fuck off, for ever, and I won't have to kill you?"

"You cunt Chancellor, you're just an old man, a has-been," spat Muwera, "I'm going to get revenge for Pascal, and kill you slowly." As the last word left his mouth he launched both his knees as hard as he could, from his prone position, into Carter's back. As Cat's head came forward, Georges managed to rock his head and neck upwards at the same time and caught Cat's nose with his forehead. The sudden burst of blood over the faces of both men, went unnoticed as Muwera was now able to push Cat off him and scramble to his feet. Talbot sprang back and up at the same time, and they circled each other briefly.

They both lunged at each other, with arms extended to each side, trying to gain an advantage. Cat tried to launch himself at the bigger man in an attempt to bring him down again, only for Georges to step out of the way, or counter with some high kicks aimed at Cat's face. Carter realised that the longer this went on, the harder it would be him to better the younger man. He needed some sort of unexpected advantage. As the clockwise circling took Cat near to the scree at the base of the hill, he saw his chance. He feinted to lunge high and right with a punch, while dipping down and rolling to his left. He went completely head over heels and came up with a cricket ball sized rock in his left hand. As Georges spun round to meet the new direction of threat, Cat swung his left hand around in a wide arc and crashed the rock into the right side of Muwera's head.

The African staggered and blood gushed down his cheek from the deep cut over his ear, but he stayed on his feet and swung his fists wildly in a desperate attempt to make contact. Carter dodged well and then hit Georges again with the rock, this time on top of his skull. He turned and managed to avoid Cat's next lunge at his head, but only by dropping suddenly to one knee in front of Talbot. While his opponent was still dazed, Cat jumped behind him and grabbed his neck in a tight arm lock with his right arm. Talbot's weakened shoulder burned with pain as he held on tight and scrambled for robust purchase behind Georges, who was now struggling to breathe. Carter brought his left arm around to complement the pressure of his right then, with a sudden shift of his whole body weight, he broke Muwera's neck, and let him slump to the ground.

This had all happened in less than three minutes and in the absence of any other traffic along that stretch of the B887. Cat dragged the body back to the Honda and using all his strength, managed to wedge it into a driving position. He then leaned in and restarted the car before reaching over and pushing down on the corpse's left boot to press the clutch, while selecting first gear with his other hand. He then positioned the body's right foot on the accelerator and pushed down while lifting the left leg. He had already turned the wheel hard to the right and the car followed that angle, until it left the road and the increasing gradient of the slope helped it pick up more speed. As it tipped forward, more weight must have shifted down onto the accelerator and the car was still speeding up with a roaring engine, when it launched itself off the slight lip of the loch to nosedive into it, about twenty feet from the bank. Carter watched for only the time it took for the Civic to completely disappear into the deep black waters of Loch Beitarsaig, and for the final ripples to settle, before turning his jeep around and heading east, as the last of the daylight went out.

-+-

******

Part Three

Chapter Forty One

"Tuck in Carter, not like you to nibble at your lunch like an anorexic robin," observed a rather red-faced Lydia Hockley-Roberts over her scrubbed oak dining table.

"I think you may have had too much claret Lids," observed Carter Talbot, lifting his own glass and sipping gently at the voluptuous wine.

"I think you're probably right... Cat or Rob or whatever we're calling you today, but then it is Christmas. So...anyway...eat up, you miserable sod."

"Sorry Lydia, I just don't seem to have much appetite today... No reflection on your cooking though...damn good effort, Darling."

"Ok, you're forgiven. Let's leave all the turkey and stuff, and snuggle up on the sofa with the last of this bottle? Then you can tell me what really happened, before you came here last Sunday."

Talbot stiffened in his chair, "I told you Lids, I followed Muwera to his hotel, then lost him. I assumed he'd gone to Crawnish, so drove down there but couldn't find hide nor hair of him. I came back to the hotel later that evening and managed to break my nose, by tripping and falling on the outside steps. I then sat in the bar until closing time. There was still no sign of Georges, so I took a room for the night, and got the first flight to London, via Glasgow, the next day."

"That's all very well Carter, but it doesn't explain why Georges Muwera seems to have vanished. Toby has been quizzing me as well as you and doesn't seem to accept that I don't know anything."

"I can't help that Lydia, it's the truth and, frankly, I don't care if that glorified thug has disappeared. A good thing for the cocaine using community of East London to have a little break in supply over the festive period."

Lydia rested her head in her cupped hands and looked deeply into the blank features of her lover, in particular the blue and black areas around his nose and eyes. "Ok Cat... The thing is, I know you're lying to me, but you are very good at it...and, honestly, I love you anyway, so that's the last time I'll mention the, 'Case of the Vanishing Drug Dealer', I promise."

"Good decision Lids, life's too short to worry about such nonsense. Did you say we had one more bottle of this claret?"

"Yes we do, in the wine rack."

"I'll go and open it then. It may make the Queen's speech almost bearable."

"Agent Talbot, isn't that tantamount to treason for men in your position?"

"Probably, but not when you're retired... Cheers!"

+

Across London, in the Muwera residence, Timothy, Thomas, and Joshua had finished their Christmas dinner, cooked by the Somali maid with enthusiasm but not much skill, and were drinking a bottle of brandy that they had found in the cocktail cabinet.

"Are you sure you looked everywhere, you two? Josh asked the others.

"We spent almost a whole fuckin' week in the wind and rain up there looking for the Boss, but wiv no luck," replied Tom.

"Well, four days anyway," added Tim, to a glare from his partner, "The hotel said 'e checked in at lunchtime, wiv that fake name 'e gave us, went out, and never turned up in the evenin'. Even his phone is dead."

"So we drove to that place where Chancellor lives and asked around," continued Tom. "There was nobody at 'is gaff, and most of the locals wouldn't talk."

"Except that fisherman-looking bloke," added Tim, "He said he'd been out walking 'is dogs when 'e saw a car outside Chancellor's place and spoke briefly to a big African, who then drove off. The car sounded like the one that the car hire place said was rented by the Boss, under the fake name, and that they didn't get back."

"We must 'av driven all round the island looking for the car and the Boss, the amount of fuckin' petrol we used up was unbelievable. Spent nearly all our cash on juice for that 'ummer fing," moaned Tom.

"After three days searching, we'd 'ad enough," said Tim. "We even went to the local Plod and asked if they knew anyfink. They took a few notes but just said they'd let us know if they heard any news. After that we said, 'fuck it, let's go home'...and 'ere we are."

"So what, my friends, do we do now?" Josh queried.

"I dunno," said Tim, "But stayin' 'ere doesn't seem sensible. Plod will keep on watchin' and followin' us when we go out."

"You're right," agreed Tom, "Wiv bofe bruvvers gone, I'd say we're out of work, my old mate."

"If we are," continued Josh, "Then at least we're entitled to some redundancy, wouldn't you say boys?"

"Wot 'ave you got in mind Josh?"

"Well, after I got your call saying you couldn't find the Boss, I've been digging around this place and I found a spare key to the safe, plus some notes stashed away here and there, and a bit of 'stock', of course."

"How much?" Tim asked.

"There's about a hundred grand in cash, plus some bags of coke. Then, of course there's some nice electronic gear in the house, plus the Hummer and the Porsche, and the boat. I say we split it, after paying off the maid to keep her sweet. What do you think?"

Tom grinned, "Nice one Josh, it'll be like our 'Christmas Box'."

"But what if Georges turns up?" Tim ventured.

"He'll find us gone...won't he...and with all his worldly goods into the bargain." Said Josh with a smile.

"Yeah, fuck it." Tom added, "Come on Tim, we deserve this."

"All right," agreed Tim, "But you can 'ave the Tank...I want the Porsche."

"I dunno if I can afford the petrol," said Tom, "I'll toss you for it?"

"So it's settled then," interrupted Josh, "You boys will fight over the cars, and I can have the boat?"

"And we do a three way split of the dosh and drugs?"

"I'm cool with that," said Josh as he topped up all their brandies and reached for a big Tesco carrier bag under his chair. "Let's count it properly," he said, tipping the contents into the middle of the large table.

On Boxing Day morning, the former employees of the Muwera brothers went their separate ways. The Somali maid got a taxi from the house to a relation in Hounslow with, to her, the enormous sum of £10,000 buried deep in her handbag.

Tim, having won the toss with Tom, revved up the Silver Porsche Turbo and, glancing at the bag on his front seat, smiled at the thought of the £30,000 in cash and two kilos of coke therein. He drove effortlessly through the gates and off to see 'his old lady', in the depths of South London. He thought she might like the new Bose hi-fi that he'd managed to squeeze into the front luggage compartment.

Tom was somewhat less high spirited than his ex-colleague and followed down the drive soon after with the Hummer. He had already taken his old employer's holdall from the boot and chucked it into one of the wheelie bins at the side of the house, replacing it with a couple of Smart TV's and three crates of wine. He also had his one third share of the cash and cocaine hidden in his small suitcase. His destination had been the West Country but the thought of trying to steer the 'Tank' through all those narrow lanes in Cornwall had put him off. He was heading for Norfolk, and a nice pub he knew in the Broads.

Joshua had waved them all off, and now finished his own preparations. It didn't involve much carrying. He had all his clothes and those items that he'd liberated from the bedrooms of the Muwera brothers, typically watches and jewellery, in two luxurious designer suitcases. He put his equal share of the salvage into the cases, then fastened them and put them by the back door. He then did a final sweep of the safe, picked up the remaining handgun lying there and put it in his jacket pocket.

After going right through the house, locking every window and door, Joshua collected up all the keys and went to the back door. Using the secondary alarm panel, he set the system and opened the door onto the rear garden. Once his cases were through it, he locked the final exit from outside, picked up the luggage and walked down the path towards the river, hearing a satisfying beep from the alarm on the way.

He loaded the cases into the cockpit of the boat, pleased that, although the late morning was cold and cloudy, there was no noticeable wind. He then took the cases below, unlocked the double wardrobe of the main sleeping cabin and tried pushing the cases in. This was a struggle as there was already a briefcase on the floor. This was what he'd put there before Tim and Tom had come home, and he grinned as he remembered the additional £80,000 he'd stashed in it, from the Muwera safe. If he was going to get this boat to Ibiza, he thought, he'd need a fair bit of cash. Strange how trusting the boys had been, he hadn't needed to clear the safe before they agreed on equal shares, they didn't even ask for a look. He knew he would have done, if the boot had been on the other foot.

Joshua took one last look up at the locked and empty house, picked the bunch of house keys off the leather cockpit seat where he'd placed them, and casually tossed them into the river. He started the engines, loosened off the ropes, and opened the throttle. The powerful engines responded and the cruiser cut a strong bow wave that curved towards the opposite bank as Joshua turned the craft towards the south.

+

Over five hundred miles away, as the crow flies, DI William Keilloh, even though not on duty, had been at his kitchen table early and was looking at a file of papers with a 'G. Muwera' label handwritten on the corner of the manilla cover. His Stornoway home did not lend itself to having a study, and his children had commandeered all bedroom space, apart from the marital bedroom, long ago.

He moved the plate with the remains of his breakfast toast to one side and tried to lay out the different loose leaf pages in the file across the table. They wouldn't all fit so he focused on the latest again:

From: tcrabbe@fco.gov.uk

To: wkeilloh@policescotland.org

Sent: Wed 24/12/14 18:20

Subject: Muwera disappearance

Billy,

I'm just about to call it a day for Christmas and thought I'd drop you a quick line. Like you and your officers (from our phone conversation today), we've had no reported sightings of Georges Muwera since our man Chancellor saw him go to the Royal Hotel in your town last Saturday. He admits following him but then, apparently, drew a blank. I've spoken to his girlfriend and she supports his story.

I would suggest that from an MI6 perspective, we can cool down this enquiry. We will send someone to the Muwera house after the long Christmas weekend and will let you know of any results. In the meantime, and with Chancellor in London for an indefinite time, I would recommend that you suspend any surveillance on his Crawnish address. Notwithstanding the use of a false identity, we are confident in proposing that you relegate this whole matter to the simple status of a missing person report. From a resources perspective we're not sure that any more attention is justified.

Many thanks for your assistance in this matter, now and previously. Please enjoy a well-deserved break over Christmas and have a good 2015.

With kindest regards,

Toby.

Keilloh's wife then interrupted his train of thought, "Everything all right Bill?"

"Aye...fine Hen. It's just this missing African guy. He was seen in Crawnish on Saturday by a reliable witness, and his hire car was logged going along that road earlier, but not ever logged going back. I'm tempted to start a serious search, men marching over the moors, divers, helicopter support, but I'm being warned off. London aren't interested."

"Well William, perhaps there are better things to worry about? But, whatever you decide to do, could you start by clearing the table? We're due visitors and I want to set the table for a cold meat lunch."

-+-

Chapter Forty Two

Ever since Christmas Day, Carter and Lydia had got into a disciplined schedule and work progressed steadily on the book. They would wake up early and he would sit at the big table with his laptop to write until late morning, while Lydia would edit what he'd written the day before. He would then go for a run on Hampstead Heath to re-energise himself, followed by a hot shower. They would have a good brunch together as their main meal of the day, and follow that with an afternoon nap, sometimes including sex.

If refreshed sufficiently, the late afternoons and evenings would occasionally involve trips to the pub but, more often, Lydia would catch up on her office emails and keep in touch with her other clients. They might watch a downloaded movie before retiring early and sleeping well. They kept to their 'no work on Sunday' rule and would walk together on the Heath or explore random parts of London, content with each other's company.

By the end of January, they had reached 1993 in Cat's life story and Lydia had been intrigued by the twists, turns, and revelations in his history. They sat at the table one morning and Lydia took charge of reviewing the additional chapters completed.

"So," she began, "After the Falklands it was back to peacetime soldiering in Germany, then alternating tours into Northern Ireland to try and keep you busy. But it's clear from your descriptions of those years that you were unfulfilled."

"When you've experienced the thrill of real combat Lydia, it's hard to be satisfied with little more than police work."

"But you had your 'distractions' didn't you? You picked up where you left off with German and Irish women, and you even got promoted to Major, when still in your twenties. That must have pleased you?"

"Not as much as you might think Lids. They said it was in recognition of my 'exemplary work in the Falklands campaign', but being a Major in a peacetime Parachute Regiment just means more bloody administration work and less action."

"Hence January 1985?"

"Yes."

"Did you go looking for this or were you picked, it's not quite clear in the manuscript."

"I thought it was."

"Let me read the salient passage back to you...

After a whole month of acting like a personnel manager, sorting out Christmas leave requests and whip rounds for charity contributions, I was more than ready when I got a call by my former CO in the Falklands - Lt.Col. Baxter - asking me to take the next transport plane from our German base to the UK, and meet him for lunch in London.

In the Dragoon Club, we had a very good lunch and Baxter went on about what a ruthless and determined officer I was, just the sort of chap the country needed to tackle the new threats facing Britain, and stuff like that.

After coffee, we repaired to the smoking room for a post-prandial whisky or two and I was introduced to a stocky man with piercing eyes called Archie Findlayson. As we enjoyed some very silky Macallan, he observed that after the bombing of the Grand Hotel in Brighton a few months before, the intelligence services had decided that 'the gloves were off' when it came to tackling the IRA. This meant that they needed decisive people to 'take the fight to the enemy'. Apparently Baxter had assured him that I was an ideal candidate for this sort of work."

"Yes, that's how it was, Lids."

"But Cat, did they just pick you out of the blue, or did you encourage them behind the scenes? It's important to the reader to know whether you were bored enough to forego your army status and career, for the uncertainties of an undercover role."

"Ok, I get it. Yes, I did write to various senior officers before then, asking about opportunities for more action and stressing that I would tackle anything exciting."

"By exciting, of course you meant dangerous?"

"To some of us Lydia, they are one and the same thing."

"So they offered you a position in MI6?"

"Well, it was more subtle than that. As I said in the next part of that chapter, they assigned me to the Foreign and Commonwealth Office as a 'Security Consultant' and then put me through the most strenuous training I'd ever had."

"Yes, but to all intents and purposes you had a Secret Intelligence Service remit, under cover of British diplomatic missions all over the world?"

"That was about the size of it. Anywhere there were 'security' problems, they wanted me to help solve them and remain discreet."

"You certainly threw yourself into your first mission, didn't you Carter?"

"You mean the Dublin assignment?"

"Quite. Once Patrick Magee was arrested for the Brighton bombing in June '85, it was clear that he and his accomplices didn't dream up the plot by themselves. Someone senior in the IRA had specifically ordered it."

"The thing is Lids, I didn't know in detail how MI6 got the background on the senior guy, I think it was from one of Magee's gang trying to get a lighter sentence. All I know is that I was seconded to the British Embassy in Dublin, and there I was given the identity and details of where he was hiding out in the Republic."

"And you blew him up!"

"Donal Cleary was an evil bastard, I have absolutely no regrets Lydia."

"Nevertheless Cat, I think that I might blur the edges a bit on this chapter. Otherwise you might be really asking for trouble from his former colleagues?"

"You're in charge Lids, I'm just telling it like it really was. I thought that's what you wanted?"

"It is Carter, but I also care for you and I don't want you to worry every time you see a strange car coming down the road at the cottage."

"Speaking of which, when are we going back? I don't want to presume on your hospitality for too long," grinned Talbot.

"We can discuss that later. For now, let's bring ourselves up to date with these chapters of yours?"

So they spent the rest of the morning reviewing the years in Carter's life from 1985 to 1993, as remembered by him. The missions included time in Malaysia, India, Pakistan, Belize, Nigeria, Sierra Leone, various parts of the Middle East, Kenya, and Bosnia. Whether it was tackling illegal logging, tribal conflicts, the supply of blood diamonds, ivory poaching, or helping the British army in the Balkans under their UN flag, Talbot had an uncanny knack of either getting results, or at least seeming not to make matters worse.

"This latest chapter Cat, number twenty-one, it seems a bit restrained or incomplete? The one where you're seconded to the cavalry in Bosnia."

"You make it sound very grand. The cavalry you refer to is no more than a squadron of four light tanks called Scimitars, operated with three man crews by the 21st Lancers, from northern England. The tanks were all painted pure white to make them stand out as UN vehicles and, supposedly thereby prevent them being shot at while on humanitarian escort duties. I was at the British Embassy in Zagreb and tasked to join them for a week, to report on the incidents of hostile fire onto convoys of food and medical supplies, from Bosnian Serb positions, in the hills overlooking the main convoy route."

"Talk me through it. Were you looking for trouble?"

"Not on this occasion, I was meant to be observing, but trouble found me."

"You say in your chapter that, *'The fire from the hills began only ten minutes along the road and amounted to continuous rounds of mortar fire, plus tracer ammunition as if from anti-aircraft guns aiming horizontally. The mortar shells were not very accurate and none of the trucks were hit in that first encounter. A couple of our tanks were grazed by the tracer fire but being anti-aircraft ammunition, it exploded in the air rather than on contact, so no real damage done.'* Doesn't sound like too much a problem."

"It wasn't, at this point. It was about 20 miles further on when the real trouble occurred. We rounded a bend and there was an enormous tree trunk across the road. The valley slopes prevented easy manoeuvring either side, and then the firing started, from the left."

"You say that the lead tank was knocked out almost immediately by a close mortar shell ripping its left track off. You were second in line, with all the trucks behind you, and the remainder of the squadron bringing up the rear."

"Yes, and it was hard to know what to do. We could see the Serb gun and mortar sites up the hillside but the rules of engagement were very restrictive. We could only return fire if we were in immediate and direct danger from incoming fire, and had orders to respond."

"You say that you, *'Encouraged your tank commander to open fire on the Serb positions,'* but that he wouldn't act without orders."

"Yeah, he was scared stiff, only a Corporal, not fair on him to have to decide really, and no orders from the squadron commander in the lead tank, who had probably lost radio contact in the blast. He used some sense though, got our driver to steer to the sheltered side of the knocked out leader and open up the cannon on the middle of the tree trunk to try and blast a way through the obstacle... I'll tell you what Lydia, why don't I read you the first version I wrote, but then changed?"

Cat then opened up another Word file on his laptop and read aloud:

'By this time, the other two tanks had driven past the immobile trucks and were trying to get through the undergrowth on the left of the road, towards the Serbs. I lost sight of them for a while behind some trees, then saw them emerge about 100 yards below the mortars and guns. Clearly whoever was in charge of the Scimitars didn't care much for the rules of engagement, and opened fire with cannon and coaxial machine gun on the twenty or so Serbian soldiers that we could see through the smoke.

Another mortar blast to our front obscured our view, and a piece of shrapnel from it caught our tank commander in the jaw. He clutched his face and dropped down into the turret. The driver moved to give him first aid as I took the commander's place behind the 20mm cannon and peered out of the turret. As the smoke cleared I could see a pick-up truck careering down the slope from where the Serbs had been. There were three men in the cab and about ten in the back, grasping onto the sides of the truck and onto personal weapons.

Clearly our two tanks had flushed them out and they were on the run. They were no direct threat to us, but I'd had enough and pulled the cocking lever on the cannon while aiming the sight just in front of the fleeing vehicle. I pulled the fire lever repeatedly and got off six rounds in a couple of seconds. All but one hit the truck and it virtually disintegrated in the clear view of the telescopic sight, with body parts flying off in all directions. The flaming wreckage slammed to a halt against a tree and some remaining bodies, flames licking them, flew over the cab onto the dusty ground.

I grabbed my SA80, jumped out of the Scimitar and ran over the intervening ground to the site of the wrecked pick-up. The petrol tank had already exploded and I couldn't see much movement. I then saw a man, face down in the dirt, smoke still coming from his baggy trousers, stretching out his hand towards an AK47. I fired three quick rounds into his back and he partly rolled over as he died. I could then see the soft features of a teenage girl on the exposed face, and felt sick at what I'd done.'

"Bloody hell Cat, that's vibrant writing, if a bit of a shock to the system."

"But it makes me sound like some sort of vigilante. I should have let them go, that girl didn't even have a uniform on. I went straight back to the Embassy after that and the FCO got me back to London to avoid any awkward questions."

"Don't worry about it Carter, I'll do a 'cut and paste' job on chapter twenty-one so that you are seen as a Maverick, but one with principles. Where do we go next with your story?"

"Well, after Bosnia, I spent a few months taking it easy in London and even took some time out to stay with Uncle Hugo, trying to clear my head."

"And then?"

"And then, is why I want to go back to the cottage. In 1994, I went to Rwanda and had life changing experiences in more ways than one. I'd imagined writing this part at the cottage ever since I started the book. I need space and peace to think, I need my 'place by the sea'. I hope you understand Lids?"

"Of course, you're fit as a fiddle now so why would you

want me in the way?" Lydia replied, trying and failing to sound supportive. "Why don't you go back tomorrow, and I'll join you whenever you let me know it's Ok?"

"Thanks Lydia, I know you're upset, but I'll make it up to you... I promise."

"You'd better, Mr Talbot."

-+-

Chapter Forty Three

As Carter drove south on the Isle of Lewis, in the jeep he'd left at Stornoway airport a few weeks before, he drove gently, enjoying the unfolding scenery. It was early lunchtime and the sun was as high as it was going to get on the 1st of February, in that latitude. In an almost cloudless sky it reflected brightly off the pale blue sea every time Talbot got a glimpse of it from the winding road. As he left the open spaces of Lewis and got into the rugged lumpiness of Harris, the sun played upon the hills and he could enjoy the snow-capped peaks and the shadowy gullies between them.

There was no traffic at all, as is fairly normal on a Hebridean Sunday, and as he turned along the Crawnish road, the police car on the corner was conspicuous by its absence. He saw on his left, with increasing regularity, pristine beaches of pale gold with the benign sea merely seeming to caress those shores encouraged by the slightest breeze. Carter couldn't help slowing as he approached the area above Loch Beitarsaig, and pulled over to stop on the left of the straight road. He didn't get out but looked intently at the faintly rippling surface of the black waters, before putting the jeep back into gear and completing the short distance to Water Cottage.

After putting the jeep into the garage, Cat let himself into the cottage with his carry-on case in one hand, and picked up the six weeks of junk mail that had accumulated on his front doormat, with the other. He went into the study, threw the post onto the desk and put his bag in the bedroom. After putting the kettle on, he went into the lounge and sat in the armchair with the best view of the sea. He let his mind wander over all that had happened since he first arrived at his 'place by the sea', and was only shaken from that reverie by the brisk sputtering noises from the kettle.

With a mug of tea in hand he returned to the chair and continued his pondering. There would be no writing today, he liked Lydia's rule. There was no pressure in just thinking for a few hours, getting a good night's sleep then throwing himself into chapter twenty-two on Monday morning. After drinking his Darjeeling, he settled back and continued to watch the waves lapping at the boulders on the shore, until he drifted into a gentle sleep.

Later that afternoon, after watching an instantly forgettable CIA-based thriller on the TV, with a toasted sandwich from bread in his freezer for company, Carter went into the study to get himself a whisky. As he poured some Bruichladdich into a tumbler, he saw the stack of post he had casually thrown onto the desk and sat down to go through it. About a dozen pieces of junk mail received short shrift and ended up in the bin, most being unopened. But there, near the bottom of the pile, was a distinctive pale blue envelope with red and blue piping around the edge, and the epithet 'Par Avion' on the top left corner.

In all his overseas postings, Carter that never received many 'blueys', not having much in the way of family or friends who would keep in touch with him. His interest was instantly roused when he saw that this Air Mail had originated in Kenya. The neat handwriting was not familiar to him but the destination was clear: 'Mr. R. Chancellor, Uisge Bothan, Crawnish, Harris, Outer Hebrides, Scotland, UK.'

Cat was careful to open the envelope without tearing and inside he found two separate letters, also on pale blue, lightweight paper, and both handwritten. He unfolded the one with the handwriting that matched the front of the envelope, and took a sip from his glass.

'Jambo Carter,' he read, *'It's the week before Christmas and I'm at home with the family. I'm sorry I've not been in touch, but this is my father's doing. I am virtually a prisoner in our house and we (Milton, Mum and I) are not allowed mobile phones or access to computers. Even if we had, I wouldn't know your number, it was lost when Milton threw away your phone during our departure from Harris. All the servants are searched at the end of each day to stop messages getting out. I'm hoping that this one makes it to you. I'm praying that you are still at the cottage after that awful day, and have recovered from your wounds? Milton blamed everybody but himself for what happened and Father seems to believe him. I have to keep the peace to protect Mum. She has written you a letter which is also enclosed.*

Mum has put up with so much over the years and now seems more unhappy than I have ever seen her. I explained what you told me about '94, that you didn't abandon her but thought she had been murdered in the carnage of those horrible days. She was so pleased that I'd found you and lights up when I tell her about you, and the cottage, and the pleasant things we did in my all too short visit! Of course, assuming that you are now in fair health, I hope that you are making good progress with your book, I know how keen you were on getting it done.

I don't know what the future holds for us. I suppose that one day, Father will relent and life can approach some degree of normality. However, at the moment his paranoia seems to be uppermost in his mind and he thinks we will abandon him given half a chance. Mum can speak for herself on that but for me, I'd love to escape and make my own life. If I try now it would be a disaster. Whether I succeeded or failed, Father would take it out on Mum. Frankly, I don't care what happens to Milton, I've seen the darkest side of him and I hate him, twin brother notwithstanding.

Obviously it would be great to hear from you, but posting anything to our house would be fraught with danger. If I get a chance to access the Internet, I intend to set up a new address: shakykenya@hotmail.com. If you get this letter, it might be worth a try emailing me on that. You never know, I might get lucky!

It's my twentieth birthday on 3rd January, but I don't suppose there will be much in the way of genuine celebration around here. Still, what is it that Alexander Pope wrote; 'Hope springs eternal in the human breast..?' We shall therefore continue to live in the hope that better times are ahead of us.

Take care Carter, and thanks for being there. I'm so sorry that it turned out the way it did. I'll never forget your friendship. Asante Sana, Shakespeare.'

Cat put the letter down on the desk and turned on his laptop before doing anything else. Within a few seconds the Wi-Fi kicked in and he had connectivity. He sent a very quick email to the address that Shakespeare had given him, showing just the words: 'Shaky, got your letter today, this is to test your new email. Regards, Cat.'

He then turned to the other letter, which was folded, glued, and had the word 'CAT' written on the back of it. He turned it over in his hands, without unfolding it, as if delaying the pleasure or protecting himself from pain. He wasn't sure which. A welcome delay came from the laptop, which beeped in receipt of an email. He looked at the screen and there, in his inbox, was the clear message subject: 'Delivery Status Notification (Failure)' and a message which made it clear that the email address of Carter's test was not yet a reality.

After another sip of his whisky, Cat opened out the second

one page letter and read it most deliberately:

'Dearest Cat,

I'm writing this in the wild hope that it will get to you and that you are well enough to read it.

This whole subterfuge is Shakespeare's idea. He said that we shouldn't hesitate to try and get in touch with you, and that if we didn't, you would probably never forgive us for suffering in silence. And suffer we have. Not so much the twins, I'm sure that Shakespeare has told you about the background to our situation and, over the years, I have always put their happiness before mine. But I have suffered terribly, not so much physically, although God knows Alphonse can be a brute if riled, but twenty years of mental torture, right from the beginning.

The last time I knew pure happiness, that happiness of a selfish nature that only being totally in love with somebody can bring, was with you. Those days in the mountains on our gorilla expedition, were blissful. I thought that I'd found the love of my life and was sure you felt the same. I couldn't wait to see you again, but it never happened. Shakespeare has told me that your friend had seen me being herded into the church and that the next day all they had found were bodies. It was true, except for me. Alphonse (or Portier as he was called then) was the officer in charge of our 'escort' and seemed to take an instant fancy to me after talking to his Sergeant, who had questioned me earlier. Much later, when drunk once, Portier told me that I was saved from the slaughter because having total power over a half Belgian and half Tutsi woman would always remind him of his complete revenge, on both groups responsible for treating his own Hutu tribe with such contempt.

The price of being saved, to my shame, was to be

repeatedly raped by Portier, the first time in the church, when his men had finished slaughtering the women and children. He was genuinely aroused by the killing and I was too petrified to resist, or even object. The symptoms of pregnancy came not too long after that, and what could I do? The country was in chaos, my family were dead, and all the Europeans had gone. For the sake of what I was carrying, I learned quickly to put up with Gatanazi and we ended up escaping to Kenya via what was then Eastern Zaire, and Tanzania, once the Hutus were defeated.

I have never before told anybody about this and Shakespeare doesn't know. If he did, he is such a good hearted young man, I have no doubt that he would not condemn me for anything. I have tried to love his brother but it is difficult, he is too much like his father. In an ideal world, Shakespeare and I would get away from here with just enough money to get our own place, somewhere that Alphonse couldn't reach us, and just try being happy. I dream of this sometimes but then wake up to the reality of being stuck, with no clear way out.

I'm not going to say any more in this letter, it's too intense for inconsequential chatter. But I will end on this note Carter. I would so love to see you again, Shakespeare said that you were truly thrilled that I was still alive, and that you are a single man. I'm sure that you have girlfriends everywhere but, I hope, perhaps none from twenty years ago? My heart has long ago forgotten what true love feels like, perhaps it will get a little nudge from you one day?

With the most tender love,

Your Nicole XXX.'

Talbot read the letter again, and again. Then, after a very large helping of Bruichladdich, he did it once more and felt his eyes watering. He swiped his shirtsleeve across the bridge of his nose and cleared the tears, then took a deep swallow of the single malt, enjoying the punishment of the smoky burn at the back of his throat.

He sat back in his chair and stared out to sea. He was oblivious to the darkening sky and the freshening wind outside and just sat there, mind racing, lifting his glass to his lips repeatedly. It was dark outside and inside the cottage, by the time Cat finished what had been at least a half full bottle of whisky and slumped in his chair.

The piercing noise of 'Communication Breakdown' by Led Zeppelin pierced his dulled brain and he remembered that he'd played about with ring tone downloads over Christmas, as he woke through the waves of spirit still coursing through his veins. He fumbled for and picked up his mobile, then tried talking into it upside down, before getting organised and grunting "Hello," as he pressed the correct part of the screen.

"Hello Carter" said a voice, "Are you Ok?"

"Erm... Yeah... I think so."

"It's Lydia... Remember me?"

"Hi Lids, sorry, had a few 'wee drams'..."

"You were going to call me, let me know you'd arrived safely...you know?"

"Was I?.. I mean, I was...yes indeed... You just beat me to it."

"Sounds like it...so, everything alright then?"

"...Yeah, fine. No bother."

"Is the cottage Ok?"

"No signs of any break-ins, if that's what you mean."

"You sound like you need a hot bath and a decent sleep... No more whisky tonight Mr Talbot, you've got to get chapter twenty-two underway tomorrow!"

"Right...yeah. Roger that, LHR HQ. I'll call you tomorrow evening, over and out."

Carter didn't hear Lydia's final remarks as he had already ended the call. She was right about the bath and the sleep, but somehow he didn't think he would feel remotely in the mood to recreate the events of April 1994, when the day dawned tomorrow.

-+-

Chapter Forty Four

Carter Talbot had been a man of action for most of his life. After he woke up early on that Monday morning, 2nd February, 2015, his instincts kicked in, despite any lingering effects from yesterday's whisky intake. As was his way, he would use whatever resources he could to help him plan whatever action was, to him, necessary. He went through some old files at the back of his bottom left desk drawer until he found one with the word 'Kenya' written on it.

Inside the file was a large folded map and Cat opened it out onto the top of his big desk, where it sagged over the side, front, and back edges. There were pencil and ink markings at certain points on the map. Some scribbles and arrows were prominent in the south-west corner, both red and black, with co-ordinates noted across the Masai Mara region, near the Tanzanian border. Looking further east there were similar doodles across the Tsavo national park but Talbot skimmed quickly over these and concentrated more closely in the area to the north of Nairobi.

He learned forward in his chair and looked closely at Nanyuki, to the west of Mount Kenya. There he saw a solid red blob with a line leading an inch away to a box with a name and an address that could feasibly have been more appropriate on a large scale map of England; 'Charlie Reid, Red Lion Pub.' Not far away was another similar marking with the label 'Tony Chalk, Kakulet Farm.' Carter smiled grimly with memories of his one assignment in Kenya and continued panning his view west, almost as far as Lake Victoria, then slightly north. He had to stand up to get a close look at an area to the west of Kitale, where he remembered Shakespeare saying his house was situated. The only words on that part of the map were the printed legend 'Mount Elgon National Park' across a large, roundish, pale green coloured area. He noticed that about two-thirds of the park was over the border in Uganda.

He moved the map off the desk onto the floor, then went onto Google on his laptop. He entered 'Mount Elgon National Park' and the map function took him to a similar, but brighter green, area as on his faded old map. Try as he might, by constantly magnifying the scale and moving the cursor all over the much enlarged area, Cat couldn't unearth any writing showing the presence of a large estate near the border, as described by Shakespeare. The dirt tracks were few and far between and didn't show as ending up anywhere specific. They just ran out in the sea of green. He hadn't expected much, but it had been worthwhile checking.

Carter now rummaged further in the file and pulled out a typed sheet with some names and telephone numbers. He looked at his watch and saw that it was around 08:30, so 11:30 in Kenya. He picked up his mobile and, remembering to apply the +254 international code, entered a number from his list. After three rings, he could hear the phone being picked up and a somewhat questioning voice, with what sounded like a Birmingham accent said, "Red Lion, hello?"

"Is that the Red Lion, Nanyuki?" Cat asked.

"It is, Charlie speaking. Who's this?"

"Someone who, memorably, saved your arse twenty five years ago Charlie, that's who!"

There were a few seconds of complete silence...then, "Fook me, that can't be Carter Talbot, can it?"

"It can, and it is, Charlie."

"No wonder, only some mad Rupert like you would use the landline nowadays."

"Sorry about that, didn't have your mobile number. They weren't even invented the last time we met, I seem to recall."

"And you never bothered to keep in touch, of course."

"Sorry again Charlie... You're still running the pub then?"

"As long as the British Army keeps training soldiers in Nanyuki, there'll be more than enough thirsty squaddies to keep the old place going."

"Have you got family now Charlie?"

"Same Kenyan wife as when I left the army, and she's given me four kids, two of each. All grown up now, two girls working locally, one boy in the pub, one still at college. Anyway Mr Talbot, you didn't ring me after twenty five years to have a gossip. You want something."

"You always were very direct, Charlie. That's why the men trusted, and respected, you."

"Cut the bullshit, Sir. What's going on?"

"It's too complicated for the phone but, essentially, I'm coming to Kenya soon and I'm going to need some help. I wonder whether any of our old anti-poaching team are still around?"

"Apart from me, and Chalkie of course, there's only one of the gang still in Nanyuki. Corporal Wells, as was, runs a garage and workshop on the Meru road."

"Tony still at his farm?"

"He is, but don't forget he's in his seventies now, Mr Talbot."

"Of course...yes...of course. Would be great to see him again though."

"Look, Sir. You know you'll be welcome here. I'll tell Mr Chalk and Wellsy that you might be paying us a little visit, we can then have a proper chat over a few beers and let's see what comes of that?"

"Perfect plan Sergeant...er Charlie. I'll let you know my arrival date, once I've booked a flight."

"Righto Mr Talbot, Sir."

They finished the call and Carter started looking online for flights to Kenya. He found that the cheapest options, and possibly those attracting less attention, didn't originate at Heathrow. He ended up booking a route from Stornoway, via Edinburgh and Amsterdam, to Nairobi, with an open return, via Istanbul and Glasgow, timed for six weeks later.

He spent most of the rest of the day Googling all manner of related topics to help gain an understanding of where he was going. He tried things that he remembered Shaky saying about his home area, while at the cottage. He tried the real and assumed Rwandan names of Shakespeare's father without any real success. He was able to discover a bit more about Kitale, the nearest town to the Kwizera estate and home, but not being a tourist or a farmer, this wasn't going to be of great assistance.

By the end of the afternoon, Carter took a break and realised that he hadn't eaten all day. After a quick visit to the kitchen he tucked into some beans on toast and remembered that, while still the worst for drink the night before, he had promised to phone Lydia today for a more sober chat. He got himself a bottle of sparkling water from the fridge and sat back at his desk, staring at the phone. What was he going to say? He ruminated on this, but only briefly. Things had changed and he couldn't pretend they hadn't.

"Hello Lydia," he said in his most friendly voice after she answered the call, "Sorry about last night, the Bruichladdich got the better of me!"

"It's Ok Cat, you've been through an awful lot. You need to let off steam sometimes."

Carter was surprised at her warmth but managed, "Thanks, you are very good to me."

"I've got to look after you Carter, you're a valuable commodity. But we probably should have a proper talk, at some point. Perhaps after you finish chapter twenty-two?"

"The thing is Lids... Something's come up."

"What do you mean? I thought you were all set to do that chapter, and I was going to leave you in peace until it was done?"

"Yes, that was the plan...but...but now I've got to go on a trip."

"A fucking 'trip'? What are you talking about? Where, and for how long?"

"Kenya, and I don't know how long for."

The line went quiet, and all Carter could hear was some restrained breathing, from which he deduced that LHR was annoyed with him but holding back. Eventually she spoke, softly but firmly:

"Carter, I'm sure that this has something to do with young Shakespeare. I know that if I ask you any more, you'll not tell me the whole story, you never do. I'll have to explain to Francis that you're suffering a mild relapse and need a bit of a rest. I just hope that whatever you've got to do, you come back safely, to me. I love you Cat."

Something in her tone stopped Talbot from finishing the call like that. He wanted to show he cared, so he asked, "You said we needed a proper chat, at some point. What about?"

"I was hoping to have that face to face Cat, not over the phone. When are you flying?"

"Wednesday morning, and not via London, so I'm afraid I can't meet you on the way."

"Which is a shame, as it is rather important news, really."

"I'm really sorry Lydia... I do care for you, and awful lot, even if I don't ever tell you. But this is something I've just got to do. People need my help and I can't just ignore that."

"I understand Carter, that's just you isn't it. The thing is, if anything went wrong, I'd never forgive myself for not telling you before you went, so here goes... I've had my suspicions for a few days, but I went to the doctor today and she confirmed. Carter Talbot, you have made me pregnant!"

-+-

Chapter Forty Five

Last night's phone call with Cat had gone on for a while after Lydia had 'dropped the bombshell'. Cat had reminded her that she'd told him she was on the pill, and it was true but, as she admitted to him, sometimes she forgot to take it. He had been understanding and she'd also sensed a bit of pride in his voice. However pleasant the conversation however, he had been resolute in sticking to the plans for his 'trip'. His view, typical of Carter, had been, 'It's something we can talk about when I get back'. His final question, almost an afterthought really, was along the lines of, 'How do you feel about it?'

This question came back to her as she sat in her taxi, stuck in London traffic, supposedly on the way to the office. Yesterday's doubts and the non-committal answer she had given to Cat, seemed like a flicker of old memory. Now, she thought to herself, she felt great. She couldn't remember ever being truly broody in her life but, somehow, the thought of being a mum - even at forty-one - made her excited. Carter had told her when they first met that he'd never had any children...that he knew about. Therefore, she pondered, as this was a first for both of them, perhaps he might share her excitement one day. Time would tell, she thought, as the taxi finally squeezed through a gap and dropped her off.

Once at her desk, Lydia turned on her screen and clicked on the 'AONAG' tab which instantly revealed the very latest draft of Carter's book, right up to the end of chapter twenty-one. He was going to Kenya and, as she'd challenged him, this must be something to do with Shakespeare. She also thought that there might be some clues about the nature of the trip from looking at an earlier chapter from when he was in Kenya before. Scrolling upwards she got as far chapter seventeen and slowed her scrolling to a stop, at the chapter title page.

Even though she'd edited the pages in recent weeks, Lydia read slowly trying to see what nuances she could pick up from the text. Carter had been assigned to the British High Commission in Nairobi early in 1990 with the specific role of helping the Kenyan government tackle the scourge of ivory poachers, who were driving the rampant slaughter of thousands of elephants. After talking to BHC officials and having various meetings with government and wildlife experts, the first action he took was to visit the British army training base in Nanyuki and, with MoD backing, recruited a small team of volunteers to help him. The names Charlie Reid and Ray Wells were mentioned often in the text as key members of the team.

According to Cat, they spent several months joining in with newly formed Kenya Wildlife Service teams trying to patrol some of the national parks and open country with the biggest elephant populations. Carter's frustration, at the outcome of their work, came through the text clearly. They would literally catch poachers red-handed, as they butchered recently killed elephants. The team would then hand them over to the police, only to hear later that they'd been given a derisory fine, or a few weeks in prison, before resuming their grisly trade. Knowing Cat as she did, Lydia smiled at the next passage.

It was after being thoroughly fed up with almost daily sightings of dead elephants, that one night I had a drink in the Red Lion with an army officer called Tony Chalk. A fair bit older than me, he had done time in a regular regiment and in the military police. Over a few Tuskers, in which I probably moaned like hell, he suggested that it wasn't entirely the poachers fault.

They were dirt poor, said Tony, and if they were being offered the equivalent of a year's wages for one pair of adult tusks, it was only human nature that they would do it. The real problem, according to Tony, was the dealers. The middle men would pay the locals, to trap and kill the elephants, then remove the tusks. These men would then load up the ivory onto trucks and drive, usually to Mombasa, for delivery to the dealers. There the agents would get their stock weighed and be paid a much higher rate than they had paid the poachers. The dealers would then secure passage on ships bound for Far East Ivory Traders in places like Hong Kong and be paid by representatives of these eventual recipients, at prices between five and ten times what they had paid the middle men.

If, suggested Tony, there was some way of targeting the dealers, the demand could fall and it would stop being worthwhile for the poachers in the first place. Of course, there were big obstacles in the way of success. One main one being the high ranking and strong connections that the dealers had with the Kenyan government, and President Moi in particular, who was a dictator in all but name. I pointed out to Chalk that, less than a year before, the same President had publicly burnt over three million dollars' worth of ivory that had been seized from poachers, as a demonstration of Kenya's commitment to fighting the scourge of poaching, by destroying stocks. Tony simply laughed that off as a publicity stunt and pointed out that the President's cousin was one of the most notorious dealers.

I mined as much extra information from Tony as I could, then asked him if he fancied joining our team for a long weekend, as we were now going try something different. He seemed up for it and I said we'd sort out a plan with the rest of the team the following night. The next day I got Reid and Wells to ensure that we had one or two heavier than normal weapons, plus extra ammunition, and supplies for five days loaded into the two Land Rovers that we used on missions.

Typical Talbot, thought Lydia as she imagined Carter with his natural enthusiasm for action, taking on a new challenge without pause for reflection. She read how they had agreed at that evening's get together, to go down to Tsavo where, not only were elephants still plentiful, but it was relatively close to Mombasa and that made their plan more workable. Two days later, Talbot, Reid, and Wells, with one Land Rover got themselves into the bush and found a big family group of elephants by the banks of the Galana River in Tsavo East. The other vehicle was waiting just off the main Mombasa highway, about forty miles to the south-east, with Tony Chalk and two volunteer Privates for company.

Lydia enjoyed how Carter, with her editing help, had built tension into the story and contrasted the dullness of the observation phase, with the intense excitement when four poachers came into the picture. She was also impressed with the restraint shown by Carter's team as they deliberately waited until one adult elephant had been shot, when they could have saved it, their thoughts being on a bigger prize. The rest of the group, who had clearly been hunted before, stampeded down the shallow banks of the river, over to the other side, then into the lush undergrowth.

Carter's team had stayed hidden in a copse of trees watching the poacher gang cut the long, curved, and dust stained tusks, from the still steaming body of the elephant. As the four local men loaded them into the back of a sturdy looking pick-up truck and covered the fresh cargo with sacks and canvas sheeting, Carter' team continued watching while edging towards their own vehicle. As soon as the poachers were paid off by the two men in the pick-up and left the scene, the truck drove up onto the dirt track that followed the river, and headed west, towards the afternoon sun. Charlie Reid got straight onto the radio and alerted Tony's team with a full description of the vehicle.

The narrative explained how the two Land Rover teams had, with the help of their radios, alternated along the highway with one always being behind the target pick-up and one ahead. They didn't always have to keep the target in plain sight until they got near to Mombasa, as there were precious few places to divert from the highway. The road was not in good condition and, as they got near to the industrial area on the way to the port, the pot holes turned into a completely broken surface. Talbot described how his two groups had kept open radio contact as they went through this area, being a maze of warehouses, or godowns as the locals called them. Lydia screwed her eyes up as Cat's story jumped to life, off the screen.

"Chalkie, to Cat, over,"

"Cat here Chalkie, over."

"Target has turned left into an unmarked road, about 400 metres behind you, am pursuing. Private Howes is at corner to guide you on your return, out."

Within ten minutes both teams were parked by one of the long sides of an old godown in, even by Mombasa standards, a very run down area. The godown itself was an old, grey, concrete block, shed style building with no rendering, no windows, and a tin roof. At a guess, I put it at around a thousand square metres. Tony had seen the target vehicle go in through the main warehouse roller shutter at the front, and left his other private, Knowles, watching around the corner. He had already done a circuit of the building and reported no other entrances or exits. The light was almost gone and activity was slight with just a few workers making their way to the main road on foot or bicycle.

Sergeant Reid voiced the thought that was uppermost in our minds, "What now, Sir."

"Good question Sergeant," I replied, "Views Tony?"

"Well..." Chalk replied slowly, "The sensible thing to do, is to keep watch here while one car goes to the local police and report what we've found."

"There's a lot of doubt in your voice there Tony." I observed.

"Indeed. That's because the local police are bound to be involved in some way, even if it's only receiving money to turn a blind eye. The other option, of course...is to take action ourselves, when it's completely dark and there are no witnesses wandering about."

"Reid, Wells, Howes, I can't order you to do this, what do you think?"

Sergeant Reid looked at the two others and they both gently nodded at him. "No need for orders Sir. We've had a little chat between us about this, and what these bastards do. It's about time they got what's coming to them, Mr Talbot."

"Thanks men. My main concern is that we don't know what we're up against once we're inside the building, but we have got the benefit of total surprise. I'm afraid it's cold rations while we wait, then if someone could relieve Knowles please. Unless they try to leave earlier, we'll go in at 22:00."

We spent the next couple of hours planning, and sorting out the equipment. We mounted a heavy machine gun on the roll bar of Chalkie's LR and ensured that the other car had both rocket propelled grenade launchers within easy reach of the crew.

All our two dozen grenades were shared out, and everyone had an automatic rifle with five full magazines each, plus a holstered Browning side arm. Corporal Wells took a large canvas bag and disappeared around the front of the building for twenty minutes, before returning with a much lighter bag.

At 21:55, as quietly as possible, we reversed the Land Rovers back to the front of the godown, picking up Private Howes from the corner, on the way. He confirmed no activity in or out of the building and there seemed to be nobody about outside, so we took up our assault positions. Tony's LR facing diagonally from the left about forty yards back, the muzzle of the 50 calibre weapon ominously projecting forward from the top and the canvas roof stripped off for action. My LR was on the adjacent diagonal to Tony's right, also stripped for action and both Reid and Wells had shouldered the RPG launchers, in the direction of the roller shutter door. The engines of our vehicles were running and the headlights were on full beam.

I looked at my watch, then over at Tony. He waved and put up one thumb. I looked down at the small plastic box device that Corporal Wells had passed me earlier, flicked a switch that was glinting silver in the light from the dashboard, then pressed a red button below the switch. For a second, nothing happened, then almost in slow motion, flames then smoke billowed out from the side edges and top of the metal shutter, accompanied by a concentrated and dramatic triple boom from the virtually simultaneous explosions of C4.

We didn't wait for the smoke to clear but started pouring fire in the direction of the warehouse entrance. The first two RPGs hit the remains of the shutter, largely completing the work of the plastic explosive charges. Reid and Wells instantly reloaded and the next two took slightly longer to explode as they went deep into the heart of the godown before impacting. Since the first explosions, Chalk's crew had kept up a sustained fire through the breach with the 50 calibre and their automatic rifles, while I had loosed off two magazines in support.

The burst of the third RPG rounds in the warehouse was the pre-arranged signal for us to move in and I slammed the gearstick forward then revved the engine. Tony's LR bounded forward on cue and we both charged at the breach in the shutter. The moment we burst through, our lights picked up little more than smoke from the various explosions but in the absence of clear targets we sprayed the interior with more rounds in every direction.

At the shouted order from me of, "Dismount," we all grabbed our personal weapons and took cover behind the vehicles with our backs to the ruined door. The smoke swirled and gradually settled in the headlight beams and we could see large stacks of tusks covering about a third of the total floor area at the rear of the building. Parked in front of the ivory was a large, maroon, E-class Mercedes and the pick-up truck we'd followed from Tsavo. There was also a set of stairs halfway along the left hand wall leading up to a platform area, and what looked like offices. The rest of the warehouse was a jumble of packing cases, ropes and other paraphernalia of warehousing anywhere, mainly scattered and damaged by the explosions.

"Tony," I called, "I can't see any bodies, what about you?"

"We've got two dead here," came his reply, "Must have been close to the door, a real mess."

"Roger that, can you take your men, and do a recce up

those stairs? We'll cover you... Wells, get on the 50 calibre please."

Lieutenant Chalk and his team, scampered, crouching, in the headlights to the foot of the stairs without incident and stopped, craning their necks to see up the stairs, eyes sensitive to the slightest movement. Wells trained the machine gun along the balcony also looking for any tell-tale sign of trouble. With all the attention being on the left, I was surprised when the next noise I heard was a sharp crack to my right front, and a simultaneous shattering of glass from closer to me. Within a second there was an identical sound, and the light in the building was now distinctly dim compared to moments before.

"Reid," I whispered, "To our right, probably behind those packing cases, someone's shooting out the headlights. Get along the wall while I keep his head down." I then pulled a grenade from my webbing and hurled it at the jumble of boxes I'd identified. Tony took advantage of the grenade bursting and his team flew up the stairs before throwing themselves flat on the steel balcony.

Meanwhile, Reid had found the dazed sniper behind the boxes and shot him twice in the chest and once in the head, before calling out, "Clear!"

"Well done Reidy," I shouted, "Now, could you demolish those vehicles please? We don't need to hang about here all night."

Back on the balcony, the other team had still not met any resistance and were now on either side of the opening to the offices. Taking no chances, three grenades were dispatched through the door and they went down on the steel floor again. Jumping to their feet they ran in and sprayed the dark interior with a few dozen rounds before Knowles tried the light switch on the wall. It stayed dark so they took out their flashlights and glanced around. There were no further bodies, just a chaotic scene of splintered plywood desks, ruptured office chairs and holes all along the chipboard walls. An inner door was still standing, although badly damaged. They were suddenly bathed in yellow light through the shattered office window for a few seconds, as they heard the cough of a small explosion followed immediately by the roar of a big one.

Back on the warehouse floor, Sergeant Reid picked himself up from behind a few protective packing cases, satisfied that his grenade in the petrol tank of the pick-up had done its job. He skirted the flames that engulfed the truck, to make his way to the Mercedes for a repeat performance.

Back in the office, and conscious that they were now beyond the covering arc of Wells on the machine gun, Chalk's team proceeded cautiously. Three more grenades through the inner door, followed by a few bursts of automatic fire, then they entered, waving their torches. They were surprised to see that this wasn't more offices but more like a large combined lounge and sleeping area. One African man was sprawled on a couch which was heavily stained with his blood. He made no sound.

Tony scanned the room and it occurred to him that there was something unusual about how such an obviously heavy mahogany dining table had ended up on its side. Then his instincts took over and he immediately dived behind a settee while screaming, "Cover," to his men. Their training kicked in and they also threw themselves down where they could as the rattle of automatic gunfire heralded a spurt of bullets from around the side of the table top. All three of Tony's team had the same thought and lobbed grenades over the edge of the table, then blasted at it until their magazines needed changing.

When the noise stopped, Tony lifted himself up and

cautiously approached the table with his reloaded weapon in front of him. He peered over the corner and then released all the breath he'd been holding in, as he saw that the three men behind the table would be giving no further trouble. They double checked that the man on the couch was also dead then went back out onto the balcony, waving to Wells and shining their torches on their faces so that he didn't think of them as threats.

Meanwhile, Sergeant Reid was having trouble with his destruction job on the Mercedes. The fuel cap was locked flush with the body and must have an internal mechanism as he couldn't see how he could easily open it. When he went to the driver's door, that was also locked. His attempts to smash the blacked-out glass with the butt of his rifle were dramatically unsuccessful, in that he ended up with a dislocated finger. I could hear Reid swearing at the "Fucking armoured, fucking glass," and seeing that Chalk's crew were waving safely from the balcony, moved towards the Merc in the light of the still burning pick-up.

In his pain and temper, Sergeant Reid had dropped his rifle and was using his right hand to hold the injured digit on his left hand, while turning his back to the car. As he did so, I could see the driver's door quickly open and a well built, suited African jumped out. He grabbed Reid quickly around the neck with a thick right arm and nuzzled a handgun quickly and sharply into the left of his neck, dragging them both backwards to lean against the car, closing the door with the weight of them as he did so.

"Who is in charge here?" shouted the man.

"That would be me," I called, now about fifteen yards from the rear of the car.

"Are you an officer?"

"I am in charge."

"How dare you come in here and disturb my business?"

"Unfortunately for you, that's our job."

"Did the police not tell you who I am?"

"The police know nothing of this operation."

His natural arrogance seemed to falter a tiny bit with that news and I pressed home the advantage, "If you're such a 'big man' why were you hiding in your car while your men were killed defending your 'business'?"

"I was just about to go home, when you and your thugs blasted your way in here. Your vehicles are blocking the exit. When my cousin, the President, hears about this, you will all be tortured to death, be in no doubt."

"I'm not sure that he will hear about this, certainly not from you anyway. Look around you, there are six of us, all highly trained by the best army in the world."

"You British, you still think you can bully us Kenyans even all those years after independence. You are not wanted here."

"Nevertheless, we are here, and I would be most grateful if you could release our colleague unharmed."

"And I would be 'most grateful' if you could order your men to put down their weapons, to avoid me having to shoot this one."

I dropped my rifle and raised the hand that had been holding it, while nodding and calling to the team, "You heard him lads, put down your weapons, and lift your arms so that he can see."

The team deliberately took their time putting down their guns, and Wells climbed down from the LR. While the ivory dealer was looking around to check on the unarmed status of my colleagues, I took the opportunity to get a little closer to him, while removing my side arm from its holster, flicking the safety catch off, and moving slightly to the side so that one of the large packing cases shielded his view of my right hand.

"Now," said the dealer, "Your colleague and I will be taking a little ride, so if you could move the Land Rovers, all will be well?"

With that, the dealer took a slight dip towards the door handle. It was all I needed and my arm came to the horizontal, aiming at the head of the big African as it turned back towards me. I squeezed quickly and his head immediately jerked backwards. His gun fell from his hand as he fell to the ground but the strong grip he had on Reid's neck took the Sergeant down with him. I ran forward and pumped two shots into the man's chest, then helped Reid to disentangle himself.

"Thank you Sir," he gasped with a smile.

"Never in any doubt Sergeant," I grinned back.

"Right you men," I shouted, "We've already been here long enough, quickly get all our spare petrol on the tusks and drive the Merc over to them as well. Reid, if you think you can find out how to open the petrol tank, perhaps you could finish the destruction?"

"Sarcasm is the lowest form of wit you know, Sir." Reid replied, having already found the switch on the dashboard.

We soon had a huge fire going onto which we threw a few dozen packing cases for good measure. By the time the six of us and our Land Rovers were out in the fresh air, Chalk leaned from his car towards mine, looked at his watch and commented over the dull roar of the conflagration, "I can't believe it Carter, less than half an hour for that whole job."

"I know," I replied, "All that adrenalin used so quickly. And our only casualty a rather feeble dislocated finger. Time to get out of town Tony, don't you think?"

"Yes, back to Nanyuki through the night, should be in time for late breakfast or early lunch at the Red Lion?"

"Brilliant idea, what could be better after a night's driving then plenty of beer and a fry up?"

Lydia, turned away from her screen and leaned back in her chair for a moment. How she envied that sense of bonding that men in combat clearly had. And that tale had been so 'Carter', humour lying so close to deadly peril and the breaking of all the rules.

She finished the chapter and it seemed that, although Talbot and his crew never admitted what they'd done, the people at the BHC put two and two together and the result was a fairly rapid departure from Kenya for Carter, and a solid denial of any British involvement.

Lydia hadn't had the highest expectations of finding clues to Carter's current 'trip' in the chapter and in that she wasn't disappointed. Certainly there was no mention of Shakespeare or any promising contacts in the story, apart from the other soldiers, who she assumed were long gone from Kenya by now. She did however, think that it might be worth trying to track down the Red Lion in Nanyuki to see if he had ventured in there on this return journey. It was clearly a favoured watering hole in those long gone days.

-+-

Chapter Forty Six

It was a very tired Carter Talbot who stumbled off a KLM 787 Dreamliner at Nairobi and, in the heavy early morning rain, darted onto the bus at the bottom of the steps. This was his third departure from an aircraft in the previous fifteen hours and, although flying through the night, he hadn't had much sleep. The packed bus soon deposited the passengers at the makeshift arrivals terminal which had been fashioned from the multi-storey car park after the airport fire, and was still serving its new purpose.

After buying his visitor's visa as he went through immigration, Carter waited for his camouflaged Bergen at the baggage carousel. He had only brought essentials, so shouldered the pack easily and strolled through customs. In the open hall that was previously a car park deck, he was looking for car hire signs and trying to block out the hundreds of noisy people around him, when he heard the repeated cry, "Bwana Talbot". Carter turned his head towards the noise and saw a very young looking, mixed race, man with a cardboard placard displaying the name 'TALBOT' in thick strokes of purple ink.

Carter looked at the man, with no sign of recognition, and moved towards him. Pointing a finger at his own chest, he said, "I'm Carter Talbot."

"I know Sir, my father showed me some photos, but said that you might be fatter now."

"And who might your cheeky fucker of a father be?"

"Charlie Reid, Sir. I'm his son, Churchill."

Carter smiled at Churchill, through his fatigue, then shook the proffered hand saying, "Pleased to meet you. But I told your Dad not to bother, I was going to get a hire car."

Churchill looked slightly hurt and muttered, "He thought you'd like to see a friendly face when you arrived, and was worried that you wouldn't remember how to get to Nanyuki after so many years away."

Talbot smiled again, and remembered his manners, "That's very kind of him, and you, to take this trouble. I'm really grateful."

"The car is this way, Bwana."

The very early Thursday morning traffic was, in the pre-dawn hour, easy enough for Churchill to get them through the capital and onto the Thika superhighway heading north. Within three hours they were approaching the garrison town of Nanyuki and Carter's mind was cast back a quarter of a century. He looked to his left and could see the huge banks of white cloud that shielded the peak of Mount Kenya from view, reflecting the morning sunlight. A kilometre out of the town to the east, they turned off the main road and down a short track which opened out into a gravel car park. A life size crimson statue of a male lion with full mane, had pride of place next to the front door of a sprawling two storey brick building with tiled roof, behind the car park. No sign was necessary, even if Carter hadn't been able to remember the place.

Churchill hooted twice, as he parked the Toyota saloon car near the statue, and the front door opened inwards. A stocky short white man with bald head, insignificant chin, and an earring in his right earlobe, strode through and smiled at the car. Churchill and Carter walked towards him and his arms opened wide in greeting. He gave Cat a massive bear hug, then stepped back, went into rigid attention and snapped a crisp salute. "Major Talbot, Sir. Welcome back to the Red Lion."

"Great salute Charlie, longest way up, shortest way down. But not necessary old friend. I wasn't even still an officer when we first met!"

"As you wish Sir, but you'll always be Major Talbot to me."

"Never mind that, is it too early for a Tusker, Charlie?"

"Never too early, and never too late, at the Red Lion. Even before I bought it, as I'm sure you remember."

"Indeed I do... Let's have a chat."

Carter noticed some new touches about the old pub. A 72 inch TV screen was fixed to one wall in clear view of the main bar, for sporting events, according to Charlie. The number of regimental pennants adorning the walls had grown exponentially as British and Commonwealth regiments being trained at the Army base just outside the town, made this a home from home. But mainly, observed Cat, it was still the same dark wood and mixture of old mismatched chairs that it had always been, and he announced himself glad of it.

Several hours later, Cat and Charlie had well and truly enjoyed each other's company after so many years. Around lunchtime they were joined by former Corporal Wells and Tony Chalk who both tried to catch up with the beer consumption. Churchill looked after the old comrades, keeping their glasses filled and bringing food when it was necessary.

By mid-afternoon, the lack of sleep, plus the excessive beer and a belly full of Churchill's selected bitings, had left Cat ready to drop where he sat. After securing a promise from everyone that they would reconvene at breakfast tomorrow for a serious discussion, Carter let Churchill get him upstairs and onto a bed, where he slept straight through until just before dawn the following day.

Early on that Friday morning, the same group reassembled in the small, private rear bar where the table had been laid for breakfast. Carter told them all he knew about Shakespeare and where he lived, about his brother and the havoc that had been wrought in Crawnish when he had come looking for his twin. He then told them about the contents of the recent air mail letters that were now stuffed into an inside pocket of his combat jacket. He shared the knowledge that Shaky had passed on regarding his father's involvement in the Rwandan genocide, and also the fact that he had never been named as a war criminal by any court.

"Mr Talbot?"

"Carter... please Wellsy," responded Cat to the quietly spoken former Corporal.

"Righto Sir... Carter?"

"Yes."

"Well, it seems that you're thinking of some kind of rescue mission, would that be right?"

"Yes, that's exactly what I'm thinking. I don't mind admitting that Nicole was the only woman I've deeply loved and that I thought she was dead for the last twenty years. Knowing that she's not only alive, but being held against her will by some murderous thug with delusions of grandeur, just eats me up, boys."

"From what you've said though, Mr Ta... Carter, the husband is well off and has an unknown number of guards protecting him on a private fenced estate."

"That's right... But I've got to do something."

"Have you thought of speaking to the authorities?" Tony Chalk asked.

"I did give that some thought Tony, but only for a couple of minutes. This is Africa, and this Gatanazi guy has been safely set on this estate for nigh on twenty years. He will have all the local police and politicians in his pocket. Plus the fact that, after Westgate, the Kenyan defence forces have been very much focused on Al Shabaab and the terrorist threat from Somalia, not chasing alleged war criminals with no hard evidence."

"What if we talked to someone in Nairobi, I've got some connections?"

"I don't think I can risk it Chalkie. Word would only have to get back to the estate that someone was asking questions, and they'd be on their guard for months."

"Fair point... Are you thinking of a repeat of the 'Mombasa Ivory Raid'?"

Carter went quiet for a moment and enjoyed the grins that accompanied the memory of their last time together. "I'm not sure we'd get away with that again," he said softly, "Not enough of us, and we're probably all too old for frontal assault on an unknown enemy."

Charlie Reid had been quiet up to this point and now volunteered his thoughts, "Look here, Carter... I, for one, am with you, whatever the plan is. I realise that we've got to box a bit clever, and we're not as young as we used to be. But we have surprise on our side and I have complete faith in you, Mr Talbot."

"Thanks Charlie. That means a lot to me."

"Mount Elgon is a long way," said Wells, "About 400 kilometres, I'd say. You'll need a couple of decent vehicles, with someone to look after them if it all goes 'tits up'. Looks like I'd better come too..."

Carter smiled at him and nodded in thanks.

Tony Chalk looked worried for a second, then opened his mouth. "I hope you don't think I'm too old Cat? You could probably do with a wise old head and, as long as you don't expect me to sprint through the bush all day, I can do my bit."

"Chalkie, you're in of course, wouldn't be the same without you."

Tony breathed a sigh of relief then went into organisation mode, "Great... Anyone know the area up there?"

"I know someone who does," offered Ray Wells, "One of my mechanics was in the Kenyan Wildlife Service and did a few months at the National Park. Good bloke, he'll join in."

"Look Gents, before we go any further," said Carter sheepishly, "I'm on a good pension from Her Majesty but just so there's no misunderstandings, I can't afford mercenary rates of pay for this mission. All costs are on me and, if we get away with it, the biggest party this pub's ever seen."

"We're all soldiers at heart here Cat," said Charlie, "I think for the sake of good order, you can pay us current British Army rates of pay, for our former ranks, and we'll be happy. Non-army guys at rates for a Private." He looked around the table and his colleagues nodded sagely.

"Thanks again gentlemen. Now, let's look at the map shall we?"

For the next half an hour they looked at a road map of northern Kenya and, via The Red Lion's Wi-Fi, some computerised maps of the target zone. They identified the general layout of the area but similar to Carter's solitary analysis earlier, they couldn't find much recorded detail on the ground, apart from some roads, the border between Kenya and Uganda, and the extent of the Mount Elgon National Park.

"Shakespeare said that his father's estate forms a sort of a triangle backing onto the eastern slopes of the mountain. It's in a chunk of what became the national park after the estate was built and fenced off, so it sort of sits within the park boundaries but not under park jurisdiction, due to some old political influence. Unfortunately it doesn't show up on any map we've seen."

"I think Mbugua, my guy, will be able throw some light on this," said Ray, "I don't know when we're thinking of going, but I can get him here later today if needed?"

"Honestly, chaps. I don't have a plan for this operation yet. I think the best way forward is to get up there as soon as we can, with plenty of kit, and find somewhere quiet as a base. Then we can do an extended recce for as long as it takes. We can agree a firm plan once we've found out all we can. What do you think?"

After common assent was expressed, Carter then asked, "What about weapons?"

Charlie then got up from the table and invited them all to follow him to the cellar. The scraping of chairs was interrupted by a rather loud, old-fashioned, tinkling bell noise from behind the bar. Charlie leaned over the bar, grabbed at the bakelite handset and stretched the cord to reach his ear, "Red Lion," he said, breezily. Then, after a couple of affirmations and a look at his colleagues, he asked the caller to hold on, put his hand over the mouthpiece and said in a half-whisper, "Cat, it's for you... Lydia?"

Carter looked a little taken aback, then smiled, took the handset and leaned on the bar to talk. "Hello Lids," he said cheerfully, "Didn't realise you were a detective?"

"You shouldn't be surprised at my resourcefulness Cat, not now you know me so well. I just wanted to check that you'd arrived safely. Everything Ok?"

"Fine, I got here yesterday, met up with some old colleagues."

"Let me guess, Chalk, Reid, and Wells? Sounds like a firm of solicitors!"

"You are thorough, Darling."

"Are you going to see Shakespeare? Don't worry, it'll be our secret."

"That is part of it, yes."

"Well, I won't pry too much. Just please take care of yourself and, if remotely possible, stay out of trouble. I don't want another round of hospital visits to see you Carter, nor months of convalescence, thanks. And, don't forget, you've got a serious reason for coming home safely, growing bigger every day."

"I know Lydia, and it's exciting for both of us. I've just got to do...what I've got to do, then I promise, home safely and prepare for being a Dad."

"Ok then, I'll leave you to it... I love you Carter."

"Bye Lydia, I'm in company at the moment, but thinking of you."

"Bye Cat," 'click'.

Before Carter could even get the phone down, Charlie had to get a quick dig in, "You, a Dad? This is a first, though but, Sir."

"It is lads, a bit scary eh? Months away yet. Anyway, we've got more pressing things to think about for now. Come on Charlie, you were taking us to the cellar, I believe?"

They went down a half flight of steps, behind the bar, into a low roofed cellar, with bare brick walls and two electric light bulbs. They followed Charlie to the rear of the room and he heaved at two aluminium beer kegs with Tusker labels glued on the side. Once they'd been moved the men saw a flat hinged hatchway with a flush ring handle to the non-hinged side. Reid reached down and lifted the hatch open, laying it back against the kegs. He then grabbed a flashlight from a shelf and shone it down into the open space.

Reflecting back the bright light was a rough wooden rack with about a dozen automatic rifles of various designs, lying diagonally on grooves in the timber. To the side was a number of ammunition boxes labelled with numbers and letters denoting the racked weapons. Charlie stepped down into the relatively small space and opened the lids of some larger boxes around him. His friends could see bazookas, RPGs, and boxes of grenades and flares of various types. There was a coffin sized box full of boots and another with an assortment of webbing and helmets. Rummaging around in the back of the basement out of sight of his colleagues, he mumbled something about his 'pride and joy', then emerged with a sniper rifle in one hand and a three inch mortar set, in the other.

"Which is it Charlie?" Carter asked.

"Which is what?" he replied.

"You were saying something about your 'pride and joy'?"

"Oh, that's too heavy to bring out on my own. It's our old friend the 50 calibre machine gun, liberated from the quartermaster after our Mombasa adventure, and sat here ever since. In full working order mind, with stacks of ammo. Tested annually, a beauty."

So the team worked on selecting which weapons to take on their mission, and many a friendly argument livened up the afternoon at the old pub. Mbugua arrived and gave them a brief geography lesson about the area they were planning to go to. They agreed that they would finish the preparation that evening and set off early on Saturday. Traffic would be relatively light and they should make it to the Mount Elgon area in one day.

As the light started to fade, Ray and Mbugua, who had made themselves scarce during the late afternoon, returned to the car park with the two vehicles they were going to use. They looked like two large, fairly modern, 4x4, Nissan Patrols, one grey and one brown. They drove them down a private track to the rear of the building and backed them up to the back door of the pub. They then came in for a nightcap with their friends, in a pub that was now filling up with off duty servicemen, out for a few Friday night bevvies.

Carter enjoyed a few beers but was quieter than the previous evening. Charlie and Ray both knew better than to quiz him but offered their support. "It will be fine Cat," said Charlie, "If anyone can do it, we can. We'll rescue Nicole and Shakespeare, in double quick time, probably before anyone notices. Then we can hide them here until the dust settles, and you can help them to wherever they want to go."

"Let's hope you're right, Charlie. There's just so much we don't know."

"We'll manage Carter, it's what we're best at."

-+-

Chapter Forty Seven

A frisson of excitement coursed through Shakespeare Kwizera as he looked up from the book he was reading late on a Friday afternoon, in the shade, by the pool at his father's ranch. Movement from the sun-kissed side of the water had reflected in the still surface and attracted his attention. That attention accelerated rapidly as he beheld Monique the hooker, slipping off a light green satin jacket and matching sarong, to perch on the edge of a sun bed in high heels and a swim suit.

She glanced over at him and his jaw dropped slightly towards his chest as he took in the view of her fabulous shiny brown body, in a cream bikini, and the full smile from her mouth that he remembered so well. He moved to put down his book and shifted as if to rise from his bed. He stopped when he saw the brief sideways shake of her head and the finger to her lips. He then noticed, coming through the sliding patio doors, a young white woman with full blond hair, in a black bikini which sharply contrasted with her very pale complexion. Shakespeare thought that it was almost as if her natural colour was pale blue, and that she needed some sunshine to just go white.

As he pondered this, his father strolled out behind the girls in a ludicrously baggy pair of Hawaiian-style shorts and a loose, white linen, collarless shirt, then moved to hug them both in a bear-like grip.

"Shakespeare my son, look at these two beauties," he shouted across the pool, while grasping their bottoms with one of his hands on each. "They are among my regulars. You don't know what you're missing," he went on, "Meet Monique, and... Russian girl, what's your name?"

The pale girl dutifully giggled and said, in a heavily

accented tone of mock disappointment, "You know I Natasha, I bin before."

"You both have, and you're early," Alphonse observed. "Sit here and enjoy the last of the sun, come to my room at seven. I'll be ready for you. Shakespeare, where are your manners."

"Sorry father," replied his son in a neutral voice, "I'm very pleased to meet you, ladies. Would you like a drink?"

An hour later, the whole patio was cast in long shadows and Natasha, being the worse for several shots of neat vodka, gently dozed on her sun bed. Shakespeare and Monique moved away onto two other beds and talked in low voices. He was thrilled when Monique confirmed that the letter he had given her nearly seven weeks before, had been posted as soon as she had returned to Nairobi. She reminded him that he owed her 50,000 bob and he smiled at her.

Shaky tried to remember how much cash he had in the locked drawer in his bedroom, and reflected that it would probably be enough, "How would you like to double that?" he asked.

"You naughty boy, you want my mouth again don't you?"

"No... I mean yes... I mean, I was thinking of something else."

"My arse will cost you more than double, it's only for special people."

"Monique, can we just forget about sex for a minute? I need another favour."

She finally shut up and listened as Shakespeare explained

what he needed her to do and that she would get her 100,000 shillings, if all went well. They finished their drinks and he left the girls to themselves while he returned to his room, inwardly thinking about just how cute Monique was, and seething about the sort of things his father was going to do to her.

Some four hours later, Shakespeare quietly left his bedroom and walked softly up to his father's suite of rooms. The door was locked so he sat down on an easy chair along the landing and, under a side table lamp, read a book. After about half an hour, he heard some metallic fumblings from the door and walked over to stand outside.

"Monique... Is that you?"

His question was answered seconds later when her smooth face appeared, in the widening crack of an opening door.

"He's had plenty of champagne," she whispered to him. "And so has Natasha. They're both snoring like pigs."

"Has he... Has he, hurt you?"

"I'm... Ok," she said softly with a forced smile. "Just do what you have to do, I'll go back in the bed and keep him occupied if he wakes up."

"Thanks Monique."

Shakespeare quickly went behind his father's big office desk and sat behind the large desktop computer screen. He reached for the mouse and a graphic pornographic image, involving what looked like an interracial orgy, flashed open in front of him. Using a separate tab he opened the browser, then a Google page in quick succession.

He searched for 'Hotmail' and quickly set up the address

he'd mentioned to Cat in his letter. He also set up an email response option within the account and saved the settings, before clearing the history of the pages he'd been on and going back to '**ebonyandivoryorgy.com**'.

He put the mouse back where he had picked it up and, as he sat waiting for the screen to fade into black, he rummaged in the desk drawers. After going through each one without finding what he was looking for, Shaky tried the filing cabinet beside the desk. It opened and inside was some alphabetic suspension folders. On a whim, he flicked through, stopped at tab 'K' and slipped his hand into the folder below. He pulled it out and looked at a bundle of keys now in his hand. A quick check through the collection of keys while standing at the door to the landing gave Shakespeare what he wanted, and he took it off the ring then pocketed it. He replaced the key ring and remaining keys back in the filing cabinet then edged towards the bedroom door.

The door was slightly ajar and in the dim glow of a TV screen, he saw that Monique was lying next to the other two and looking towards him. He attracted her attention with his hand until she slipped gently out of the bed and followed him into the office.

"You've been great Monique." He whispered to her, while holding out a fat envelope. She didn't look at it but slid it into the waistband at the back of her knickers. She then held his shoulders and, standing on tip toe, gave him a genuinely tender kiss. "Go" she said and she moved to the door to the landing, locking it again after he'd quietly left.

Nicole was woken by some light tapping at her door moments later, and she heard her son's voice as she got out of bed and let him in.

"Mum, I thought you should know," he said breathlessly,

"I've done the new email address and got a spare key for Father's study. We might be able to get the odd message to and from Carter."

His mother looked concerned and tapped his arm, saying, "Well done Darling, just be careful...please."

"I will...we can't carry on like this...I had to do something."

"I know... Get some sleep Son, and be patient."

"Honestly Mum, patience is getting boring now, we need to take some chances. Trust me."

"I do Darling. Good night."

-+-

Chapter Forty Eight

Early the next morning, four hundred kilometres to the east, six men started the serious business of loading up their two vehicles for a 'camping trip' to the Mount Elgon National Park. Interestingly for nature enthusiasts, they packed a wide assortment of highly destructive weapons and these all went into the false floors in each Nissan Patrol. With the covers on the floors firmly in place, all the camping equipment and other kit went on top and filled the rear of each vehicle. As a finishing touch, Charlie Reid wedged an open half case of Johnnie Walker Red Label on top of each pile of luggage.

"Nice thought Charlie," said Cat, "But if you want to take so much whisky, why not put it all in one case and save space?"

Charlie just looked at Talbot and tapped the side of his nose in a knowing way, without any comment. Carter knew well enough to shut up and they finished their packing by putting personal backpacks on the spare rear seat in each car.

When all were happy, they went back inside and had a massive cooked breakfast, with giant mugs of tea. Charlie went upstairs to say goodbye to his wife and the others went into corners with their mobiles for similar farewells. Carter took out his iPad and, via the Red Lion's Wi-Fi, tried emailing 'shakykenya@hotmail.com'. He was pleasantly surprised when, instead of the failure message he expected, a clearly automated email popped up:

'Thanks for the email. If you're Cat, then we are Ok. Situation much the same. Only limited access to emails but I will read them at some point. Hope you are Ok? Shaky.'

Carter thought for a few moments, then composed a reply and touched 'Send'. He finished his tea and was rejoined by his colleagues around their breakfast table. Ray Wells placed a pair of walkie-talkie units on the table and Tony picked one up.

"Thanks Ray," he said, "In terms of comms, these will do while we're travelling. As agreed last night, I'll take the lead car with Churchill and Mbugua. Cat... You, Charlie and Ray follow."

Cat picked up the other WT unit and asked, "Call signs Tony?"

"Well, this is a rescue mission and it has an international flavour, so the puppets on Tracy Island come to mind." Chalk smiled, "We'll be 'Thunderbird One' so T1, and you boys can be 'Thunderbird Two', T2."

"Nice one Chalky... But who the fuck is going to be 'Brains'?" Charlie enquired.

They set off with the sun behind them and the cloud clad bulk of Mount Kenya to their left. Ray was driving Cat's Patrol, with him in the other front seat and Charlie in the back. Their WT crackled into life, "Tango One, Tango Two, radio check, over." Carter picked it up and held the button, "Tango Two, Tango One, comms OK, over." "Thank you Tango Two, these haven't got much of a range gents, any problems, all keep your mobiles on. We stop for gas and a breather at Eldoret, ETA five hours, Tango One, out."

They were about half way to Eldoret, on an empty bit of road north of Nakuru, when Cat noticed the brake lights of Chalkie's vehicle flashing three times. This was their signal for possible trouble ahead and he reached for the

WT, "Tango Two, Tango One, problems Tony? Over." "Tango One, Tango Two, police check point ahead, stick together, out."

Carter could now see that their lead car was being flagged down by a blue uniformed, white capped policeman while another officer stood behind him with an automatic rifle held across his chest. Although they hadn't waved his car towards the verge, Cat told Ray to follow Tony's lead and pull over. The unarmed officer spoke briefly to Churchill, who was driving Tony's car, then strolled purposefully back to the second one. "Leave this to me, Sir," said Ray quietly from the driver's seat, as he lowered his window.

The policeman, they could now see from his arm, was a sergeant and he came up close to Ray before saying, loudly, in English, "I did not ask you to stop, do you have something to tell me?"

Ray answered him in what to Cat sounded like fluent Kiswahili, but he had no idea what was said. The conversation went back and forth briefly before the officer walked back to the car in front. "Routine check point, gents," said Wells. "I told him we were travelling together, that's why I stopped. Stuck to the story, we're on a camping holiday to Mt. Elgon. He seemed Ok, said that if we had anything to hide, we would have just driven on."

Through the windscreen, they could see that Tony had got out of the lead car and was going back to the tailgate with the sergeant. He opened both rear doors, and gesticulated at the various bags and equipment stacked up therein. The officer leaned further forward and pointed, then they could see Tony laughing as he reached into the pile and rummaged. His hand quickly emerged with a bottle of whisky which he passed to the sergeant, now also laughing. They shook hands and the policeman returned to his armed colleague, showing off the proceeds of his search. Both officers enthusiastically waved the vehicles forward and saluted as they drove off.

"I see now Charlie, why you put the whisky in last, and in both cars."

Before Charlie could respond, the WT crackled again, "Tango One to Tango Two, regret to advise the loss of one Private J. Walker, of the Scots Guards. We must make sure that his sacrifice is not in vain. Tango One, out."

The journey continued with all on board both cars wearing a grin, as they ate up the miles. They beat their five hour estimate by half an hour and when they stopped at a filling station in Eldoret for diesel and a toilet break, they agreed that some cold soft drinks and snacks would take the place of lunch, so that they could carry on and reach the target area well before dark.

They continued towards the north-west through the early afternoon until they saw a metal sign saying 'Welcome to Kitale' and Thunderbird One pulled over to the dusty verge, just past the sign. Carter, who was taking his turn in the driver's seat of Thunderbird Two, pulled in behind it and turned off the engine. Everyone got out of both vehicles to gather around Cat's car bonnet, as he spread a map of the area out on the still hot metal.

"Mbugua," he said, "Can you remind us how you remember the layout of the park?"

"Yes, Bwana, the main gate is at Chorlim and is not far from Kitale. We need to go west out of town on the Suam road and, just before the road turns north, about here," he explained, jabbing at the map for emphasis, "Is Mount Elgon Park Road on the left. If we get to Endebess, we've missed the turn. Assuming we find the Park Road we follow it and go through the gate, as paying tourists of course."

"And the Kwizera ranch? Any recollection where that might be?" Cat asked.

"I've never seen it, but I phoned an old colleague and he remembers a private, fenced-off estate, due west of where the park road runs out. It becomes pretty much a dirt track after that and after a few miles of forest, the trees thin out and you're in a dusty area as you get higher up the slopes of the mountain. He isn't sure who lives there but he remembers that park rangers weren't welcome."

"Thanks Mbugua, how can we verify, chaps?"

"Ask at the gate?" Churchill suggested.

"Really Son?" said Charlie, "And let word get back to the ranch that people are asking questions about them? No, we need something more subtle."

"I could pop into the club?" Tony proffered.

"Club?" Charlie repeated.

"There's a Kitale Club here somewhere, they played Nanyuki Club at golf now and then in the old days. Bound to be an old mzungu or two who I could ask on the quiet."

"Ok," said Cat, "That can't be too hard to find. Ray, have quick look on the GPS can you? Let's go."

Within five minutes the two Nissan's were parked in the Kitale Club car park and Tony had gone inside alone. Twenty minutes later he emerged, slightly more red-faced than when he'd entered. He went over to Cat's window and told him, "Cost me a couple of large gin and tonics, but got what we needed. Mbugua was right about the ranch. If we don't hang about, we can get through the

Chorlim gate before it closes for the evening."

The team left the club and continued on their route. Their navigation was faultless and they found the main gate just as it was closing. It took Tony's persuasive powers with Johnnie Walker again for the KWS guards to allow them to pay their entry fees and proceed. The Rangers kindly pointed out the way to the official campsites, for which they were thanked and after a few miles saw a rough sign to the 'Saltlick Campsite'. They ignored it and pressed on.

They hadn't expected the foliage to be so lush and their speed gradually slowed as they got deeper into the park. After many miles of twists and turns, the surrounding vegetation began to show gaps in it and they noticed that they were climbing steadily. They got to a small ridge and the maintained road just seemed to peter out at a rough timber gate between some solid looking baobab trees. There was a very rusty metal sign on the gate that said 'No Through Road' but they could clearly see a dirt track, beyond the gate.

Mbugua jumped out of the lead car, opened the barrier and waved the team through. He then remounted after closing the gate, and they drove on for a couple of miles until stopping in a copse of jacaranda trees.

Once they were all gathered again around the bonnet of Thunderbird Two, Cat briefed the others, "We've got about an hour until nightfall and I don't think we should be visible from the road. Well, when I say 'road' you know what I mean. Let's take the cars cross country to the north for about a mile. We can set up camp, organise watches, and cook some well-earned supper. We can then discuss our options, and firm up a plan for tomorrow. Is that Ok with everyone?" There was a general mumbling of assent and they gently drove the Patrols through the bushes to a slight plateau with good tree cover to the south but a decent view of the mountain, beyond the forest to the west.

Within an hour, two four man tents were up with their entrances facing each other, and a fire was blazing on the ground between them. Churchill was crouched over the fire and had set up a metal frame, from which dangled a round black metal pot. He stirred the contents of the karoga and faint bubbling noises from within, competed with the spitting of the branches on the fire. Ray had set up a perimeter trip wire just inside the line of trees to the south, stretching around both sides of the camp to end at the edge of the plateau. At intervals along the wire, he dangled small bunches of bells.

Carter had, in the meantime, used one of the GPS satellite phones to send another email message to Shakespeare. In return he got a repeat of the automatic response he had seen that morning, and nothing more. He sent a quick text to Lydia saying that all was well, that she shouldn't worry, and that he was thinking of her. He then put the phone on top of his sleeping bag in the tent he was sharing with Reid Senior and Wells, before going to sit by the fire and break out some cold beer from their icebox.

The rest of the team gathered around the fire and, between swigs of Tusker from the bottles handed round by Cat, they ladled chicken curry from the karoga into enamel bowls. They tucked in with spoons and agreed that Churchill made a very good Chicken Madras.

Charlie Reid gave a very satisfied belch as he sat back against a tree stump and stretched his legs. "What's the plan, Carter?" he said.

"I don't know yet Charlie, the problem is that we don't yet know enough about what we're facing. We're in desperate need of more local intelligence. I've tried emailing Shaky but he must have very restricted access, so no joy there.

The risks involved in just going straight for the ranch down the only track are too high. I couldn't bear to report any casualties to your families, or put Nicole and Shakespeare in any more danger."

"But we could get a good idea of the target by, shall we say, turning up there by accident?" Tony suggested.

"What have you got in mind Tony? If all six of us arrive at their doorstep, surely they'll be suspicious of our motives?" Carter replied.

"Exactly, that's why I'll put on my doddery old bastard act. If I pretend to be some eccentric wildlife photographer, who has lost his bearings and is in need of help, I can discover plenty about the layout and the people, then report back."

"Worth a shot Tony," Ray observed, "And you're pretty good with that camera of yours."

"I could go with Bwana Chalk?" Mbugua offered. "Surely he wouldn't be out here on his own? He would have a faithful servant to help him in the bush. I could do that."

"Great idea," said Ray, "And, just before you get near the entrance, you could put a kink in the fuel line or something, to make the car run ragged, as an excuse to ask for help."

"Sounds good...take one of the satellite phones with you...just in case," said Talbot. "If you're sure that you're Ok with this, Tony?"

"I wouldn't have suggested it otherwise Cat. I might be in my seventies, but I've still got all my marbles."

"So, you two can set off after breakfast tomorrow then?"

Carter said, "And we'll throw one of the tents back in your car so it looks like you're genuinely camping. We'll rest here until you get back."

"All agreed then," said Charlie, climbing to his feet, "I'll get a bottle and we can toast good luck to Tony and Mbugua's mission."

The whole party agreed that this was essential to success and they passed around one of the Johnnie Walker bottles, until it was empty. There was plenty of banter and reminiscing, as a second bottle loosened tongues. Charlie regaled them all with stories about his childhood in the Black Country of the West Midlands. Ray pitched in with episodes of life as a football-loving Essex boy, and Tony brought them back to the present with his tale of finding new love after years of widowhood, with an Englishwoman returned to Kenya. His colleagues enjoyed the story of how Emily Verity, someone he'd adored when she was married to someone else in his days as a young army officer, met him again after her daughter came to Kenya to track down a former lover who had deceived her. In the autumn of their lives she had decided to leave England and move to his farm only last year, to be with him, 'to the end', as she had put it.

The second whisky bottle was empty and drowsiness, after a long day, took hold while the fire went down to an orange glow framed by grey logs, wrinkled black. "I'll take first watch," offered Carter, "One hour each should take us to first light. Goodnight gentlemen."

-+-

Chapter Forty Nine

The Sunday mid-morning sun was in the eyes of the two askaris looking through the small windows of the Kwizera ranch gate house, out onto the dusty slopes to the east. In spite of this limiting effect on their vision, they could see a small, rising dust-cloud about three kilometres along the direction of the track leading to the gate. As it slowly got bigger, one picked up a pair of binoculars and asked the other, "Are we expecting any deliveries?" His colleague looked at a printed list pinned to the cork notice board on the wall and confirmed, "None until tomorrow."

Although the target of their view moved closer, it seemed to be travelling slowly and, as it got to within hearing distance, the askaris could plainly hear an erratic throaty coughing coming from the engine of a large 4x4 vehicle. The askari with the binoculars kept them trained on the struggling car and told the other one to call 'the boss'. He picked up a handset and pressed an intercom button. "What is it?" asked a grumpy voice through the speaker. "Corporal, there is a big car coming up the track, nobody is expected," replied the askari. "I'm on my way," grumbled the corporal.

The brown Nissan Patrol spluttered to a stop right outside the black metal gates. The red dust, thrown up by its passage, started settling on and around the car. A window in the concrete wall to the left side of the gates opened and a harsh voice with little Kenyan accent called out, "Who are you, and what do you want?"

A tall, thin, old mzungu, dressed in a somewhat worn olive green safari suit, got out of the front passenger door and stood by the car, stretching his arms high over his head, then windmilling them around, while flexing his back from side to side. After a while, the voice called again more loudly, "I asked you, who are you, and what do you want?" It then added, "This is private property."

"I heard you, I'm just stretching my aching joints... Hours bouncing over unmade tracks at my age, make me rather sore." He then walked over and looked up at the window above his head. "The thing is, old boy, we seem to be having a spot of car trouble and we could do with a bit of help. As for who I am, my name is Anthony Chalk and I'm a wildlife photographer on a bit of a photo shoot. This is my man Mbugua." He waved with a flourish at the black face behind the steering wheel.

"I told you, this is private property. Strangers are not allowed in," came the voice.

"Even in an emergency?" Tony asked quietly.

The window now yielded a face, peering out and down at Tony. "I'm sorry M'zee, but we are under orders not to let strangers in."

Tony, noticing the stripes on the man's arm which was now resting on the window ledge, whispered gently, "It would only be for a few minutes Corporal. Mbugua there is a good mechanic but there is something he needs that isn't in his toolkit. And I would also be grateful to share your, no doubt expert, knowledge to see where I am on the map so that we can find the proper way up the mountain."

"How grateful?" responded the Corporal, his voice somewhat softened by the pleading tone of Chalk's voice.

"Well, I'm a poor old man nowadays and anyway, I wouldn't want to insult a professional like you by offering money. However, can I ask you Corporal... Do you have a favourite whisky?"

Two minutes later, the Patrol was inside the gate and in the shade of the guard house, with the bonnet up. Mbugua was bent over the engine while Tony unfolded his sparse map of the area on the ground and allowed the Corporal to fill in a few blanks for him with a biro.

Up near the house, Milton Kwizera was walking back to the front steps of the main building from the farm manager's cottage and, glancing left, he noticed the front gates just closing. He then noticed a brown car, that was not one of theirs, just inside the gates and started walking quickly down the slope towards what he had seen. He patted the holster on his hip as he marched, his face set grimly on the scene before him.

+

At roughly the same time, on that same Sunday morning, Lydia Hockley-Roberts was standing at Heathrow airport, terminal five, gate A12.

After her phone call with Carter on Friday, she had to talk to someone so she took Francis to the Printer's Devil, and treated him to a few whiskies. In her condition she rationed herself to one glass of wine then some sparkling water. She explained the delay in the writing process and that their author had gone to Kenya without telling her why, on the eve of starting the chapter about Rwanda. Francis had shared with her that he remembered Carter once, after a real skinful at the club, going on about the horrors he had experienced in Kigali during the genocide, and how he had lost someone really close in those events. When Francis had asked him to share the story a few days later, when sober, he had clammed up.

"The point is, Lydia," he had said to her, "His Rwanda posting wasn't that long after his Kenya one so perhaps there is a link somewhere? He never mentioned it to me again, so I don't know any more. Anyway, why are you drinking water?"

"Just being sensible...for a change," she had smiled back at him. "I'm going to take some leave Francis, if that's Ok? I'm going to visit Kenya and see if I can find Mr Talbot. I know where he's staying and if he's gone into the bush, I'll be a nice surprise for him when he gets back."

"Fuck me Lydia, if that's you being sensible, I'm not sure I want to experience one of your wild moments!"

She smiled as she remembered that conversation, and picked up her hand luggage to begin the boarding of flight BA 65 to Nairobi.

+

On that same Sunday morning, Shakespeare Kwizera had extended his usual breakfast spell by the pool and was reading a biography of Nelson Mandela, while itching for an opportunity to get into his father's study. Monique and Natasha had gone back to Nairobi the day before and he hadn't seen Alphonse so far today. He'd seen Milton going out early to see the farm manager and his mother had gone back to her room after breakfast.

He finished a chapter and thought it might be worth having a scout around to see if his father had slipped out unnoticed. At the end of the corridor, as he got to the bottom of the stairs he was nearly flattened by the speeding bulk of his dad rushing down them and pulling a shirt over his head at the same time. "Out of the way, Boy," he cried as he made for the front door. Shakespeare stood aside and looked out of one of the windows. In the distance, at the gate, he could just make out a vehicle and some people standing around it. Alphonse strode purposefully towards the scene.

Shakespeare was curious and went to follow, but checked himself and then darted up the stairs. He didn't need the key as his father's study door was wide open. As usual there was porn on the screen that had been paused. He minimised it and went to his new Hotmail account via Google. He saw two entries in the inbox, both from Cat and opened them excitedly. The earliest, dated two days ago read:

'Hello Bardy, I'm in Nanyuki and have come to Kenya to help you and your mum. That is, of course, if you want me to help? We plan to come to your area over the weekend then stay for as long as it takes. We will be careful not to arouse too much suspicion. When we've worked out a plan, I'll let you know. Take care, both of you. Cat.'

Shaky then looked at the second one, from last night:

'We're in the National park and are discreetly camped off the track to your place. There are six of us in two Nissan Patrols (grey and brown). We will be doing some reconnaissance then will share our ideas with you. With utmost care, you and your mum should be prepared for a fast getaway, but otherwise act completely normally. Cat.'

Looking out of the tinted study window down the long drive, Shaky saw that his father hadn't yet reached the group by the gate. He grabbed a telescope from a bookshelf and focused on the scene. That definitely looked like a brown Patrol with its bonnet up, but the tall, slightly stooped, mzungu next to it wasn't Carter Talbot. Three of his father's askaris were standing around and he could make out Milton gesticulating in all directions.

Shakespeare made the most of his chance and spent the next five minutes composing, what he hoped would be, a helpful email. He clicked on 'send' then closed Hotmail and Google, before restoring the frozen pornographic image to the screen. He placed the telescope exactly where he had found it, left the room with the door still wide open, and deliberately resisted the temptation to join his brother and father at the gate by resuming his liaison with Mr Mandela at the swimming pool.

+

Down at the gate, both members of the Kwizera family were shouting. The son was swearing at the white guest for his 'impudence' in 'tricking' his way into their private property and not having the right equipment when travelling through the bush. His father, sweating profusely and out of breath, was berating the corporal whose head was hanging forward, partly to avoid the spittle flying out of Alphonse's mouth as he raged. Stopping to take a much needed breath, Alphonse darted into the gatehouse and returned with the bottle of Johnnie Walker Red Label.

"You like fucking whisky do you?" he screamed at the corporal. "Well... DO YOU?"

Tony tried to interject, "Look, Gentlemen... This is all my fault, I ju..."

"Shut the fuck up you old cunt," shouted Milton, putting his hand on his holster.

"I'm still waiting for an answer," Alphonse said, more quietly this time.

"I'm sorry, Bwana."

"SORRY! I'll give you sorry..." The big Rwandan then brought his right arm, that was holding the bottle, around in an arc and smashed it over the bowed head of the corporal. Glass, whisky and blood spattered in all directions and, with a surprised sounding groan, the corporal dropped to the ground.

For a few seconds everyone froze. Then Tony knelt down and put two fingers on the side of the corporal's neck for about half a minute. "He's alive, for the moment," said Tony looking directly at Alphonse, "But will need patching up and lots of ice for the swelling. God knows what long term damage you've done to him."

Showing no remorse whatsoever, Alphonse replied, "He brought it on himself, with your help...M'zee."

Tony opened his mouth to reply but Alphonse raised his hand to signal that he was still talking, and continued, "Now, I suggest that you get very quickly on your way...and don't even think of coming back."

Mbugua, who had been standing by the engine compartment, then spoke. "Of course, we will be pleased to go, but I beg to remind you that I need some heavy duty tape to fix the tiny leak in our fuel line."

Everyone could smell the diesel as the drips had now formed a growing stain beneath the Nissan, and Milton ordered one of the askaris to run over to the workshop to get the required item. He then turned to Tony and said. "You have got five minutes to finish up and get out, otherwise there will be real trouble."

Tony fixed him in a stare and replied, as softly as his churning desire to punch the little shit allowed, "And we wouldn't want 'real' trouble, now would we?" He then got back into the passenger seat of the car.

The Kwizera's then walked together, back up the hill towards the house while the askaris carried their corporal into the gatehouse, then one went to get the senior house-girl, who doubled as a medic on the ranch.

Once Mbugua had the gaffer tape, he quickly repaired the self-inflicted leak in the fuel system. Meanwhile, with the body of a big digital camera on his lap, Tony had pointed the connected small and flexible lens tube around the top of the dashboard, taking photographs in every direction.

Mbugua got back in and the engine started first time, settling into an even growl. A guard opened the gates for them and they headed back the way they had come, with Tony taking many more pictures of the gradually receding estate, through the back window.

+

Shakespeare made Nicole some lunch a couple of hours after the unwelcome visitors had left, and the two of them sat at a breakfast bar in the kitchen, knowing that this was one place where Alphonse and Milton would be highly unlikely to visit.

As Nicole forked small portions of pasta into her mouth, her son told her about Carter's emails and that he had seen, from a distance, one of Cat's colleagues at their gate.

"Sheila told me that your father almost killed one of the guards," she replied. "Apparently he let the man and his servant in, and got a bottle over his head for it. She had to put twelve stitches in his scalp and he's not been able to speak yet."

"I didn't see that, but...how typical of father...I'm sorry Mum, but he's a savage."

"You don't have to apologise Son, I should be saying sorry for not standing up to him more in the past."

Shakespeare touched his mother on the forearm and smiled at her. "You've always done your best, Mum, I know that. Anyway, Cat's here and he seems determined to get us out."

"Yes, but how many more people will suffer because of it?"

"Are you saying that you'd rather stay?"

"Of course not... I just fear for our staff here. If we get away, he'll take it out on them."

"Mum..." Shakespeare's head dropped slightly, "I've already emailed back to Carter, telling him that we'll be ready at a moment's notice and giving him some information to help him and his team. If I get the chance, I'll tell him about your concerns."

"Thanks Darling, I'll pack one bag, you do the same." She looked thoughtfully over her half empty dish. "Carter Talbot...after all these years, I can't believe he's really here, well...out there in the bush somewhere, you know what I mean."

"He'll be so pleased to see you again too Mum, his eyes would sparkle when he spoke about you. He'll come, and we'll be safe...I just know it."

"I hope you're right, Son."

-+-

Chapter Fifty

At Camp Tusker, named by Charlie after the growing number of empty cans of the Kenyan lager piling up while they waited for the return of Tony and Mbugua, Churchill was the first to see the fast-moving red billow, blowing towards them from the west, heralding the recce team's imminent return.

With his binoculars, Carter scanned the range of dusty gullies spreading down from the top of the mountain, the line of trees that blocked his view of the lower slopes, then back towards the open area below the small escarpment on which he stood, "They seem in a bit of a hurry, hope everything's Ok?" he said, to no-one in particular. Then in a rather lazy, but still effective, imitation of John Le Mesurier as Sergeant Wilson in Dad's Army, he drawled, "I say you chaps...would you mind awfully, just...sort of...ah...standing to...if you'd be so kind?"

"You heard the Gentlemen," shouted Charlie at Ray and Churchill, while grabbing an automatic rifle, "STAND TO!"

The other three ran for weapons, then all took cover on the perimeter facing the direction from which the vehicle was expected. "Just to be on the safe side, eh Charlie?" Cat said softly to Charlie through an acacia bush, behind whose edges they were both sheltering.

"Quite right, Sir." Reid replied.

The brown Nissan growled its way through the thinnest part of the undergrowth and pulled over by its grey relative, near one of the tents. The four defenders of Camp Tusker breathed a collective sigh of relief and got to their feet as they saw Tony and Mbugua dismounting from the

Patrol. Tony looked a bit redder than normal, but otherwise all seemed well with the pair.

"Quick briefing Mr Chalk?"

"Sure, just need a piss first," responded Tony, already on his way to the tree line at the back of the camp. When he returned, the other five were sitting around the unlit fire, already prepared for later, and six more cans of Tusker were being opened.

"What's the story?" Carter asked.

Chalk seemed to switch straight away into reconnaissance talk and painted a verbal picture for his colleagues of the Kwizera ranch.

"Target is what we thought, a very wide triangle of high, barbed fences, as far as we can see, with the hypotenuse along the leading edge facing the south east. The gate is roughly at the centre of this part of the perimeter and is solid steel plate set on rolled steel hinges. Concrete block work surrounds with gatehouse accommodation for maximum of four guards. Main house is just under one click to the north west of the gate and a barrack block set about halfway between. From the window count, possibly twelve to sixteen more guards, line comms link gate, barracks, and main house. Guards look fit and smart, although prone to persuasion, so perhaps bored stiff."

"Weapons Tony?" Wells queried.

"None being held, but gun rack in gatehouse had three AK47s in it."

"Anything else Chalkie?"

"We've got plenty of photos, so if someone gives Mbugua

an iPad, he can download them for viewing."

"Well done you two," beamed Carter, "Great job, but you look a bit flushed Tony... Are you actually going to tell us what happened?"

So, as they all sipped on their cold cans, Tony regaled them with the tale of entry by bribery and the unfortunate recipient of said bribe being bottled to the ground by, who he assumed to be, the owner of the house. Certainly, according to Chalk, the rest of the people there had been terrified, even the cocky, strutting, little bastard who must be the brother of Shakespeare that Carter that told them about. He then told Cat, with a somewhat pained look, what Milton had called him, and Mbugua couldn't stop himself grinning. "M'zee," he said, "The askaris respected you. The young man is crazed by power, he is no good and will come to a sticky end, as you British say."

"Thanks, Mbugua, you've put the incident firmly in perspective. Anyway Cat, I hope that helps, no chance to recce further than the gate I'm afraid."

"Luckily, probably while you were distracting the men of the house, Shaky has managed to get an email out to me. Combined with what you've discovered, it might give us something to go on. Let me read it to you."

"Then you can look at the photos. Taken under virtually battlefield conditions, you know?"

"Ok Tony..." he smiled, "Message reads:

'Cat, it's very exciting to know that you and your team are out there somewhere. I think some of them must be at the gate right now, so I'm taking this opportunity to try and help. The house is high and looks down on everything to the south and east up to the trees. The fence is the same all the way around, even behind the house in the thick mountainside vegetation. It's electrified as well and in a power cut the generator kicks in.

Apart from the main entrance, there is only one other gate and that is at the point of the triangle right behind the house, where the fence goes along the lower slopes of the mountain. Mum had it put in so that she could go up to the waterfall on the rear heights of the volcano.

The guards are split into 3 teams of 6. This means that there is always one section on duty and two resting. While on duty there are always at least 2 on the front gate plus an NCO on call usually up at the house watching me and Mum, one on the rear gate, and two constantly patrolling the inside of the perimeter for breakages or intruders. One of the other teams are in the barracks relaxing but ready for action, the third team is off duty and may be away briefly with their families. The teams rotate every eight hours. The NCOs are ex Rwandan army, been with my father forever, the other soldiers are locals, trained by my dad and his NCO cronies.

Mum is fully aware of your earlier emails and is as excited as me. I don't know when I'll get another chance to send anything but tell me what to do, if you can. We'll do our best and, as you instructed, try to keep a low profile in the meantime. Bardy.' That's the lot gents, what do you think?"

"I think that we're up against someone who knows what they're about, Carter."

"Yes, it seems that way, doesn't it Charlie?"

"Yes, Sir."

"But out of all the information from Shakespeare, what

stands out as an opportunity, would you say? Anybody?"

"That's a long fence Cat, and lightly guarded, surely plenty of opportunities to break through?" Ray offered.

"Yes, true. But more than that, and I know I've had more time to think about this than the rest of you so I'll tell you... The back gate was put in at the request of Nicole. So perhaps she can use it again to go up to the waterfall? If she does and knows what to look for, even if she's guarded, we have a great opportunity to let her find a mobile phone. Then we're in a good position to drive events."

"Fair play to you, Mr Talbot," remarked Wells, "That Sandhurst education wasn't wasted on you, was it Sir? But what about a signal, it's pretty remote around here?"

"I remember Shaky getting texts from home, before the big storm, when he was staying with me, so it should work. We'll use my mobile, but test it near the fence before hiding it. If we're not all together, we've got the satellite phones to stay in touch."

"I can feel a plan taking shape Carter," said Tony, "Now, here's my iPad, with the shots of the front of the estate and inside the gate."

The tablet was passed around and they all got a feel of the place where Tony and Mbugua had been that morning. Some half a dozen photos were of the backs of two stocky black men, one larger than the other, and in the background was a pale building, clearly a house. "We were not formally introduced, but they are Messrs Kwizera, senior and junior. Borderline psychopaths, if I'm any judge."

Cat looked at them carefully. The younger, smaller one

was definitely Milton. As for the father, Carter looked repeatedly at the images with a furrowed brow and a degree of hatred which was clear to his colleagues. Tony broke the spell by holding out a beer can. "I know what you're thinking Cat, focus on the mission, you'll get your chance," he said quietly. "Thanks Tony," said Carter, taking the Tusker and drawing deeply from it.

Later, over a meal of mince, onions and beans, all cooked together in the big pot, they planned their next move. It all depended on getting a message to Shakespeare, but they wanted to be ready if and when they got that done, as well as preparing a plan B.

"First, we need to know where this waterfall is, then we've got to get there," suggested Carter. "Mbugua, what can you tell us?"

"There are some big ones on the northern slopes, in the Ugandan part of the park. These are for tourists and you couldn't easily walk there from the house. If it's the small one I'm thinking of, it's about five kilometres behind the house, on the eastern slopes of the mountain, hidden in the folds of the volcano and thick forest. From here about twenty kilometres to the north west, mostly on foot, there's no easy way through for vehicles once you get to the forest."

"Right," responded Cat, "So if we're walking, especially through the forest, we're going to need a full day to get up there. But we could get a bit nearer this afternoon?"

"Sir?" Wells queried.

"Tony reckons that on the other side of the next ridge of trees to the west, we could get a good, if distant, view of the ranch, and we'd be a few clicks nearer to where we need to go tomorrow. So, we can break camp now, move everything to there and set up shop deep in the trees. We set off at first light to the north east, where that line of trees joins the thicker forest. We'll make the waterfall by sundown and take it from there."

"All of us Cat?" Tony asked.

"No Tony. No offence but I couldn't put you through that, you've done enough already. I'm suggesting that you stay with the vehicles and Churchill can stay with you. We need Mbugua as a guide, but you two can keep watch on the house, keep us informed of comings and goings."

Everyone looked at Tony Chalk, who graciously and with an almost imperceptible nod of gratitude, replied, "Good decision, Carter."

"Right you lot," said Talbot as he clasped his hands together in front of his face, "Let's get moving, we want to be out of here in 30 minutes, and have everything set up on the new site before it gets dark. I'll send an email to Bardy."

-+-

Chapter Fifty One

Lydia awoke while it was still dark on the morning after her flight to Nairobi. She found herself in a luxurious hotel room and felt fully energised from her early night, fortified only with plenty of cups of lemon tea and a late night toasted sandwich from room service. She had done some quick research online at Heathrow before boarding the plane, and had settled on the Sankara Hotel in the busy business district of Westlands. It seemed to have a great reputation on Trip Advisor, and the taxi there had been an easy drive after the hectic arrivals hall. She had commented to the driver that she had heard about Nairobi traffic being horribly busy, to which his response confirmed her own thoughts, "It usually is Madam, but Sunday night is OK."

On arrival she had been struggling with her luggage as she came through the security screening, when a charming Asian man in a smart suit approached her from the check-in desk and waved an arm at the concierge desk. "Good evening Madam," he beamed at her, "Let me get someone to help you. Welcome to the Sankara. I am the General Manager and you must tell me if you ever need my help." With her bags neatly whisked away by a young assistant, Lydia smiled back at the Manager whose eyes shined with warmth and flirtation. "Thanks very much, you're very kind," she said.

"Karibu Sana," he said, then noticing her hesitation added, "You're very welcome."

Lydia, who had read up on a few Kiswahili phrases on the flight, replied confidently, "Asante Sana," and turned towards the check-in desk.

Later that evening, she had called the number on the

General Manager's business card and asked him to arrange a reliable car and driver to take her to Nanyuki. Moshi had told her to relax as he would personally sort it out on her behalf.

So, after pondering on the night before, a refreshing shower, and an omelette served in her room. Lydia went down to reception in a loose fitting jump suit and met her driver. Samuel was introduced by Moshi who had already arranged for her luggage to be put in the car. After paying her bill, she gave Moshi a big hug and thanked him for being the most perfect of hosts, before following Samuel into the car park.

+

On that same Monday morning, at first light, Carter, Charlie, Ray, and Mbugua picked up their heavy Bergen packs and set off to the north from Camp Tusker Two. They had spent the late afternoon and evening of the previous day setting up the new camp about 100 metres back from the edge of the tree line, from which there was a clear view of the gates of the Kwizera ranch about three kilometres to the West.

They had chosen their equipment and weapons with care and a sense of variety. They'd estimated rations for up to one week and each had a Browning 9mm handgun which they concealed under their combat jackets. They had decided against overtly carrying larger weapons in case they bumped into KWS rangers who had orders to shoot poachers.

Charlie, however, had dismantled the sniper rifle and wrapped the parts in plastic bags and stuffed them in his Bergen, 'just in case of trouble', as he put it. Plenty of ammunition, grenades, some C4 explosive, night goggles, binoculars, compasses, and sleeping bags completed their inventory. To keep in touch with Base camp they had a satellite phone and various mobiles in case they could get a signal. They had drawn up a rough map of the target and its surroundings, based on Mbugua's memory, the view from the new camp site, the photos, and Shaky's email.

The going was immediately slow as they stayed well within tree cover and relied on compasses to follow the inconclusive gaps through the forest. The undergrowth was tangled but there were usually ways between the trees and only occasionally did they need to revert to their pangas to hack a breach. The air hung heavy with moisture and Mbugua explained that the rainfall in this area was one of the highest averages in Kenya.

After six hours they reckoned they were over half way and they had certainly seemed to be climbing steadily for the last two hours. They stopped and got out their water bottles. Ray passed around a bunch of bananas from his pack and they had two each for energy.

Cat opened the map and they estimated where they thought they were. They then looked at the GPS screen on the satellite phone and it seemed to roughly agree, in that the co-ordinates and level of slope appeared to suggest they were about ten clicks from their start point. Carter made the observation that they probably had about seven clicks to go to the waterfall and Mbugua agreed that this was a good estimate.

"The slope will get steeper from here," explained Mbugua. "We'll be climbing nearly another 1,000 metres in height as we go forward, and it will be slower."

"Roger that," was Charlie's retort, "It's nearly 13:00 now so five hours, and a bit, of daylight left... Piece of cake, as long as we don't hang about admiring the view."

"Wise words Charlie, let's get moving again," said Cat, levering his pack over his shoulders.

+

At the Kwizera house that morning, Nicole and Shakespeare sat together as normal, having breakfast by the pool. As they were alone, and the house-girls were out of hearing distance, Nicole started to discuss their situation. Although her son thought it best to only say a bare minimum, he couldn't ignore his mother's enthusiasm.

"I know you're excited Mum, but if only one word about this gets to Father, he'll make sure it is stopped and Carter's team could be in all sorts of trouble. Let's just try to pretend it's not happening."

"I hear you Son, but just listen for a moment. If anything happens and you get a chance to get away, just take it and don't worry about me. I can cope here if I have to, knowing that you're safe."

"You know I wouldn't leave you Mum. Anyway, they'll be nothing happening at all if I can't get to Dad's computer again."

"It's the second Monday of the month, sometimes your father goes into Kitale and plays cards with the local MP, the Chief of Police, and some hangers-on. He didn't go in January, but perhaps tonight?"

"Fingers crossed, eh? Oh, and Mum, you don't need to stuff those rolls in your bag. I know you, you'll think we might need food for our escape. Trust me, the last thing we'll be, if it happens, is hungry."

+

In his own room, where he had been served his breakfast by one of the house-girls, Milton looked out of the window and took in the view down to the gate. The problems yesterday, with the unwelcome visitors, had preyed on his mind overnight. He didn't care much that the Corporal was still unable to talk but there was something about the way that the old mzungu had been looking around, that made him uneasy.

He got dressed and went to his father's study. He rapped on the door and tried the handle. It was open and he entered unbidden. His father looked up from his desk and leaned back in his chair. "Hello Son, what is it?" he said, forcing a half smile across his expansive, shiny, cheeks.

"Good morning Father, I just thought I'd call in for a chat."

"Really... I thought you were still cross with me, for curtailing your 'activities'?"

"Well, as I said before, I can understand...for Shakespeare's disobedience. But I have only ever tried to do what's best for you, and I feel that...perhaps...I could be allowed...some, 'leeway'?"

Alphonse looked into the eyes of his son standing there, and could see a spark of rebellion behind the blinking. "You showed loyalty yesterday, with those 'visitors'. In fact, you could have probably handled the incident without me. I trust you Milton, but I'm keeping you hemmed in here for a couple more weeks." He saw the spark start to ignite and quickly raised his hand. "This is for your own good, there are still awkward questions being raised about that old elephant."

"I'm still not sure about that old mzungu, Father," Milton said in a rush. "There was something about him. He seemed too...interested, in where he was and who we were."

"What are you suggesting Milton?"

"I don't really know, perhaps they came on purpose, looking for some excuse to weigh us up?"

"Anything else?" replied his father, slowly.

"Not really, Mother and Shakespeare don't really speak to me anymore, but then, I'm not sure I'm bothered."

"They don't speak to me either, Son. I'm hoping that the sulking will eventually wear off and they'll appreciate all I've done for them. I hope they don't try and do anything stupid."

"I'll keep a closer eye on them...if you like, Father?"

"That might make sense, just in case there is something going on outside."

"I'll do that, Papa. You know you can rely on me."

"Mm, I do hope so Milton."

-+-

Chapter Fifty Two

The back bar of the Red Lion in Nanyuki was buzzing with noise, as only a room full of women can do. To Emily Verity, the older of the two white ladies around the table, all the Kenyan girls seemed to be having simultaneous conversations with everybody else, in a sort of sing-song language which she didn't understand, but knew to be Kimeru.

Lydia Hockley-Roberts, who had arrived at lunchtime and was sitting opposite Emily, decided to intervene and put her hands in the air for effect. The chatter slackened off.

"Ladies, ladies...sorry, but I can't understand what you're saying and would love to be part of the conversation this evening," she said. "As I've only just met you, do you think we could do some introductions?" she continued.

"Good idea Lydia," volunteered Emily in a quiet but strong voice, "I'll start, although some of you have seen me before. I'm Emily Verity and I am an old friend of Tony Chalk, living with him at his farm, having spent most of my later life in England."

"Asante Emily," said a buxom Kenyan woman with a big smile in a round dark face. "I am Brenda Reid, married to Charlie. We've run this pub ever since he left the army and married me. My son Churchill has gone up country with his dad, my other son is at college, but my two beautiful daughters are right here, Christine and Abigail."

The mixed race girls looked shy for a brief moment then shared their mother's smile. "I'm Christine, karibu Lydia," said one in full make up, wearing tight silver leggings and a low cut scarlet glittery top. "I work at the gym in town," she added while shaking her long plaits of red and black hair.

The girl next to her was as slim as her sister and dressed in a smart navy skirt suit. She looked around the table with wide bright eyes. "I'm Abbie," she said. "Very pleased to meet you. I'm a PA for the MD of a property company here in Nanyuki."

Next to Abbie was another Kenyan woman of around Brenda's age. She was wearing a spectacularly multi-coloured, full length, 'dera' that seemed to flow in the air as she moved over to the bar to get another wine bottle. She turned from the bar and said through plump lips, "Hi, I'm Judy Wells, married to Ray. I do all the book-keeping for the garage business and look after our dogs. Our son is away in Nairobi working for an insurance company."

All eyes turned on Lydia, who took a brief moment to compose herself then announced, "Thanks to all of you, especially Brenda who has given me her best room, in which I've had a nice snooze this afternoon." She lifted her glass of juice towards Mrs Reid. "I feel that you've made me so welcome. My name is Lydia Hockley-Roberts and I've been helping Carter Talbot with his book. We're also... that is to say we... have a... relationship. Look, there's no subtle way to say this, I'm having his baby."

The room erupted in cheers and hugs and the noise level resumed its former level, then exceeded it as the girls, having discovered that Cat didn't know Lydia was here, argued about how to surprise him.

+

"I could do with a pint...or failing that, a breather," puffed Charlie as he trudged through thin lasers of light dancing on the thick foliage of the forest, and glistening off tiny droplets of moisture on wide shiny leaves. All three of his colleagues grunted their assent and they stopped to draw deeply on the thin mountain air.

"What...do you think, Mbugua," gasped Carter whose injuries of last year had made this a serious struggle for him. "We can't be far off, surely?"

"Yes Bwana, you're right, very soon."

"Didn't you say that an hour ago?" Ray challenged him.

"Yes indeed, I was being positive Bwana."

"Ok boys," interrupted Charlie, "From when we reached the slopes, we started off to the north west. Since then we've been gradually coming round to the west, with the steepest slope up to our right."

"So we're getting nearer the back of the ranch," observed Cat.

"Yes, but with no points of reference within the trees, we can't be sure how close. I'd guess about five clicks."

"According to the GPS we've now travelled more than our estimated distance to the waterfall, at lunchtime," added Ray to the conversation.

The group looked around in all directions, but all they could see were more trees and bushes, with small gaps between it.

"Bwana," said Mbugua, "I remember it being set back in a deep upright fold in the rock face. You think it's just another side of the mountain but between the trees it goes back on itself, so you can't see the water unless you're in the gap. If we take the steepest route here we should be close."

"Right," said Carter with a glance at this watch, "It's past 17:00 so we really need to find it in the next hour lads. Let's go...onwards and upwards, as they say."

After another twenty minutes of forceful exertion, the four stood with heaving chests on a small outcrop of rock, from which they had a reasonable view up the side of the mountain for a couple of hundred yards to east and west.

Mbugua looked excited and pointed to their left, where a vertical line of green was half broken by an outcropping edge of rock. "There Bwanas," he said, "If we go straight ahead, then left, we'll find the gap, on our right hand side."

They instantly forgot the lack of breath in their lungs and moved quickly to follow the young Kenya. In another ten minutes, deep in the shadow formed by the mountain that now seemed to engulf them, they went anti clockwise into a vertical crack that had clearly been carved in the mountainside, by the elements.

They heard the fall before they saw it, not roaring but just a soft, permanent, flushing noise, getting louder as they pushed through the thick undergrowth that the water had encouraged over millennia.

Finally, they were rewarded for their efforts as they slipped between some wide grass that was higher than the tallest of them, and down to a tiny beach of shale. They looked up and could see water tumbling gently out of a wide hole in the rock face, some hundred feet above their heads. The stream hit a couple of outcrops on the way down before splashing into the oval shaped pool at the bottom and sending endless eddies out to the banks.

A small family of monkeys, playing on the opposite beach, looked warily at the newcomers but didn't move away.

"Well done Mbugua," said Cat, "Good job. I don't know about you blokes, but I'm going to have a quick dip." He quickly threw his pack and clothes on the beach, yanked off his boots and jumped in. "Fuck me, it's cold," he shouted at his team.

"You'll soon warm up if there's a crocodile in there, Mr Talbot," shouted back Ray, "You should have checked first, I think."

Carter looked around quickly and, as casually as his scrambled steps up the shale would allow, tried to look nonchalant. "Well, that's me feeling much better," he said as he dried himself on a clean tee shirt from his pack.

"Well, if it's good enough for Cat, it's good enough for me," said Charlie who followed Cat's lead and was joined by the other two, splashing around like children.

When they were all dry and dressed, two of them got waterproof ground sheets out of their Bergens and they quickly made a rough camp with one sheet under four laid out sleeping bags, and the other one over, on a small patch of flattened grass next to the beach.

They built a small fire on the beach, just enough to boil water in their mess tins and sprinkle sachets of high energy combat rations into them. They sat quietly eating the resultant hot mush, without great enthusiasm until Charlie lightened the mood by producing a good sized steel hip flask from his pack and passing it around. "I put some of the whisky in this, thought it might come in handy," he said, taking his second swallow.

"Ok Gents, we've made it to here," said Carter. "We need to get our bearings, scout around a little, make sure we've got entry points covered. Then I'll get an email off to

Shakespeare and check in with Tony. After that... We wait."

+

It had been dark for a couple of hours or so, when Shakespeare went from his bedroom to the kitchen for some snacks. He had eaten dinner with his mother early and now felt the need for a cold beer and some peanuts. He bumped into Milton in the corridor and couldn't avoid grunting a greeting.

"Hello Brother," replied Milton, "You look as restless as I feel."

"I'm Ok," was Shakespeare's non-committal response, "Just a bit hungry."

"You're as bored as I am, so don't pretend otherwise."

"I've got my books, and they're usually better company than you'll ever be."

"Oh yes, your books will help you find a girlfriend and get a life, won't they Shakespeare," Milton sneered.

"What's wrong Milton, will father not let you out, in spite of all your crawling to him recently?"

"That's all you know Brother... In fact Father is going to be relying on me a lot more in the future, he told me this morning. In fact, the only reason I didn't go with him to join his poker group tonight, is because I...er...there's a movie on DSTV that I wanted to watch."

Shakespeare looked down to avoid his brother seeing his reaction, then mumbled, "Well, good for you Brother," then continued his journey to the kitchen. He patiently got a Tusker from the fridge and purposefully poured some peanuts from a large bag in the larder into a bowl. He sat down on a high stool at the breakfast bar and thoughtfully sipped and crunched in silence.

Feeling composed, Shaky went back to his room and extracted the key to his father's study. He walked quietly along the corridor and up the stairs. He knocked on his father's study door, just in case Milton's news had been wrong, and met with silence he used the key, re-locking the door from the inside.

He kept the room light off, to avoid anyone outside noticing and, managing to get the screen on, he worked in its reflected glow.

The first unread email from Cat, was dated and timed from the night before:

'Bardy, our guys got safely back from your gate and we've moved camp so that we can keep an eye on your place from the front, but still stay hidden.

Me plus 3 of the team are setting off on foot at first light tomorrow (Monday) heading for the waterfall that you mentioned in your last email. We plan to get there by nightfall and will send another message.

The plan is that we want to hide a phone at the fall and if your mum can somehow get there, we've got proper communication and can plan further.

I'll be in touch tomorrow night.

Cat'

The second email was sent only two hours earlier:

'Bardy,

We've made it to the waterfall and are camped here. We've got supplies for a week so don't panic if you can't do anything immediately.

Assuming that Nicole can get here, and if she does will be guarded, we will be concealed in the trees on the slope to the right of the fall as you look at it. The phone will be wrapped in plastic bags and hidden under a rock, ten paces to the left of a tree stump that's almost on the edge of the left bank of the pool. She can't miss it.

If you can let us know when she's coming, great, if not, no worries, we'll stay vigilant. If there's no way she'll be allowed out, try and let us know. If we don't hear anything after four days, we'll try something else.

Take care,

Cat.'

He took his time composing a reply, then re-read it:

'Carter,

Messages received and understood. As soon as I've sent this, I'll print them and give the details to Mum before burning. Mum might get away with an escorted walk to the waterfall, as she used to go regularly. I've not been since I was a boy and to suddenly show interest would probably arouse too much suspicion.

As you say, if we can have the phone we can talk and await the right opportunity. Bide our time, as it were. Mum wanted me to say that whatever happens we must be careful not to endanger our staff. Most of them are not like father and Milton, it's hard to get work around here, they are basically good people.

Thanks, from the bottom of my heart, for what you are doing for us.

Shakespeare.'

He clicked on 'send', then printed the email trail and picked up the paper. He folded the two sheets together like a letter and stuck one end of the bundle into the back of his waistband, before restoring everything back to normal and exiting the study. He put the keys quickly in his pocket and was on the penultimate step at the bottom of the staircase when Milton walked into the hall.

"What were you doing upstairs, Professor?" he asked.

"Nothing, I just wanted to speak to Dad..." Shakespeare replied tentatively while staying head-on to his twin. "Silly really, it was only when there was no answer to my knocking that I remembered you saying he was out tonight...at his card game wasn't it?"

Milton looked long and hard at his sibling..."Yes, that's right. Your memory is clearly not what it was, Brother." he said with a degree of finality, and carried on walking to his own room.

Shakespeare finally breathed out and, wiping a hand across his forehead, went to his mother's room. After they had read and re-read the emails, Shakespeare held the sheets over a candle until ignited, then put them in the ensuite enamel hand basin, until they were ready to be crumbled and washed away.

"I'll ask your father tomorrow morning if he minds me going to the waterfall," said Nicole.

"We'd better hope that he manages to beat all his cronies tonight then, and take a lot of their money," replied Shakespeare thoughtfully.

-+-

Chapter Fifty Three

Carter was on the last watch of the night and, as the waterfall was almost at the end of a 'cul-de-sac', had positioned himself between it and the way they had come in, just like his three colleagues before him. The only sound he could hear was the gentle rhythm of the water on the surface of the pool, and Charlie's soft snoring from their makeshift group bed about thirty yards away. Nothing had disturbed the peace of their camp all night.

The angle of the gap in the rock face through which they'd arrived meant that he couldn't see the sun as it breached the eastern horizon, but the sky started to lighten and he looked at his watch, 06:07. They'd done two hours watch each and he could wake the team up. He decided to let them awake naturally and leaned on a tree trunk to look again at Bardy's message of last night on the screen of the satellite phone. He turned on the device and noticed an icon telling him he had a text message. He opened it and read:

'Hello Cat, surprise, surprise! Lydia here. I've just enjoyed a splendid night at the Red Lion, Nanyuki with various ladies whose men are with you. Brenda give me this number. Please don't hate me for coming, I just wanted to show support, and be waiting for you when you get back from your mission. Love, LHR plus one, Xx'

He quickly re-read Shakespeare's message then turned the phone back off again, knowing that they only had one charger pack and one spare battery to last them several days.

He couldn't help smiling at what Lydia had done and felt comforted by the fact that, if not near, she was at least in the same country as him. The prospect of future fatherhood had also, at the back of his mind, began to seem like an exciting challenge to come.

But now, there were more pressing issues to consider, like where in these trees might be a polite place to go for a dump. He felt in one of his pockets for tissue paper and thought he should go and wake his colleagues after all.

An hour later, the team sat around a small fire in the same spot as the previous night. Everyone had made the best of the limited facilities, cold water splash washes from the pool being the height of sophistication in terms of male grooming that morning. After the water in their mess tins boiled they made tea individually, then Charlie, after rummaging in his Bergen, turned to the fire with what looked like a large, hollowed out, aluminium discus. He produced something akin to a wire coat hanger bent into a handle and clipped it to the discus with the concave side up, then rested it on top of the fire.

"Charlie, what are you up to?" Ray asked.

His friend didn't answer, just turned back to one of the side pockets in his pack and pulled out a big plastic packet which he slit open with the hunting knife from his belt.

"On this morning's menu," he said proudly, "I thought that bacon rather than C-rations might be preferred." With that, he put slice after slice into his makeshift frying pan and the team were mesmerised by the sizzling sound and drifting smell.

"Top man Charlie," said Carter, toasting the man reverently with his mess tin full of tea.

After breakfast and a complete tidy up, including rolling up the sleeping bags and groundsheets, they cleared the area, put all their kit behind the trees on the upper slope behind the pool, and sat down on the beach.

"Right Gents," said Cat, "Sitrep time. We know that Shakespeare and Nicole have got our message and that she will be trying to get up here at some point. What we don't yet know is when that might be. That means, unfortunately, that we need to be on constant alert and I think a two men on/two men off, or on admin, approach will be best. Me and Ray can be one pair, Charlie and Mbugua the other. Four hours on, four hours off.

Within each pair, one man will need to be on picket duty and I've already found a spot this morning, while you lot were getting washed. After the turning into the waterfall the route west gets a bit easier to travel, perhaps people used to come here for water in the past, I don't know. Anyway, about half a click towards where we know the ranch house to be, the path, such as it is, goes past a pile of rocks that probably fell down the mountain years ago. There are all sorts of small trees sprouting out of this heap and it gives a discreet vantage point to see anyone coming our way. You can't see the ranch as the trees are too dense but you can see about half a click along the track, time enough to get a message texted to your partner back here, who can alert the other pair. Clear?"

"Clear," they said in unison.

"The pair not on watch can do the camp admin, making sure that everything is cleared away so that any visitors won't know we're here, cooking, and catching some sleep here and there. I've already put the mobile phone under the rock for Nicole. By the way, I checked with Tony last night and the only visitor at the ranch yesterday was what looked like a supermarket delivery truck. Through the night goggles they saw a big 4x4 leave the gates in the evening and not get back until the early hours of the morning, occupants unknown. Finally, for now, we need to agree what to do, if and when Nicole comes here. She's bound to be guarded and we know that she doesn't want anyone hurt, so I think we just watch and learn. If she doesn't return as expected, Shaky could be in danger. If anything goes wrong, just follow my lead. Everyone happy?"

The group agreed that they were indeed happy, and set about their business.

+

Nicole went to the staff housing late that morning to find her husband's driver and ask some questions. Satisfied with the answers she made her way to the kitchen and got one of the house-girls to cook some chicken, 'Just the way M'zee likes it.' She got out a tray and took a bottle of champagne out of the fridge, placing it on the tray with one flute. When the joints of barbecued chicken were ready, she piled them on a dish, added it to the tray with an empty dish for the bones, and picked it up herself.

She went gingerly along the corridor and up the stairs, knocking strongly on her husband's door. She heard no answer so tried the handle. It opened and she went into the study, before turning towards the bedroom door which was open and going inside while calling, "Alphonse, are you awake?" She go to the side of the bed before his eyes flickered open in his fat face. She could smell the whisky fumes in the air around him.

"Nicole?" he croaked suspiciously, "What are you doing here."

"I've brought you some breakfast...your favourite, and a little something to help you celebrate."

The residues of sleep and whisky lay heavy on Alphonse's

head as he struggled to sit up on his array of pillows, strewn around the headboard.

"Celebrate?" he asked, the tone of suspicion still present.

"Yes, everyone's talking about how you fleeced all those no good public figures last night, took them for a few hundred thousand bob, so they say."

"But why do you care?"

"In spite of everything Alphonse, you are still my husband and whatever we may have said to each other in the past, I want what's best for my family...the whole family."

"So, do you want to celebrate with me? I notice you've only brought one glass."

"I would never presume, my dear, that you would welcome my company."

He looked intensely at her face, trying to see malice or deviousness, but only finding a smile of serenity and comfort.

"Get yourself a glass from the cabinet over there, I'll open it," he said grasping the bottle by the neck and fiddling with the foil top.

He couldn't help but inspect, through his bleary eyes, the wire and cork, checking for any tampering that may have occurred. He could find no evidence, so opened the bottle with a flourish and poured the chilled bubbles into the two glasses that Nicole held out to him over the bed.

"This is a nice gesture Nicole, but I know you too well. You're after something, aren't you?"

"Husband," she smiled, "You do indeed me know me well, better than I know myself sometimes, and yes, there is one small favour that I'd ask." She paused for effect and took a delicate sip of the wine.

"Go on," he urged.

"You know how I used to love going up to the waterfall? I'd sit with a book or some headphones and just enjoy the coolness for a couple of hours."

"I vaguely remember."

"Well, I haven't been for a while and you told me not to leave the ranch for anything, at the moment. I just wonder if you might let me go back there for the occasional visit, while the weather is so hot."

Alphonse took a deep swallow of the delicious champagne and burped with satisfaction.

"I'm not totally without feelings, you know," he replied, "Ok, Wife, you may go... But Shakespeare stays in the house, and you'll be guarded on your 'trip', for your own protection of course. I'll ask Milton to escort you, perhaps you and he might 'build some bridges', for the sake of...the family?"

"Thank you Alphonse, that's very kind. When can I go?"

"No time like the present is there? Why not this afternoon?"

For the briefest of moments, Nicole's cool failed her with some rapid blinking, before she responded with, "Thank you Husband, a good idea, would you like to come?"

Alphonse swigged again at his flute, and looked around

the room while saying, "I don't think so Dear, I've got some...work to do on the computer, you know how it is?"

Nicole, who knew exactly the sort of 'work' that her husband planned to do on his computer, smiled again at him. "As you wish, perhaps we can talk again at dinner, tonight?"

"Sure...why not, you can tell me about your walk?"

"Until this evening then," said Nicole, leaving her husband to the remains of the Taittinger and his own sordid pleasures.

She went straight to Shakespeare's room and told him the news.

"There's no way we can let Cat know in advance, if you're going today," observed Nicole's son. "If Dad's got the sort of hangover you describe, plus the champagne, he won't be moving from his rooms until probably tomorrow."

"But we can't miss this chance, and Cat said they'd be vigilant."

"You're right," said Shakespeare holding onto both her upper arms and then hugging her tight. "Just be careful," he added as he released her from his grip, "And be wary of Milton, you know what he's like. When are you setting off?"

"About noon, after an early lunch. It usually take me just over an hour to walk there, then I can enjoy the afternoon, in spite of your brother, and get back in daylight."

"Wish I could come."

"So do I Son, so do I."

+

As Carter had done the last watch before dawn, he and Ray were 'off' watch until 14:00. Charlie had gone down the track to take up picket duty and his partner Mbugua was sitting by the pool with phone in hand, having just done a comms check at 10:30.

Ray and Cat had been repositioning some foliage to camouflage the place up the slope where their equipment was stored, and at the same time creating an observation post adjacent to it. They had hollowed out a scrape in the soil between two trees and put some green netting over the spot, then interlaced all manner of branches, ferns, and grasses into the net. All four of the team were wearing green and brown disruptive pattern material, combat suits. The end result was that any of them, crawling under the net from the rear, would have a good view of the fall and pool through the front while remaining unseen by any visitors below. Cat had decided that whoever was in the OP would have the sniper rifle which Charlie had lovingly assembled.

Once the OP was ready, called OP2 as Charlie was at the first one on the track, they encouraged Mbugua to try it out and he took position. They tested their handiwork from all angles and agreed that they couldn't see him. They then went up behind Mbugua in OP2 to the very end of the slope about fifty yards further, where it ran out against the sheer cliff of this part of the mountain. There were some thick bushes sprouting in a cleft near the rock face and behind them they laid out two sleeping bags for off duty use.

Ray then laid down on one of the bags, while Carter sat on the other and sent a brief reply to Lydia's text: 'Lids, there's no point telling you that you shouldn't be here, you wouldn't listen. Can't phone for battery life reasons. I'm secretly touched that you've taken the trouble and I keep thinking ahead to what life as a Dad is going to be like. Look after yourself with all those Meru women, you can see how easily they lead people astray! Cheers, Cat Xx'

-+-

Chapter Fifty Four

Milton, who had been summoned to his father's study earlier, sat brooding over a bowl of soup at a table by the swimming pool, dabbing sporadically at the contents with a spoon. His mother sat opposite, also spooning chicken soup and dunking bread into it.

"I can't believe I have to guard you all afternoon, it's like being a babysitter," he grumbled through his next mouthful.

"Milton," said Nicole with infinite patience, "Your father thought that some time together might do us good, let us talk."

"About what?"

"I don't know, the future? What you plan to do with your life?"

"My immediate plan involved a day on the Play Station and a few beers, perhaps cooling off in the pool later, as I'm not allowed out."

"Well this is going out, the waterfall is lovely."

"Lovely for you, boring for me."

"I've taking a couple of books, including one you might like."

"Forgive me for not jumping with joy, you know I can't be bothered with books."

"This one is a small part of our family's history, and might be worth having a look at."

"If you say so, and I can't find anything else to do."

"Well, I've finished," said Nicole putting down her spoon in the empty bowl. "Shall we go?"

"If we must...just wait while I get my revolver."

Nicole packed some fruit and water into her day pack, which was already bulging with books and a cushion then put it over her shoulder and put her long hair under a wide brimmed khaki hat. Her baggy white linen jump suit and powder blue hiking boots completed the outfit.

Milton came back, twenty minutes later. He was in his safari outfit with holstered Colt on his hip, spare rounds in the bullet shaped loops on the belt, and a green Tilly hat with one side of the brim secured up on the side of the crown, Australian style. Over his shoulder was what looked like a camera case for a chunky Nikon or suchlike.

Shakespeare appeared to be disinterested as he watched from his chair on the other side of the pool. He saw them get up and waved to them, calling over to wish them a good time, before going back to his book. Mother and son went towards the rear of the house and exited via a back door, heading towards the gate in the fence a couple of hundred yards up the slope of the land. The guard saw Milton, saluted, and let them through.

It was getting close to 13:40 when Charlie Reid reached for his water bottle to try and stop himself dozing off. He'd been on watch, wedged into the cracks between three overlapping boulders, since 10:00 and although he was screened pretty well from the path, the overhead sun had plenty of gaps in the spindly young trees, warming him to the point of discomfort.

As he put the bottle back in his webbing, he picked up the binoculars again and aimed them at the path to the west. He refocused briefly and then he saw them. Two figures in hats. As they got closer he made out a young stocky African stomping behind a lighter coloured woman, who was walking with an elegance that seemed incongruous to her rugged surroundings.

He immediately picked his mobile from his pocket and turned on the screen. He pressed some screen keys quickly and glanced at the drafted message to Mbugua, 'Incoming towards OP1 at 13:41, assume N. + 1, he with sidearm,' before touching the send button. He then got lower behind his rocks and trees as the two came parallel with his position and he heard the woman say, "Only half a kilometre from here." Charlie could make out a rather grumpy grunt in reply from the African, who he now saw was probably not long out of his teens. He watched them until they were out of sight to the east then, as had been agreed, waited for further instructions.

Mbugua, in the cosiness of his foxhole, had succumbed to the overhead sun and nodded off. He therefore didn't hear the beep signifying the text from Charlie and continued to doze. Cat and Ray were sprawled on their sleeping bags, saving energy for their watch, which was due shortly.

Ten minutes later, Nicole and Milton arrived at the waterfall and looked around. Because of the height of the mountainside around the fall, the sun could only directly reach the surface of the pool for the three or four hours in the middle of the day. It was already darkening the western bank of the pool as Nicole looked for the tree stump by the water's edge and, having located it, went into the sunny patch to its right and sat on the beach. She pulled two books from her bag and offered one to Milton who shook his head, sat on the tree stump and started fumbling with the camera case. He pulled out a game console and started playing almost immediately.

The scene was quiet for a few minutes, then the troop of monkeys who had not been around since the evening before, came back from the northern edge of the trees and started some raucous chatter on the bank opposite Milton.

Carter, disturbed from his snooze by the monkeys' yelling, came around even more quickly when he looked at his watch and saw that it was now just past 14:00. Standard procedure was to wake the new watch ten minutes before their due time. He guessed that something wasn't right and woke Ray with one hand shaking his shoulder, and the other across his mouth. He moved one hand from Ray's shoulder to his own lips and put his index finger vertically in front of them. Ray got up quietly and they moved gently out from behind the bushes, while keeping prone on the ground.

Meanwhile, Mbugua was being woken up by the monkey's noise that had now reached a crescendo right below his OP. As he looked up, he saw the new arrivals by the pool and noticed that the African man was standing and pointing a heavy looking revolver directly at his position. Mbugua instinctively pulled back the cocking lever on his rifle and aimed at the man, very concerned that he had been spotted.

Several things then happened almost at once. With a shout of, "YOU NOISY BASTARDS" half drowned by the monkeys' screeching, the man by the pool fired three quick shots towards Mbugua and some dirt shot up in the air from the impact on the slope below him. He squeezed off a shot at the man by the pool, who quickly darted towards the woman on the beach and grabbed her around the neck. Cat and Ray then appeared on the slope behind the OP, sidearms in their hands and half ran, half slid down the slope to the west bank of the pool. The monkeys scattered back to the trees they had come from and Milton pulled his mother to her feet, with his left arm still around her neck and his right hand pointing his Colt at her right temple.

Cat and Ray scrambled to their feet and pointed their Brownings across the pool at Nicole and Milton. Carter tried to take charge, "We meet again Milton, but you're the one outnumbered this time. Why don't you just drop it. Nobody's been hurt so far and I've got a trained sniper, you can't see, with your head in his sights."

"Clearly not that well trained, he missed me in the open, and now I've got a shield. I don't think he'll risk that shot somehow. Now, I suggest that you two," he motioned at Ray with a nod of his head, "Stand closer together where I can see you."

Ray looked at Cat, who nodded almost imperceptibly, then moved closer to him on the bank. They still had their weapons raised at Milton who started to, very slowly, back towards the way out, his revolver still touching the side of Nicole's head. Her eyes looked imploringly at Carter and he itched to get a clear shot at the man who had injured him so much only a few months ago. But he couldn't do it, Milton was clever, constantly moving this way and that, lowering his position behind his mother and adjusting the angle of his weapon to prevent him becoming an easy target. Cat and Ray couldn't move any further forward as they were already on the bank of the pool and could only go sideways.

Cat knew he had to play for time. "Milton, can't we sort this out another way? We're not interested in you," he shouted.

"Well why did your 'sniper' try and shoot me?" Milton asked and stopped moving backwards.

"Mbugua," called Cat over his shoulder, "Why did you shoot at this man?"

From the deep thicket up the slope came the reply. "He fired at me Bwana, three times."

"I was trying to sh...scare the monkeys away," Milton mumbled.

"So, a complete misunderstanding then?" Cat suggested.

"Bullshit, you're not here by coincidence."

"This isn't a revenge thing, Milton, we've come to see your mother and brother."

"And you do it by ambushing us like terrorists? Fuck off, we're leaving." Milton made another step backwards to the narrowest part of the single track path out of the cleft. It was the last move he ever made and suddenly a red and grey mess emerged from the front of his head, as a loud crack echoed around the walls of the waterfall, and the body of Milton Kwizera crashed to the path, taking his mother with him. Just behind where they had been standing, was the chunky figure of Charlie Reid, holding a smoking Browning.

"I don't think you are leaving, somehow," said Charlie as he bent down and disentangled Nicole from her son. Cat and Ray had run around the pool and we're now gathering around the others. Nicole was splattered with some of the mess from Milton's exit wound, but unharmed physically. As she was brought to her feet and someone was helping with a handkerchief dipped in the pool to clean her, she turned to Charlie and slapped him very hard across his face. "You killed my son," she said, "But you saved me." Then she hugged him gently before turning away to have a more thorough wash.

"Shock Charlie. It's a strange thing," said Carter.

"Right enough Skipper. By the way, sorry for disobeying orders and all that."

"Sorry, Charlie?"

"Standing orders at the OP on the path, 'Once you've reported any insurgents, wait for further instructions'. The thing is Mr Talbot, I didn't get any instructions, and after hearing four gunshots, I thought you might need my help."

"How right you were."

"Oh, and I still owed you one from that little unpleasantness at Mombasa, all those years ago. That should even the score, Sir."

"Thanks again Charlie. But now what do we do?"

"First things first I think. That lady is going to be very upset, her son is dead so we should do the right thing by him, and her...in my opinion, Carter."

"You're right, let me talk to her."

"Take your time, Sir, you'll need it."

-+-

Chapter Fifty Five

Carter Talbot couldn't take his eyes of the face of Nicole Kwizera. He was nodding supportively, his lips were moving with words of comfort, but he had no precise knowledge of what he was saying. They were sat by the beach, near where the fall splashed into the pool and this dulled their voices from the others nearby. She wasn't crying but Cat could see that her eyelids were going to be insufficient to hold back the force of tears welling up behind her eyes.

He put an arm around her shoulders and pulled her close to his chest. For a fleeting moment she held back, then surrendered to the need for release and sobbed, without restraint, into his jacket. Carter held on, silently, letting her shed the anguish into him. Over her heaving head he could see that his men were scraping a shallow grave between the trees to the north side of the pool.

He felt her spasms of grief slow after a while, and just kept holding her, saying nothing. Eventually, Nicole partly lifted and turned her head, "Does this remind you of Virunga, Cat?" she asked.

"Virunga?" he replied slowly, as he trawled his memory. "The gorillas...of course," he assured her. "Everything so lush, and peaceful...and the water, just like our little camp...all those years ago."

"It's why I like to come here," she said, looking at him dreamily. "I never told anyone, but I would sometimes just come here on my own, lie on my back, and remember those days. The bliss...before the horror."

"And bliss it was, Nicole, for me just as much as you. I never really loved anyone else after that. Perhaps it was just too perfect?"

Nicole looked distracted and distant, "I brought a book with me today, to give to Milton, thought it might soften him somehow. It's all about love in the midst of the genocide, I couldn't think that anyone would read it and not be touched. He didn't even look at it."

"I might have read it?"

"A Sunday at the Pool in Kigali."

"Yes," it was Carter's turn to be distant, "I cried when I read it, years after it all happened...everything seemed to come back."

She said nothing, sat up straighter and turned slightly away from him towards the opposite bank. "Are they burying Milton?"

"Only for now, so nothing can come and...disturb his body. They'll wrap him in a groundsheet first. You can decide later, what you want to do..."

They made their way around the pool to where Charlie, Ray, and Mbugua had contrived a temporary grave out of the root rich soil. They lifted the bundle within the groundsheet and placed it gently inside. Ray stuck the blade of his portable entrenching tool into the pile of fresh earth and carefully tipped some onto the body. As he did so, they all heard the distinct sound of a mobile phone ringing. The sound emanated from the groundsheet and they all looked at Cat, then back at the body. The ringing continued and they looked at Cat again.

He said quietly, "Sorry about that, Nicole. Lads, let's just stop for a moment and retrieve that phone shall we?"

"The weird thing is that Alphonse wouldn't let them replace their phones and took mine off me."

"Perhaps, as Milton was looking after you today, he was given one for emergencies?"

No more was said and Charlie rummaged inside the groundsheet, removing his hand which was clutching a phone that had, by now, stopped ringing. He glanced at Cat and Nicole, then passed it to her. She looked at the screen and Carter spoke, "If it's your husband, he'll try again. When he does, answer and say that Milton's had an accident, he's unconscious and you were just on the way back to get help."

"But what about Sha..."

The phone started ringing again and vibrating in Nicole's hand. She looked at Carter, then at the screen, and touched it to answer. She said nothing for a few seconds, then, "No, he's had an accident... He's unconscious, he was...climbing up the rocks...tripped, hit his head." The group around her could hear the muffled voice coming back to her and rising in intensity, even though they couldn't make out all the words. Nicole answered back, "I didn't know you'd given him a phone did I? I was leaving for help when I heard it ring in his pocket." There was real anger audible from the other end of the line and everyone standing around Nicole heard the final comment of, "Don't fucking move, we're coming," before a click terminated the call.

"I don't think he believed me," said Nicole, while holding out the phone.

"But, he'll be here in... How long Nicole?"

"Less than an hour, if they hurry. He's bound to bring his

two Rwandan sergeants, they're so loyal to him. His corporal is immobile with a head wound."

"Yes, we heard about that," answered Cat, "What about his other soldiers?"

"The others are all local Kenyan's. Alphonse and his cronies have trained them but they look on it as just a job, they're not cruel like their masters."

"But will he bring some?" Cat responded, with perceptible impatience.

"Carter..." said Nicole despairingly, "I'm not a soldier, I don't know. What I do know, is that one of my son's is dead and the other one could be in all sorts of danger. What about Shakespeare?"

Talbot looked guilty and softened his tone, "Sorry Nicole, yes, assuming that he won't be invited on the rescue mission by your husband, Shakespeare is going to be stuck at the ranch. Can we also assume that as soon as he gets the chance, he will be on email?"

"Yes," said Nicole, "He's got a key to his father's study and I'm sure he'll access it the moment Alphonse leaves the house."

Carter turned to his team, "Right Lads, we need to do two things. Prepare a reception committee for our imminent visitors, and create a diversion to help get Shaky out. Charlie, sort out a discreet defensive position, I'm going to send an email then give Tony a ring. Can you quickly cover this up first," he said, glancing back down at the grave.

Charlie quickly took Mbugua to one side and spoke quietly to him. "You're looking sorry for yourself, don't worry.

That was my fault, giving you the sniper's rifle. I didn't think we'd have company so soon, and I would have time to train you on it when we were off watch."

"Thanks Bwana, in the KWS I only learnt how to use a standard old Lee Enfield."

Charlie patted the Kenyan on the back and they finished filling, then disguising with foliage, the grave beneath the trees. Charlie then said to Mbugua, "I've got an important job for you," and briefed him quickly.

+

Shakespeare was lounging on a sun bed on that warm afternoon, trying to relax but restless with the thoughts of his mother and whether she would get the phone back safely from her trip to the waterfall. He was surprised from his pondering by the growing voice of his father, shouting from inside the house into a mobile phone, "Meet me at the back gate in ten minutes, bring your section and get everyone else on guard...I smell trouble."

Alphonse Kwizera then loomed into Shakespeare's view, stuffing his phone into the breast pocket of a tight, dark green, battledress. He saw his son lying there and bustled over to him, an AK47 swinging from his other hand.

"Is there a problem Father?"

"Nothing I can't handle, Kijana."

"Is it mother?"

"I said, I'm dealing with it. You, stay right here. Gahigi will be in charge while I have to go out for a while." He checked the double magazine on the rifle for emphasis, and slammed it back into the weapon.

Shakespeare bit his lip to avoid saying anything and watched as his father walked quickly along the corridor towards the rear of the house. He forced himself to wait for a few moments then quickly went to his room and got the key he needed. As he walked to the hallway he heard loud voices in Kinyarwanda and saw the two Rwandan sergeants at the bottom of the stairs.

"Sergeant Ngabo and Sergeant Gahigi," he said, "You must be looking for my father?"

"Yes," they said in unison.

"He's gone to the back gate, I'm sure he'll brief you there."

The two stocky, dark men, in similar uniforms to his father's and carrying identical weapons, looked at each other then went back out of the front door. Shakespeare could see through the window that Ngabo's section of six men was formed up outside and the two sergeants led them around the side of the house, out of his view. He ran upstairs, with key at the ready, and was quickly in front of his father's computer screen.

'Bardy, things have kicked off here at the waterfall,' the email read. 'Milton started shooting, your mother's safe, your father's on his way. You must try and get out as soon as you can. Tony will be creating a diversion at the front gate at 16:00. If you get the chance, join him. If not, try the back gate and join us at the fall. Take care, Cat.'

Shakespeare read the email one more time then glanced at the time in the corner of the screen, already past three o'clock. He needed to be ready.

Within a minute he was back in his room, and had changed so that he was better prepared for whatever happened later.

He had walking boots on, and a safari suit over a tee shirt, with a hat stuffed into a pocket. He put his remaining cash, plus his passport, into another pocket, picked up a book and went to sit at the small poolside bar. Sergeant Gahigi found him there and, tapping his holstered handgun for emphasis, made it clear to Shakespeare that M'zee had ordered him to watch his son, who wasn't to leave the compound.

+

Portier Gatanazi was struggling for breath as he, and his squad of askaris, hurried upwards from the back gate of his ranch along the rough winding path towards the waterfall. He shouted, "Ngabo, let's rest for a moment."

Sergeant Ngabo, who was at the head of the small column, held up his right hand and the soldiers stopped walking. They had only gone a couple of kilometres but their Bwana had taken a large red handkerchief from his pocket and was wiping his face and neck, to soak up the heavy perspiration. He made his way to the front of the group, still mopping his shiny black brow, and spoke more quietly to the NCO.

"Are we... half way, Ngabo?" he asked, continuing to puff.

"Nearly Bwana, three more kilometres to go."

"From here on... you stay by my side... send these six in front. There's something wrong about this, I'm sure of it."

"Bwana Kwizera, I have been with you many years. If you think there is danger, then there is danger. We can be careful, let these Kenyan boys be at risk."

Gatanazi took a big swig from his water canteen, put it back on his belt then told them all to move on, and keep their eyes open for anything unusual. He tried calling Nicole again, but after many rings it went unanswered.

They marched on, with weapons carried in skirmishing order for ready use. After around half an hour, they halted, at their sergeant's command, next to a jumble of rocks and young trees on the left of the path.

"Bwana," said Ngabo, "It's only half a kilometre from here."

"Ok, we'll wait here, send half the squad ahead. Get them to search around and report back here, all of them."

Behind the rocks and trees, Mbugua listened intently to this conversation until it finished and transcribed it to a text which he sent to Charlie. He heard the remaining members of the group from the ranch settling down to wait as their weapons clattered on wood and stone. He removed his sidearm from its holster, and sat, without making a sound, between two rocks facing the mountain.

+

Tony Chalk looked at his watch again. It was now 15:55 and all was set for the diversion. Churchill was at the wheel of one of the Nissan's and Tony was standing on the back seat with his head through the big retractable sunroof. Crudely but solidly, Charlie's 'pride and joy' was mounted on the front of the car roof, with steel bolts through the machine gun's legs and into the metal roof support, prepared by Ray, under the grey skin.

"Righto Churchill," called Tony as he slid on some wraparound sunglasses, "Let's roll. Full speed ahead and don't stop for anything."

They bounded over the rough ground and were soon on the

track to the front gate of the ranch. Having done the journey before, Tony knew that there would be quite a bit of dust thrown up and he hoped that this cloud would disrupt a clear vision of the vehicle from the gate, so they wouldn't immediately see what was coming.

There wasn't much time for subtlety and when they got to about four hundred metres from the gate, Tony cocked the 50 calibre weapon and made sure that the ammunition belt was loose and free. At one hundred metres, he aimed the barrel straight at the bottom of the double black gates with both hands on the grips, and pressed the butterfly trigger. He could feel in his arms the pumping action as the gun spat rounds with incredible velocity, and the recoil forced the barrel upwards. The noise of gunfire dwarfed the growling engine and Tony could see big patches of shiny metal flickering on the gates as the bullets flaked off the painted surface with every hit. At twenty metres, Churchill began a prearranged turn to the right and Tony let go of the trigger.

He reached down into a canvas bag hanging near him and pulled out two grenades. He held one in each hand and pulled out the pins with his teeth, before lobbing them towards the entrance. They exploded against the gates as Churchill completed the turn and was coming around for another run. Tony got back on the gun and started firing again, this time at the brickwork on each side of the gate posts.

He threw two more grenades as Churchill turned again, this time to the left, and they retreated some four hundred yards and stopped, after facing the ranch once more. Tony opened another belt of ammunition and fed one end into the machine gun. He then picked up his binoculars and studied the target. The gates were a mass of indentations and scarred metal, while the brickwork to the sides had chunks missing from the facings and scruffy piles of rubble on the ground. He couldn't see that they had actually punctured the gates or walls, but he could see some steel gun barrels pointing through the gatehouse windows in their direction.

"I'm thinking one more run Churchill, what do you think?"

"You're the boss Tony, let's do it."

"Just to be on the safe side, let's just make it difficult for those guys in the gatehouse," said Chalk as he got out of the Patrol and opened its rear doors. Following a few metallic noises from behind, Churchill heard four high pitched coughs in succession. He then heard a clattering and the rear doors slamming shut, before hearing soft explosions in front of him and seeing smoke billowing out from four distinct points in his field of vision.

"Come on Churchill, kanyangia my friend!"

"I am stepping on it, Tony," he replied as they hurtled for one more pass at the gates. The smoke shells thrown by the mortar has created the desired affect and Tony expended another belt of ammo and two more grenades at the embattled target area. They heard some ragged return fire from the gatehouse windows but raced away unscathed and returned along the track to a safe distance. There, again with the vehicle facing the ranch, Tony keep vigil on the gates and sent Cat a text.

+

When the sound of heavy calibre gunfire had started at 4 o'clock, Shakespeare looked at his minder and saw Sergeant Gahigi tense with nervous energy then fumble for a phone in his tunic. He touched a button.

"Bwana Kwizera, Gahigi here. Gunfire Sir, sounds like it's

coming from beyond the main gate." There was some nodding then, "Yes, Sir," from the sergeant who pocketed his phone, got up from the chair and picked up his Kalashnikov.

"I must go and see what's happening then report to M'zee."

"I'll come too, you could use my help," offered Shakespeare.

Gahigi sneered at the young man then, pointing his rifle in his general direction, replied, "You... Kijana, are to stay here and not move, says your father."

Shaky lifted both hands with palms outward and said, "Ok, Ok, I was just trying to help."

Gahigi then moved swiftly away and, after a few moments, Bardy followed the direction he'd taken. From the windows by the front door, he saw the Rwandan jogging down the slope to the gates, shouting as he ran. He went outside, then in the opposite direction.

He got to the gate in the back fence, just as an askari joined his colleague guarding the portal. Shakespeare ran up to them, gesticulating over his shoulder vigorously.

"You two," he shouted imperiously as he approached, "I've just been with Sergeant Gahigi, all men are to go to the front gate immediately. We are under attack. You've heard the gunfire."

The newly arrived guard replied, "We need to hear it from Gahigi himself, our orders were to watch this gate."

"Look," Shakespeare said more gently, "I know you're scared and you'd rather stay away from the shooting, but if you don't go now, I'll have to tell my father that you were afraid to fight...what do you think he would do to cowards?"

The men exchanged knowing glances and, as if to help them make the right decision, Shakespeare added, "Don't worry, I take full responsibility for this. Off you go...and hurry."

The men hastened off down the slope and when they looked back over their shoulders, Shakespeare was standing stiffly by the gate. Two minutes later he was through it and hurrying towards the waterfall.

-+-

Chapter Fifty Six

It was well past 3 o'clock when Milton's phone rang again, in Nicole's hand. She was sitting on the poolside stump waiting for the men to finalise their plans in a huddle nearby. Cat heard the noise and looked over at her, shaking his head vigorously. She ignored the call and stood up to join the three men.

"It's best to maximise his confusion at this point," said Carter to assist her apparent uncertainty. "We know he's on his way and need to be prepared... So... I want you to have this, just in case." With that, he handed her his 9mm Browning and showed her quickly how to use it.

"What about you, Cat?" Nicole asked as she lowered the pistol.

"I've got Milton's '45, which would be too heavy for you, and his belt of ammunition, I'll be more than Ok."

Cat and his two colleagues spent the next half an hour checking various firing positions and talking in staccato military language. Just before 16:00, a 'text received' beep sounded on Charlie's mobile and he quickly shared Mbugua's information with Ray and Carter. "Three men coming from OP1 now," he said, "Five others, including the Boss and a sergeant, waiting near Mbugua."

"Ok boys, positions please," said Cat, in a lisping musical director style, then he clapped his hands twice for effect. Nicole and Ray stayed where they were on the beach nearest to the entrance to the waterfall, while Charlie and Ray vanished into the undergrowth and trees on either side of the entrance.

Just over five minutes later, the leading askari entered the cleft in the mountain and beheld the waterfall to his left. He moved forward and two others followed him, their weapons moving around in all directions as they scanned their surroundings. They could see the back of Nicole as she knelt on the beach over someone lying on the ground, but from their angle could only see the trousers and boots of that someone.

One of them called out, "Madam, we are here."

She didn't turn around but called over her shoulder, "Have you got a stretcher?"

"Er... Yes... Or rather, the others have got it."

"Others? You mean you aren't all together? My son needs urgent medical help right now and you come empty handed. Get it quickly you buffoon!"

The first askari turned immediately and started to jog back towards the entrance. As he got to the narrowest gap between the bushes on either side, he could feel his jogging feet make no direct contact with the ground as he was hoisted sideways, his rifle flew into the undergrowth, and a hand was clamped hard across his mouth. That hand was quickly replaced with a handkerchief stuffed into his mouth and instantly bound with three turns of gaffer tape around his head and across his lips. His hands were pulled behind him and were bound with the same tape, as were his legs across his ankles. He was then sat behind a fat tree facing the wooded slopes of the mountain and a final few stretches of tape secured him to the trunk.

His two fellows, oblivious to the whereabouts of their comrade, approached the rear of Nicole and one said, "Madam, we are getting the stretcher, is Bwana Milton alright? I see his head is covered."

"He lives, I am keeping his wounds shaded."

"What can we do, to help matters, Madam?"

"To help matters, my old son, you can both drop your rifles immediately and put your hands on your heads," said a voice behind them. As, in their confusion, they did not immediately obey, the nearest one got a jab in the back of his head from the snub nose of a Browning automatic. Then, in an instant, the figure in front of Nicole threw off the towel over his head, jumped to his feet and brandished an identical weapon, repeating the call for action to the astonished askaris.

Having obeyed the order, the newcomers were rewarded by being trussed in the same way, and taped to the same tree, as their colleague.

Carter emerged from the bushes having checked the bindings of their captives and said, "Well done Charlie, well done Lazarus... I mean Ray. Nicole, brilliant, are you Ok?"

"My heart was pounding in my chest, I'm not sure I could do that again, Cat."

"I don't think it would work again, not with five of them. Let's see what news we get from Mbugua...and...hold on..." He fished his phone from his jacket, "Here's something from Tony, listen up, 'Diversion over, plenty of noise and havoc at the gates, no casualties on either side as far as we can tell, but no sign of Shakespeare. Think it best to retire gracefully?' What do we tell him, team?"

"If he's sitting outside the ranch, he could get in trouble if they decide to get their vehicles out and chase him," offered Ray.

"But what if Shakespeare comes out of the front and Tony's not there?" Nicole asked.

"I'm sure that if he was coming out of the front gates he'd have done it by now, but I'll ask Tony to stick around for ten more minutes, then disappear if there's no sign of our friend, or if they come after him. I'll tell him to make his way along the fence to the east as far as he can go then turn north west towards us, once the fence turns back on itself." Cat called Tony and repeated the instructions.

Almost immediately there was a text from Mbugua to Charlie, and he gave them very few words, 'They're all coming, now'.

+

In the gatehouse at the ranch, Sergeant Gahigi was peering carefully out of a window frame showing signs of heavy damage. He could still see the grey 4x4 that had sprung upon the front of the ranch with such force, now moved back to about a kilometre from the gates, facing them.

He pondered his next course of action. Although the gates were externally damaged, the thickness of the steel had resisted being breached by the heavy bullets and the grenades. No one was hurt and he had not yet phoned M'zee Kwizera. He considered himself a good soldier but not a reckless one. The overwhelming thought in his mind was that if he called the Boss, he and his section would be ordered to leave the compound in their jeeps and attack the attackers. He knew what 50 calibre rounds could do to an unarmoured vehicle and had no desire to be sitting in one when it did.

After wrestling with his conscience, Gahigi told his men to keep a careful watch on the car outside and tell him the moment it moved. He then slumped down in a chair and swigged warm Coke from a bottle. There was still some liquid left, when one of his men called him back to the window. He breathed a sigh of relief, the car had turned to the east and was driving slowly away. He still couldn't understand why they'd attacked in the first place but told his squad to take a jeep and drive along the inside of the fence, to the east, and report to him if their perimeter was attacked.

He then remembered he was meant to be watching the Bwana's boy and strolled up the track towards the house to find him.

+

Carter and his crew knew that they had only five minutes to get organised and few words were spoken as they moved to their planned positions.

Charlie went to a stubby tree just in front of the three askaris prisoners and took a position behind it where he had a view of the entrance path.

Ray went to the tree cover between the entrance and the waterfall itself, on the opposite side to Charlie, and laid down behind a jumble of broken branches, through which he could see the entrance and the pool.

Cat took Nicole to the bushes right up the slope beyond the pool, where they had laid the two sleeping bags and insisted that she stay there. Nicole wanted to help but was told that if things got messy, she was most at risk, like when Milton used her as a hostage. Carter told her to keep her gun at the ready, with the safety catch off. He then took his place in OP2 which gave him a commanding view of the whole scene and he cradled the sniper rifle as he settled down, hidden from view.

The team at the waterfall knew that the five men, searching for their missing comrades, were coming, from the shouted orders of their leader cutting through the quiet of the late afternoon. "Keep your eyes open," he bellowed, "They can't have vanished into thin air." As this tirade continued, the first soldier came into the secluded oasis and looked around nervously.

"Where the hell is my wife and son?" Alphonse called to the three men at the front from his position back near the entrance. Sergeant Ngabo, standing between his Boss and the three askaris, offered the obvious answer, "There's no sign of them Bwana."

As the NCO turned back to face the front, he felt an incredible pain in his left thigh, and heard a resounding crack echo around the waterfall. He instinctively tried dropping to his knees, but managed to fall sideways to his left and screamed as he grabbed at the epicentre of the pain with his left hand.

The three askaris threw themselves on the ground and pointed their rifles at the general direction the noise had come from. The echoes made this problematic and they ended up with rifles angled across 270 degrees. Bwana Kwizera ran behind a tree to his left which now acted as a barrier between him and the slope beyond the pool, where he thought the shot had come from.

In OP2, Carter had reloaded and was surveying the scene. He could see that Gatanazi was well protected but only about twenty yards from Ray. He could easily pick off the askaris if he chose to. Charlie was out of the picture at the moment and Mbugua would be coming back as instructed. Time for a bit of a chat, he thought.

Without moving, Cat projected his voice and it echoed around the walls of the pool, "Portier Gatanazi, listen carefully. Your son Milton is dead, your wife Nicole is well and safe. Your son Shakespeare should be on his way here. You, are finished here and the best thing for you is to walk away. You, and your men, can live if you all lay down to your weapons and go back to your house. You can take your wounded man back on your stretcher, we will not interfere. All you must do, is let Nicole and Shakespeare go. What do you say?"

"I say this," roared the old Rwandan, as he leaned half around the right of his shielding tree and loosed off half a magazine of his AK47 in Cat's direction. There were several impacts, just above Carter's head, into the branches and he instinctively wriggled deeper in the OP.

The askaris had now focused their three gun barrels in Cat's direction, and the Sergeant lay on his back, moaning quietly as he clutched his thigh with bloodied hands. Carter looked towards where he knew Ray was concealed but couldn't signal him adequately from his prone position. He retrieved the satellite phone from a pocket and sent a short text to Wells, copied in to Reid and Mbugua, 'Ray, I'll keep his head down, see if you can get near and behind him. Charlie, cover the askaris. Mbugua, stay by the entrance and keep watch for Shaky.'

Carter then adjusted the sights slightly and focused on the fat tree, behind which the lumbering bulk of Gatanazi was mostly hidden. He could just make out the barrel of his rifle and the top of his right boot between all the leaves and ferns linking the trees together. He aimed for the rifle barrel and squeezed the trigger. The bullet missed but the rifle and the boot disappeared from sight. From the other side of the trunk now appeared a couple of inches of the green clad left buttock belonging to his target. Cat adjusted his aim and fired again. Through the telescopic lens he saw the bottom of the Rwandan jerk forward and heard an inadvertent yelp. Clearly, he had pierced the man's body and, Cat hoped, perhaps his arrogance too.

Carter opened his mouth and called across again. "Portier, my men are all around you, we don't want any more bloodshed. My offer still stands, walk away or you won't ever leave this place." There was no reply, and Cat noticed from a ruffling of the foliage on left and right of his field of vision, that Charlie and Ray were manoeuvring into better positions.

Carter fired off another shot, this time deliberately into the tree shielding Gatanazi, the high powered round made a satisfying smack into the timber which mixed with the echoing gunshot around the scene. "I'm going to count slowly to ten, Gatanazi," called Cat. "By the time I finish, if you haven't surrendered, you will all be shot. You three askaris on the ground, if you leave your weapons where they are, you can walk away unharmed...now."

"ONE,"

Charlie, from his new hiding place thirty yards to the left of Gatanazi, took the initiative and called out a translation of Carter's surrender order, in Kiswahili.

"TWO,"

The men on the ground conferred in whispers, looking anxiously over their shoulders to their master's tree.

"THREE,"

The wounded sergeant, pointedly threw his Kalashnikov clumsily in Carter's direction, then lay back, cursing and whining in pain.

"FOUR,"

A quick shot came from Gatanazi, aimed at Ngabo and spat up some dirt about six inches from his head. Carter quickly responded with a shot at head height which hit the left edge of Portier's tree and sent splinters of bark flying sideways.

"FIVE,"

Gatanazi, unwilling to risk another sneaky shot, shouted out from behind the acacia, "You cowardly bastard Ngabo. When this is over, I'll kill you like a dog."

"SIX,"

The askaris, from their frantic head movements and furious whispering, looked in panic and this wasn't helped when their bwana shouted at them, "The same goes for you three, if you don't fight back."

"SEVEN,"

Further discussions among the Kenyan soldiers, and Cat could see that Ray was now within ten yards of Gatanazi.

"EIGHT,"

The askaris very deliberately pushed their rifles as far forward as they could, then slid backwards away from them, before putting their hands behind their heads. Carter banged off another round at the acacia's trunk and Charlie fired off three shots from his handgun in the same direction while shouting from behind some bushes, "Come over here, kujeni hapa." Then, noticing their hesitation to get up, he called angrily, "Do it NOW, harakisheni," and fired three more shots to cover them as they sprinted towards his voice.

"NINE,"

Cat again fired into the tree to help Ray get even closer to the target, unnoticed.

"TEN"

A volley of shots sounded and echoed around the mountain walls as the three Englishmen all fired repeatedly at the already battered acacia tree. "CEASE FIRING," shouted Carter, then softened his voice as the echoes died away. "It's over, Portier," he called. "You're a soldier, you know I'm right... Give it up."

Nothing happened, and Cat thought that perhaps their shooting had secured some hits. He got up and started down the slope, eyes firmly on the tree. Then an AK47 flew out from behind the tree. Ray moved out into the open to pick it up, and also gather those abandoned by the askaris and their sergeant.

Charlie was holding the three soldiers at gunpoint near the entrance when Mbugua and Shakespeare walked cautiously along the path towards the waterfall. "Well done Mbugua," said Charlie, "Can you help me tie these lads up please? You must be Shakespeare?" he added to the wide-eyed young man following. "Make yourself useful and check on the bindings of the three boys taped to a tree through there, could you?"

Meanwhile Nicole, having heard the goings on from her location at the back of the upper bushes, was now coming down the slope, 9mm still in hand. She joined Carter who stood with his rifle pointed at her husband, who now limped out towards the beach. He was holding his, normally holstered, sidearm by the barrel and threw it onto the ground in front of Cat.

Nicole could see plenty of blood soaking the left side of

Portier's left leg but apart from being covered in wood clippings and leaves, he looked otherwise unharmed, and extremely angry. The wounded sergeant got the force of Gatanazi's glare as he looked with disdain at Ngabo on the ground behind Cat. They were then joined by Shakespeare who couldn't help a smirk at his father, before a warm smile at his mother and Carter.

"So...what now, Mr Clever Mzungu," asked Portier with bitter sarcasm, his hands casually behind his head as instructed by Cat.

"Well, I'd imagine your former enemies in Rwanda, might want to have a word or two with a war criminal like you? What do you think?"

Gatanazi didn't answer, but grimaced in pain and moved his left hand down to his bleeding buttock. "Can I take the weight off my...where you shot me?"

Cat passed his rifle to Shakespeare and stepped forward to help the big man, lifting his right arm towards the Rwandan's shoulder so as to assist him in getting to the ground. As Carter touched Gatanazi's shoulder blade his captive's left hand moved swiftly from his buttock, to the back of his waistband and forward towards Cat's torso. There were two immediate muffled shots and Carter's body jerked back as he bent double, then went down.

Nicole screamed and didn't stop to think, she raised her hand holding Cat's Browning towards her husband and pulled the trigger. A red hole appeared in his chest, the noise echoed, and the man she had known as Alphonse for twenty years staggered backwards. He went to lift his small gun towards her but she fired again, and again, and again. His chest was now a mess of holes, blood and torn cloth and he fell backwards dropping his weapon. Still not satisfied that he could do her no harm, she stood over him and looked into his face as he gasped desperately for air. Her last shot was through his open mouth, and his efforts to get breath into his ruptured lungs, stopped for good.

-+-

Chapter Fifty Seven

Charlie Reid and Ray Wells had been well trained in military first aid and had, on occasion, been forced to use those skills. As they stripped away Carter's tunic and shirt on the grass next to the beach, and applied pressure to the two bleeding holes in his abdomen, they knew it was bad and Ray told their still conscious friend exactly that.

"Bollocks," said Charlie, "Flesh wounds, Sir."

"It's a shame that you're wrong Charlie," gasped Talbot, "Just like it's a shame that I fell for that old bastard's tricks. I tell you lads, I'm losing my touch...my killer instinct has deserted me. Spare gun under the back of his jacket...bloody hell!"

"Tiny little thing too Cat, Sig Sauer Mosquito .22," added Ray, knowing that he had to keep him talking.

"I've been in touch with Tony," said Charlie, "He can't get the Patrol up to here but he'll get as near as he can, then jog up. He's a good medic Sir."

"Yes Charlie...but, sadly, he's not God."

His friends finished applying field dressings and bound his whole abdomen in multiple layers of bandage. Then Ray offered him a morphine syrette, and Carter cracked a smile. "I had some real fun, once upon a time, with one of those... I don't think I'll have it yet. If this is a one way ticket...I don't think I want to take the trip with a brain like a zombie...I'm really thirsty boys."

Charlie and Ray looked at each other, then back at Cat. "Just to rinse your mouth, Mr Talbot, we don't know what damage has been done...in there."

"From the pool lads...please."

Nicole and Shakespeare, who had been hanging back while his comrades tended Carter, then sat down on the ground next to him. She put someone's jacket over his bare chest and bandaged abdomen while her son held the freshly filled canteen against his lips.

"Thanks Nicole," said Carter, clearly in pain. "If it hadn't been for you...others might have been hurt."

"I feel terrible, if you hadn't come, you wouldn't be...in this mess now."

"I just wish...just wish...I'd somehow found you again twenty years ago. We'd have been so good...together... Mind you, then perhaps you wouldn't have had your boys, and this young man here is a credit to you...Nicole."

"He's a credit to you too Carter."

"What?...what do you mean?"

"I've always known he was different...so different to his brother. I often thought that...well, you and me in Virunga, that we might have made something special. It was only two days later that Alphonse raped me... Although they were born twins they are...were... so different. Colouring, attitude, sense of humour, likes, dislikes, habits. I never said a word to anyone about this but I sometimes would hear comments from the house-girls about Shakespeare being more of a 'Point Five' than a full African."

Shakespeare looked agog as his mother continued pouring out her bottled up emotions. She finished by saying to Carter, as she stroked his forehead, "So, for all these years

I suspected that my twin boys had different fathers, and that this one here...was your son. Now I've seen you together, I know deep in my heart and soul...that I was right."

Shakespeare, still shocked, managed to be practical. "We can do DNA tests, when all this is over...to find out for sure?"

Carter weakly held up his hand to Shakespeare and the young man took it in his. "Nice idea, Bardy...but not sure I'm going to make it. The boys have...patched me up well, but I've seen enough...of these wounds to know... The internal bleeding, in the end...it's too much...for the body to cope with."

"Don't say that Carter. If you're my Dad, you owe me some time I think. I want to go fishing again, and play chess, and drink single malt... I love you..." The tears rolled down the boyish face as he held on tight to Cat's hand.

Nicole joined in the crying and kissed Carter's face again and again, as she dripped salt tears onto his cheeks. His breath was getting more laboured but the three of them talked about little things and big things, like him being an expectant father, for another hour and a half, his comrades keeping a respectful distance.

They were clearing up the site, digging another grave next to Milton's, and tending to the wounded thigh of Sergeant Ngabo when Tony and Churchill arrived dripping with sweat and puffing like steam trains. "We crashed through as much bush as we could...and ran up the last three miles of jungle...homing in on your GPS signal," said Tony, rushing his words between breaths. "How's Cat?"

"Alive...just," said Charlie, nodding in the direction of the three figures by the pool. Tony went over with his medical pack and turned to his old friend, whose face had gone very pale. "We're going to try and move you Carter. If we can get you to the Nissan, and find some open space, we can get the flying doctors in, to get you to Nairobi, I've already called them."

Carter looked through half closed eyes at Tony and smiled grimly, "Nice try Chalkie, but there's no time mate. I can feel...it's like I've got lights inside me...and they're being switched off...one by one. Like when a theatre empties out...after a performance."

Tony put his hand on Cat's face and looked into the swollen faces of the man's son and of his long lost lover. "And, my old friend, what a great performance it's been. I hear you Carter, you just rest for a while."

"Tony...I think I'll have that morphine now...Charlie's got some."

The rest of the team gathered round the small group and Tony gently jabbed the syrette into Carter's thigh and felt it leech out. "You always were a thrill seeker, Sir," Charlie said.

Cat smiled and his eyes flickered open, then fixed on Shakespeare.

"Son," he said, "Go to Lydia...tell her I'm sorry...that I won't be doing...the missing chapters...of the book...but make sure...it gets finished...Archie Findlayson...can fill in a lot of the gaps...look after your Mum...and your new half brother or sister."

"You can rely on me...Dad," answered Shakespeare through more tears.

"Nicole," Carter Aragorn Talbot struggled with his words, "...You were the one...the love of my life...the one...whose face...will be the last thing I ever see...I love you." She kissed his mouth as he closed his eyes, and slipped into a dream, never to awake.

-+-

Epilogue

The people of Crawnish hadn't seen so many people in their hamlet since the media attention they got a year ago, just after the 'happenings' at Uisge Bothan. Finn, the barman at the Dion, had been told a couple of days previously, by the rather posh Englishwoman who now sometimes stayed at Water Cottage, that there were going to be visitors that weekend. His suppliers in Stornoway had sent a van that morning and he now had extra barrels of heavy and lager, plus some cases of wine and a few extra spirit bottles, in the lean-to at the back of the little bar.

It was Saturday 24rd October 2015, and a variety of private cars, plus several taxis, had been driving into Crawnish all morning. The drive at Water Cottage was already full of vehicles when the taxi van carrying Charlie Reid pulled up at the bottom of it. The driver went as far as Mrs McArthur's shop and did a three point turn before depositing the Reid family at the end of the drive. They took in this first sight of Carter Talbot's former home, reflected in the pale autumn sunlight of late morning, and Charlie tried to envisage the mayhem here, that Cat had told him about.

Inside the cottage, Lydia Hockley-Roberts checked the cot next to the double bed and called out gently over her shoulder, "Carla, could you bring the baby bag please?"

Now LHR's full time secretary, the former receptionist at Riveting Read arrived a moment later and passed the multi-coloured bag over to her boss who said, "I thought we'd better change her before it all gets hectic."

Carla sniffed the air and concurred, then went to a drawer built into the base of the cot and pulled out a lemon yellow, thick quilted, romper suit with built in hood and mittens. "Is this the outfit you had in mind Lydia?"

"Oh yes... Cat would have liked her in that. Five weeks old, she's going to look brilliant."

Once the baby was clean and wrapped lovingly in fresh nappy and romper, Carla wrapped her in a soft blanket and followed Lydia to the lounge. In the hallway, the Reid's had just come in and were hovering at the edge of the lounge door. "It's looking a bit crowded in there Lydia," smiled Brenda Reid.

"Never mind, you get to meet my daughter first," Lydia beamed back as she looked back at Carla and shuffled to the side to let her and the baby come forward.

"Reid family... this is Daisy... Daisy, these are some of your dad's best friends, Charlie, Brenda, Churchill, Christine, and Abigail."

Daisy greeted her mum's guests with a yawn and without opening her eyes. "You've clearly made a good impression on her. Could your other son not make it, Brenda?"

"Well, he never met Cat, and someone's got to keep the pub open, so he's taken a week off college to help out."

"God knows what we'll go back to," grunted Charlie with a resigned note but a wry grin.

Tony Chalk stuck his weather-beaten face out of the lounge door, "Is Reid hogging the star of the show? Typical," he said waving an empty coffee mug. "Charlie, if you're having a brew, I wouldn't mind another one, old chap."

"I'll do that, Tony," offered Churchill, taking the mug and turning to the kitchen, "I'm sure you old men have got lots to gossip about."

Lydia, Carla, and Daisy, squeezed into the lounge and Lydia looked around the room. A year ago, she'd never even heard of most of the people here. But now, they meant more to her than anyone she could think of. Next to Tony was Emily Verity, delicately holding her tea cup. Ray and Judy Wells were standing behind one of Cat's armchairs, with Mbugua. Sitting in the armchair was the beautiful and serene Nicole Kwizera, with her son perched on the left arm of the chair. Standing just behind him, with her manicured hand on his shoulder, was a tall Kenyan girl with a very short dress and high heels. Shakespeare's friend Terry was adjacent to Monique and leaning back against the wall, while by the fireplace was DI Billy Keilloh, nursing a china mug. Monopolising the other armchair was LHR's favourite publisher, Sebastian, with his perfectly dressed press secretary, Charlotte, elegantly crossing her legs as she perched next to him.

"Thanks, everyone, for coming," Lydia said softly, "And sorry for the squeeze in here. Luckily, it looks like a bright day outside. So, when our final guests arrive, we can spread out in the front garden. First of all, I'd like you to meet Daisy, who has decided that this special day won't be interrupting her beauty sleep."

Carla tilted the bundle in her arms and slowly rotated clockwise so that everyone could see the dozing baby. Murmurings about how pretty she was, rippled around the small room.

"Cat named her, just before... When Nicole and Shakespeare were with him at the end. He left the middle name to me, so they told me. Assuming that you don't mind," Lydia looked into the face of the woman in the armchair, "I thought... Nicole, would be good?"

All eyes turned to the Rwandan, who smiled and replied, "Daisy Nicole... it sounds lovely, and I'd be honoured."

Lydia went over and kissed Nicole on both cheeks, then fleetingly on the mouth, "Thank you... thank you so much," she added with a slight quiver in her voice. She then took a quick glance at her wrist and said, "Just gone twelve. If you could finish your drinks, the others should be here by now, and we can go outside. Don't forget to wrap up well, it looks sunny but this is still the Hebrides."

As her friends gathered outside, Lydia and Carla kept them shepherded along the front wall of the cottage. The reason for this became apparent a few minutes later as they all looked up to see the source of a rapidly increasing, fast chopping noise. A small, four seater, helicopter descended out of the sun and gently came down on the grass at the front of the cottage, near the edge by the road. When the rotors had stopped, three men in dark overcoats climbed out and Lydia went over to welcome them.

They walked back over to the waiting group while the pilot sat in the cockpit and pulled out a book. "For those who haven't met these gentlemen before," Lydia announced, "This is my boss, Frank Rafferty, his friend Archie Findlayson, from the Foreign Office, and Toby Crabbe, also with the FCO. When I told them what we were thinking of doing, they couldn't keep away."

Lydia gently herded the gathering to the middle of the space between the cottage and the helicopter, where a shallow square hole, less than a metre square, had been dug in the rocky soil. She asked, "If you could all stand around here please and, Shakespeare, could you get the necessary for me?"

As they waited for Shakespeare's return, Lydia, while scanning all their faces, "Honestly, I don't know how this is going to work out today for me. I want to be positive, but if I break down, please understand."

The young Kenyan came back from the house with two black bags, one big and one not so big. He put them on the ground in front of Lydia, who looked up and started to speak.

"I only met Carter Talbot, or for Charlotte's purposes - Robin Chancellor, about eighteen months ago and it's fair to say he made a strong impression on me. In fact I fell for him, a lot. Cat liked me, yes, but I loved him, right from the start. Frank here, told me that Carter had a great story to tell and that I was to help him write it. He wanted somewhere remote, so I found him this cottage and he started work. You all know what happened here and how 'Robin Chancellor' became a bit of reluctant hero in the eyes of the media.

After that I came here and, for a few wonderful weeks, I helped him to get well again and to get really stuck into his book. He never said he loved me but I think that, in his own way, he did. In any event, he gave me Daisy and I love him even more for that. He planned out the unwritten chapters of the book but hadn't done the pivotal one when he chose to go to Kenya to help Nicole and Shakespeare. I felt that I had to go after him.

When the boys came back to Charlie's pub and told me what had happened to Cat, it broke my heart. Thank you to all of you who helped me through that and, as a pregnant 41 year old, to focus on what was then important, our child to be. I remember going to Nicole's home and seeing Carter before he was cremated. He still seemed to be smiling.

Anyway, Shakespeare and I had a chat and he told me

some of what Cat had said to him in his last hour or so. How he'd wanted the book to be finished, how his old boss in the FCO could help. So, Shakespeare came back to England with me, we spoke to Frank and Archie and finished the book in six months. Sebastian here, bit our hand off to publish it and advance orders suggest it's going to be a massive bestseller. All rights to the title having been documented to Carter's descendants.

Ladies and Gentlemen, hot off the press, courtesy of Sebastian, here is the first hardback version of 'An Officer, Not A Gentleman', written by, it says here, 'Robin Chancellor and Shakespeare Kwizera'." With that announcement, Lydia reached into the smaller of the two bags at her feet and pulled out a pristine book and passed it to the person on her left. "Could you all please just write Carter a message in here, inside covers, dedication page, wherever you want?"

As the people around the hole in the ground fumbled for pens, Lydia reached into the larger bag and pulled out a big, olive green painted metal box, then continued.

"You all know that Carter wasn't the least bit religious, his exact words to me on the subject summed it up rather nicely, 'It's all a load of bollocks, Lids' he told me. So, after he was cremated without ceremony, I came up with the idea that his remains should be remembered by us, the nearest thing he's got to family and friends, and put somewhere meaningful. He loved this cottage, and it is just so sad that he wasn't here much.

But, now he can be, for ever. Charlie has donated his most sturdy ammunition box and, in this smaller grenade box, are Cat's ashes. They are going into the bigger box along with the signed book and anything else that any of you want to add. We'll then bury it here, so that he can be near the cottage and the sea. While the book is going round, it would be lovely if anyone else wants to say anything?"

Nicole signalled with the wave of a black gloved hand that she'd like to speak and everyone paid close attention.

"I just want to make sure that I tell Carter, while he's sitting in the ground here, not to worry. Thanks to him, I have a new life, one without fear and one where, with the help of my son, I can be happy, even without the one man who loved me completely. He should know that a half sibling DNA test last week on Shakespeare and Daisy showed that they do, indeed, have the same father. They are therefore the ones due all the book royalties, and I know Lydia has set up a trust for when Daisy is eighteen.

In case anyone was wondering, the deaths of my other son, husband, and 'mystery mzungu visitor' were reported by me to the Kitale Chief of Police and Senior Magistrate, to have stemmed from an argument on a hunting trip. As all the participants died, there was no need for a serious investigation. This decision was helped by large contributions to police and legal profession charities in the town, via those important men, as you can imagine.

Our home is now being converted into a wildlife conservancy and all our former guards have taken jobs with us as Rangers, even the ones somewhat traumatised by their experiences at the waterfall. They seem to like it a lot more and even Portier's old Rwandan soldiers have changed their ways. Shakespeare and I are now supporting wildlife and helping the local community to encourage visitors to our beautiful part of Kenya. We are building a new tented camp in the grounds of the ranch and are calling it the Talbot Game Lodge. Any of you are welcome any time, at no charge.

As for putting something in the box, I haven't got any photos of Carter and me together, but to help him remember our happiest time, here's a leaflet for Gorilla Trekking in Virunga Forest." She leaned forward, dropped the flyer and murmured, "Goodbye Carter."

Shakespeare then took half a pace forward and started talking, quietly at first but then more firmly, to try and look in control.

"I've not got much to add, except that meeting Carter for that first time, on this very spot, changed my life. And changed it for the better. More importantly, he was able to help my mum, who was so unhappy...before. I'll always be proud of him, but also very sad that I only discovered that he helped bring me into the world, at the point he was leaving it.

I'm flattered to be named as a co-author with him, as all I did was to write the Rwandan chapter based on what Cat had told me in the pub. It was seared in my mind and Frank told me that this came across in the words I used. He said it took the reader to the heart of my father and what he became in later years... A much softer individual than he was before 1994, and meeting my mother. I would have thought that Lydia and Archie deserve much more credit than me. She put it all together and he filled in the detail for the later chapters.

Anyway, I'm sending Carter off with a bottle of his all-time favourite single malt. He didn't have any when I visited, but I've tracked some down." Shakespeare got, from the small bag on the ground, a sealed bottle of 24 year old Springbank, and put it in the ammo box.

The portly figure of Sir Archibald Findlayson, long serving member of the FCO and the Secret Intelligence Service, thrust his hands deeper into his overcoat pocket, then coughed and said, "On behalf of HMG, I should like to say something, especially for young Charlotte over there. This is all a bit unusual and hasn't turned out the way any of us really wanted. However, we must remember that although this book is being sold as fiction, under that assumed name, there's actually quite bit of reality in there. Not that the press need to know that, nor Cat's real name, understood Charlotte?"

The young press secretary nodded in silence, then spoke up, "Of course, Sir Archibald."

"My part in the later chapters," he continued, "Was just to paint the picture for Lydia to write the stuff, then muddy the waters if she got too close to anything embarrassing. All in all, I think the old girl has done rather well and I shall treasure my copy. Oh yes... Er...well done Cat, and here's a letter of commendation from Her Majesty, for exemplary service... Still, she doesn't know the half of it," He chuckled, as he dropped it in the box.

Everyone ended up saying something, apart from Billy Keilloh who'd been asked along by Toby Crabbe mainly to ensure they could deal easily with any untoward arrivals of uninvited guests, or press who had got wind of proceedings. And everyone put something in the metal box, with Terry Arnott getting a good chuckle from the gathering for putting four cans of an organic beer called 'Norfolk 'n' Chemicals' in the collection. With his north-eastern accent on the product name and the fact that he admitted never meeting Cat and being only there for Shaky, he lightened the mood considerably.

Lydia, by now, had got the book back and was glancing at all the comments scribbled in by her guests. As she read them she could feel her eyes suddenly filling with tears. Eventually, she could not hold them back and sobbed uncontrollably. Arms came around her and handkerchiefs dabbed at her eyes and face. Nicole, in particular, whispered soothing words in her ear until she was composed. Lydia reached into her coat pocket and added two photographs to the box. They were from those she and Cat had taken of each other on Crawnish beach, when writing their names in the sand.

The ammo box was now quite heavy and there was just room in it for the book to be added before Charlie stepped forward and locked it up. He laid it gently in the hole, stepped back and handed Lydia and Nicole a small trowel each, from the pile of earth at the side. The two friends both spooned soil and pebbles from the heap over the green box and, after three trowels full each, they passed the trowels around so that everyone could take part.

Once the hole was full and patted neatly down, Shakespeare rolled a good sized boulder from the side of the garden, over the newly filled in excavation. He stood tall, breathing heavily from the exertion, and said to the gathering, "So that he's not disturbed." He then went on to announce that the pub was only a short walk away and was open for the rest of the day, and all night if required. Food and drink was all laid on.

As they all moved to leave the grounds of the cottage for the delights of the Dion, Tony sensed some sombreness in his colleagues. He turned to Charlie and Ray and conspiratorially whispered to them, "I'll tell you what boys, if any of Cat's soul is left in that box, he'll have got a great view up that Monique's dress!"

They laughed loud and long as they headed for the pub, leaving Carter's remains and tributes in the ground behind them, secure in his place by the sea.

-+-

THE END

******

About the Author

After starting work at sixteen in Lloyd's of London, Simon Clayton has spent the last forty-one years working in the insurance industry in Europe and East Africa. During that time he was married for twenty-seven years, has a grown up British son, a young African one, and his fiancee will be delivering identical twin boys in December 2015.

He got all his professional qualifications later in life and has been lucky enough to be successful in his field, holding a succession of CEO positions and directorships in the industry. He is British and is currently living and working in Kenya, with a holiday cottage on the Isle of Skye. He is a bad golfer, a supporter of Tottenham Hotspur, and an avid fan of good single malt whisky. His first novel, "Less Than One a Year", was published in March 2014.

CPSIA information can be obtained
at www.ICGtesting.com
Printed in the USA
BVOW09s0913061117
499662BV00003B/448/P